LAIRD *of* BALLANCLAIRE

Books by Jackie Ivie

Laird of Ballanclaire

A Perfect Knight for Love

Knight Everlasting

A Knight and White Satin

Once Upon a Knight

A Knight Well Spent

Heat of the Knight

The Knight Before Christmas

Tender Is the Knight

Lady of the Knight

"A Knight Beyond Black" in *Highland Hunger*

LAIRD Of BALLANCLAIRE

Jackie Ivie

ZEBRA BOOKS
KENSINGTON PUBLISHING CORP.
http://www.kensingtonbooks.com

To Barbara—for helping me craft this story.
Elise—for helping me make it better.

Laird of Ballanclaire *would not be*
the book it is without you both.

And a special thanks to complete strangers—such as Mario,
an ex-professor from Rome, who allowed me to pick his brain
about everything from ancient societies to pagan ceremonies
during an entire flight from Seattle to Anchorage
on a long, dark night.

OCTOBER 1771—THE LOFT

Chapter One

She was going to have to think of a better punishment, because denial wasn't working.

Constant shoved the butter paddle, mumbling and keeping rhythm the entire time. "One, two, three, four! I hate my name. I hate my name. One, two, three, four! Hate, hate, *hate* it! And he knows it! One, two, three . . . oh! The little runt will be lucky to get fresh bread, let alone butter!"

She looked up to spear her tormentor with a glare. He was nearly out of sight. Already. Constant grimaced and turned to her sister Prudence's youngest daughter.

"Hester? Be a dear and go and see what he's up to." Constant wiped at the moisture beneath her cap before swiping it on her skirt. Despite the chill in the air, Constant had worked up a sweat. Wasn't that grand?

"No!"

The little girl leaped from the porch, her petticoat bright in contrast to the dark skirt she wore.

"No? Why, you little—!" Constant dropped the paddle and grabbed at her skirts.

"Oh . . . let her go. She only speaks so to get you

chasing. Besides . . . she's checking on Henry. And isn't that what you wanted?"

Constant bit back a reply and watched the little girl's progress from the edge of the porch. It was just like her next-older sister to interfere.

"Have I asked for your assist, Charity?" Constant turned back to the churn.

"Don't get all uppity with me, Constant Ridgely. Is it my fault I cannot be of help?"

Oh, how she longed to answer with the proper words! Constant's inner turmoil transferred to the churn. Of course it wasn't Charity's fault that she could hardly negotiate stairs over her bulk. Nor was it anyone's fault her baby was overdue. Constant stopped her motions and cupped a hand to her forehead to scan the yard.

"You see? Now I've lost both of them." Constant sighed and put both hands on her ample hips. If she were expecting a child, it would have been birthed by now.

"How far can they go? You know they won't miss sup, although we'll be fortunate if anyone eats, at this rate."

"If I don't finish my chores, we might starve? Is that what you're saying?" Constant bent back to the butter churn.

"I didn't say that," Charity replied.

"Did too. You spend every waking moment speaking of my laziness!"

"I do not!" Charity replied.

"Do so!"

Constant pounded at the churn, feeling the resistance in the cream. Her last strokes had been angrily delivered, quickening it to butter.

"Girls! Cease this bickering! It's upsetting to the babe. Any change, Charity?"

Their mother stepped from the steamy warmth of the

house, the sharpness of her voice belying her worried expression.

"None. But I'd have a better time of it if I had more peace," Charity replied. "I can't even sit on the porch without being disturbed."

Constant barely had time to look innocent before Mother turned.

"Of course you would. As for you, Constant . . . I'm ashamed at your actions. Whatever possessed you?"

"Constant only thinks of herself, Mother. She doesn't care for anyone else. It must chafe that Thomas Ester-brook hasn't declared—"

"You leave Thomas out of this!" Constant cried, goaded into revealing how unrepentant she really was.

"Constant!" Mother stepped in front of Charity. "I can think of more chores today, young woman . . . chores your father has put off. Do you take my meaning?"

Of course she did. Until Henry was of an age where he could help, Constant had most of the chores. No wonder she was big and strong! She hefted the ax, chopped and carried wood, cleaned out stables, handled the livestock . . . she ought to feel lucky she looked feminine at all.

"Apologize, and then go hunt down Henry. You know better than to let him run free. Honestly, Constant! I don't know what . . ."

Constant watched the dirt sift through the floorboard at her feet while her mother continued admonishing her. She should've kept her tongue.

"We're waiting, Constant."

She swallowed. "I'm sorry I spoke as I did, Charity." *Charity? The woman hasn't a charitable bone in her frame.*

"Thank you, Constant. That was prettily said. Now fetch Henry before your father hears of this. You're in luck he's hunting. And what of Hester? What have you done with her? Prudence will be back from shopping in Boston on the morrow and you've lost her daughter, too?"

"She sent Hester running after Henry. I just hope nothing happens to them."

Charity had best stay hidden behind their mother if she wished to escape with those words.

"You couldn't! You didn't! Of all the thoughtless . . . reckless—"

Mother said more. Constant didn't stay to hear about her laziness, her misguided judgment, her lack of decorum, her thoughtlessness—she'd heard it all so many times.

It wasn't that Thomas Esterbrook wasn't going to offer for her, either. They'd been promised to each other since they could talk. They'd grown up together, and until she'd grown taller than Thomas, they'd been inseparable. Then she started outweighing him, but that couldn't be the reason he didn't come courting . . . could it? Of course not. Charity was just jealous. Thomas was so much better-looking than all the other boys. *Boys?* Why had she thought that? He was already eighteen.

Constant shoved the toe of her boot into the dry dirt of the lane as she walked, her thoughts delaying her. Thomas was just caught up in his work with his family print shop. That's why she rarely saw him anymore.

"Henry! Hester!" She scanned the trees lining the lane. Falling leaves left the limbs near-naked, but there was still enough concealment for two impish children.

"I—I think he's dead, Henry!"

Constant could just make out two heads of red hair in a leaf-choked gully. Henry knew better than this! There was always danger of flash flooding, and he'd been told time and again to stay away.

"He doesn't move . . . watch!"

Hester squealed as Henry must be putting motion to his words. Stupid children! If they were playing with an animal, Mother would harangue Constant for hours.

"He's not dead. See?"

Constant stumbled through the leaves, her passage so loud she was amazed the children didn't hear. Henry's head disappeared. Fear caused Constant to trip, sliding over the edge of the wash, coming to rest beside what felt like a very large, disembodied, stiff feathered object. And then she saw the dried blood mixed through the down.

"Get help . . . lad!" Words wheezed from the feather-covered form that held on to Henry with one arm.

"Constant! Don't just sit there! Make him let me go! Help me! Constant!" Henry's terror made his voice squeak.

"Con . . . stant?"

Whatever strength he had must've been spent. The man's arm dropped. Constant's brother fell. She'd never seen a man tarred and feathered before, but she instantly knew what had happened. She also guessed why. The only ones earning this kind of punishment were tax revenue agents who wouldn't take no for an answer.

"Help me . . . please?"

He licked his lips, looked into her eyes, and Constant's heart skipped a beat. Raggedly. She hadn't been around men much. And she'd never been needed by one. She should grab the children and leave. Report him to her mother. She shouldn't get involved. She was a dutiful daughter . . . and then a tremor ran through him, his eyes narrowing in what could be pain.

"I beg you, lass . . ."

Constant hushed him with a finger to his lips. A spark shot through her lower arm, tingling and enervating. Surprising. He was frowning as if he'd felt it, too. And that's what decided her.

"Who is he?" Hester asked.

Constant looked at her coconspirators. "Help me get him to an out-shed so we can find out. Can you keep a secret?"

Henry and Hester beamed and nodded rapidly. Constant squatted beside the man, gripped his arm in one of hers, lifted his chest so she could maneuver beneath him, and tried to stand. He was much heavier than she expected. Constant's legs trembled and then collapsed, dropping him. His grunt held pain. Bleary, red-rimmed eyes showed how much.

"I'll be back," she whispered. "I promise."

She pushed from him and scrambled to her feet, the children at her heels. "Come, children! We've got to steal a quilt from the line! Henry! Scout ahead. Don't let anyone see us!"

Within the hour they had the man not only rolled into a quilt but inside a shed, too. But then she didn't know what to do. She had an injured man on her hands, two five-year-olds for help, and a houseful of gossipy, backstabbing women. The only good news looked to be that the men, gone hunting, weren't expected until the end of the week. That gave her four days. Worse, she still had to finish her chores and get supper, all the while pretending nothing out of the ordinary was happening.

The evening was as worrisome as she'd anticipated. She expected either Henry or Hester to blurt something at any moment. That they kept each other company made it easier. Their whispering looked normal, as was their inability to sit still. But the real reason nobody noticed was that Charity finally went into labor.

As an unwed daughter, Constant wasn't required to assist with childbirth. She got every other chore instead. Without supervision, she tossed dishes from wash water to rinse, flung the drying cloth about them, and clattered them into cabinets with haste. Night had fallen as she placed the remainder of sup in the cooling house, folded sheets, stoked the fire, pumped buckets and more buckets of water for heating, told any within hearing that she was going out to feed animals with Henry and Hester, and then she was out.

Her hands were shaking as she turned the hasp on the padlock. She fully expected he'd be dead. She warned the children to stay out long enough for her to check, and then she crept in.

They'd put him in the shed for drying hides. It had an unpalatable odor that wasn't conducive to a sick ward, but she hadn't many options. She didn't know what the punishment for harboring a revenue agent was. She might be tarred and feathered, too. Or . . . at the very least, be put in the stocks.

The mound of quilt hadn't moved. Constant knelt beside it, touched the man's cheek, and then put her palm beneath his nose. Warm breath made her own restart. She hadn't even realized she'd held it.

"It's all right, Henry and Hester. You can come in. Bring the lard."

"Lard?" The feather-covered form spoke.

"I don't know about removing tar. I thought we'd try lard."

He chuckled, then stilled with a quick intake of breath.

"I'm going to try it on your shoulder."

There was blood oozing between some of the feathers coating him. Constant swallowed any reaction and slid fingers full of grease onto his shoulder. Feathers came off while the black, leatherlike sheath over his skin appeared to soften.

"Does . . . it work?" he asked.

"I can't tell."

"Did you bring . . . water?"

"Water won't work," she replied.

"To . . . drink."

"Oh. Henry? Pull a bucket from the well. Can you do that for me?"

Henry dashed off before she finished. Constant put another layer of grease on the featherless portion of the man's shoulder before she picked up a cheesecloth and wiped at it again. All that happened was the grease came off. The tar was immobile.

"Well?" he asked.

She sighed and dropped the cheesecloth in her lap. "It doesn't work."

"Peel it. It makes horrid scars . . . but it comes off."

"Won't that hurt?"

"You think . . . it does na' . . . already?"

"Oh."

He had an odd accent she couldn't place. Nor should she try. Constant looked at the softened ridge of tar covering his shoulder. From that small portion she could tell how strong he was. This was a fully grown male. Virile. Mature. Muscled. Extremely muscled. And he was right at her fingertips. That was a new experience. Heady. Exciting. Illicit. Scary.

"Go on, lass. You can do it."

"Are you a handsome sort?"

He choked, and caught it with another intake of breath. "To some," he finally answered.

"It would be a shame to damage you, then. Let me see . . ." She eased a fingernail beneath a crack in the tar. Then she lifted it. He stiffened the moment she tried.

"Jesu'!"

The curse came through gritted teeth and Hester put her hands to her ears. Constant removed her fingernail.

She bent closer to lift the tar piece just slightly. She could see a layer of fine hair between the tar and his skin.

"I have an idea. I'll be right back. Don't move."

"Doona' move, she says . . . when I'm tarred . . . into position. You're a strange angel of mercy, my love."

My love? Her ears heard it as she squatted next to him. She had to clear her throat to get Hester's attention.

"Come with me, Hester."

"Doona' leave me alone . . . with the lad."

"I won't. Look. Here's Henry. He's got some water. You'd best not drink too much, sir. Uh . . . until we have some of this off . . . uh . . ."

"The parts I'll be needing. I ken."

Constant's face reddened so much it burned. Henry dipped a cup and handed it to her.

"I'm going to ease my arm under your head and lift you. Ready?"

He stiffened when she did it. She guessed the black mass on him was pulling and tearing with each movement. She only hoped when she had it off, there wouldn't be too many open wounds to deal with. *If* she got it off.

He drained the cup she held to his lips. His light brown eyes thanked her, although they were still so red-rimmed, the color was hard to decipher. One thing was clear, though. If his eyes were any indicator, he was definitely a handsome sort.

"Come along, Henry and Hester. We've got to feed our patient. We also have to get a paring knife. One of my apple ones. Come on," she directed as she stood up.

"A knife?" Henry asked.

"I have an idea. It may work. It may not. It's better than the alternative."

"Con . . . stant?" The man choked on her name and she bent close to him.

"Yes?"

"Doona' let the bairns see this." He fell back with a groan.

Constant frowned slightly. Even said oddly, using an unfamiliar word, she knew what he meant. But she didn't have a choice. If she didn't let the children follow her, they'd be telling, and then she'd be in terrible trouble. They were all she had, and that was that. Her frown cleared.

"Come along, you two. We've got to steal our man some sup. I fancy a bit of pumpkin bread, a piece of squab pie, and some cider. That might work." She bent near his ear. "I'll return. I promise."

She didn't hear his reply or even if he gave one.

No one was about when they raided the kitchens and no one noticed that Hester and Henry still weren't abed, thanks to Charity. Moans filtered through the hall and into the kitchen, masking their activities.

Constant took her smallest knife, a sharpening stone, and a candle with her. If she didn't miss her guess, it was going to be a long night.

Chapter Two

Her patient hadn't moved. She shut the door, told both children to find a comfortable spot if they wanted to stay, and knelt next to the man.

"I'm here," she whispered. Then she opened the lamp to light it with her candle. The fright in his eyes startled her. Constant lit the wick and set it beside her knee. "It's all right. I need it to see."

"Oh."

"I'm going to try to cut the tar away."

"Cut?"

The fright was back in his eyes again. Constant had never felt such power. She wasn't certain she liked it.

"Yes," she replied finally. "Cut."

She put her left hand on his shoulder as if it were one big apple, put the blade of her paring knife beneath the edge of the tar she'd greased, and did the best skinning job she could manage. A thin strip of tar came up, curling as it did so, and if she didn't miss her guess, beneath it was unblemished skin. Constant bent and checked. It was definitely skin, unblemished and slightly pink, but otherwise undamaged. She did it again, scraping another swath that left just a trace of rawness.

"It works," she cried. "Sweet heaven, it works!"

"You should start with . . . my back."

"Why?"

He swiveled his head to look at her. "To prevent black rot. 'Tis likely a mass of dried blood by now."

Constant gulped, met his eyes, and gulped again. "Blood?"

"I dinna' stand still while this was done to me, lass. I fought. Took a few lashes with a whip or two. Mayhap three. I was na' counting at the time."

"Oh."

"I'll also need . . . a support."

"Support?"

"I'll need to roll onto my belly. I doona' wish . . . a broken rib puncturing anything."

"They broke your ribs?" Her voice carried shock and horror. She couldn't prevent it.

"I'm . . . na' entirely certain. My chest is afire when I breathe. And my lungs gurgle. Both bad signs. I'm probably lucky. They meant . . . a lot worse."

His lungs gurgled? She shouldn't even have him here. He should be at a surgeon. She was playing in God's territory. "I don't think I should do this," she told him.

"Please, lass? There's nae one else. And . . . I can pay."

"I don't want your silver. I'm more worried over failure. I've set broken bones before and handled cuts and scrapes, but for this . . . you need a doctor."

"Please?"

Constant stood. Looked him over for a bit. And then she sighed. He was right. There wasn't anyone else. Even if she sent for Doctor Thatcher, it would take days. He was out with the hunting party.

"Children? Keep an eye on him. Don't let him move."

His response was probably a laugh, but it ended up as a cough that did sound as though it contained liquid.

Constant ran, checked the barn, and then the wood-pile. The best she could manage was a halved log. With the flat edge on the ground, it should support him. She was going to need hot water, too. Luck was still her ally. Nobody was about when she filched a bucket from the hearth. All of which took longer than she expected. He hadn't moved. The children had, though. They were both crouched near his head.

"Henry! Hester!"

"His name's Kam," they said in unison.

Constant frowned. *Kam?* What sort of name was that? And what parent would put such a name on their off-spring?

"She's back?" the man asked.

"I've brought a log. It's the best I can do. Back away, children, so he can roll onto it."

"If . . . I can."

"I'll help. Here."

Constant put the log next to him, took his right hand, and pulled so hard she fell on her backside, much to Henry and Hester's amusement. The man rocked amid a medley of groans and half-spoken curses. He was huffing, his eyes were scrunched shut, and some of the tar had flaked off the skin around them. Then he opened them, surprising her with the sheen of moisture on the golden-brown color. And that caused her heart to give another odd flutter.

"You're going to have to help me. I can't do it alone. You're too heavy."

"Try . . . pushing." He wheezed the words.

Constant went to the other side of him and pushed. He rocked, grunted, and called out several unsavory things that had Hester openmouthed. Constant crawled to the wall beside him, braced her back against it, put both boots on his closest shoulder and heaved. He actually rolled, amidst a great deal more cursing and feathers flicking about. And that's where he stayed, in a slightly bowed position as he lay facedown over the log to keep his ribs from contact with the floor.

"You all right?" Constant asked.

"I think . . . I'm about to be ill," he muttered.

"I'll get a bucket."

"Just get your skean . . . and start your carving."

"Skean?"

"Begging pardon, lass. I keep forgetting. A skean is a knife. Get your knife."

It wasn't dried blood seeping from the feathered mess on his back. It was wet. Constant watched her hands tremble. She had to breathe slowly and deeply. She wouldn't be any good to him if she couldn't hold a steady knife. She went to her knees, steadied her left hand on the skin she'd already revealed, and started paring. It didn't work. The tar wouldn't peel. The knife blade skidded along, grabbing at chunks, and the more she scraped, the more he stiffened. The more times he stiffened and groaned, the worse he shook beneath her, and all that happened was her knife got slippery with blood.

"I can't do this! I'm sorry." Constant lifted her hands and put the knife aside, swiping at the blood with a piece of cheesecloth. She was afraid every bit of her tears sounded in her voice.

"You canna' stop now," he said. "Please? I'm begging you."

"But I don't know what's wrong. It won't come up anymore."

"You dinna' . . . grease it up."

"Of course. The lard." Constant turned to her niece. "Hester? Do we still have the lard tub? Bring it here, please."

"Grease is verra good for a burn, anyway, Constant, love. It'll be all right," he informed her.

"Burn?"

"Cold tar does na' stick verra well."

"Oh, sweet Lord, now I think I'll be ill."

He chuckled, but it turned into another cough, this one sounding wetter than before. Constant scooped a gob of lard and spread it on a small area with her left hand. She couldn't afford to get her right hand slicked up again. It had to wield the knife.

And it worked.

Thank the Lord! Constant settled into place and went to work in earnest. She concentrated on greasing up feathers, wiping them off, and then peeling tar, doing her best to avoid noticing the sections of raw flesh. Constant gulped more than once to steady her stomach. It was laborious and onerous, and it was well past midnight before she had the tar on his back removed to his waist. And that just highlighted a myriad of stripes from a whipping.

She'd lost her audience hours earlier. Both children were asleep, snuggled together for warmth near the man's feet. Constant had been so occupied she hadn't noticed the feeling of frost in the air. She didn't think the man had either. She didn't even think he was conscious anymore.

Constant unbent stiff limbs and frowned at the water bucket. It had been hot hours ago. Not anymore. She was going to have to go for another one. She got to her knees.

"Doona' . . . leave me," he whispered.

"I have to leave. I have to get warm water. You need

washing and bandaging. Actually, you need a doctor. I should have gone for him the moment we found you."

"This doctor . . . of yours? His name Thatcher?"

"Yes," she answered. "Yes, it is."

"Then you're observing a bit of his handiwork. Fetching him will na' help me."

"Doctor Thatcher helped tar you? Mercy! Why? What did you do?"

"If I tell you, will you leave?"

"Is it bad?" she asked.

"Na' to some," he replied.

"You're not a revenue agent?"

"Nae," he answered.

"Then, why?"

"Thatcher . . . has a verra lovely young wife. She offered."

Constant went stiff everywhere. She held her breath. She let it out and then pulled in another one. "You—you're an adulterer? I'm risking severe punishment and worse—for an adulterer?"

"I dinna' say I took her up on the offer, Constant, love."

"I've got to wash your back now. I'm going to use cold water. I was worried about how it would hurt. I'm surprised at myself. I truly am. I want you to know this beforehand."

He didn't answer. She dunked a clean piece of cheese-cloth into the bucket and wrung it out. She got her emotions under control before swabbing at the outside edge of his wound. Part of her emotion was due to the way he jerked from the first touch, part was because he was injured and she didn't want to hurt him, and part of it was because if she didn't finish this, he wasn't going to get well. And then he wouldn't leave.

Before she was finished washing his shoulder, she

realized his injuries were just as bad as they looked. His back was a mass of bruising and a crooked latticework of open wounds that needed cleaning, medicating, and bandaging if they were going to heal properly. Whoever had whipped him made certain to break skin. Each time she dipped the rag the water darkened, until finally it was unusable.

She would have explained that she was leaving to get a fresh bucketful, but she was never speaking to him again.

There was nobody about in the kitchen, and there was hot water bubbling in every bucket on the hearth. Constant put her empty bucket down and stole a fresh one. Somewhere in the house she heard Charity moaning. Constant didn't stay around to verify anything. She had to get the man named Kam better. She had to get him out of the shed, and she had to get him off her mind.

The door to the shed creaked a bit when she got back. Hester and Henry were still sleeping, and the man was still stretched out, his shoulders elevated atop the log, his head hanging to the floor.

"You . . . came back," he said.

"Of course. I've little choice now."

Constant knelt beside him and dipped her rag. She had one side of his back washed, and started on the other one. She'd been right earlier. He was muscular. And large. His back was immense, covered with more muscle than she'd ever seen. Of course, she only had her sisters' husbands for contrast; as well as their father, who was smaller than Constant; and Thomas Esterbrook, who was fairly thin, although most young men at the age of eighteen were. Then again, she'd never seen a man lying stretched out before her. Maybe in that position any man appeared extraordinarily large.

"Is it . . . bad?" he asked.

Constant dipped her rag and washed the area where a belt should be holding his pants up. He didn't have any spare flesh there, either, only a thick ridge of muscle.

"Well?"

"I am not speaking to you ever again, sir," she answered.

He snorted. "Doona' call me that. My name is Kameron. 'Tis a family name. Auld Gaelic. But I'd like it if you'd call me Kam."

"I don't want to know your name," she replied.

"Why?"

"Because I was stupid."

He stiffened as she cleaned. Constant lightened her touch.

"You're na' stupid. I am. I lied, too."

Constant narrowed her eyes. "An adulterer . . . and a liar?"

"I dinna' commit adultery with anyone, Constant."

"You should call me Mistress Ridgely. That would be right and proper."

"Right . . . and proper? Now?" He wheezed out a breath that sounded like a laugh. "I really think you should call me Kam."

"Why?"

"Because I'm asking you to."

"Why?" she repeated.

"Because . . . we'll be getting verra familiar with each other fairly soon, and I'd feel much better about it if you'd call me by my name. Fair?"

Constant narrowed her eyes. "I don't know what you're talking about."

"They took my clothing, lass. All of it."

Her hands halted, her eyes widened, and she forgot to breathe for a moment. She concentrated on dipping the rag, wringing it out, and then finishing her chore.

She forced her mind to a complete blank and then ordered her own throat to swallow.

"Dinna' you hear me?" he asked quietly.

"I already told you I'm not speaking to you ever again. I don't understand why you didn't hear it the first time . . . *sir.*"

"Well, at least I know why they call you Constant."

"They call me that because it's my name," she replied.

"What kind of name is that?"

"Mine. I just told you."

"Who would name a child that? And why?"

"Punishment," she replied. "I am going to bandage you now. I brought more cheesecloth and a bedsheet. It shouldn't be missed, especially since I do all the laundry anymore."

"Punishment? What sort of sin requires naming a daughter Constant?"

"My parents have eight daughters. I'm one of them."

"Eight? Good . . . *Lord.*"

The third word was higher-toned because she'd started layering the bandaging on his back. It must pain something terrible. It also wasn't going to be easy to get the tar from his chest. She wondered if he knew.

"We should have done your chest first," she said.

"Nae doubt . . . but my back hurt worse. I'm thankful to you, Constant. When this is all over, I'll prove it to you."

"No. When this is all over, I want you to disappear. I am going to forget that I was stupid enough to feel mercy toward a man like you. I will forget I ever met you, or helped you. That will be thanks enough . . . *sir.*"

"Are you finished bandaging?" he asked when she'd finished her speech.

"I can't secure it until we have your chest peeled. I would think that much is obvious."

"Fair enough." He coughed again.

Constant waited. "Well?" she finally asked.

"Well, what?"

"Are you going to turn over for me, or do you want me to shove at you again?"

He groaned. "I doona' think I can. Please?"

"I can't get the tar from your chest if you're on it."

"I ken as much."

Constant sat on her heels and looked over her handiwork. He needed to stay off his back for at least a day to give it time to start healing. She looked over at the two little cousins. They were absolute angels when asleep. She looked at the bucket of pink-stained water. She looked at the massive back and shoulders of the man at her knees. She looked at the yellow feather-covered mass of his lower body. She gulped.

"You ken what needs doing, Constant."

"I'm thinking," she replied.

"Think faster. It'll be morn soon, and you've got to get me hidden afore then."

"I don't have to do anything of the sort."

"You have to find a better spot to hide me. You ken that."

"Why?"

"Because young bairns canna' keep big secrets."

She glanced at the sleeping duo again. "Can't you just leave? Find some other naïve girl to assist you?"

"I canna' walk. If you saw my legs you'd ken the reason."

"What happened to your legs?"

"Finish taking this off and see for yourself."

Constant narrowed her eyes. "We don't have time for word games. I have to get you hidden, remember?"

"Good lass," he answered. "Thank you."

"I am doing this for self-preservation, sir, and no other reason. I want you to know that."

"Constant, if you will get me hidden and help me get well, I will more than disappear. I'll forget directions to your hamlet. I swear."

"You do more than your share of swearing already, sir."

"Kam," he said, softly.

"I'll be back. Don't move."

He huffed a breath in what might have been amusement. "You ask the strangest thing. Does it look as if I can move?"

She stood and looked him over. "No," she said finally. "I suppose not. I'll devise something. I'll return."

It was dawn before she managed to move him to his new home, rolling him in the quilt and using their plowhorse, Eustace, for help. Kam was grunting and swearing through most of it. He had no room to complain. At least he'd get to sleep the day away. Constant was going to be at the beck and call of the entire household while guarding her own tongue. She had to keep her brother and her niece from guessing her patient's new location, and she was going to have to pretend that she'd gotten a good night's sleep as well.

She eased the wooden platform over the hayloft, clicking her tongue to Eustace, to back him. Kameron dangled above the fresh hay for a span before he dropped. Then all she had to do was unhook Eustace, put the wagon back against the barn wall, and run back to the shed. She regretted having anything to do with the tarred man. Back when she'd thought he was just an English revenue agent, she'd had second thoughts about helping him. Now that she'd talked to him and seen some of him, she had third and fourth ones. She should've run home and told her mother what the children found.

She certainly wasn't keeping him secret so she could have him all to herself. That kind of idea was for wicked young women with nothing else to occupy them. Constant was helping him because she was a God-fearing, churchgoing human being, who had a charitable and merciful side. *That's* why she was helping him.

She almost had herself convinced of it when she curled next to Henry and Hester to catch a nap.

Chapter Three

Constant hushed her aching muscles, pushed the damp rag over her face and neck, and gathered foodstuffs in a basket. She was purloining enough for three meals, but her patient was probably hungry. He hadn't reached the size he was by not eating. She was going on guesswork, however. She'd checked on him only once, when she'd gone to fetch more wood for the fire.

He'd been sleeping.

She was ready to drop from exhaustion, and the source of her problem was sleeping. Constant thinned her lips before adding several pats of butter to the feast she was gathering.

Hester and Henry had been upset to find the man had fled during the night. Hester had even cried over the poor bird-man named Kam. Constant cautioned both not to say another word when she'd carried Hester back to the house. The admonition hadn't done much good, but luckily no one believed there had been a bird-man in the shed.

Constant hadn't time to fret over any of it, however. Her mother ran her all day: gathering eggs, milking the three Jerseys they owned, cooking a breakfast for ten, serving it, cleaning up, gathering laundry, and keeping pails of water heating on the fire. Charity wasn't moaning anymore, either. She was a lot louder. Then it was time to fix luncheon, serve it, clean it up. Prepare vegetables, meat, and barley to get a stew going, finish baking bread, and serve supper. Charity hadn't had her baby yet and everyone worried. Near dark, she was doing a lot of screaming between her crying episodes, too.

It hadn't taken much to persuade Henry to go to his room. He'd been scarce all day, and Constant had kissed him before he retired. And after that, she was supposed to be gaining her own bed. The entire house felt different somehow. Charity wasn't as loud, but the hushed whispers from the master bedroom at the back of the upstairs hall were worse than the screaming. Nobody noticed as Constant snuck down the stairs, tied up some food in her apron, purloined another pail of heated water, took her mother's honey-herb salve jar, and slid out the back kitchen door. Not a soul saw her.

Constant lifted the latch of the barn door and pulled it open. The harvest moon was framed in the hayloft window, pouring moonlight into the loft. She hitched her skirts and started climbing the ladder.

"Constant? Is that you?"

"Hush!" Worry made the sound loud. She put a leg over the top rung and settled her bucket into a solid spot in the loft. It took a few more moments to find the flint and light the wick of the stable lamp she'd purloined. And then she turned to find him.

"Sir?"

"You came back." He sounded surprised and relieved.

"Yes," she replied. She started brushing straw away from the spot where she'd put him but couldn't locate anything that looked like a hulk of a man. "Sir?" she said again.

"Near the wall. I had to hide. The lad, Henry, is verra inquisitive."

"Henry was up here?"

"More than once. He seems to believe I hadn't the strength to walk on my own, and that you'd hide me. He also thinks you'd use your hayloft. Why is it called your hayloft?"

"Where are you?" she asked again, moving her hands in a circular motion.

"Call me Kam and I'll tell you."

"We haven't time for games. I have to get that tar off you. I have to get you well. And then I have to get you away from here."

"Who's Charity?" he asked.

"My elder sister. And trust me. She doesn't fit her name."

"What's wrong with her?"

"She's birthing her first child. Being very loud and complaining over it. That's the only reason no one is paying much attention to other things."

"Like what?"

"Lard disappearing. Me, eating enough for four. Hester's story about a bird-man that disappeared from the shed. Things like that."

She heard him chuckle slightly. "You should reassure the lad. He thinks Charity's dying."

"How do you know all this?"

"He spoke of it to someone. I dinna' hear an answer. Does he speak to himself oft?"

"He probably had Stream with him." Constant connected with a foot. She ran her hand up his leg, lightly grazing feathers and then brushing hay from him.

"Who's Stream?"

"My younger sister."

"Your parents had strange ideas on the naming of their children."

"Are you hungry?"

She had brushed away the hay and was arranging food in front of him. He'd moved quite a span. He was still lying facedown atop the log she'd brought last night. It appeared he'd shoved forward until the log was propped against the barn wall, with him on it.

"I think I could eat Eustace. Whole."

He shoved a huge chunk of bread into his mouth and swigged it down with a good gulp of water from the canteen she'd brought.

"You know the horse's name?"

He swallowed. "Naught is wrong with my ears, Constant. Or my eyes. I heard you last night when you moved me. The horse obeys your every command. Why is that?"

She shrugged. "We till fields together. He must mind my voice because he always hears it."

"You? You till the fields, too? What does everyone else do?"

"My father has only one son. He was a sickly baby. He's but five years old. My father is old and ill. My brothers-in-law assist, but if I don't help till the soil every spring and bring the harvest in every fall, we don't eat. Who else is going to do it?"

"You bake this?" He gestured with the half loaf he hadn't shoved into his mouth yet.

"Yes," she answered.

"It's good. You make the stew, too?"

"Yes."

She was pulling the bucket over. Her first task was removing his dressing. Then she could wash the wound and rebandage. It took some time. Constant realized it hurt as Kameron stiffened off and on while she saturated the cloth clinging to every welt. The volume and depth of them were a shame. He had such an impressive, well-muscled back. The stripes would probably scar. She wondered if that would bother him, and then why she cared. She had the honey-herb jar opened and let some dribble onto him before another thought arose: Mother always swore about the benefits of her salve. This was going to be a good test of it. That was certain.

"What are you doing?"

"Coating you with honey."

He choked on his bite of stew. "Honey?"

"Mother swears by its restorative powers. You're going to need restorative powers on this back or it'll scar badly."

"I'm prepared for a head-to-toe scarring, Constant, love."

"Not if I can help it," she replied under her breath. He was much too glorious-looking to be mutilated and disfigured, based on the parts of him she could see. "There. It's done. You can stop fussing."

"Will na' my bandaging stick something terrible?"

"Of course," she replied.

"And will it na' need to be soaked free?"

"Yes."

"Then . . . I doona' understand why you bother."

"It will stick and it will have to be soaked off, and that's the chore I'm setting myself tomorrow night, the night after that, and the night after that. By then we'll know if it works."

"You'll drop with exhaustion afore then."

"Probably," she replied.

"Then you'd best na' do it. I doona' mind a bit of scarring, especially on my back. Might make me appear a bit rakish, now that I mull it."

"Rakish?"

"Aside from which, who sees a man's back?"

"Your wife, for one."

"I doona' have one," he said between bites.

"You don't? That is not good."

"Actually, to my way of thinking, it's verra good."

"A man your age should have a wife. He should have a few babes, too. He shouldn't be unwed, naked beneath a cloak of tar and feathers, being tended by a young, unmarried woman. He shouldn't."

"A man my age?" he replied. "*My age?* I think I'm offended, Constant. Truly offended. And that's difficult to comprehend."

"Why haven't you wed?"

"I doona' ken for certain. Limited selection. Na' enough pressure," he answered.

"Pressure?"

"It's a long story. Canna' we talk of something else?"

"How old are you?" she asked.

"Twenty-eight. Almost twenty-nine."

"Twenty-eight? Good heavens! You're almost old enough to be a grandfather."

"Oh. Please," he said, in a sarcastic fashion.

"You have a problem with marriage?"

"Nae."

"You have a problem with responsibility?"

"Nae," he replied again, in the same tone.

"Then, why aren't you wed?"

"I already told you. The selection is too broad, and at the same time, too blasted narrow. And I doona' wish to speak more on it. Agreed?"

She thought about that for a few moments. "I'm sorry I asked," she finally replied.

"So am I."

"I'm going to start on your feathers now."

"Well, doona' let me delay you."

The answer was flippant and accompanied by another slurping sound as he took a bite of stew. Constant pulled the tub of lard over to her side. If she worked through the night she might be able to get most of the tar from him. And if she did that, he'd be leaving sooner.

"Do you have the care of the animals, too?"

"What?" she asked.

"I'm attempting a change of subject."

"We don't have a subject."

"Verra well, then, I'm attempting to find a subject. One that does na' include talk of marriage and all the chains that accompany it. And one that veers away from my present state of undress and incapacity. So . . . do you? Take care of the horses, goats, pigs, cows, cats, dogs, and whatever else you have on this farm?"

"Chickens," she said, thinning her lips.

"Chickens?"

"You asked what else we have. The answer is chickens."

"Oh. And do you take care of them all?"

"Most of the time."

"You're verra humble, Constant. It's odd. I'm eating the results of your culinary skills, I'm on the receiving end of your compassion, and I heard Henry talking and playing all day. He does na' seem to have a bone devoted to responsibility."

"He's the long-awaited heir in a household of eight sisters. And he was a sickly baby."

"Oh. I see. He's God's gift, then?"

She sighed and looked from his feet to his head and back. "I'm afraid this is going to be a bit difficult. You may not want to do much talking."

"On the contrary, I'm speaking for a reason."

"What is it?" she asked.

"So, Constant, tell me, doona' you have sisters to help you? What's this Stream do?"

"You're not going to tell me the reason?"

"Uh . . . nae. I'm invoking patient's privilege. So, tell me about this Stream. She is na' much help to you. Why?"

"She's an invalid."

"Oh." He was silent for a bit. She heard him slurp more of her stew. For some reason, his appreciation of it made her warm all over. She wondered what that meant. "I'm sorry," he said finally.

"Don't be. She was born that way. We accept it."

"I can still be sorry."

Constant sat on her heels and looked over the length of man at her knees. "I think I'm going to need quiet now," she said.

"Why?"

"Because I've never seen . . . what I'm about to."

He choked again, and this time he coughed for some time afterward. Constant watched his back undulate with it.

"I probably should have you send a message to my garrison. On second thought, that's what I'll do. Can you get some paper, ink, and a quill?"

"I can't send a message to any English-held anything."

"You canna' read or write?"

He was almost worse than dealing with Charity. "I'll have you know I read and write. I do both quite well. I even speak two foreign languages: Spanish and French. I was taught by my sister Hope. She married a learned man. She wants to be a schoolmarm."

"Oh. My mistake. So, why canna' you get a message off for me?" he asked.

"Because it would be disloyal."

"Disloyal? To whom? We're all loyal British subjects . . . are na' we?"

"Disloyal to my father. He had business with Doctor Thatcher this week, and that means what I'm doing right now, for you, will not go unpunished in my family. *If* it's found out."

He sucked in his breath. "Your name is Ridgely? That is what you said?"

"Yes," she answered.

"God damn! Jesu' Christ! And his Mother Mary! And bloody hell to top it off!"

"Mind your profanity, sir!"

"For the love of—! Constant. I was ever profane. I'd apologize, but I'll probably just spout more, and then I'd have to apologize more, and then I'll just do it again."

"Well, I'm not used to it."

"Fine. I apologize, but that does na' change it."

"What?"

"Your father. Ridgely. Does he write articles for the *Colonial Register*? Some bits of trash about sedition and rights of citizens? That sort of blather?"

"It isn't blather!"

"Sweet Saint Jude. I'm covered with tar that your father heated to the correct burning, scarring temperature so those men could pour it all over a soldier doing little more than tipping a pint at an inn . . . and you defend it?"

"I already told you he's ill. Old. He couldn't do any such thing," Constant retorted defensively.

"If you write that sort of drivel, you light the spark behind every one of these uprisings. Inflammatory words spark insurrections, my dearest Constant."

"Perhaps your country shouldn't try to cheat colonies half a world away, then."

"You share your father's sentiments?"

"I was born in the colonies, sir. I've never been to England. I have no desire to, either. I'm not English."

"Neither am I," he replied.

Constant frowned. "I don't understand."

"I'm a Highlander. Black Watch regiment."

"A . . . Highlander?"

"From Scotland. And damn proud of it. Oh. Bother. You'll pardon the profane portion of that, will na' you?"

Constant's face fell. "Aren't you a soldier . . . in King George's regiment?"

"That does na' mean I'm English."

"There's a difference?"

He sighed heavily. "Keep me jailed in this tar long enough and I'll have time to explain."

"I'm not keeping you anywhere."

He sighed. "You're right, Constant, love. And it's dense of me to get you angered right now."

"I'm not angry," she replied.

"Good."

"I just need you to be quiet."

"I doona' think I can. We should probably change the subject again, though."

"To what?"

"I would like to ken why it is that you're na' looking at a man's nakedness every night of your life. That's what I'd like to hear."

She was hot with the blush. She put every bit of affront into her voice. "I am not wed!"

"Well, you should be. You're old enough. I've seen how young they like them in this uncivilized, backwater colony. I'm finding it difficult to believe that our sovereign is actually preparing to quell the insurgency over here."

"Insurgency?"

"When colonists rebel against their country it's called

insurgency. It's also treason. It's whispered about on every street corner of your cities, bandied about in every tavern, and it's lauded in your little news rags, like the *Colonial Register*. All of which is treasonous by law."

"I know what insurgency is, and you're wrong. What you just described sounds like free men with a voice. If that is treason, then the word needs another definition."

He sighed hugely, reaching for his mug of water. "I thought we changed the subject."

"Find one more to my liking than looking at a man's behind, then."

His reaction was probably a chuckle. He shouldn't have been drinking at the time, she thought, watching him cough and choke again. It was some time before he said anything. She waited.

"Verra well, Constant. We'll leave off arguing finer points of treason and the law. I'm at a disadvantage at the moment. I canna' face you and argue."

She smiled at that. "Does that mean you're going to be quiet, finally?"

"Quiet?" He tipped his head as if considering it. "I might, if you answer my question first."

"What was it?" she replied.

"Why have you na' wed?"

Constant had a handful of grease and was hovering above the well-feathered rump, trying to gather her courage. She knew what she had to do. She knew it wasn't going to be easy. She knew it made her warm with the blush. Nothing helped. She swallowed.

"I have no offers," she answered.

"Really? The men in this country are more dense than I suspected."

She reddened even more, closed her eyes, and plopped her greased hand on his buttocks. It was just as embarrassing as she'd suspected it would be. She felt him stiffen as she picked up the cheesecloth and wiped him free of feathers. And then she opened her eyes.

Oh no! That is much worse! More man than she'd ever seen was displayed right in front of her, covered only by the thin sheen of black tar.

"You should na' be doing this," he said.

"No, I shouldn't. Why, I'll probably have lost my virtue before I'm finished, too."

He chuckled. "Na' from this position, sweet."

"Sir—"

"Kam," he interrupted her. "It's my name, Constant. Please use it. Please?"

Constant picked up her knife and started sharpening.

"I doona' like the sound of that," he said.

"What?"

"I may na' be a colonist, Constant, but I'm still human. You're starting to make me verra nervous. I dinna' ask for this. I did little more than drink overmuch in the wrong den of seditious souls. Now I'm covered with a rock-hard substance, weak as a new bairn. I've some verra angered ribs, I'm na' certain my legs survived the burns, I've my bare backside in the air, and a young lass who detests me is sharpening her knife prior to carving on me. I doona' see much to like. Do you?"

"You liked my stew," she answered. "Kameron."

Saying his name gave her chills. It was almost as strange as the tingle she got when her left hand rested on him. She took a deep breath and slid her knife under the layer of tar. The skin she uncovered was as unblemished as his shoulder and a lot pinker. Her embarrassment deepened. If he said one word, she was going to choke.

She wiped the knife and slid the blade along his flesh, slipping the tar away just like an apple peel. It even curled as it lifted. Constant watched that, and ordered her mind and eyes not to see what she was revealing. And knew it was impossible.

She had to stop more than once to dab at her forehead, upper lip, and then her fingers. Her hands were shaking, too. It was so excruciatingly embarrassing it brought tears. She only hoped he didn't hear it. And then it was finished. She was finally done, and she sniffed loudly against her sleeve. Then she put her hands to her eyes and tried to hold it in.

"I doona' believe I can ever repay this, Connie," he whispered.

"Please . . . don't say a word," she answered, her voice breaking midway through the sentence.

"I doona' believe I've ever met anyone like you."

"Please?"

She was shuddering with holding the weeping in, and going nearly sleepless for two days and a night was taking its toll. Aside from that, she usually wasn't the type to cry. She was the one everyone counted on to be stoic, passionless, and strong.

"Is there a blanket or some such, to cover me?"

"Uh . . ." she looked up, wondering at the stupidity behind his having to ask such a question. She hadn't considered what she'd put on him once he was without his covering of feathers and tar. She started untying her apron. "I've got an apron," she answered.

"It's a verra good thing I'm secure in my manhood," he replied. "I would na' survive being naked afore a strange lass and then having to wear her apron. My mother would na' be able to show her face in society if she knew."

"You've a mother?" Constant sniffed the last of the tears away and tucked her apron about him. And for some reason, it helped.

"Contrary to appearances . . . I was na' hatched," he replied dryly.

She snorted in amusement. It cleared her nose out and then she had to wipe it against her sleeve.

"I promise you, I'll make this up to you."

"You'll do that when you walk out of my life."

"I only hope that's possible, love," he answered.

She blushed and reached for the lard. "I've been doing some thinking, and you shouldn't be calling me such endearments," she replied.

"Probably na'. But you should na' be with a near-naked man in your hayloft, either. Tell me something we should be doing."

Chapter Four

Constant rocked back on her heels and considered him. She'd gotten through peeling his backside. It couldn't get worse. And she was stalling. She got a gob of lard and started spreading it down the back of one thigh. She stopped when her hand rubbed against a large strip of rope midway to his knee.

"There's a binding on you."

"You doona' say? How odd," he answered flippantly.

"They tied you?"

He ignored her question. "You've quite the hand in the kitchen, Connie, love. Your bread is most fragrant. Thick. Soft. Better than my sire's chef. I wonder if the man will survive the insult once I inform him."

"My name isn't Connie."

"Well, that's what I'm going to call you. It's more informal."

"Constant. My name is Constant."

"I think I ken why they named you such. You bring constant joy into their lives"—he paused for a moment, as if for theatrical effect—"obviously."

"You would be wrong."

"So, why did they name you Constant?"

"Why did they tie you?"

"Because I'm verra large, verra strong, and I'm a devil when attacked. Would na' you have tied me?"

"Why were they so vicious?" He must have had his mouth full, because he didn't say anything while she wiped at the feather-grease mixture on his upper thigh. "And what did you really do?" she continued, working at the rope with her knife.

"You probably should na' cut through that . . . just yet," he replied.

"Why not?"

"Offhand, I'd say it's doing a fair job of holding my leg in one place and keeping it straight. Rather like a splint."

Constant dropped the knife. Her eyes flew wide and she looked up at him. He'd swiveled his neck to look at her and more tar had fallen off his face. He had fairly full lips and a perfectly defined, square jaw. He had a small cleft in his chin, too. Her mind went absolutely blank.

"What?" he asked.

She shook her head. She couldn't think of one intelligible thing to say.

"Well, if you're na' going to speak with me anymore, this is going to be a hellishly long night."

Constant cleared her throat. It actually helped. "I didn't say I wouldn't speak to you."

"Good. Then, go on with your story. Tell me why they named you Constant."

"I already told you. It was punishment."

His eyebrows wrinkled. Although they had tar sticking to them, she could tell they were a light brown color. She wondered if they matched his hair.

"Explain," he said.

"My older sisters are Felicity, Prudence, Hope, Patience,

Faith, and Charity. Father told my mother the last four were named for his virtues, because all she presented him with were daughters."

"And?" he prompted.

"He told her if she presented him with any more daughters, he was going to start naming them exactly as he saw it."

"And that was?"

"You can't tell? Constant Stream . . . Of Daughters."

"Good Lord! You canna' mean he would have named a child Of?"

"Don't know. Henry came next. Father said he should have come up with his threat years earlier, since they got too old to try again."

"Thank heaven. I pity the poor girl they might have produced."

"Do you have any sisters?" she asked.

"Nae," he replied.

"Brothers?"

"Nae," he replied again.

"You're an only child?"

"That's what occurs when one has no siblings, so . . . aye."

He was smiling in order to make the sarcasm more palatable, but Constant narrowed her eyes. He was incredibly handsome, but he was also without morals and lacked any sense of how to treat the girl who still had carving to do on his body.

"Has your father passed on, then? Your mother?" she asked.

"Na' to my knowledge," he answered with the flippant tone he wielded so quickly and easily.

"I'm sorry, then."

"You're sorry my parents are both living?"

"I didn't mean that. I meant I'm sorry they couldn't have other children besides you."

He smiled wryly. It made her mouth go instantly dry. She looked away.

"My mother produced an heir. Me. She fulfilled her duty. She was na' about to put herself through anything like that again."

"I don't understand."

"What doona' you understand, love?"

She turned back to him and frowned. "My name is Constant. You will use it when speaking to me, please."

"You make this butter?" he asked, putting a bite of bread in his mouth and chewing it. "It's verra good. Perfectly salted."

"Cows make butter," she replied.

He grinned. That was even worse. She should be grateful black tar still clung to his cheeks, his nose, and his forehead.

"Did you churn it, then?"

She nodded.

"You're quite a catch, Constant Ridgely. I'm surprised the gents round here have na' spotted it. They must be blind. Deaf. And care little about the taste of their food."

She reached between his thighs to retrieve her knife. She had to avert her face to do it. Then she was peeling at his upper legs. The tar came up easily. She assumed it was because he had more hair there, which kept it from sticking as much. It wasn't long before she had both legs clear almost to the backs of his knees.

He was tensing the more she touched him, though. The flesh was weeping a clear liquid with every movement of her knife, too. She had trouble controlling the trembling of her own hands. Her tears weren't caused by embarrassment now. They were caused by his suffering.

"I'm not certain I can finish this . . . Kameron," she told him when she slid grease down to his ankle, being as gentle as possible; and yet still he went ramrod stiff.

"Most surgeons . . . doona' weep for their patients, Connie."

"I'm not a surgeon," she replied.

"So tell me . . . do you have a gent, Connie girl?"

He was shuddering so hard, the question came in chunks.

"Yes."

"What's . . . his name?"

"I don't think I should tell you."

"It's . . . all right. I'm . . . na' jealous," he answered, huffing between each word.

She shook her head slightly. "I'm not going to tell you because of who he is and who you are. That would be stupid."

"And just . . . who . . . am I?"

"A British soldier."

"I'm na' British, Connie, love."

"Dearest God." Constant breathed the words as she made the first slice of her knife at the tar behind one knee. The skin wasn't unblemished and clear. It wasn't even skin. It was flesh that was wet with a clear liquid.

"What is it?"

"I'm so sorry, Kameron." She sniffed and wiped her eyes on her sleeve so she could see. "I'm not certain where to put my knife. Everywhere I try . . . skin comes up with it."

"I'm burned, Connie. It's probably dead skin, anyway. Besides, they did me a bit of a favor, actually."

"A favor?"

"They left me tied."

"That was a favor?"

"Aye. Na' only was tar unable to reach the skin behind those ropes, but they gave my legs support in the event they're broken. I doona' think they did it apurpose. They dinna' realize how much they helped me, and I was in nae fit condition to alert them."

"You think . . . they're broken?"

"Perhaps one. I doona' ken for certain. I'm pretending I doona' have much feeling in them at the moment. It's almost working."

"Is that why you won't be quiet as I asked?"

"Bright girl. Remind me to search out the young gents in this country and knock some sense into them . . . leaving you unclaimed and available. Why, they'd best mind themselves. I'm na' immune to your charms, myself."

"Oh, I hardly think so, sir!"

"Kam," he reminded her. "And what's wrong with me having an eye on your charms?"

"Well . . . you're a British soldier, you're too old, you speak funny, and you've got a very slick tongue. If I didn't think it to keep your mind off your pain, I'd accuse you of being a liar, too."

"I keep telling you. I'm na' British. I'm Scot. There's a huge difference, sweet."

"Constant." She said it through gritted teeth.

"You're na' verra flattering, love. You deflate a man with few words. I speak funny and I'm too auld? Remind me to recommend your bedside manner to all my injured friends. And even if all that is true, how does any of it make me a liar?"

"You speak of charms. And I haven't got any." She peeled another bit of tar up and sighed with relief when it came easily, being attached more to rope than skin.

"Oh, you have plenty," he answered. "Trust me."

"Yes, I know." She put her knife beneath another

ridge of tar. "I'm strong. I'm built solid . . . like a man. I work hard. I bake and cook and I tend farm animals. I can till and harvest a field. Spin fabric. Sew. All wonderful exploits, I'm certain."

"You doona' look . . . in a mirror oft, do you?"

"Why would I do that? I know what I'll see."

"Describe it for me," he asked.

"Why?"

"It'll help keep my mind off other things." He sucked in air through closed teeth.

"Other things?"

"Like my current state. My immobility. How much this pains. Things akin to that."

"Oh, Kameron. I'm sorry."

He shook his head. "That sort of reaction is na' working. I need my mind *off* my current state. So . . . I'll try another tack. What do you do about here for entertainment?"

"Entertainment?"

"You ken . . . dice. Board games. Cards. You have any cards?"

"Of course not!"

"Why? Are they against the law?"

"Drinking and gaming are vices. As are adultery and philandering."

"You mean I'm on Puritan soil?"

"The Puritans live up Salem way. Past Boston. Now, that city has all sorts of vices. Not like here. We're God-fearing Christians around here."

"Of course you are. That makes it odd that I was in a drinking establishment when this all started. So you may be God-fearing and Christian, but you are na' teetotalers. You drink. I know you do. I've seen you."

"The menfolk might. I don't know. I'm not one."

"That is definitely one of your charms, Connie."

"What?"

She looked up from the area at the back of one calf. He was a mass of stained, charred ropes as she neared his ankles, but little wounded skin. That made the peeling easier and quicker.

"You're a lass. That's a good thing in the current state of my affairs. I shudder to think what this would be like with a young lad working . . . where you've been."

Constant looked up at his body, past the apron-draped backside, the cheesecloth-covered back, and took in black-framed lines of suffering etched on his face.

"We probably shouldn't talk this way," she said.

"You're shy," he replied.

She looked back down. "We go to church," she said finally.

"What?"

"You asked what we do for entertainment. We go to church."

"Too much singing, threatening, and complaining takes place at church. That is hardly entertainment. Think of something else."

"Well . . . we get together when we can. Now that it's harvest time, we do it more often."

"Tell me about these get-togethers," he requested.

"They're for socializing."

"What on earth do you colonists call socializing?"

"We meet at each other's homes; discuss the latest gossip, the newest dress patterns. Who is engaged, who is expecting a child. News like that."

"Oh. Sort of like a ladies' tea."

"It probably would be like that if we had enough money to afford the exorbitant tax. We haven't had tea in months."

He groaned. "Must we return to that again?"

Constant looked up from her ministrations. He was facing forward again, slumped over the log.

"We also have barn raisings. We attended one last month, at the Jacob Pryor place."

"Barn raising? That sounds like work."

"Oh, it isn't. It's great entertainment. The men compete in teams, to see who can get a side up the fastest and the best made."

"Do you ever do anything together?"

"I just told you we do. A team is more than one."

"I mean male to female, as in dancing. Do you never have balls?"

"Balls?"

"Where everyone dresses formally, puts on airs, and nae one is required to do more than dance and speak pretty words?"

"Sounds stiff and very British to me," she replied.

He made a sound close to exasperation. Constant ignored it. She had one leg completely peeled. She mopped at her forehead before starting on the other knee.

"I think they have fancy-dress balls in the city. I've heard tales. I've just never attended one."

"Why na'? Are you too young?"

"I have too much to do, and no fancy dress."

"I've decided my method of payment to you, Constant, my love. I'll see you clothed elegantly and beautifully, and then I'll escort you to a fancy-dress ball. I promise."

She blew out a sigh. "You're going to leave, remember? That was our bargain. You've got a garrison to return to. Laws to uphold. Taxes to collect. Colonists to bully. Trouble could break out any moment. We won't be allowed to dance. We'll be near-enemies. Why, I've as much chance of dancing with you at a ball as I have of . . . of . . . well, of wedding my own beau at this point."

"What's wrong with the fellow?"

Constant started peeling at his other knee, disgusted to be saying anything. "I outgrew him," she answered.

"Is he your age?"

"Yes."

"Give him a couple of years. He'll sprout. Most lads do."

"There're at least four other girls trying to catch his eye." She tried to keep the wistful note from her voice but knew she didn't succeed. "I haven't got a couple of years. I probably don't have but another season before he'll be engaging himself to one of them, instead."

"Good riddance to him, then! If he canna' see the prize right in front of his nose, then he deserves to lose it."

Constant smirked. "Besides, we don't need balls. We do other things to get together. We have quilting bees. I belong to three of them."

"What is a quilting bee?"

"It's a group who go from house to house, chatting and socializing and putting stitches into quilts. That way everyone gets new quilts each year, and it's quicker than sewing them by yourself."

"Boring," he replied.

Constant stopped slicing. It wasn't because of his remark; it was the leg beneath her. The ropes were cutting into swollen, tight flesh, and there wasn't a speck of his leg that wasn't a mottled purple color. She'd sprained an ankle before. She knew what they felt and looked like. He'd be lucky if it was broken.

"Oh, Kameron," she whispered. "How do you manage to talk as if—"

"When are you going to call me Kam?" he interrupted.

"That's too . . . informal."

"You have seen my naked arse, Constant Ridgely, and you're talking formality?"

Her lips tightened. "I don't think you're amusing," she replied.

"Good. Use that emotion to get this over with, then. Doona' stop and quail on me now, Connie, love."

"But . . . it has to pain. I may hurt it worse no matter what I do."

"Go on then. Finish. Assess the damage later. It could be worse. You could have left me there."

"I'll try to be gentle."

"I ken. You're a verra gentle person. The man who claims you will be gaining a treasure. I'll help you find him, too. I promise. Oh. You want me to disappear. I forgot. Go on, love. Take up your knife and cut away. I doona' offer such a thing to many lasses. There would be too many takers."

"You've got a strange sense of humor," she said.

"Always did. And worry does na' change anything. Naught will. So . . . if I have to live without my lower legs, it will be my own fault, now will na' it?"

"What did you do?" she asked.

"I was dense. Extremely so, now that I ponder it."

"Dense?"

"Aye. I recall entering one of your little sedition-minded, treason-filled and populated drinking establishments, and I remember wearing my uniform."

"Were you drinking?"

"I was na' just drinking, I was well into a good drunk."

"Oh, dear God."

"There's naught ungodly about drinking, Constant."

"If you hadn't been drinking, would this have happened to you?" she asked.

"You have me there. Bright lass, as I've made mention. I suppose my answer will have to be that it might have happened, but I'd have given better than I received. At least one of them would be wearing feathers, too. So tell me, Constant, my love, how bad is it?"

She had the last of the tar off and didn't know how he'd guessed. He was bound from above the knees to his ankles, and one leg was blackish purple and twice the size of the other. The healthy one looked all right. More than all right, it looked as well muscled and strong as the rest of him, but she couldn't tell him any of *that*.

"Well?" he prompted.

"I think . . . one leg is fine."

"Is the injured one setting straight?"

"How am I supposed to tell?"

"Ankles. Are they together? Side by side?"

She surveyed them. "Yes."

"I might just be in luck."

"I should go for the surgeon. I should, really."

He swiveled his head to look at her. "And I already told you. Thatcher was there."

Constant shook her head. "He doesn't drink."

"He may na', but he had few qualms about joining a mob. Trust me."

"We can't just leave it, though. What if it doesn't set straight?"

"Are you that worried about me?" he asked.

Constant looked at those golden-brown eyes and blurted out the truth. "It would be a pure shame, I think," she whispered.

"A shame?"

"To have damage done to any part of you."

"What?" He sounded strange.

"You may be the most handsome man . . . I've ever seen, Kameron. To have any part of you damaged is more than I can contemplate. I have to make certain it isn't so."

She shouldn't have said it. Her entire body felt hot. He flushed, too. At least, there was a pink tint to his shoulders, his chin, and neck.

"With such sugared words, Constant, love, it's a verra good thing I'm na' on my back at this moment. A verra good thing. I might get ideas."

Her brows went together. "About what?" she asked.

His lips twitched. Then he turned forward and picked up another slice of bread and addressed his next words to the barn wall. "When we find your husband, have him tell you. Fair? So, tell me . . . which part of me do you plan to uncover next?"

Constant's eyes widened and her breath came quick enough to be called gasping. She had to control it before she answered. "I was thinking . . . I might pour . . . honey on your legs," she said.

"You think that might help a break, do you?"

"It might salve your burns. Aside from which, the air has to hurt. It does, doesn't it? If we get the spots covered, it might not hurt as much."

"What makes you think . . . it hurts?"

She tipped the jar and watched the honey-herb mixture ooze onto the weeping, whitish-looking skin between the ropes. He went so stiff at the first touch that his body arched up from the straw, putting the brunt of his weight on his forearms. Tears stung her eyes again. She didn't think she could answer. She was trembling before she finished getting the bandages on him.

"That . . . was na' pleasant," he croaked between the heaving breaths he was taking.

"I'm sorry," she whispered.

"I ken. I only hope my front is na' as burned."

"Oh no! I never even thought of that!"

"We'll look at it tomorrow night. Fair enough? 'Tis late, and you need some sleep."

"I don't have time for sleep."

"Make time. I'd rather you had some afore you continue carving on me. Think of that."

"I still have to get the feathers from you. I have to peel the tar away. I have to get you covered again. I have to get you better—"

"You've tortured me enough for one night, Constant, love. Let it wait. Please? I doona' think I can take much more right now."

The tears overflowed. She put the heels of her hands to her eye sockets to stop them, but it didn't work.

"Connie, please. Doona' weep. I'm na' worth it. I'm a detestable Highlander masquerading as a soldier, remember? I'm a philanderer, a profaner, and further . . . I drink to excess. Come along, love. Cease crying. Please?"

She shuddered through another breath and put her arm across her face to shield it while she wiped at her eyes. He was right. He was all those things. She was simply tired, and it was well past midnight already.

"See? That's better. We'll just do a little work on my arms and call it a night. You agree?"

"Your arms?"

"I doona' think I took much burn up here. That happens when tar is poured on you as you dangle upside down from an available tree limb. It hits your feet first, your head last. At least, I think that's how it happened. I was na' fully conscious at the time. Either way, my arms doona' feel burned, but I canna' move them easily."

"They're hurt, too?"

"Nae. Uh . . . I have hair on them. It pulls with each and every move. Verra annoying. It feels as if I'm encased in a suit of armor, complete with horsehair shirt. Verra scratchy. I doona' ken how my forebears stood it. It's na' pleasant. I would also like the opportunity to relieve myself at some point, without having to ask you to assist. I doona' think I could bear that. In fact, I'm perishing at the thought."

He wasn't looking anywhere near her, thankfully. She wasn't crying anymore. She couldn't. She was much too embarrassed. She knew her face was red.

"So, tell me. Are you going to stay like that, or are you going to help me get this stuff off my arms?"

She picked up the tub of lard and crawled forward.

Chapter Five

Constant hadn't much time to think of her patient the entire next day. Charity had finally had her baby. It was a girl. That news was accompanied by consternation and wailing whenever it was spoken of. Constant rolled her eyes as she finished gathering clean clothing in the laundry.

It wasn't so much the child's gender they were worrying over, nor was it Charity's husband John Becon's reaction when he found out. The women in the house were more upset that Charity wasn't recovering well. She might not be able to bear more children. That was upsetting everyone except Charity and Constant, but for different reasons. Charity was said to be relieved at never having to go through such agony again. Constant was less vocal, but she was relieved, too. There was enough of John Becon and his insufferable arrogance already in the world. She thought it might be a blessing.

Constant finished the supper dishes, dragged out the laundry tub, and started filling it with heated water for an impromptu bath. She was alone. Everyone was asleep, exhausted over the vigil at Charity's bedside. Henry didn't argue when he was sent to bed, either. That was odd, if she thought of it. He always argued over having to do things he didn't want to do, and going to bed was definitely one of them.

Constant pulled down her best working gown. It was a hand-me-down, as were all her clothes, but it hadn't one patch on it, and the pinkish color Charity had dyed into it still clung to each fiber. It also had a frilled apron. Constant blushed as she tossed that atop her pile, recalling where her other apron was.

It wasn't much later that she was climbing up the rungs to the loft, a blanket looped atop one shoulder, her wet hair braided and wrapped about her head beneath her cap, her apron tied around a bundle of supper for him, and another bucket of warm water in her hand. It was going to be a chore to get the honey-dried bandages from him, but it was one she actually looked forward to.

She set her bundles down and lit the wick on her lamp, noticing for the first time how much frost was in the air. That wasn't good, because she hadn't seen to her patient. He hadn't much to wear. Then again, she reassured herself, he slept in a hayloft full of straw. If he got cold, he should know what to do about it.

She knew where to find him this time. Constant smiled slightly. He was asleep and he hadn't any straw atop him. He probably needed it. He was propped up on the log, although he'd pulled some of the quilt beneath him and onto the wood, making it more comfortable. He had her apron tucked around him. His arms were just as muscled and strong-looking as she'd seen last night. It was especially noticeable now that he hadn't any hair on them.

Her smile got bigger. The tar on his arms had come up easily, but he'd been complaining the entire time of how much body hair she was removing with every motion of her knife. He seemed to think she removed it closer to his skin than she had to. On purpose. She hadn't known men worried over that sort of thing, and she didn't have anyone to ask. She went for her bucket and started unrolling another hank of cheesecloth as she considered him.

The bandage on his back was crusty with her honey mixture, but there wasn't any sign of blood. Constant knelt at his side and dipped a bit of cloth to dampen the bandage on his back. She had to push his hair out of the way first, and then she held the soaked cloth to his bandage to soften it. His hair wasn't brown as she'd suspected it would be. It was greasy-looking, but looked to be a white-blond shade. It looked thick and long, too. It probably reached the middle of his back when he had it properly tied back. She lifted the rag and put it into the bucket to soak up more water.

She was almost to his back again when he turned his neck and smiled up at her. Constant's eyes widened, her mouth dropped open, and her body started ringing with alarm. He hadn't a speck of tar on his face or in the hair she'd been admiring, and he was worse than handsome. He was beautiful.

"Hello, Constant," he said with a quirk to those lips.

She dropped the rag and put both hands over her mouth. It didn't help, but at least it hid some of her reaction. "Oh, sweet heaven," she replied.

"I hope your reaction has a bit to do with my appearance."

"I-I," she stammered, and then her throat closed off.

"If so . . . then every bit of bother today would be worth it."

He was still grinning, and on the man that had been revealed, it was incredible. The tar hadn't scarred one bit of his face. It wouldn't have dared. Constant looked at the lushly lashed brown eyes she'd already noticed, the cleft chin at the juncture of a perfectly chiseled jawline, the lightly tanned skin, the full lips, and despite his claim of being twenty-eight years old, there wasn't one hint of a line anywhere.

"What is it?" he asked.

She was feeling the shock evaporate, replaced by unreasonable anger. She felt as though some massive joke had been played out at her expense and she didn't like it. She didn't like it one bit.

"Nothing," she replied stiffly and moved her hands from her face. She still had to get the rest of the feathers and tar from him. She had to soak the bandages off and put honey-herb mixture back on him. She'd yet to handle the most embarrassing task of her life: getting the tar-feather mixture from his masculine area, unless he felt capable to do it himself.

He'd damn well better be capable!

She was amazed at her sudden thought. She had been taught better. She never cursed, even to herself. Now she had to repent. And it was all his fault! He wasn't supposed to be so striking he made her entire insides feel like mixed-up jam! *Damn it!* She swore to herself again. This time on purpose. If she had to repent for using unfit language, she might as well get some in. She had her jaw clenched as she soaked the bandage on his back.

"A little more gentleness, if you please," he said, stiffening a bit.

"What?"

"I said . . . ouch!"

She lifted her hands from him the moment he jerked. She was being ridiculous and she knew it. She had to sit back, look at the vaulted ceiling of the barn, and take gulping breaths. And that didn't even work. Nothing did.

"I'm sorry, lass," he said.

"For what?"

"Surprising you. I thought you'd be pleased."

He wasn't looking her way, but she didn't look to verify it. She knew it by the way his shoulders moved.

"Oh, it is a surprise," she said. "A rather horrid one."

"If you're na' pleased, just say so."

"I already called you the most handsome man I'd ever seen. It appears I was mistaken."

"A simple 'I'm na' pleased' would be sufficient," he replied.

"But no," she continued, watching her own hands quiver above his bandaged back. "You're not only the most handsome man I've ever seen, you're probably one of the most handsome ever born. What a horrible surprise."

She didn't dare look anywhere but at his back. Tears of mortification were stinging her lids and making every breath burn.

"The way I look is a horrible surprise? I doona' believe I've ever heard it said that way afore. You're named Constant because you're constantly surprising. That's the true reason, is na' it?"

"I am going to try to peel off the rest of your tar and feathers now, Kameron. I'm going to finish my chore and then I'm going to wash my hands of you and hope we never meet again."

"Damn. You really are na' pleased."

"I am not pleased," she retorted.

"Why ever na'?"

"Because an English soldier is supposed to be ugly."

He snorted but caught the sound before it turned into a full laugh. "Good thing I'm na' English, then. Oh . . . Christ! That hurts. Uh . . . apologies. I mean, by heaven that hurts."

"I haven't touched you," she replied.

"'Tis . . . my ribs. I keep forgetting."

"Oh." It was all she could think of.

"You can start soaking the bandage now. I will na' move. I promise."

"I don't think I can," she answered.

"What? Why?"

"Because of what you've done."

"What have I done? I shaved everything from my face. I cut tar out of my hair. I rubbed myself with your lard, plucked feathers, and made everything in my chest ache. That's what I did. On second thought, it was na' worth it for me, either."

He was stiff with anger. That was a better reason than pain. Constant looked over the entire length of him. It didn't help. She returned her gaze to her own lap.

"You've made my work harder," she whispered.

He looked at her again. She knew, because the hard ridge of muscle at his waist pulled a bit at the motion. She didn't move her eyes from her own entwined hands.

"How?"

"I'm the seventh of eight girls. I have never before seen a—a man. Not this close, and definitely not this . . . intimately. I was not even allowed into the upstairs rooms while Charity was in labor." Her voice was drying up. She looked over at him and her heart did a dive into the pit of her stomach. She swallowed.

"And?" he prompted.

"I still have to get the rest of this tar and feather mixture from you. It wasn't easy. I proved that last night." She couldn't control the blush, but he wasn't as angry anymore.

"And?" he asked again.

"It's harder now that I know."

"Now that you know what?"

"That you're this . . . ." she began, and her voice just stopped.

"Handsome? Or, would it be striking? Large? Perhaps

more toward overpowering? Brawny? Maybe just strong? Manly? It could be that, too. Which?"

"All . . . of that." She whispered the words, but he heard them.

He was openly grinning now. Constant couldn't keep eye contact. She dropped her gaze back to her lap.

"I see now, lass. You're pleased. You just doona' ken how to show it. You've na' had much contact with men, and I surprised you. I could apologize for startling you with my appearance, but I will na' bother. Most women find me attractive. In fact, now that I think on it—*all* of them do."

"I can leave you like this," she replied.

He sighed hugely, and then caught his breath with what was probably pain. "Oh . . . verra well. I'll be a good patient and keep my mouth shut and try to pretend that I'm an ugly auld soldier. I want you to ken in advance that it's na' going to be easy."

"Kameron?"

"Aye?"

"I'm going to need you to be quiet now."

He sighed again, softer this time. "Verra well. Begin. Do your worst. I'll attempt to ignore how much it pains, with my own imagination for company."

Constant reached for the cloth. Despite the chill in the air and the dampness of the material in her hands, she felt absolutely scorched, and only because she'd had been in contact with his bandage! She sighed and dropped the cloth into the bucket. Her hands weren't cooperating. She picked up the rag and held it limply above the bucket and tried narrowing her eyes. That didn't work, either. All that happened was the man at her knees shimmered with the lamplight.

She moved to soak the honey-encrusted bandage off and a strange buzzing sensation seemed to be affecting her palms. No matter how often she touched him, the vibration came again, and with it her fingers tingled, her wrists warmed, and her entire body flushed. It was terrible and odd, and thrilling and frightening at the same time. And she didn't know what she was supposed to do about it.

The bandage came up, most of the honey-herb mixture with it. Constant peered at him for a bit. She didn't know if the salve had helped. She reached for the jar and dribbled some more over him, following the latticework of wounds across his back.

"Connie?" he asked.

She folded four layers of cheesecloth together to put over his back and had it in place before she answered. It was a lot of cloth, but she was doing the laundry. She could simply wash it and hang it out. She was already debating if she'd have time in the morning. That way no one would ever know.

"Yes?" she answered as nonchalantly as possible.

"What do you look like beneath the shapeless sacks you wear?"

Her eyes flew wide and she inhaled cold air. It was a good thing she had her hands in the bucket of tepid water, where he couldn't see them jerk. This time she didn't bother wringing out the cheesecloth before pressing it atop the old layers on his legs. She was rougher than she meant to be, but her hands didn't feel like her own at all. She watched him tense.

"You're not to ask such a thing." She managed to get the words through her teeth.

"Well, my own imagination . . . palls on me after a time."

She was choking. Her eyes were wide and she stared, unseeing, at the length of bandage right in front of her. "Please don't do this," she implored.

"Why?"

"Because . . . I'm asking you not to."

"Oh, verra well. You're impossible to flirt with, Constant. You probably doona' even ken the meaning of the word."

"Of course I know what flirting is. It's pretending an attraction to engage someone's interest when you don't truly want it."

"Wrong," he answered.

"Can't you be a little quiet? At least until I get this off?"

His leg bandages came up easily. The skin didn't look any worse than last night. She had honey-herb salve dribbled all over before he spoke again. His voice sounded lower than before and trembled slightly.

"Perhaps if you flirted with this beau of yours, he would na' even look at those other lasses."

"How do you pretend interest if you really feel it?"

She kept her attention on the length of cheesecloth she was preparing for his legs where the swelling was still severe. The top of the skin was flaky and whitish. She hoped he wouldn't lose his leg. It would be especially cruel for someone who looked like him.

"Flirting is na' pretending. It's making the other person aware that there's someone of the opposite gender who finds them interesting, if na' downright intriguing."

"How do you do that?"

"Come here. I'll show you. We'll practice."

"I haven't got your bandage in place," she replied.

"Verra well. Finish. And then come here to talk with me for a bit. I'll show you how to flirt and you can practice on me."

She gulped. "I can't do that. I still have work to do. I

have to puzzle out how I'm going to get the front of your legs peeled. We probably shouldn't wait much longer."

"Why?"

"Tar on open wounds can't be good. If they fester and poison, you might lose your legs."

"I doona' think there's much danger of anything except severe dry skin, Connie, love."

"You . . . don't?"

"I'm hazarding a guess they poured it first all down my back. At least, that's what it feels like. I'm grateful. And lucky."

"Why?"

"I'm grateful they dinna' burn all of me, and I'm lucky it cooled before reaching . . . uh, certain parts. Na' that it does na' itch and annoy, but I think 'tis little more than blisters. Besides which, I doona' wish to put anything on my back just yet. It's painful. Makes the front of my legs feel like faeries trifled with them."

"Oh."

It was easier to give him short answers, she decided. They didn't give things away; like how little sense he made, and how it felt to look over a broad measure of the back he'd just spoken about.

"So, come up here. Sit for a spell and keep me company while I sample what you've brought me to eat. You did bring me sup, dinna' you?"

Constant went to get the food she'd tied in her frilly apron. "I brought roast turkey, apple-nut salad, pickled beets, potatoes and gravy—although I mixed them together to travel better—and a half loaf of bread. You like my bread, as I recall." She opened her apron and spread it for him.

"Please doona' tell me you cooked all this."

"I won't," she answered. "Besides, it wouldn't be true. I didn't cook anything in the salad."

He grinned to show he heard; then attacked his food. She should have brought him something earlier, she realized. As he shoveled it in so quickly, Constant wondered if he could even taste it. She sat on the straw beside him, her feet tucked under her knees, and waited. He had a healthy appetite. He polished off everything except one apple. But that was to be expected. He even drank the entire quart of cider she'd brought. She shook her head.

"What?" he asked when he brought the jar back down.

"I'm surprised at how much you eat."

"I get one meal a day and it's a delight on the tongue. You think I'd waste it?"

"I'm sorry. I never thought about that. I should have brought some for you to save for morn. That isn't very considerate of me, is it?"

"You're an angel of mercy, Connie. Forgive my words. The verra last thing I wish is to make you feel bad. Your cooking is amazing, you are constantly amazing, and I spend most of the day sleeping, anyway. Unlike you. Did you get any?"

"Any what?"

She wasn't pretending the confusion. It was difficult to concentrate when he turned the full extent of his golden-brown gaze on her. She wondered if he knew, then answered her own question. Of course, he knew. He had said he attracted not some, or even most, of the ladies, but all of them. *All.* She only wished it wasn't most likely true.

"Sleep," he answered.

"A couple of hours, I think." She moved her gaze to her entwined hands.

"You need more. I doona' wish your carving hand shaking from lack of rest. Think of how that will affect me."

Constant couldn't answer. The last thing she was pondering was lack of sleep.

"So. Are you ready to experience a little flirting?"

"Uh . . ." She didn't have an answer. She was afraid of what her body was experiencing already. The idea he could make her feel interesting and intriguing sent everything to an even higher pulse-pounding tremble.

"Look at me," he said.

She shook her head.

"We canna' entice this beau if we doona' look at him. Have you considered that?"

She shook her head again. It felt as though her entire body was covered with a fine sheen of perspiration. It would probably reflect in the oil lamp, and what excuse was she supposed to give? The air had a bite of frost in it and she was overheated. It was as impossible as it was faintly illicit, and just a tad exciting.

"What's his name?"

"Thomas." She croaked out the name. It was the best she could manage.

"Thomas. The fellow has a lass like you waiting for him and he looks elsewhere. He's a fool. You ken that?"

She glanced up and gulped.

Chapter Six

"We'll start again, and go a little slower. You ready?"

She bit at the tip of her tongue and nodded.

"Tell me. And be honest. Keep looking at me. Good. Now . . . tell me what you see."

At least she thought that was what he said. Her ears didn't hear a thing over her own pulse. Constant held his gaze for a count of four before she dropped hers. She suffered through another blush.

"Constant?" he asked in a tone she hadn't heard before.

"Yes?"

"We canna' flirt with this fellow if we canna' look him in the eye."

"I think . . . I should go now," she answered.

"Look at me first. I promise I will na' move. You have my word as a Highlander. My solemn word. 'Tis a far-fetched notion anyway, since I'm still half covered with hardened tar and the accompanying feathers."

"We . . . should work on that," she replied.

"Tomorrow. I'll put some weight on my back tomorrow. On one condition."

Her head came back up and she looked as levelly as

possible at him. The lantern was somewhere behind her, putting her in semi-shadow, while his face was alight with the yellow glow. It had the same lighting effect on his eyes. They looked more akin to topaz. She would have gulped if her mouth and throat hadn't gone instantly dry.

"Better," he replied.

"What . . . is your condition?"

"That you learn how to use your gaze on a particular Thomas fellow who is being a bit stubborn."

"This is foolish," she replied.

He didn't say anything. He let his eyes do it for him, moving his gaze slowly and deliberately over her lips, down her throat, lingering at her bodice, before they slid to her entwined hands at her folded knees. It felt as intimate as a caress. At least, she thought it must be what a caress was like. It also felt as if everywhere he'd looked on her body was alert and ready.

She very nearly crossed her arms in front of her breasts as the reaction there startled and embarrassed her. The one thing stopping her was if she made any such move, he'd know he'd embarrassed and startled her. She knew he was aware of it, anyway.

He brought his gaze back the same way. Constant's eyes were wide as he returned the full measure of his attention to her, and she was having a difficult time pulling in, then letting out, each breath.

"Well?" he asked.

"Uh . . ." She tried to answer, but not much else came out.

"Did I make you aware of me, Constant, love?" he continued, in the same low tone.

She nodded her head.

"As a man?" he continued, lifting one brow.

She nodded again. It was safer, and her throat wasn't working well enough to speak.

"Do you ken why?"

"Uh . . ." she replied again.

"We'll answer that later. Now, look into my eyes again and tell me what you see. Look deep this time."

Constant ignored the loud pounding of her heartbeat in her ears and did what he asked. His eyes were well spaced and lushly fringed with dark lashes. "They're gold," she replied finally.

He was smiling. Her breathing grew shallow. Constant forced in another breath, only to release it the moment she did. Then she had to do it again as he looked back at her.

"I think they're described as brown," he replied.

"No," she answered. "They're gold, and sometimes they look almost amber."

His eyebrows lifted higher. "Amber?"

She nodded.

"This could be a good thing for our little plot."

"What plot?" she whispered.

"To entice the recalcitrant Thomas to your bed."

Her gasp was audible and she dropped her eyes again. She had to. The blush was too intense. She'd envisioned for a scant moment a man in her bed, but it wasn't Thomas Esterbrook.

"With the blessing of the church, of course," Kameron continued, clearing his throat. "I could claim innocence of the thought I just planted in your head, but since I did it on purpose, what would be the point?"

"What?"

"Look back at me, Constant."

She shook her head. *Look at him again?* She couldn't. She wondered with a strange sort of detached amazement what was wrong with her breasts. They felt larger, heavier, and the tips were even sensitive to the cloth that covered them. Looking toward Kameron was beyond her imagination at the moment.

"Your shyness could be a fairly large stumbling block for our poor Thomas," he said.

"What?"

"Your beau. Thomas. He canna' ask a question if you will na' look at him."

"I look at him. He never looks at me," she replied.

"That's what we're attempting to rectify."

"What? How?"

"Looking him in the eye. Enticing him. Dinna' I just entice you?"

"Uh . . ." Her face was red again. She could feel it.

"Dinna' I just make you aware of me as a male?"

"I already said yes." Her answer was directed toward the clasped hands at her knees.

"True. You did. Now, for the best part. Dinna' parts of your body tell you of it, as well?"

"I *really* think I should go." The first part of her statement came out as a squeak. The last part was a whisper.

He chuckled. "It's all right, love. Trust me. Such a response is natural and good and exactly as Our Maker intended. I promise. I also promise that I'll do naught to harm or frighten you. How could I do such to my own angel of mercy?"

"I'm not an angel," she replied.

"You are. I just have to get that blind Thomas fellow to see it."

"He's not blind," she replied. "He's as sharp-eyed as they come. He takes the marksman prize every season."

"You defend him. That's good. He may be a first-class marksman, but he's woefully inept at seeing what he's looking at."

"Why do you say that?"

"Because any man with sense kens the proper traits

to look for in a future wife. They look for compassion, warmth, charm, a frame that will birth bairns well—doona' quail on me now, Constant—where was I? Oh, yes. They should look for good health, a good disposition, and add in a heavy dose of culinary skills. It's also nice to find skills with needle and thread, spindle and wool-comb. Nae man likes to go threadbare. This is what a man should look for. And this is what our lad, Thomas, is na' seeing."

It was chilly in the loft, but Constant wasn't aware of it. She was overheated from the reaction of her own body. But his words about needle and thread jogged her memory. She cleared her throat.

"That reminds me. I brought a blanket for you. I forgot it last night. I wasn't thinking."

He let out a long breath and then he shrugged. At least, she thought he did, because it came with an accompanying groan and a mumbled curse followed by an apology.

"Are you cold?" he asked, finally.

She shook her head.

"I'm na' either. Why is that, you think?"

She looked up, locked gazes with him for the barest moment, and looked away again. Then she shrugged.

"It's the autumn season. It's the middle of the night. We're in a loft with an open window, and if you huff a breath out, you can see it. Yet, we're na' cold?"

"You're half covered with tar still," she offered.

"True, but it's on the side I'm lying on. Which does mean there's na' much on this side of me. I'm verra nearly naked, love."

She choked on the reply and moved backward so rapidly, she fell from her folded knees onto her backside, her farm boots landing right next to him. Constant rocked back to face him, holding her skirts in place. He was chuckling.

"I—" she began.

"Doona' leave me." He put a hand out to hold on to her ankle. Constant looked from his hand, up his shaved expanse of arm where muscles were flexing as if for her benefit, and right into very amused golden eyes. "Please?" he asked.

She lifted her chin. "You reminded me on purpose."

"True enough. It worked well, too. Dinna' it?"

"I don't know," she answered. It was true. She didn't.

"I was bringing you back to the subject at hand, and you are a verra astute student. That will also bode well."

"Also?" she asked.

"Along with the romantic nature you've been keeping hidden. Verra well hidden, I might add."

"Romantic?"

"That's what I said. And that's exactly what I meant. You are a romantic, my dear."

"I am not. I till and harvest fields, and work from dawn to dusk at my chores. I haven't time for anything remotely romantic."

"You probably daydream through most of it, too," he answered. "Tell the truth now."

Her ankle was warm where his hand was still attached. That was especially strange since she had boots on, and he was holding on to leather.

"What makes . . . you say so?" she asked.

"You called my eyes amber. Verra romantic word for a dull color, amber. You were na' even aware of the word as you used it. That made it something you did subconsciously, without thinking. You probably apply romantic descriptions to menial things all through every day of your existence. Tell me I'm wrong. I'd like to argue the point with you."

She was staring. "How do you know?" she finally asked.

Her answer was a swift grin, and then he winked. Her body responded all the way to her toes and back. Constant only hoped it wasn't as visible as it felt.

"I make it my business to look beneath the surface, love. I'm good at it. There's a wealth of information people keep hidden. Sometimes from others. Sometimes from themselves. You're in the latter category."

"I don't think I like it," she answered.

"What? That I can tell what a person might be thinking, or why he's about to do something? It's a talent I have. Tell me another of yours."

"Another?"

"You are definitely the most talented cook I've run across in this country of yours. I'm just impressed that I had the good sense to fall into your ditch from where I was slung across my horse. You did see a horse, dinna' you?"

"No," she answered.

"That's depressing. I guess he was na' very loyal. It's a good thing he was military issue. I'd hate to claim him as one from my own stables."

Constant's lips twitched despite herself.

Kameron's expression sobered as he watched her. "You probably underprice yourself, Constant, love."

"What are you talking about now?"

"Pricing. In the marriage mart. That's what lasses do. They price themselves. They tend to attract the men worthy of the price they set. You probably haven't a clue what I'm talking about, do you?"

She shook her head.

"If you see a beautiful rug for sale and the owner is asking a pittance for it, what happens to your opinion of the rug?"

She scrunched her face in thought. "I would wonder what's wrong with it."

His smile was back in full force. "Verra good. I knew you were quick. I'm glad it's borne out for me. I doona' much like being wrong."

"I don't understand."

"Have you been available for this Thomas before?"

"I don't think I like your meaning," she replied in a very careful, emotionless tone.

Kameron narrowed his eyes in thought and lost any hint of joviality. He was even more handsome with that sort of expression. If any of her sisters could see him, they'd most likely swoon.

And if they saw his current lack of attire, they would for certain.

She put the thought away the instant it occurred, but it was too late. Her eyes flicked down the length of him, to his feet and back. When she came back to his eyes, his eyebrows were lifted, and there was the slightest hint of color high in his cheeks. It made the amber of his eyes glow.

"I think you need to keep to the subject at hand, Constant, love," he said softly.

"What?"

"I am verra aware of you as a woman now. You did well."

The flush heated her right to the roots of her hair. She had to drop her eyes, although there wasn't much safe to look at. He still had her boot, his arm was still extremely muscled, and she already knew what his eyes looked like. She closed hers to keep any reaction exactly where it belonged . . . inside. When she opened them and looked up, he was still watching her, and those golden eyes were exactly as leonine and warm as she'd already imagined.

"I meant, if your Thomas comes calling, do you go to meet him immediately or do you make him wait?"

"He never comes calling," she answered.

"When do you meet this fellow?"

She shrugged. "Church. Quilting bees."

"Your Thomas is a quilter? Good Lord."

Her eyes flew open at the insult. "His mother is notorious for being the best with a needle in the area."

"Oh. My mistake," he replied, with what she recognized was a sarcastic tone.

"Let go of my foot," she said finally.

"Why?"

"Because I've finished here."

"I'm getting a little too close to the truth of this Thomas lad, am I?" he asked softly.

"You are not!"

"If you rarely see him, and you doona' look at him, and he doesn't come calling, what by the saints makes him your beau?"

Constant swallowed around a knot that contained tears. "I really . . . should be going. There's still time to get a few hours of sleep."

He released her foot. "I'm stealing your food, your goodwill, and your sleep. I am na' a very pleasant patient, am I?"

"No."

He grinned. "It's a good thing I'm pleasant to look at then, is na' it?"

Constant's eyes widened and she gaped. She couldn't think of one thing to reply. Not one.

"Come, Constant, confess. You wanted me to look like this, dinna' you?"

"It never crossed my mind," she answered, as evenly as possible.

"You're na' a verra convincing liar, Connie, love. I would na' take it up as a profession, if I were you."

Constant wrinkled her brow again. "Lying isn't a profession."

"Oh yes, it is. Some people doona' even ken when they've chosen it as one. You would probably know a few if I described them."

"Who?"

"Oh, I doona' go by names. I use types. There's your snobbish types that wed for security or wealth, or perhaps both, but they do it without emotion. You ken any of them?"

Charity, was her instant thought. She nodded.

"You think they doona' lie with each and every caress? Each and every kiss? Every intimate gesture they receive and then force themselves to return?"

Constant's eyes flew wide. *Charity caressed John Becon . . . intimately?* She hadn't ever thought about it. Everything that Kam had pegged as a romantic in her was shuddering. She nearly gagged. John Becon was older than their father, fat, pompous, had horrible teeth, worse breath, smelled . . . and that was with his clothes on.

"How about the type that goes about pretending to be brave, when they long to run and hide? They're verra good at that, too. They put on a good front, especially if they are well fortified with spirits. I imagine some of my mob friends fit that category. You ken any of them, Constant?"

She nodded.

"They're pretty good at lying, would na' you say? You could actually say they've chosen lying as a profession. I bet half doona' even realize it, because they're lying to themselves, too."

"How do you know this?"

"It's my talent. I can usually spot a liar the moment I meet them, which is why I told you what a terrible one you are. Those turquoise eyes doona' hide a thing."

"My eyes are not turquoise," she replied, although her voice didn't sound like her.

"What color are they, then? In your opinion, of course."

"I don't know . . . blue?"

He tilted his head slightly and considered her. Without once blinking. Constant couldn't take that much of his undivided attention without it showing somewhere on her body for him to read. She looked down at the boot he was no longer holding.

"You forgot the darker, bluish-green streaks in them," he said softly.

Her eyes widened. She didn't dare look up.

"They're also perfectly clear and honest, and impossible to hide a thing behind."

Her face was beet red. It had to be if the heat behind her eyes and nose was an indication.

"You should look in the mirror more, love."

"You shouldn't use such endearments," she whispered.

"Probably na', but it's too late to change, and I want to give you something to daydream about while you work tomorrow."

She twisted her hands together to hide the trembling. "Are you dallying with me?" she asked her entwined fingers.

"Na' yet. But I was definitely considering it."

"What?" Surprise choked the word. And something else. Something she was avoiding. She couldn't fancy herself feeling anything for a tarred-and-feathered soldier named Kameron. It was against everything loyal in her. It was dangerous. There wasn't a soul who knew she was alone all night with a very handsome, very virile, and very exposed man. It was also thrilling. Exciting. Tantalizing. She trembled. Stilled. "But . . . why?" she asked.

"I'm beginning to suspect the reason behind this fellow's obstinacy in na' snatching you up the moment you were old enough. I'm hoping to jolt some sense into him without having to meet him and actually knock it into him."

Constant's eyes were huge as she raised them to him again. "Why would you do such a thing?"

"Because the only other way to gain his attention is to pursue you myself. There's naught like a bit of jealousy to make a man's heart pump harder, get his interest piqued and his sense of possessiveness aroused."

"Surely . . . you jest."

"Nae. I doona'. I just will na' have the opportunity. I'm a soldier, remember? Your Thomas is probably a member of the little colonial militia that's causing all the trouble. I canna' just waltz into one of your barn-raising affairs with you on my arm . . . although it is a thought."

Constant had to shut her eyes or he'd be able to read her response. She very nearly lost control. Arriving at any function with such a handsome man would be more than she could envision. It was going to cause her some trouble every time she thought of it.

"All of which brings me back to why I'm making you daydream about me. It serves my purpose at present."

Constant narrowed her eyes and regarded him. He was holding himself up with his elbows, his upper body resting on the log, his well-developed lower back outlined by her apron. He had his head tipped sideways to speak to her as she sat near his right shoulder. He was easily the best-looking man she'd ever seen. Once he was well and standing beside her, he was probably so much man that she'd faint, and she had never done that in her life.

"I don't understand," she said.

"If you constantly find your thoughts on me, I'll ken I've succeeded."

"At what?"

"Flirting with you, of course. A good dose should teach you what to expect. And what to do. And then you'll be able to use it on this Thomas fellow. You can make him think about you all day, just like I'm making you think about me. You'll tell me if it works?"

"I haven't even seen Thomas for over a month," she replied.

"That is na' what I meant. Try harder, Constant."

Kameron had a devastating smile, filling the gap between his lips with perfectly spaced, white teeth. Constant suppressed her own answering smile with difficulty. She'd never had such a conversation with another person before in her life. He made every nerve ending tingle, until even her scalp itched. He made her throat alternate between tight constriction and blubbering uselessness. He sent her from pale shock to heated blushes. She already knew she'd be thinking about him every minute of the entire day.

"I think . . . I'd better go," she said, finally.

"You can do the same thing to your Thomas. I promise."

"What thing?"

"What you're feeling. We can make Thomas go through the same emotions."

"I never said I felt anything," she replied.

"Those beautiful turquoise eyes do. Run along, love. You probably have to be up at dawn, or before. That gives you about three hours of sleep. And mind you keep from wasting any of it dreaming."

"I won't," she replied and got to her feet with the same sort of stiffness that was in her voice. She gathered the empty bowl that had held his sup and wrapped it back up. She avoided looking anywhere near him, although it wasn't easy. She was winding the wick back into the oil in her lantern when he spoke again.

"Constant?"

"Yes?" she answered, waiting for her eyes to adjust to the change in light. Kameron hadn't been accurate, either. She had maybe one hour before the sun was up.

"You said you brought a blanket?"

"Yes."

"Would you put it over me afore you go?"

She tightened her jaw and favored him with the look she usually gave Charity. It only worked because she couldn't actually see him. "Now?"

"It's fairly cold, of a sudden. I fancy I ken why, but I'll leave it unvoiced. I've given you enough to think about already."

He didn't even mention how she was going to feel spreading a blanket over his semi-nakedness, by touch alone.

Chapter Seven

Despite what she'd thought might happen, Constant found the day passed in a blur of activity. Henry was even helpful to her, especially when doing outside chores such as chopping the wood and bringing the cows in for milking. He didn't once chide her over her name, either. There were no comments about her being in "constant trouble," or what a "constant problem" she was, or even what a "constant source of aggravation" she was. Constant didn't stop to question it. She couldn't. She didn't even notice when he was there or when he wasn't.

She hadn't got more than an hour of sleep, and yet felt perfectly refreshed. She surprised their mother more than once with her industriousness, and for once there was no undercurrent of reprimand in her mother's remarks. Constant smiled through every chore. She baked, cooked, swept, made beds, and handled dishes. She even bade Charity and her new daughter a good morn, and a good afternoon later when she took up her sister's tray.

She was aware of only one thing, and it seemed to grow with a hum inside of her, until her hands couldn't seem to keep up. Through the entire day, every thought was of golden eyes set in the most handsome face, crowned by such a glorious length of white-blond hair, it undoubtedly got him more than a few second glances. She was running through her immense series of chores for a reason. She was hastening toward the night and Kam. She could hardly wait to talk with him again, and feel the anticipatory reaction he told her was flirting. And she longed to feel his skin beneath her fingers.

She also longed to reveal more of him. If his back was so gloriously muscled and vast, wouldn't the front of him be even better? She guessed he'd probably have the same golden fur on his chest that he'd had covering his arms. He wasn't going to keep it. She was in charge of the shaving, wasn't she? Her lips twisted and she had to duck her head in embarrassment at her own thoughts. If his arms were that muscular and strong, wouldn't his chest be even more so?

Constant stilled her hands in the washing tub full of supper dishes, lost in thought. She rubbed her hands over the hard surface of a tankard, running her thumbs along the ridges and indentations the silversmith had hammered into it. She wondered if Kam's chest would feel as hard to the touch. Instinctively she knew it would, although it would be warm and alive under her fingers.

She actually felt her fingers tingling with the thought before dipping the vessel into the cold rinse water to soothe the feeling away. She snickered at her own thoughts and checked the round, slightly distorted image of her own reflection in the tankard's side. Constant had long, thick, brown hair. It was always worn close under her cap, but wisps of it were curling about her face and eyes—eyes that didn't look the least bit plain blue.

He calls my eyes turquoise.

The humming sensation intensified. Such a strange emotion didn't seem to be a bad thing at all. It made her day fly by, her chores almost nonexistent, and any missing sleep became little more than an afterthought. Every moment felt like a waste of time, until she could be with him.

Kameron. She said his name in her thoughts for the thousandth time. *Kameron. Great, golden-eyed Kameron . . . what?* Constant stilled as she realized she didn't even know his last name. Then she shrugged. It hardly mattered. She probably shouldn't know it. It was safer. There wasn't a future involved with any of this. She knew it. He knew it.

But nothing stopped the humming feeling. Her entire body felt as though it was vibrating as sundown grew closer. The commonsensible Constant told herself she was a fool and a simpleton. The dreamy-eyed romantic in her knew she was foolish, and didn't care.

Kameron had raised her awareness of him to such a degree it was almost frightening, if she thought of it. So she didn't. She shrugged off any negative thoughts, closed her eyes, and saw him so clearly, she was surprised when she opened her eyes to find the kitchen wall staring back at her.

She knew the man named Kam was off-limits. She knew he was going to be the enemy. She knew he was teaching her the art of flirtation so she could use it on Thomas Esterbrook, although she was having difficulty bringing Thomas's face to mind. She knew everyone would be horrified at what she was imagining, and yet it made the entire day more sunny and bright than a late October day had any right to be.

She wondered if such secret thoughts made her a sinner. She'd had exactly three secret nights to know him, and already she wondered such a thing? She was in trouble if the answer was affirmative, because she had no plans to stop thinking about Kam anytime soon.

There would be time enough for any regrets after he got better and disappeared.

Constant dried the dishes, in a reflective mood, then she shrugged the feeling off. She wasn't going to regret a moment of time with him. She was going to commit every bit of it to memory, and wasting time over the dishes wasn't going to get her any more moments.

Constant's senses were heightened as she sponged off in the room she shared with Stream. She knew Stream slept; she was overtired from all the fuss in the house. She'd never been strong, and the spindly body she'd been born into wasn't up to such things as newborns. Constant smiled at her sister's sleeping frame.

She toyed with wearing her night rail before closing her eyes against such sinful thoughts. She was tending to an invalid, not going to an assignation. In truth, except for a comment Charity had once made in jest, Constant didn't even know what an assignation was. All she knew was their mother had chided Charity over such lustful thoughts.

Constant returned to the kitchen and ladled gravy over Kameron's feast of turkey pot pie and wondered if what she'd been feeling all day was lust. If it was, it was obvious why lust was such a problem. Her body felt different, especially her breasts, and she'd just grown into the size of them. She knew their purpose; breasts were to feed her as-yet-unborn children—although Charity didn't look like she was enjoying the chore both times that Constant had interrupted her.

That is the only purpose, isn't it?

She was still mulling it as she made her way to the barn and rolled her skirts beneath her apron tie in preparation for the climb into the loft, a pail of water in her free hand. Tonight was a cloud-filled night, promising a hint of snow. It was colder in the loft than she remembered,

too. Constant eyed the open window with a frown before
opening her apron and putting the pail down. She
should have had the sense to bring horse blankets up
with her. She couldn't keep purloining from the linen
cabinet, especially since it was closing in on winter and
every blanket was in use, but there were good, stout horse
blankets right below her. One would be sure to fit across
the open window. Constant shook her head and climbed
back down to fetch one.

It was a good thing she hadn't taken all the tar and
feathers from him yet, because it was probably helping
to keep him warm. Constant climbed back to the loft
and put the blanket against the window and shoved
horseshoe nails into the upper corners, pushing them
into the window frame with ease. It covered the opening,
but didn't let in much light. She'd just knelt to light her
oil lamp when she heard his groan. Her hand stopped.

"Kameron?" she whispered.

"Here."

His voice sounded strange. Rough. Her hand trembled and she had trouble with the wick. She let it flare
brightly for a bit, catching fire, before winding the wick
back down into the oil, dimming it. It was strange: here
she was prolonging the moment that she'd been rushing
toward all day. Constant swiveled her head and narrowed
her eyes to find him, and then went to her knees with a
jolt beside him.

There was a tint of blood on his honey-encrusted back
and it had reached the apron, staining it a brownish
color.

"Sweet heaven, what happened to you?"

He groaned again in reply. He was leaning over his
log, exactly as she'd left him, except the blanket she'd
given him was down around his lower legs.

"Did someone find you?"

"Nae," he replied.

"Then . . . what?"

"I turned over." His voice was deeper than usual, and he still spoke into the straw.

Constant stared for a moment, then clucked her tongue. "Why would you do such a fool thing as that?"

"I promised I'd put some weight on my back."

"You promised to try."

"Well, I tried. I failed."

Constant frowned. If the honey-herb salve had been working, he might have undone it. She pulled the pail over and dipped a rag.

"This might hurt, I'm afraid," she said before putting the dampened cloth on his back.

He flinched. "I'm sorry."

"You should be. You've undone all my work. I only hope it doesn't scar."

The packed honey brought some scabbing with it. She watched fresh blood fill the stripes on his back. She was afraid he could hear the sympathetic tears in her voice.

"It was already going to scar, Constant, love." His voice was gentle.

"Not if I can help it," she replied, and set her jaw.

"Why?" He swiveled his head, using his shoulders, which made the blood seepage worse. Constant put the cloth onto him and held it there.

"You've got to lie still. I can't stop the bleeding otherwise. Whatever possessed you to do such a thing without my help?"

She had to look away from his face if she wanted to keep her voice steady. Lines of pain were etched on his forehead and cheeks.

"I should na' be here. I'm causing undue trouble for you. I've put you in a dangerous position. Compromising. If it's discovered that you've harbored a young, unmarried gent, it will na' go well. I ken how strict you colonists are. I ken the rules. By having you attend me . . . without anyone else present . . . I've placed you at risk. I canna' stay here much longer. And that's why I tried."

"It's been three days, Kameron. You can't rush Mother Nature," she replied softly.

He continued as if she hadn't spoken. "And . . . I wanted you to be proud of me."

Constant's hands trembled atop his back. She had all the honey mixture wiped off and just sat there, holding the cloth in place. She was afraid she'd heard him wrong, yet knew that she hadn't.

"I don't . . . know how to answer to such a thing," she finally answered, feeling as tongue-tied and awkward as before.

"With as much reserve as possible, I suppose. Damn me! I should na' have been so lax! I should have seen this coming. I should have done a hundred things different."

"Nobody can heal in three days."

"Nae. Having this done to me in the first place. I'm nae a spring pup, still wet behind the ears. I should have seen it coming and avoided it."

"Oh, that."

Constant lifted the cloth. The damage might not be as bad as she'd thought. The wounds from his lashing had been knitting well. There was a puckering of pink skin about the edges, although he'd disturbed scabs by moving about as he had. She tipped the honey jar and drizzled honey across the skin again.

"So . . . did you think about me today?" he asked without looking her way.

Her fingers lost feeling and she nearly dropped the jar on him. The same sensitivity was happening to her breasts again, too. Constant caught her lower lip in her teeth and sucked on it.

"A bit," she finally answered.

"I thought about you continuously. That is na' a good thing."

If daydreaming about him had put her in an untouchable realm of fantasy, finding out he'd been doing the same jolted her into the present with a rush. Suddenly the loft was very defined and focused, no matter where she put her gaze. Constant didn't have a prayer of holding on to the jar, and watched with unblinking eyes as it thudded onto the straw beside her.

"What?"

"Nothing," he said.

The apron was filthy with dried blood, and Constant looked at it as if seeing it for the first time. "I'm going to have to get you something different to wear," she said finally.

"True enough. That would be an excellent place to start."

"Start what?"

"Saving us from this tomfoolery."

"What tomfoolery?" she questioned.

"You look in a mirror yet?" he asked.

"No, but I did look in the side of a tankard."

He shook his head. She watched the white-blond, lanky strands of hair graze his shoulders. "Na' good enough. 'Tis distorted and confusing. You need to look in a real mirror. Then you would na' have to ask questions a simpleton could answer."

"You're being very rude for someone who still needs tar and feathers removed, I would say," she replied.

"Good. That's an improvement."

"To what?"

She didn't understand one thing. Constant rocked back onto her heels and considered him.

"About this covering for me. You have access to material? A hank of cloth? It does na' even have to be trousers. I'll fashion a *feileadh-breacan.*"

"A what?"

"Highland wear. It'll be hell to don properly, but it should suffice, even if I do shock every colonist I run across."

"How will you get to your garrison if you do that?"

"Bright lass. As always. You have trousers then?"

"I'm afraid not. Even my father is smaller than I," she replied.

"Oh. I'm certain that's enormous."

There was a strangely snide tone in his voice. She stared.

"Not . . . exactly enormous. But I am large. One of the reasons Thomas doesn't offer for me is because I'm bigger than he is."

"The fellow's a dwarf."

"He is not! He simply hasn't finished growing yet."

"Well, at least you still defend him. That's more than I dared hope."

"I don't understand you at all, Kameron."

"I have no excuse to offer, Constant," he replied. "Other than the obvious. I'm used to a certain amount of feminine attention, I'm locked in a loft with a verra pretty girl, and I'm still verra much a male. With the cursed needs that accompany all of that. You'll have to pardon me, I'm afraid. Either that, or hit me with something."

Constant forgot how to breathe for a moment. Then,

when she remembered, it felt like an entire lungful of winter frost. *He called me very pretty!* Whatever had been the trouble with the increased awareness and sensitivity of her breasts was happening to her entire body. She hugged her arms about herself and made herself breathe in and out.

"Forget I said any of that, will you?" he asked.

"How . . . can I do that?"

He sighed. She watched his back rise and fall with it. The honey mixture stayed in place and then showed the slightest hint of blood. She busied herself with folding more cheesecloth and then put it on his back. She reached for her knife and started sharpening it.

"What do you think you're doing?" he asked.

"Getting ready to get more of the tar off. Just as I said I would."

"I canna' put any weight on my back, Constant. I'm na' so certain I dinna' crack a rib or two. It's na' possible to remove any tonight."

"Doesn't it itch?"

"Almost unbearably."

"Then I'll get it off you. Besides . . ." *I want to see if the front of you is as manly as the back.* She couldn't finish speaking. Her thoughts were making her body alternate between flamelike heat and ice-cold chill. Heat. Chill. Fire. Ice.

"Besides what?" he asked.

"Oh . . . nothing."

"Christ. Oh, bother. Apologies."

Then he swore some more before speaking in a language she'd never heard before. Constant continued sharpening the knife until he quieted.

"Besides, I have an idea. Can you lift yourself with your arms?"

"How do you think I move? Wishful thinking?"

His tone was as rude as his words. Constant narrowed her eyes. She tested the knife on a blade of straw. It cut easily and cleanly. It was as sharp as it was going to get.

"Lift yourself. I'm going to get beneath you and shave your chest."

"You are na'!"

"I most certainly am. And if you possess any hair, it won't be difficult to get the tar off."

"I will na' sit idle while you shave every bit of hair off me! Do you ken how long it took to grow in the first place? I canna' even grow a decent beard. I'm a tow-head, for pity's sake."

Constant's brows knit. "What does that mean?"

"White-blond. Towheads canna' grow much hair, and when we do, it's pale and hard to spot. I'll have you know that women expect certain things of a man. One of them is hair on his chest. I'd rather be scarred head to toe than hairless as a newly birthed bairn."

A flush rolled over his shoulders and disappeared beneath the bandage on his back.

"But you told me you weren't married," she said.

Kam made a sound that resembled cursing, but there weren't any words to it. Constant slid onto her back to lie beside him.

"You are na' getting beneath me, Constant. I forbid it."

"Oh yes, I am. I'm shaving your chest. And I can't get to it if I don't get beneath you. Now, lift up so I can apply the lard."

"I am strong enough to raise myself, but I canna' hold it that long. What do you take me for, a mule?"

"We'll do a little at a time. Now, lift." She poked the handle of the knife at his side and was rewarded with his instant movement.

"You enjoy having me at your beck and call, doona' you?"

He growled, but moved to place his hands, palm-down, beneath each shoulder. Constant watched the muscles flex in his shaved arm, and had to close her eyes for a moment.

"I am trying to heal you, Kameron."

"Right," he muttered, and pushed himself up.

Constant slid a hand into the lard bucket and smoothed it over the feather mixture coating the closest section of his chest. Feathers came away in her hand, even before she used the cloth to wipe at them. Tar was hanging in pieces from what appeared to be a very muscular, lightly haired chest. She bit her lip to keep her reaction in. It would be an easy process to go fetch scissors and cut the clinging tar from him.

That would also result in letting him keep almost all of his precious chest hair. She sucked in her cheeks as she considered. Then she put her left hand on him to steady herself, and started shaving.

Chapter Eight

"Back away, Constant. I'm coming down."

Constant slithered out from under him as Kameron lowered back to the log. She'd known her time was about up. The trembling in his arms had increased the longer she'd slid her blade along his skin. That was her first indication he was tiring. She'd let it go on for some time though, because it disguised her own shaking.

She was having difficulty keeping the knife against his skin, and not just due to all the muscular ridges on his chest. It was more because the skin she revealed wasn't white, injured, or remotely infirm. It was supple, clear, and unblemished, and it was tanned, as if he went shirtless often. She wiped the tar, hair, and lard mixture from the knife blade onto the dirty cheesecloth and watched her own hand quiver.

"Ready to go again?" he asked.

"I brought turkey pot pie for you," she told the straw.

"Good. I'll think on filling my belly. It might work."

"With what?"

"Instead of the obvious. Are you ready or na'?"

She was blushing and afraid to consider why. She watched him lift and hold himself up. His leg wasn't broken. She knew that for certain, as he held himself anchored with all ten toes.

"Constant, I doona' grow any lighter, and consequently holding myself up does na' become easier, with your idleness."

"Oh."

She lay on her back and scooted her head beneath him. In little time, she had the upper chest uncovered and was ready to start on what looked to be solid bumps of muscle beneath the skin of his abdomen. Only it got more difficult the longer she worked. Constant's entire left palm kept tingling where it was propped against him, and her right was having trouble gripping the knife properly. He also smelled suspiciously like rose water, but that was impossible.

Her head was wedged against his stomach, placing her bodice beneath one of his armpits as she finished the area about his rib cage. She was as careful as possible, but still he tensed as she scraped at his ribs. She ran her fingers along the shaved skin, feeling for any uneven bones as well as thoroughly enjoying how the striations of muscle seemed to tense and release with the slightest touch of her fingertips.

"Looking for something?" he asked, his voice tight and sarcastic-sounding.

She rotated her head along the ridges of his shaved chest to look at where he'd tipped his head down to watch her. "I'm testing your ribs. They appear to all match up, although this one—and maybe this one here—have swelling on them. I think they're cracked. We probably should wrap you."

He sucked in air as she touched the lumps. She didn't have to guess at the pain she caused him. His body tensed with it. She scooted out from under him and waited as he eased back down onto the log again.

"Cracked." He finally repeated the word when the silence grew to absorb even the sound of her breathing.

"I think so. It's bad, but could be worse. You're lucky you're a man. We've put down animals for less."

He turned and put those beautiful lips into a smile. "You certainly do dampen a man's enthusiasm, Constant, my love."

"What . . . does that mean?" *And it couldn't be what it sounded!*

"More than I'll admit at present. So . . . you think two of them are cracked?"

She nodded. "They're healing straight, though. As far as I could tell."

"That's truly what you were doing?"

"Uh . . . yes." She wasn't going to say a thing about how much her hands were still tingling from the experience of touching him as intimately as she had. "Why?"

"I appear to have developed an overactive imagination"— he paused before finishing—"obviously."

Constant's brows drew together. She knew she wasn't the type to make any man enthusiastic, especially a man like Kameron. There had to be another meaning. She just couldn't decipher it.

"What have you brought for me to eat tonight?"

She searched his face. He had a blank look on his perfectly formed features.

"There's turkey pot pie with peas and carrots and potatoes. Um . . . gravy . . . some pickled beets, and rolls. Buttermilk to drink. Honeyed cranberries for dessert. I think."

He was grinning. "You think? You certain you've na' forgotten anything?"

Constant had to look down at the straw-covered floor. "You wish to eat now, or finish with your chest?" She spoke to the hay, her voice halting and stupid-sounding to her own ears.

"Your choice."

She glanced up. He had his head cocked toward her, resting it atop the log, his arms in the position to lift again, putting definition to the muscle. And those golden-brown eyes were impossible to look at for any amount of time. Constant dropped her gaze again. She should have run for the scissors.

"Well?"

"We'll finish," she whispered.

"Fair enough." He took a huff of breath and pushed up.

This time when she ran her knife along the array of muscles in his abdomen, the knife shaved more than hair. Constant had to stop her ministrations and wait to see if the area darkened with blood. She didn't tell him of it, though. She was watching her own handiwork with wide eyes. She shouldn't have dimmed the light as much as she had.

"What color is your hair, Constant?"

She moved her eyes from his belly to his face. Even in the dim light she could see that he was looking right at her.

"Brown. You've seen it," she replied.

"You always wear a mob-cap affair. If I've seen it, I've lost recollection. Refresh my memory. Describe it for me."

"I just did. It's brown."

"But what sort of brown? Light brown? Dark brown? Medium brown? Does it contain reddish highlights? Strands of gold? Darker auburn? What?"

"Oh . . . dark brown, I guess." She moved her gaze back to where she'd scraped at him. The area looked pinkish, but hadn't bloodied.

"Dark brown? And here I thought you a romantic.

So . . . what else is it, besides dark brown? Is it curly? Straight? Thick? Thin? Stringy? Which?"

"Um . . . wavy. My father calls it unruly, whenever he notices me. It never stays in a braid long."

"When your father notices you? Does that mean what it sounds like?"

"I was his seventh disappointment. He never speaks to any of the others. I am the exception, I guess."

"Why are you so lucky?"

She reached for the tub of lard resting beside her hip and got three fingers full of the stuff. "I help him with the chores, remember? I required instruction more than once. I wasn't the best student at the time."

"That better na' mean what I think it means, either," he replied.

"What?"

"He dinna' beat you, did he?"

"I required the strap more than once. I probably deserved it. I didn't want to do heavy field work. I didn't want to till soil. I didn't want to grow great muscles like I have." She ran her hands along his left side as she spoke, from the thick cording of muscle at his waist to his armpit, thinly spreading the grease. That way she wouldn't have to dip more. She could tell he sucked in a breath and then held it. She felt the motion under her fingertips and where her forehead rested against him.

"You are *not* shaving me there," he said, letting the air back out when she moved her hands from him and wiped at the feathers with her cloth.

She giggled. *Men care about hair even there?*

"And you're to cease that, too."

"What?"

"Your laughter. You can cease laughing at me. I'm na' immune. Nae man's fond of being laughed at. You ken?"

"It bothers you?"

Constant wasn't following their words. She was considering the tar glued all along his supple-looking side.

"Aye."

"I'm sorry. I didn't know."

"The hell you dinna'."

He said it so softly, she thought she might have heard wrong. She nearly giggled again.

"Are all men so vain?"

"Vain? What? I am *na'* vain. I've rarely been so insulted. Vain. Me."

The arms holding him aloft wavered slightly. She wouldn't have time to get this tar off before he collapsed.

"A girl laughs at you and you get all stiff and offended. I call that vanity. If you suffer vanity, then you are vain. Simple."

His arms trembled, then stilled. "If I'm stiff anywhere, Constant, love, it's because I'm a failure at self-control at the moment. It most certainly is na' because I am vain. Trust me."

"If I were a man . . . and I looked like you . . ." She ran her hand along the tar she was going to scrape off next. Her voice lowered as she spoke. "I would be vain. Very much so."

He started shaking again. Since she had her head wedged against his abdomen, she felt every tremor.

"You need to move out, Constant. I am coming down. Now." The words came through what sounded like clenched teeth.

She scooted out, and a moment later he was again stretched out on the straw, his head resting on the log as he considered her.

"Your Thomas fellow is an ass. A full-fledged, mule-headed ass. I vow, when I've regained my strength and movement, I am going to search him out and knock it into his thick skull, too."

Constant gaped.

"And I will need more covering afore you take one more touch anywhere on me. Anywhere. You ken?"

Her brows rose. Her eyes widened.

"Good. You do understand. Did you bring me anything more to wear?"

She'd been avoiding that problem. She'd been debating using the length of homespun she'd woven back when she was too small to be of help with fields and farm animals and chopping wood. The material was coarse, but maybe he wouldn't notice how rough and amateurish it looked. She could use it to fashion him a pair of breeches, when she found the time. And desire. She hadn't had the inclination, because he had fine, strong thighs, a back with muscle everywhere, and shoulders twice the size of any she'd ever envisioned. She didn't want any of that covered over just yet. Besides, she told herself, she still had to drizzle honey-herb mixture over the burned skin on his legs. She couldn't do that if he wore clothing.

"No," she replied.

"Give up that apron, then. I'm na' moving without something."

"I can't." It wasn't even hers. It was one of Charity's best. Constant had borrowed it from her sister's bureau. Charity certainly wasn't in any need of an apron at the moment. She'd also chosen this one because it was beautifully stitched and lacy. Constant blushed.

"Well, you're going to have to do something, or we have finished for the evening."

"But we're almost done," she argued.

"Oh, you are more than done, love."

His low tone sent gooseflesh rippling over her shoulders, down both arms, centering in the tips of her breasts. Constant nearly covered herself as she watched his glance flick to her bosom before returning to her face. He had a tight look about his lips when he did, too. He didn't say anything, and she didn't think she had a voice anymore.

He licked his lips and then swiveled his head away, looking over at the slanted wood of the barn roof rather than at her.

"Perhaps I had best start my feast," he said finally. "I need a break from your attentions. What did you bring me, again?"

"You can have my pantaloons," she replied.

"*What?*"

The word was choked out as he moved his head back toward her, the white-blond mane of hair brushing his shoulders. Constant wasn't just blushing, she was probably purple. She had to be, if the heat behind her own eyes was any indication. "I wear pantaloons. They're drawers. We girls—"

"I ken what pantaloons are," he growled. "Unlike you, I most certainty am na' a virgin. I can barely recall a time when I was, actually."

"You're a fornicator?"

"Full-fledged," he responded. "Although 'tis na' entirely my fault."

"How can fornication not be a man's fault?"

"Ah. Churchgoers. Got to love them. They're always so sanctimonious. Self-righteous. A congregation of pious busybodies. I'll tell you how. What if women are the instigators? Answer me that. Well? How am I to blame if they hand me invitations to their chambers? With full directions. I would say if they do so, then they invite it, and consequently, I canna' be totally at fault, now can I?"

"Women . . . invite—" Her voice choked off.

"Aye. They do. Continually."

"To . . . their chambers?"

"Aye."

"Did they know? What you . . . uh, you—had in mind?"

He was probably trying not to laugh. "They had a verra good idea," he responded finally.

"You ravished them?"

The eyes he turned on her were lidded to the point his eyelashes shadowed the gold color to black. "If anyone was ravished, darling, it was me. That's what inviting a single man to a married lady's bedchamber is for."

"Married? Heavens! England is as sinful as they say." Constant was shocked. It sounded in every syllable.

"It's nae different than other places. You hear of the French court? In the Bourbon dynasty, they take sin to a whole new level. Trust me. Or watch the ancient regime yourself. When they allow you to visit again."

"Allow? What do you speak of now? I know my history. France is friendly to us. We can visit anytime we like."

"Only because of British troops."

"What makes you say such a falsehood?"

"If a Frenchman welcomes colonists, it's because Britain helped you ungrateful colonists win the Indian wars a decade or so ago. What do you think the additional taxes are levied for?"

"Supporting the wicked lifestyles of the rich and titled. You just described some of it. I am not stupid."

"I would never call you such, Constant. You are miserably misinformed, however."

"My beau works at the press. My father writes a column for it. I'm well-read. I am not misinformed."

"You read seditious drivel, designed to incite. The truth got lost somewhere, Constant. England is na' taxing the colonies without reason. The country needs to pay for their defense during the French-Indian war."

"You're wrong," she replied, although she didn't truly

know. If there'd been anything resembling a war between the Indian natives and the French, it hadn't been mentioned in Thomas's family's newspaper. She would have heard of it, too.

He sighed. "Forget France for the moment. I doona' need an argument with you, although any other time in my past it would be working splendidly at what I do need."

"And what is that?"

"My mind off certain things. It usually works."

"What . . . certain things?"

He regarded her for several moments. Constant couldn't hold the gaze and had to drop hers onto her hands.

"You seem to believe Britain is the mother country of all vices. I was trying to convince you that sort of thinking is wrong, but I wasted my breath."

"You got something else, too," she replied, looking up.

"Oh, really. And what would that be?"

"You got me angry."

He grinned. Constant's heart took a nosedive into the region of her stomach, where it joined the throbbing mass of nerve endings there. The worst part was that it wasn't an unpleasant sensation.

"I am trying to concentrate on other things, Constant, love. Remarking on any kind of emotional state you're suffering is na' helping. Quite the opposite, I need warn you."

If he was trying to confuse, titillate, and mystify her, he succeeded. She wondered if this was part of what he described as flirting. So she sucked in a breath and just asked it. "Is this part of flirting?"

"What?"

"What you're doing?"

"And just what is it I am doing?"

"Making me very aware of you as a man." She used as even a tone as possible, given her acute embarrassment at saying anything so bold.

He groaned, and it sounded worse than when he was in pain. "Constant, you are aptly named after all, I think."

"Why?"

"Because you seem to do everything with a constant consistency of purpose, only it constantly intensifies, too. You bring a man to the brink, and then you just hold him there, constantly dangling it, constantly reminding him, constantly holding it just out of his reach."

She went white. She didn't dare believe what he was talking about. It was senseless. Absurd. She wasn't the type to bring a man to the brink of anything, least of all what he was implying.

"Are you speaking . . . of fornication?" she finally asked.

"Of course."

"With me?"

"You see any other woman about?"

"But . . . why?"

"Why? What fool asks a question like that?"

Tears glittered in her eyes at the roughness of his voice and the harshness of his words.

"Forgive me, Constant, love. I'm more than a brute. I am a bear. You're an innocent. I'm doing my best to remember that. And you will na' look in a mirror to find out why I have to."

"I don't want to look in a mirror. I don't have to. I have seen myself. I know what I look like. I know it very well. My family tells me of it. Constantly, if you like the word so much. I'm very plain. I'm very large. I've a large nose, large eyes, large mouth, and a large body designed more for hard work than creating anything like what you describe . . . in any man . . . let alone one as handsome as you."

She almost got through all of it before tears stole her voice. Constant felt them slip from her eyes before she closed them. She was absolutely and completely mortified. There wasn't a better word to describe it.

"Good Lord. Who could have said such things to you? Damn them! And damn and blast my impotence in not being able to go and ram a fist down their throats for it! And I'm na' asking your pardon for that bit of profanity, either, so doona' ask for one."

She opened her eyes at that. He looked as angry as he sounded. Although she'd not thought it possible, he was even more amazing while he glared at her. He had his jaw set, a nerve pulsing out one side, and what looked like every muscle tensed everywhere along his frame, too.

"Come here."

It wasn't a request. She shook her head.

"I said come here, and I meant it. Now."

"Why?" she whispered.

"Because I've got some fool to thank for filling your head with stuff and nonsense, and you're too pigheaded to look in a mirror and see the truth for yourself. Now, come here, or I'm ripping all your handiwork out and coming over there to you."

It seemed impossible for her eyes to go wider, but they did. "You can't move," she replied.

"I use my arms. I'm quite proficient at it. How do you think I relieve myself?"

Her face was burning with intense embarrassment and her eyes stung with the last of her tears. She couldn't get one word through her throat.

"Are you going to continue challenging me, or are you coming here?"

"I—" She began to answer him, but her voice just stopped.

"Verra well, Constant. But please recollect. You were warned."

He lifted himself with his arms again and shifted. She watched the cheesecloth ripple with the movement. Constant scooted nearer to him.

"Finally. You do obey. Now, lie down. Fit your feet to where mine are."

She was trembling. This time it wasn't remotely pleasant.

"And you can cease looking at me as if I'll harm you. I have na' developed a taste for virgins, in spite of my stupidity in regaling you with my exploits. Lie down."

"Here?"

"Right here. Right next to me. Match your feet to mine and lie back. Stretch out as big and large as you can."

"Now?"

He blew a sigh across her cheek. She felt the tremor in it, probably from the effort of holding himself aloft. "Aye. Right now. Could you cease being a constant irritant, and just do as you're told?"

She set her lips, scooted down until her feet were right next to his, and told herself to ignore that her dress slid to her knees with the motion. She heard him suck in air, though. She wondered why.

"Now, lie down. On your back. Match yourself to my entire length. Show me this huge frame you claim to have."

Fresh tears blurred the view of her booted feet. She swallowed.

"Well? Are you going to show me this great big frame of yours, or will I have to force the issue? I warn you, it will na' be pretty if you choose the latter. Go on, Constant

Ridgely. Cease wasting time. Show me your tremendous size."

"You . . . are cruel." She tried stanching the agony. It sounded in her voice although she was doing everything in her power to keep it to herself.

"Nae. What's been done to your confidence and self-worth is cruel. I'm going to correct it. I only hope I'm man enough to stop once I've started."

"You aren't going to ravish me, are you?" she asked.

"Only in my dreams, darling."

Chapter Nine

She thought she'd heard it, but that was impossible. Absurd. Wishful thinking. And sinful. Wicked. Wondrous. Unbelievable.

Constant forced herself to lie still as he lowered himself, although he was moving about more than that should warrant. She realized he was maneuvering the log out of the way when he commanded her to tip her face up and look at him.

"Why?" she asked.

"You really are a constant irritant, are na' you? Now, look at me, or by hell I'll force the issue. And I'm tired of threatening. This is na' easy. In fact, it's damned difficult. Do you realize how you smell to me?"

She looked sideways and saw her eyes were level with the middle of his upper arm. Constant was a good five and a half feet tall. She was the tallest in her family. She was the heaviest. She knew Kam was large, but not this large. She had to angle her head until her neck bent, just to meet his eyes. He was looking down at her with the softest, gentlest expression in his eyes she'd ever seen, even from her mother when Henry was born and placed in her arms.

"Now, what was all that blather about being large?" His voice was soft, feathering the breath across her forehead. "You look nigh invisible next to me."

"But, you're enormous," she replied.

He smiled. "True. Always was. 'Tis a family trait. What of it?"

"All this proves is that I am small next to you. But everyone probably is."

"Nae."

She felt him move his arm. He put his forefinger under her chin to keep her head tipped up to him.

"What this proves is that you are na' as gigantic as you believe, or have been told. And tormented over. Men my height and weight are na' normal, true, but they are about, looking for a woman your size. Do you ken what it's like to find a woman matching a man like me? Most women look like porcelain dolls that I'm afeard to touch. You ken?"

"Most women are like dolls to a man like you?"

He closed his eyes for a moment, a fleeting look that was probably frustration passed over his features, and then he opened his eyes again.

"You are na' large, Constant. You never were, except to a small-sized family and a dwarf named Thomas, whom I would like to thrash the moment I recover."

"No, please. You mustn't. No one is to know of this. Of us. Of my actions . . . with you."

"I would na' do anything to harm you, Constant. Ever. Rest assured of that. You've my word. And that means any threats I utter, as well as any overtures I make, are as empty as my head. All of which makes this even more torturous for me."

"What is?" She was mystified again, and it was worse than before because every inch on one side of her body seemed to be in contact with his.

"You are small to me, Constant, except in all the right places. That makes you desirable. Extremely so. I'm losing sleep over it and there's nae end in sight. Constant dreams. Constant arousal. Constant self-denial. Aye. Those are the correct terms when added to your name, Constant, love. You were named extremely well and aptly by your parents. They've my compliments."

Constant was aglow with his admissions, although he couldn't really mean what he said. Could he?

"I must keep on subject, or I will deserve another bath in hot tar. You say you have large eyes? That much is true, I'm afraid. Right now, I'm wishful you had a third one, however."

"What? Why?"

"For the love of—you need ask?"

"I ask about things I don't know. I don't know anything about men. I haven't been in contact with one until you." That got her another groan, but he didn't say anything. Constant just shrugged her shoulders and blazed on with her words. "You're acting very strange and I have no one to ask. I don't have any older brothers, and I'd never ask my father. And I can't ask a woman. You're impossible to describe without them guessing . . . uh, something. I'm sorry if it makes me sound stupid."

"Not stupid, Constant, love . . . just enticing. Damn and blast! Stop me before I say another foul word."

"Enticing is a foul word?"

"It's right in there with fornication. Doona' doubt it."

She gave him another wide-eyed look. He shut his eyes, tightly enough to cause little lines about them, while the groan that went through him shook her.

"What else did you complain of? Large eyes? We covered that. You have verra large eyes. I have to tell you, that's na' all. Your large eyes are bordered in lush black lashes. That made me suspect your hair was na' the same light shade as your brother's. You've been gifted with verra long, verra black lashes, Constant. 'Tis a gift of nature other women would be on their knees in thankfulness over . . . after spending hours preening in their mirrors. Such lashes are perfect for flirting. They create shadows that draw a man's gaze. Yours do. They send shadows onto your cheeks when you're concentrating, such as when you carved on my chest. How do I ken that? Because I noted it. And I held my tongue. And now that you've forced my hand, I canna' seem to stay the words. You should've just looked in a damned—oh. Begging pardon, I forgot. You should've looked in any mirror when I told you to, and saved me from this."

Constant brushed her eyelashes with a finger. She'd never wasted time looking at her reflection in any detail. She hadn't known eyelashes were for anything except shielding one's eyes from the sun's harsh glare. She hadn't known men looked at things like that.

"Another thing about those large eyes of yours, they're breathtaking. Beyond enticing. Let me put you straight about it in nae uncertain terms. You have large eyes. Aye. You have large, turquoise-colored eyes. They are wide and compelling and incredibly difficult to look away from once ensnared. They are too honest, as well. They show everything. This is especially true when I've said something shocking. They darken to a near slate color sometimes. I'm afraid I ken when it happens. I'm terrified that I also ken why. That is a constant problem for me, Mistress Constant Ridgely. Constant problem. Constant enticement. Constant fascination. Constant frustration."

His voice stopped and he was frowning. His eyes were still scrunched shut. It just couldn't be true. The man she'd had all to herself was saying things she'd reserved for her daydreams. Her heart was pumping with more energy than it had all day, her cheeks were probably chafing at the heat, and she didn't want to miss one word. She knew her memories were all she'd have in the future.

"Since I canna' go with my first inclination and beat the person or persons responsible for your jaundiced viewpoint of yourself, Constant Ridgely, I am going to try to correct it. You are na' large. You are na' undesirable. You are definitely na' *plain*. You're so far from that word it should be hiding in embarrassment."

She snorted. She couldn't help it.

"Oh God."

He mumbled the words and then went taut, right beside her. Since she was still touching him, she felt it. She probably should have moved away, but it was too exciting to stay right where she was, her head tipped upward to watch Kameron's handsome face while she listened to the amazing words coming from between his perfectly formed lips.

"I'm going to convince you of your attractiveness, Constant Ridgely. I'm stating it in as near truth as I can without compromising you. This is what I will do. I started this, and I will finish it. Then, I would na' bring it up again if I were you. Unless you wish consequences."

"But—"

"I'm beyond arguing, love. Maybe later, once I've supped, and you're gone, and I'm attired in your cast-off pantaloons—that you're planning to take straight off your own flesh—oh my God, perish the thought!"

A tremor seized him and Constant felt every bit of it. His reaction came from thinking of her flesh-warmed underthings wrapped about him? *Oh my!*

His shaking subsided, then stilled. Constant watched as he puffed each breath in, then out. She wondered what a kiss from him would feel like. *A kiss isn't so bad*, she told herself. *It isn't permanent. It doesn't make one any less a virgin. It certainly doesn't make one impure. Does it?* That troubled the Constant who spent the day doing chores. But she was a far cry from the Constant who had her entire right side pressed against Kameron.

"You should have figured out all these things about yourself already, Mistress Constant, and saved me the torment of having to inform you about them. Where was I, anyway?"

Constant choked on her reaction as he sucked in air with such a kisslike pucker of his lips, she was totally riveted. It was a good thing he was answering his own question; she certainly couldn't.

"Oh, I remember. Your nose. You describe your nose as large, too. I say again, na' in comparison. A smaller nose would look incongruous. It would be lost. Your nose is just right. Trust me."

He still had his eyes closed. She watched him lick his lips prior to sucking them both into his mouth, then sliding them out. Her eyes didn't move from the sight. An icy cold shockwave went from the roots of her hair to her leather-booted feet beside his, and then back, although it settled in the area below her rib cage and just sat there, pounding with every heartbeat.

"Your mouth is also large, Constant. I think it was designed that way on purpose. Do you have any idea what large, luscious lips such as you possess can do to a man?"

She shook her head. She didn't trust her voice. She was afraid of what might come out. He opened his eyes and looked at her then. The light was shadowing him. Not her. She watched him look her over.

"I was afraid of this," he told her.

"What?"

The word was mouthed. She couldn't put sound to her own whisper. Her voice was missing. It was probably lost in the knot in her throat.

"What large, luscious lips such as you possess can do to a man. I just remarked on it. Dinna' you listen? And if na', you need to start, because I'm doing my best here to ignore it."

"Why?"

"Because I will heal. I will leave this little loft. I'll rejoin my regiment. I'll go back to my life. All of which . . . you will na'."

"I know," Constant replied.

"We will na' meet again. You'll find some large, handsome, farmer type to marry. Or you can still pursue the undeserving Thomas." His words weren't as soft or gentle as they had been. "Either way, you'll forget me. You'll forget this. Everything will fade."

"You too," she said.

"I'm afeard 'tis too late for any of that in regards to me."

She smiled and raised both eyebrows, and then teased. "Oh, I agree. I doona' think there is a farmer in the land that will offer for you."

"Have you ever been kissed, Constant?"

He'd read her mind! *Oh. My.* "Uh . . . no," she replied.

"Would you like to be?"

"I—"

She had to drop her eyes. The answer was probably written so clearly on her face, he could decipher it. The slight indentation in his chin drew her gaze back. Then his overly full lips. She licked her own and watched his eyes widen.

"If the answer is nae, doona' do that again, please."

"What?"

"Constant arousal. Constant enticement. Constant promise. Constant Ridgely, you are constant, all right. You are a viciously desirable creature, too. I should have chosen a different gully to fall into."

"I cannot believe you are saying these things to me."

"Please doona' tell me I've failed. I may be rusty, but I canna' be that inept."

"At what?"

"Making certain you're aware of your own attractiveness. That is the task I set myself, remember? Do you recollect the bit about the rug seller?"

Constant wrinkled her brow. "The one about underpricing?"

"I doona' want you doing the same. Ever. There is naught wrong with you, Constant Ridgely. Your Thomas is na' worth the wait, especially if he puts four other lasses before you. If he is na' brought up to scratch afore Christmas, find another beau. They're out there. They're bigger than you. They're strong, too. They're marriageable."

"I don't know any of them, though."

"Then look farther afield. Go to Boston. You'll see. Tell your parents you need a new wardrobe or some such."

"A new wardrobe? I'm a farmer's daughter. My family has land and property, but little ready funds. I wear hand-me-downs. We don't get wardrobes."

"Well, start. It's a feminine requirement to get entirely new clothes in the latest styles. Every season. Without fail. How else would dressmakers stay employed? And haberdashers. Shoe makers. Parasol designers. Et cetera."

"How . . . wasteful."

"The man who weds you will receive a treasure. I

hope he kens it. For that reason, I'm halting the lesson tonight. Treasures doona' handle desecration well, and I'm afraid I've a mind to do something that might promote that very thing."

"What you said tonight . . . was just a lesson?"

He sucked in on both cheeks and wouldn't meet her eyes. "I canna' answer that."

"Why not?"

"Because I'm na' as truthful as you are, and there is nae correct answer. If I say it was a lesson, will that demean my words and make you doubt your own beauty? Conversely, if I say it was nae lesson, will that be even more dangerous for us? What is my answer, Constant? What? You tell me."

Doubt her own beauty? Constant was reeling with what he'd just said. And he didn't even notice.

"So tell me, Constant, love, didn't you say something earlier about—?"

"Pantaloons?" she offered, rolling to her knees.

"Good Lord, nae! I speak of sup. You mentioned turkey pot pie . . . and something about rolls? You did say something about rolls, dinna' you?"

"You'll have to wrap them about you. I am not your size."

Constant lifted the back of her dress where he couldn't see and pulled the undergarment down to her knees. Kameron's mouth gaped open.

"You do need something to put around yourself, don't you?" she asked.

No answer. Just the openmouthed fish look he kept giving her. Constant swiveled to place her back to him and peeled the pantaloons over her boots. She turned back around and handed them out to him. He didn't move. He didn't even blink. She had to fold them neatly and put them on the straw beside him. Then she crawled over to get his supper.

She felt his eyes on her the entire time, or actually, it felt as though they were burning right through her dress to where her pantaloons should be. It was discomfiting, and more than once brought a blush to her cheeks as she assembled and then brought his supper over.

"Doona' so much as think of sitting anywhere near me," he said in a tight voice she'd never heard anyone use before.

She spread out the apron and scooted back about four feet, which appeared to be outside his reach. Then she crossed her legs, tucked her feet beneath her knees, and made certain the whole was covered with her skirt.

"Is that better?" she asked, with what she hoped was the same controlled tone he was using.

He glared straight at her, frightening her with the intensity from those golden-brown orbs. "Nae, it is na' better, Nurse Constant, but it will have to do."

"I'm not a nurse," Constant replied.

"Bloody good thing. Or if you take it up, work on your own kind. Should our country take this damned rebellion to war, stay away from our wounded. Lay your own lads low with ministrations such as you practice."

"I am that bad?" Constant hated the sound of tears in her voice as much as she hated how they felt gathering in her eyes. She should've known she'd be incompetent at this, too.

An expletive came through his clenched teeth. And then another. And then a moment of silence before he spoke. "Forgive me, Connie, love. I am na' myself this eve. You are na' bad. Ever. You are that damned good."

"You can't be saying such things to me," she whispered.

He sighed hugely, his breath feathering her skin

from more than a yard away. She looked in the general direction of his face, although she wasn't sure she could meet his eyes. The light molded and shadowed every bit of him into ridges and valleys of mystery. She held her breath and tried not to look, but it was hopeless.

"You're right. I canna' be. I should na' be. I have only my lack of control to blame. I hope you can forgive me."

She couldn't answer. She was concentrating on breathing normally, while he shoved a lock of his white-blond hair off his shoulder. She found herself wondering what it felt like between his fingers, and found hers actually tingling at the thought.

"You have ever been in control of yourself, though. Except, mayhap, when you were unconscious. I would tell you if it weren't true. I promise."

"That is na' the control I am referring to."

"You can't possibly mean—," she began.

"You need a husband, Constant Ridgely. You really do. A big, strapping one. One that could bend me in two just for imagining the things I have been imagining—let alone voicing some of them."

"I don't think they come that big. Or if they do, I'm not likely to run across one."

He narrowed his eyes at that. "I canna' believe my own stupidity."

"About what now?"

"Everything. Starting with getting tarred and feathered. Although, now that I think on it, if I'd have known my torture would result in meeting you, I might na' have fought it."

"You wouldn't?"

"Na' in the least. I'd probably have the use of my legs, too . . . but that would na' be a good thing at this juncture."

"You'd be able to walk."

"If I were more mobile, right here and right now, we would be in trouble. Extreme trouble."

He turned back to face the feast she'd spread out for him. She heard him grunt with pain as he lifted his arms over the log. She knew it was probably from his ribs, and the movement he forced on them. She watched him for a few more moments, and then she had to ask.

"From who?"

He had a mouthful of food, and she had to wait for him to swallow. "From who . . . what?"

"Who would we be in trouble from?"

"Oh. Myself. This is good pie. Everything you do is good, though. I hope you realize that by now."

She watched him shovel in a whole nine-inch pie in what appeared to be three bites. She waited until he swallowed before speaking again. "You would be in trouble from yourself?" she asked, wrinkling her forehead.

"I already am, but it makes me a fool to voice it. I'm beginning to think my trouble is going to have degrees to it. It's going to constantly increase, too. Another constant thing about you. I really like your name, actually. It's so descriptive of everything about you." Then he saluted her.

"Why are you acting like this?"

"Like what?"

"Like my brother does."

He pulled the buttermilk tureen from his mouth as he looked over his shoulder at her. "The pip, Henry?"

She nodded.

"I think I'm insulted again." He choked. "Nae. This time I am insulted. Are you likening me to a five-year-old now?"

"No. Only remarking that you're using my name against me. He does it when he cannot get his way with me. I don't know what your excuse is."

"The same as his, actually."

He shoved an entire roll into his mouth the moment he finished speaking. Constant watched him and thought the tremors running through his frame were from laughter. When he finished the roll, he kept trying to hold it in. Then he just leaned farther over the log and shook with repressed amusement, although the snorts and grunts were loud anyway.

Chapter Ten

The following day had a slowness to it that defied description. Every chore felt even more endless. That was one reason Constance procrastinated over them. Chores were onerous, lengthy, boring, and—despite what the reverend said—busy hands didn't do a thing for her wandering mind . . . or the sins she was envisioning.

If this was what Kameron had been referring to when he was teaching her about flirting, it was a devastating condition; akin to sleepwalking. If troops could be made to suffer such a thing, the outcome of battle would be a foregone conclusion: the soldiers would be useless.

Constant took her hand from the stretched clothesline so quickly it twanged. Could that be what Kam meant when he told her not to nurse any of his soldiers? He couldn't possibly mean she put him into the same emotional state . . . could he?

There was no one she could ask. She'd told Stream nearly the whole of it, but her sister simply nodded and smiled, as she always did. She was a comfort to talk to, but Stream didn't have any answers. No one did.

Only once did Constant ask her mother about any of it. They were assessing the contents of the smokehouse for what meat would suffice, since turkey was starting to pall on everyone's palate. Constant got brave and asked Mother what it meant if a man wanted his way with a woman.

Constant had been troubled, ever since Kam said it, that it meant exactly what she suspected. But it didn't seem possible. The handsome, self-assured Scotsman couldn't possibly want such a thing with her. Mother was indignant, and banned Constant from receiving any visits from young men for a month. That was no punishment. She never received visitors, and the last thing she wanted was a visit from Thomas, anyway.

She'd had to avert her face to keep any of that from showing, however. She hadn't been able to stop her entire body from flushing. It was a good thing it was dim inside the smokehouse.

But nothing made the day go any faster!

Each minute passed by with excruciating slowness, and heightened her awareness. Constant had never been more aware of everything. The air-dried sheets radiated stiff and cold as she folded them. The butter felt slick and moist, melting with a smattering of bubbles when she spread it on toast. Every bite of her oatmeal had a separate taste and texture. She'd tarried over her bowl, letting the bites languish on her tongue until she could swear she tasted each separate oat.

She had an even worse time just before the noon meal. Mother wanted a pig put on a spit for roasting outside. Constant blushed ceaselessly while working with the meat, first impaling it, then guiding it onto the spit, and finally smoothing salted honey into the flesh. She couldn't think beyond how firm and supple it felt, rather like Kameron. Mother had even scolded Constant to cease fondling the meat and put it over the flame, for goodness' sake.

Her visit with Charity was the worst, however. The new mother had developed a cough, and while that was worrisome, her apathy was more so. She was pale and listless in the bed, sending back most of her food untouched. Mother merely clucked her tongue over it, and took the new baby. According to Mother, Charity was suffering from a common condition called blues, although nothing about Charity looked that color.

At the lunch meal, Constant tipped Charity's door open with her hip, balancing the food tray. Her sister looked over from a position against the headboard, and frowned.

"What do you want?"

"I've brought a nice soup of lentils and beef broth. There's a slice of bread, too. Fresh baked. I hope you enjoy it." Constant adopted the most cheerful tone she could manage.

"When you learn how to make bread, I'll enjoy it."

Constant's smile wavered for a moment. She put the tray on the table next to Charity's bed and shrugged. "Fair enough," she replied finally.

Charity's frown deepened. She had her best feature, the Ridgely reddish-gold hair, brushed back and secured under a bed cap, leaving her colorless and plain. She hadn't been a raving beauty before, although her willowy figure had captured one of the richest, most influential of the landed gentry; but at least she'd had color to her cheeks and a saucy way with her lips.

"What? No ready retort? No nasty words of argument? This is most unlike you," Charity said.

"If my bread displeases, forgive me. It must be the birth that changes your taste. No one else complains."

"You're acting differently. I just can't decide if it's for the better or not."

"It's a lovely day, isn't it?" Constant moved to open the drapes.

"Leave them be! It's gloomy, it's cold, and the sky's dark with clouds. It's the most miserable fall on record. It has to be." Charity's voice dropped to a whisper.

"No, truly. The sun is out, turning everything to mist. I swear, 'twas difficult finding Jezebel this morning to bring her in for milking. That one was aptly named, for certain. She runs from me, but everyone knows she has buckets of milk to give."

"Are you meaning something with that statement?" Charity asked.

"No."

Constant turned from the drapes. Her sister was looking for someone to argue with. Normally, Constant was a ready participant. Today, however, only her body was there; her mind was yards away. It was in the barn loft, on a freshly shaved, massive chest that rippled everywhere with muscle. Constant closed her eyes on an image so clear she swore she could actually smell him, and then she reopened her eyes to Charity.

"If you don't require anything else, I'll be about my chores."

"My, my. You've certainly changed," Charity remarked.

"I'm no different than before, except . . . mayhap more charitable?"

"I don't need your charity, or anyone else's!"

"You've got color to your face again. It's an improvement."

"Do you wish to wear my soup?" Charity asked icily, lifting the bowl with both hands.

"Not especially. You should try it. It's good. If it makes it more palatable for you, tell yourself Mother made it."

Charity lowered the bowl back to the tray. Constant

was surprised to see her sister's arms trembling. Perhaps that was it. She was weak. Then she realized Charity was crying. She'd rarely seen her sister cry. Constant's eyes widened.

"Oh, cease staring and let me enjoy my misery."

Constant walked back to the bed, pulled open a drawer in the nightstand, and handed Charity a handkerchief embroidered with a nosegay. "Do you wish me to fetch Mother?" she asked.

Charity shook her head.

"Do you want me to leave?"

Charity again shook her head. Constant sat on the edge of the bed and waited.

Charity was right about the day, although the curtains hid it. It was dull and gray, with heavy clouds full of snow. It was also invigorating when breathing in a chestful of frost-filled air. The pig Constant was due to turn was smoking and putting the most heavenly odor into the air, while everywhere she looked it was crisp and bright. The day even seemed to have a sound to it. The leaves crunched underfoot, the fire snapped, and when she blew out a breath, it made a noise as well as a misty cloud. It was truly beautiful to see and experience.

And her sister called it miserable.

Charity blew her nose, sniffed again, and Constant turned back to her. Charity had more color, but it seemed to have gone right to the end of her nose and around each swollen eye. Constant looked her sister over critically. She wondered if what Kam had told her was correct, and if Charity's misery was attached to the lie she was living.

"Has Thomas come by, at last?" her sister asked.

"Thomas?"

"Your beau."

Constant smiled slightly. "No. Why do you ask?"

"You're acting . . . strange. If I didn't know better, I'd say you were seeing a beau. And since only one man on the earth knows you exist, it has to be Esterbrook, no?"

Constant turned back to the bureau. There was definitely another man who knew about her existence. And if Charity got one glimpse of him, she'd be green with envy instead of this blue color Mother had spoken of. That was such a pleasant thought that Constant had to quickly make certain there wasn't any expression of it on her face.

"I have no beau, so I could hardly be seeing one," she replied finally.

"Your Thomas chose another? I'd say I'm sorry, but you're better off without him. You're better off without any man. Trust me."

That sobered her. Constant looked back at her sister. "Is it that bad? Truly?"

"Are you asking of the marriage *bed*?" Charity spat the word.

Constant's heart felt as if it dropped into her stomach and started pounding from there. "It isn't that bad. It can't be. Mother had nine children. Tell me it isn't that bad."

"Are you asking of the birthing, or the making of the baby? Ask the question straight, and I'll give you the same when I answer."

"I—uh . . . perhaps I should wait and ask my husband."

"Once that happens, it's too late. I know what you're asking now. You wish to know of the mating act itself, don't you?"

"Well, I—I mean, not . . . especially. I've seen animals. I don't need to ask that."

"It's worse than anything you've witnessed."

"It can't be."

"Oh yes, it can."

"Then why does everyone keep doing it? I mean—"

Constant's voice stopped. Her cheeks were so warm, they burned. She watched her sister's eyebrows lift. And then Charity's eyes narrowed.

"They do it because men like it. They're bigger. Well, most men are, with the exception of little Esterbrook. They're stronger. They force a woman. It's not pleasant."

"Is that why it's called a man having his way with a woman?"

Charity drew her head back a bit in surprise. "Have you stooped to listening at keyholes now?"

Constant gulped. She'd known it was sinful. Wrong. Illicit. She didn't need Mother's censure, followed by Charity's ugly words. She stood. "I have to go now. I have to turn the spit. I'm roasting a small pig. It'll be a welcome change from turkey, Mother says."

"It hurts," Charity said.

Constant put her hands together for something to hold on to. "Hurts?" she repeated.

"Bad. It burns. The entire time. Every time. You can beg, too. It doesn't stop him. There's a part on every male that's like a weapon. It grows and it hardens . . . and it hurts, and they don't care."

"A weapon?" The word was almost unintelligible.

"That's what I said. They pry your legs apart and force it into the deepest part of you. It's not pleasant. It's not. It's painful. It's humiliating, and it's awful, and then they use it for what seems to go on forever."

"I . . . had better go now." Constant walked to the door.

"The man gets above you. He holds you down. He doesn't ask if it's all right. He doesn't do any stroking, or any soft gestures, or even speak with loving words. No.

All he does is get atop you, shove your legs open, and insert his part in you. It's horrible, I tell you. Horrible!"

Charity's voice had risen and she'd started crying again, the words garbled and shrill but still understandable. They were terrifying to hear. They also brought Mother.

"Constant!" Mother had already assigned blame as she opened the door. "You are not to upset your sister."

"She taunted me with my duties. I don't want to go back with John, Mother! I don't!"

"Constant, how could you?"

"But, I—" Constant began, only to be interrupted by Charity.

"Yes, she did. She asked me what it meant when a man wanted his way with a woman. She forced the issue! I don't want to talk about it ever again! Make her go!"

There was no defense Constant could mount. She'd already asked the same question of her mother in the smokehouse. So she ducked her head and waited for the discipline.

"We'll discuss this later, young lady. Now, hie yourself back to the kitchen. I think we need more candles made. Get Henry to help you melt wax. Now. Charity? Calm yourself. That's a love . . ."

That was the punishment? Making candles? They already had more than three gross of them on the shelves. They put a pleasant, mild smell into the air. It was quiet in the alcove off the kitchen. It wasn't punishment, especially as it came on the heels of escaping Charity's bedroom.

Constant's heart felt as heavy as her step when she approached the loft. She'd waited until past midnight. It didn't feel remotely like last night, and she knew why.

She'd started the day with wonder, and now felt only trepidation and fear. She didn't feel like herself. Even her hands had felt awkward and ill-equipped to carve a platter full of pork slices, a heaping mound of scalloped potatoes, green beans, and four slices of bread. She'd finished the platter off with a bowl of spiced apples.

The clouds had held off snowing. It wouldn't be long, though. The day had been too crisp, still, and mild. That was usually the harbinger of snow. Constant filled her chest with cold air and pushed the barn door open. She shut it with her foot and put the tray down in order to toss two more blankets over her shoulder.

It was warmer in the barn. The animals made it so. Constant approached the ladder with feet that dragged.

"Constant? Is that you?"

She didn't answer the insistent whisper. She fumbled in the dark for the ladder rung, and wondered how she was supposed to finish getting the tar from him now.

"By God, it had better be you."

"It's me," she replied.

"What's wrong?"

Constant stopped, one foot on the ladder, and one still on the barn floor. *He knows something is wrong already?* That wasn't good. In fact, it was so far from good as to be disastrous.

"Constant?"

She cleared her throat. "I've brought pork tonight."

"I ken. I've smelled it all day. It'll be delicious. Of course, if you had a hand in it, anything would be."

Her hands shook. The one balancing his tray made the bowl of spiced apples clank against the platter. *He wants to hurt me*, she reminded herself.

"Something's happened, hasn't it?"

She reached the top rung, put the tray down, dumped the blankets, and moved about on her knees, finding the oil lamp by feel. She delayed answering him until she got the flint sparked and the lamp lit. She felt his eyes on her the moment it was done. When she glanced his way, she wasn't surprised to find it to be true, although he had them narrowed thoughtfully. Unfortunately, all that did was make him more dramatic and intense-looking. And dangerous.

Constant looked down.

"What has been done to you now, lass?"

"Nothing," she replied.

"That is such a bald lie I'm surprised you'd try it on me. Now, speak up. What's been done to you?"

Constant's eyes filled with tears. She blinked them back, but more came to take their place. "You—you want to hurt me," she whispered brokenly.

She heard his sharp intake of breath. "Never. As God is my witness, I'll never harm you, Constant, love. Ever. I swear to it."

She looked up at him, although moisture blurred the view. "But . . . every man wants to hurt. That's what they want. That's what you want."

"Who on earth have you been talking to? Wait a minute. You have na' been talking about me, have you?"

She shook her head.

"You certain you've na' said a word about me?"

She looked down at her entwined fingers. "Not . . . directly," she whispered.

"Verra well. What have you been saying indirectly?"

"I asked . . . uh—what it meant—uh . . ." She couldn't finish it.

"Yes?" he prompted.

Constant's face was flaming. "I'd better go. I've got to fetch something. I've an idea."

"You asked . . . what?"

Constant tried not to look at him but failed. He was

the most handsome, immense, virile-looking male she'd ever seen, let alone envisioned, and he wanted to forni-cate with her. He wanted to put that male weapon part of himself in her, even knowing it would hurt. Her face probably showed every bit of her line of thinking. He had his eyebrows raised as he waited. Constant backed to the ladder, displacing straw as she went. She only wished she could tear her gaze from his. She shook her head.

"Constant—" He said her name in a threatening fashion.

She ignored him, ducked her head, and pushed a foot over the side and onto a rung of the ladder. She was down three of them before she heard his reaction. The thumping of her heartbeat had been drowning him out.

"You are na' leaving me, are you? But why, love? What did I do? What does it mean—I'd hurt you? Oh, lass, doona' go. If my presence here has caused you harm, I'll crawl as far as I can from you. I swear that, too. Constant, wait! Please?"

The sound of shuffling made her look back. Her eyes went wide and every thought flew right out the top of her head. She was actually grateful she had the smooth wooden sides of the ladder in both hands for balance. She couldn't do a thing about the drop of her jaw, however.

Kameron was much more mobile than she'd given him credit for. He was lunging toward her with awkward-looking motions, using his outstretched hands to drag himself toward her across the loft floor. He stopped an arm's length away and just stayed there, his chest heaving with effort. He'd pulled his white-blond hair back, using what appeared to be the ribbon waist-tie from her pan-taloons. There wasn't a speck of hair on that perfectly molded face or body to temper any of his impact.

"Constant?"

His position put him slightly above her. If he wasn't

still moving with each breath, she'd think herself in the company of a marble statue like the ones she'd been told existed in faraway places like Rome and Greece. Constant forced her eyes to close, then open. She blinked again. Nothing changed. All she could think of was how amazing it would be when he could stand beside her, and how much she wanted that very thing.

"Constant?" he said again, and this time his breath feathered across her nose and cheekbones.

Her reply was more a croak than a word. "Yes?"

"Have I been found out?"

She shook her head.

"This new fear of my hurting you . . . have I done so?"

She shook her head again.

"I will na', either. I give you my solemn word. You believe me?"

She was caught by his eyes. Because the lamp was behind him, the light haloed his head and came slithering from around his black, tar-coated sides, over the newly shaved ridges of his torso and chest, and touched the crests of each muscle, then his jaw, and finally, the tip of his nose. She couldn't see the color of his eyes from that vantage point, but her mind colored them golden brown, anyway.

She nodded.

"Then doona' leave me. Please?"

"I'll be right back," she replied.

His jaw hardened. "I promise I'll be more restrained. I'll lie about nicely while you shave whatever portion of my frame you wish. I'll soften my approach. Why, I'll even pretend to sleep when you're here. Forget I offered that. You're the lone one I have to talk with, although I should have kept my words to myself."

"What words?" Constant asked.

"I've been a fool to speak of things you're innocent of.

And if you'll come back up that ladder and join me, I'll stop. Every day in your loft is arguably the longest in my existence. I only get through them with thoughts of spending the eve with you. You canna' leave me. Please? I'm begging you."

He emphasized the final word by pulling himself to the spot right in front of her. Constant had no trouble blinking then, and her eyes seemed to flutter, making him more difficult to look at.

"I'm only going for a couple of saddles."

"Saddles?" he repeated.

She had to drop her eyes. He was too close, too immense, and much too masculine. She was beginning to think that if what he wanted did hurt her, it would be worth the pain. That must be what made married couples, such as her parents, continue mating until there were nine children from their union. Constant should've known Charity wasn't telling her the entire truth.

"I'm getting them to—to brace you. I think I can get the rest of your feathers and tarring off that way. Uh . . . except for your male—"

"Doona' mention one part of that," he interrupted her, using a rough-edged voice. "I already took care of it. I had to. The itch was unbearable."

Constant brought her eyes back to him. He appeared to be looking everywhere but at her. She watched him flush. At least, that's what she suspected caused the darker tone creeping over his chest and spotting each cheek. She sucked in on her cheeks to still the reaction. She felt giddy with it. *He is blushing? Real men blush?*

"I apologize most humbly, Constant. I hope you can forgive my rash tongue. I'm a simpleton with a like mind. I should na' have said one word about how things are atween a man and a woman. Especially to my verra own angel." He cleared his throat. "Anyway, for what it's worth, I shaved myself in the unmentionable area already. I'd have finished the entire job if I'd been able to reach and abide the pain at the time."

"When did you do this?"

"Feels like a month ago. Maybe two."

She tipped her head. "You've been here four days, Kameron."

"The passage of time changes when one has nothing to concentrate on save one's own stupidity. Trust me. You're just going for saddles, then? You're truly na' leaving?"

"I'm not leaving," she answered, and went down a step, then another.

"I believe you, but I think I'll stay and watch. I've tired of holding myself aloft, anyway."

He dropped. She heard his grunt. And that hastened her descent.

Chapter Eleven

"So, tell me, Constant . . . and stop me if you doona' wish to answer, but I'm puzzling something. I canna' decipher the answer, and I'm deuced curious."

"Then ask."

"You spoke about hurting you."

Constant's hands stilled on the top of his foot. Kameron was stretched out on two saddles, one at his hips, the other at his ankles. She'd been keeping as busy as possible with the lard, the cheesecloth, the tar, and the knife, trying to remain detached and businesslike. Nothing worked. She was extremely aware of Kameron. She knew every bite he took as he silently devoured every bit of food on his platter. She heard every breath filling and leaving his body—although it was difficult over the pounding sound of her own heart—and she felt every blush her body put her through.

She worked on the front of his legs, where there was only a hint of blisters beneath the tar. Constant kept her tongue in her cheek as she shaved the black from him. Kam was going to look strange when he agreed to let her cut the ropes binding his legs together; there were going to be stripes of hairless flesh all the way down his legs. It didn't bother her unduly. He wasn't going to be scar-free from the burns at the back anyway, for nothing survived the scalding tar there.

She'd been avoiding finishing his chest. She wasn't willing to go where he could see her up close. Every time she put her hands on him, the odd vibration happened, going from her fingertips through her wrists and elbows, and from there into her upper arms and shoulders. Her breasts were painfully aware of each twinge, and her nipples had, more than once, hardened against the starched linen of her best underslip. When that happened, all she could do was lift her hands from him, catch and hold her breath, and wait for the sensation to subside enough that she could continue with her task.

She was afraid he knew it, too.

"Well?" He turned his head to look down at her.

Constant tried ignoring him. She shoved her tongue between her teeth and lips and concentrated. She had a very large foot in her hand. Overly large. That was going to be troublesome. There wasn't a pair of boots remotely near his size on the farm. And here she'd thought outfitting him with trousers would be difficult. She'd used every bit of her homespun on his trousers. She had one leg stitched already. The material she'd created back then was rudimentary in workmanship with uneven holes and gaps throughout, but it was better than what he wore now.

Oh my!

Constant made the mistake of taking her eyes off his foot and glancing toward the part of him she'd shaved the first night. Her pantaloons didn't do much toward disguising one inch of him, and what was worse, he had his lace-covered buttocks elevated over the curve of one saddle.

Constant blushed again, closed her eyes, gulped, and

then opened her eyes again, returning to the foot in her hand. It didn't dampen her trembling. She could only hope he didn't notice.

"Are you ignoring me, Constant?"

His whisper had as much power as a shout, she decided, and was as devastating. The foot shook for a moment before she opened her fingers and let it drop.

"I'm trying to finish, and you are not helping." She used her best admonishing tone, sounding a bit like Mother.

"Oh. I see. Verra well, then. My apologies."

He turned forward. Constant tried again, closing her eyes for a moment, breathing deeply, swallowing. Then she opened her eyes and picked up his foot again. She shouldn't be surprised at the size of it. The man was enormous. His foot had to be, too. It only stood to reason. She'd have to fashion shoes for him from something, though. Her eyes sharpened as the last of the tar came off. The bottom of his foot had taken severe punishment. It didn't look like any of his other injuries. Not only was it burned by the tar, but the flesh was raw with what appeared to be branding marks.

"What did you do to your foot?" she asked, turning it toward the light in order to look closer.

"I had a bit of a run-in with your local blacksmith while getting trussed, beaten, tarred, and then feathered. He appeared to have the same opinion of a Scot soldier as the rest of you. At least I think that's what happened," he replied.

"You don't know?"

"I was na' fully conscious. It was probably better."

"You must have frightened them."

She could tell he was looking at her again as she examined his arch and heel, where the vague outline of an oxen-yoke symbol could be seen amidst the raw swelling. She knew who used such a brand, and what it signified. It was imbedded into both saddles Kameron was perched on.

That particular brand belonged to Daniel Hallowell, Prudence's husband, and Constant's own brother-in-law. That could only mean one thing, and her mind refused to accept it. Kameron was an enemy of her family. She was committing an act of betrayal.

There was something more, too.

Prudence's husband was the most congenial, happy-spirited, and compassionate man Constant had ever met. He always had a warm handshake and a kind word. All the children adored him. Those traits were the mark of a good man. Constant hadn't needed to be told so. She knew it, just as she'd known instinctively that Daniel Hallowell was trustworthy, upstanding, and honorable. She'd known it when she perched atop his lap when she was a child, and she knew it now.

Constant's frown deepened and her quavering intensified. First Doctor Thatcher set upon him, and now the blacksmith? And how many others? And why? Why did all of them attack Kameron?

Because he might have deserved it?

"What is it, Constant?"

She looked up from the horrible revelation and met his gaze. He smiled slightly, and her heart did such a nosedive, it was painful. She swallowed, refusing to admit the other truth in front of her face. It was betraying everything she knew. It was wrong. It was wicked, and absurd, and impossible. She couldn't be in love. She would never fall in love with such a man. She just couldn't!

Constant gulped, her eyes filling with tears even as he watched. She couldn't be such a fool. She couldn't fall in love. She didn't even know for sure what love was. She couldn't love him. She wouldn't. She didn't.

"Constant?"

It felt as though she'd fallen headlong into the roasting fire, while at the same time plunging right into a snowbank. It felt bad. It felt as if her heart were getting squeezed in a great big fist. She was in agony over her gullibility, her foolishness, and what she knew was her own treachery. And all of it was overridden by this horrible yet wonderful amazement that had to be love. She didn't dare let him guess what she was feeling. Constant swallowed and kept swallowing, trying to send the gut-choking sobs back to wherever they came from.

Dearest God! She couldn't love him. She wasn't a romantic type, regardless of what he called her. She was a solid, well-grounded, churchgoing, law-abiding young woman. She'd been waiting for her beau to ask for her hand. She was a boring sort; sensible if argumentative, plain in face and form. She always had been. Such a girl wasn't capable of falling in love with an enemy of everything she believed in, just because he was the most handsome man she'd ever seen.

Kameron was more than handsome, though. He was the epitome of it. Women fell for him by the droves. He'd told her so. That had to be the reason. How could she resist? He had years of experience in enticing women. And she'd been unprepared and defenseless.

"Is it that bad?"

His voice broke through her thoughts. She closed her eyes and kept gulping.

"Lie down, Constant. On your back. Now."

"Why?"

"You look as if you're about to faint. Trust me. Lie

back. Breathe shallowly. In quick little spurts. That's an order."

She did. Constant lay on her back on the straw and watched the roof of the barn spiral above her with a detached sense of wonder, while the ringing sound of bells echoed in her ears.

"Are you all right?"

Kameron's face came into view, and Constant's eyes widened as he loomed over her.

"Constant? What is it, love? What?"

She put her hands to her eyes and started sobbing. She felt him drop onto the straw beside her. And then he brought her right against him, gathering her close, both arms wrapped about her waist to hold her to him, although he grunted when she came into contact with his injured ribs.

"There, love. Let it out. You've been doing too much for too long, for too many others. You must forgive me for adding to your burden."

His soft words made her cry harder. So did the knowledge that her head was pillowed against his chest, her nose squarely settled against where his heartbeat thumped rhythmically from between mounds of muscle. He tightened his arms about her and rocked slightly. Constant had never felt the like. She felt warm, secure, protected, and terrible about feeling any of it at the same time.

"It's all right, love. It'll pass. It's been trying for you. You've done too much. I have added to it. I should've been able to get to the fort. I should've borrowed your horse and made my own way there. I've been dense."

She shook her head, sliding her nose and cheeks against shaved skin, reveling in what happened next. Heat spread from the contact—warmer than a newly set fire. Sparks chased after that—akin to those rocketing off of blazing kindling. She was adrift in liquid—the sensation the same as when she floated in the pond on the hottest summer days. And she was completely surrounded by a glow, as if she'd just been wrapped in a newly knitted afghan. All of it combined into an amazement of experience she could almost taste. It was better than fresh-baked bread with a pat of melting butter; more wonderful than fresh-churned ice cream; outdoing even pecan pie. Every one of her most cherished sensations seemed to meld and coalesce into one huge, overwhelming one. And it just kept growing until it seemed to encompass her.

"Then . . . it's my feet? I had nae idea they looked so bad. Forgive me for that, as well. I should've prepared you. I forgot all about them. I can barely feel anything from any part of my lower legs. I thought it a blessing, actually."

She shook her head again. Her nose rubbed against him, and now humming filled each ear, replacing the ringing.

"That isn't it, either?"

She shook her head again. Constant forgot all about why she was crying. He was very warm. He was very large. He was very solid. And all of that was very wrong.

"My feet are na' that bad, then?"

She shook her head again. She felt, rather than heard, him sigh.

"That's good to hear. I'd rather na' be a cripple . . . along with everything else I am."

She sniffed loudly.

"I'd offer you a handkerchief, but I'm a bit short on material of that sort at the moment. Actually, I'm woefully short of any sort of material at the moment. All of which I'd be best off na' saying another word about . . . curse me, anyway."

She sniffed again; then giggled nervously.

His arms loosened. "Well, that's a better reaction than your first one, I have to admit. I'll even allow a bit of laughter at my expense if it makes you feel better."

Her entire being was caught in the whirl of new experience. She'd turned her hands so that they weren't shoved against her eyes any longer, but were molded about the muscles of his upper chest. She listened as his heartbeat grew louder and stronger and quicker right against her nose.

"You're all right now?" he asked.

She moved her head in the affirmative. She felt and heard him groan. Then one of his hands moved along her back, sliding up her spine to her mobcap. She had her eyes tightly closed as he cradled her head, a thumb rubbing against the space below an ear.

"Constant?" he whispered.

The thumb moved until he had it beneath her chin, lifting it so she'd have to look up at him.

"I need you to look at me. Say something. Anything."

She couldn't reply. And she couldn't open her eyes.

"You've lovely eyes, Constant Ridgely. Truly. I spoke of them already. And I should cease speaking. Please look at me. Help me with this."

She'd never been this close to any man, and never one she'd just admitted she loved. She didn't dare look at him. The finger at her chin trembled, and she felt his breath at her nose half a second before she felt it on her chin, then her cheek.

"Damn me, anyway."

She felt the hint of each word against her mouth. And then his lips touched hers, pressing lightly at first, and then more fully, molding to them. A roar went through her, turning her entire being into one throbbing, tensile mass, wrapped around a core of amazement. He tilted her head, using his mouth in a caressing motion to suck on her lower lip, taste it, shape it, and then release it in order to do the same thing to her upper lip.

She forgot to breathe. She refused to think. She was afraid she could hear singing now, but it wasn't anything except a high, perfectly pitched, drawn-out note, and it seemed to go on forever.

And then he released her, lifting away with the lightest of motions. Constant's mouth didn't feel like hers. Her lips felt swollen, and sensitive to the point she could feel the weight of air on them. Kameron was breathing hard. Each breath huffed across the bridge of her nose, and his chest moved with the same cadence. Constant stayed perfectly still, eyes closed, lips pulsing, and every sense heightened. She was completely and totally attuned to everything, even the light hissing noise the lamp was making.

The arms holding her shook. Constant finally opened her eyes. Kameron's lips were still pursed slightly, showcasing how full and almost feminine-looking they were. He had his brows raised and his eyes were wide. He looked stunned: shocked and stunned, and yet pleased. A surge of emotion rose to her cheeks and then fell, landing in the bottom of her belly as he just stared at her.

"Oh my," she whispered, through lips that garbled the words.

He blinked slowly and carefully. Then he sucked in his cheeks and narrowed his eyes. She'd thought him handsome before. It had been an understatement.

"We . . . I mean *I* should na' have done that."

"You kissed me," she replied.

His lips twisted, and then he smiled, exposing white teeth. "True. I did. I just kissed you."

"Why?"

"Uh—" He lifted his head, looking over hers. Constant watched his throat as he gulped. Then he looked back down at her. The high note had been replaced by a low timbre.

"I doona' think it a good idea if I answer that."

"Why?" she repeated, wrinkling her forehead.

"Perhaps you'd best na' ask that, either."

"But, why?"

"Because I am na' the one you need, and I'm doing my best to ignore it," he said finally.

"You mean . . . you didn't want to?"

She regretted the words the moment she said them. Especially as he squeezed his eyes shut and sighed with such emotion, it moved her. Then he opened his eyes and met her gaze. He didn't look as stunned or pleased as he had before. He wasn't smiling, either.

"Constant, you've got such trusting turquoise eyes, they frighten me. You've got very lush, tempting lips. I was afraid of how they'd taste, and I was na' far wrong. You are every inch a woman—in every sense—and you're still in my arms, reminding me of it. I'm just a man who sees and kens what a desirable woman you are. And it's a mistake for me to tell you all this."

He finished, and the buzzing noise in her ears stopped at the same moment. There was nothing but absolute silence. Then they heard a snort from a horse below them. She let her pent-up breath out.

"Oh my," she whispered.

He groaned, and the sound came from the depths of the chest she was being held against. She felt it reverberate through her. Then he stole whatever else she might have said, catching it with lips that weren't interested in being gentle, or loving, or tender, or anything other than possessive and passionate and intense. It didn't frighten her at all. It had quite the opposite effect.

She was the one clinging to him. Then she was moving her hands, running her palms over him. Her touch produced hard nubs where his nipples were, and the groans coming from him deepened. His lips weren't remotely feminine. They were hard and demanding, alternately sucking and then nibbling on hers. Then he opened her lips with his tongue and explored.

Constant's gasp helped him. She instinctively arched her neck to allow him greater access. Her will wasn't her own anymore. His wasn't, either. They were in the control of something so basic and undeniable and all-encompassing, she wasn't capable of fighting it.

Then his hands were at the back of her head, holding her in place. The moan that surged from her seemed to inflame him further. She felt him pull the mobcap away, entwining the fingers of one hand through her coiled braids while the other started threading down each and every hook at her back, releasing her dress and then caressing skin barely covered by her chemise.

Constant's entire being whirled with too many sensations from too many places at once. He created a vortex of pleasure with his lips and tongue. He was starting a wellspring of want where his hand rotated in an ever tighter circle at her back, and his fingers at the base of her neck created rivulets of shivers that didn't stop until they reached the bottoms of her toes in the bottoms of her boots.

"Oh, dearest God . . . oh, Constant. Oh, love."

She thought she heard his mumbled words as he moved his head, sending the kiss deeper. Constant helped him. She reached with one arm to encircle his neck, pulling herself up so their mouths were level.

In the far reaches of her mind she sensed his hand delving lower, sliding beneath the restriction of her waistband to mold around her buttocks, cupping first one, then the other, and then he was using a kneading motion to move her, shifting her up and back down along a large, hard, and incredibly strange part of himself.

"Oh, Constant . . . oh, dearest—"

He released his lips from hers, and then he was sliding them along her cheek to her ear. Constant cried aloud as he reached her neck, just before she tipped her head to give him greater access.

Shivers raced everywhere: her head to her belly, her throat to her breasts, her buttocks to the backs of her knees. From somewhere she registered that if what he was doing was going to hurt her, it was going to be the most pleasurable pain imaginable.

"Oh . . . my God. Oh, Constant. Oh, love! Constant . . . wait! We must cease . . . damn everything. We have to stop. Oh . . . Constant. Love."

Kam continued mumbling, but it was a garbled litany of words that alternately cursed and adored. She instinctively began sliding her loins against where she was pressed, curving until the pressure was exactly where she needed it. That strange, hard part of him responded, seeming to have its own will, not remotely interested in ceasing.

Constant hooked one leg about his waist as they lay side by side. She knew what she needed. She knew where she needed it. She only wished there weren't three layers of clothing separating them.

"Oh . . . sweet—Constant, you must stop! We canna'— I was na' thinking! We must—"

In answer to the plea she moved, instinct guiding her, and the resulting chaos of delight at her very core frightened and excited her. Constant latched herself to him, rocking her apex against his loins. Harder. Faster. Keening a cry into the air as the amazement hit, then crested, and then waned. Her actions started a shuddering within him so severe it moved them along the loft floor.

"You must stop! You must! Oh, Constant, nae! Na' there! Dear God, na' there! Not—"

Constant had moved her hand down, across the rippled muscles of his abdomen. He might be mouthing words of denial, but the rest of him didn't agree. His hips were lunging up to meet her.

"Oh, Christ . . . nae! Doona'—*ah*!"

His last word was a cry, deep in its intensity. It throbbed through the space, emboldening her. Daring her. Mystifying her. She wrapped her hand around where the pantaloons were completely pulled awry. It was hard. Rigid. Throbbing. She'd felt its movement, and now she experienced it. Her hand wound around the top of his lace- and linen-covered rod, adjusting to the size of him. The shape. Strength. Thickness. Kameron had tensed at the first touch, locking every muscle until he really did resemble a statue, and even that didn't stop her.

She'd just completed a downward motion with her hand, experiencing the full extent of him, when the muted jingle of a harness came through the blanketed window. It was followed by muffled voices.

Constant and Kameron both lifted their heads, locking gazes. For an instant she wasn't capable of saying or thinking a single thing. All she was aware of was the thunderstruck look on his face. She knew hers mirrored it. Then it was gone.

"The light!" he whispered.

Constant was already there, leaping over the saddle to land flat on her front, pulling the wick into the oil so fast it made a hissing noise, as if it shushed her.

Chapter Twelve

The barn door slid open, easily lighting the interior. Constant saw why immediately. It was snowing, the reflected light filling the interior with an iridescent glow.

"I'll be but a moment, gentlemen. I've only to find my lantern and light the wick. Now . . . this is odd."

Constant's father's voice faded as he searched for and found the hook beside the door where the lantern always hung. Except now. The lantern was still at her fingertips.

"I'll need to speak with my daughter, it seems. Gentlemen? Bring the horses in out of the elements."

There was more said, then the sounds of horses being unsaddled. Creaking noises. More voices. Constant didn't comprehend much of it. She still felt like she was aglow, every nerve ending tormenting her. She could swear she felt every piece of straw prickling her, even through her clothing. Her fingers still held to the ornate key in the lantern, and it felt hard, thick, erotic, and chilled against them.

Constant swallowed. *Erotic?* Where had she come up with that word? It probably described the arch in her back as she'd clung to Kameron. It was probably very like the feel of his hard frame against hers, and the way he'd slid his palm along her lower back before holding her buttocks to pull her against him.

She swallowed again.

"The turncoat should've gone back to his barracks. That's what any sane man would have done."

That voice belonged to Thomas Esterbrook. Constant caught her breath at the realization.

"He couldn't have moved that far, Master Esterbrook. You should know. 'Twas your rifle butt breaking his legs."

There was a bit of mumbling Constant took as agreement. The sound was cautionary. The impression illicit. She had to concentrate to make sense of it.

". . . is what's done. We're facing arrest should it become known. Come along, men. If I'm not mistaken, we've the remnants of a pork sup to dine on."

"Sounds good. Smells better." That was probably Charity's husband, but Constant couldn't be certain.

"Which is fairly odd, if I think on it."

That was definitely John Becon, she decided as he spoke again.

"What is, Friend Becon?" Constant's father asked.

"Smelling pork . . . in your stable."

Constant's entire body went stiff. Cold. Frightened.

"You see spies behind every bush, Friend Becon. Every single one. Of course it smells of pork. My wife had one roasting all day, and every outbuilding smells of it. Come. I've rooms aplenty with beds. Real beds. We need our rest, and dry clothing."

"We'll catch him, won't we?"

A voice Constant couldn't place spoke that question. She eased her breath out.

"We've no choice now. We have to get to him first. Blast the man for not taking his horse back to his garrison, where we could've found him! Anyone else would have."

That was Prudence's husband. Constant recognized the voice, but not the tone. She'd never heard such disgust and spite.

"He's probably dead. Exposure will have done what his wounds failed to. Not that we'll cease searching. We've too much at stake. Master Ridgely? You promise us a pork repast? Lead the way, old friend. I'm in dire need of a filling."

"Aye. We know. We've been listening to your belly for miles."

That was the surgeon and her father again. There was a bit of chuckling, and then Thomas spoke again.

"You think he's dead? Truly? That's a shame."

"You thinking it better if he lives to tell about it? That would be worse for us all. Dead men tell no tales, you know."

"I was only thinking as how it would be a pure shame if he was already dead, and I didn't have a hand in it."

Constant felt horror invading her body. Replacing the warm ecstasy of moments earlier with such a cold feeling, she thought for a moment she was going to lose control of the bile churning warningly in her belly. She put a hand over her mouth.

"You already had a part in it, young Master Esterbrook. He wasn't walking when last I saw him."

"I didn't do it very well, then. You heard. He's still missing, and there's a sizable sum being offered by the British for his return. A reward for a blasted turncoat! Should have minded his own business."

"Well, he didn't, and we reacted. And now we're all

responsible. All of which means we'd better find him first. We all agreed?"

There were murmurs of assent. Constant was trembling. She didn't realize how badly until one of the men below her spoke up.

"What's that?"

Instant silence greeted the question. Constant bit on her fingers to still any further sound and forced her body to still.

"That rustling? I have rats. What barn doesn't?"

"We should still check. No harm in checking, is there?"

The lower steps of the ladder creaked. Constant swore they'd hear her heartbeat. It was deafening to her.

"John Becon? You hear whispers in the wind and now spies in the lofts. Cease this, and get down."

"Yes. Come. We've a tasty sup, warm beds, and a new-born to see. I understand your daughter is a healthy child. You're to be congratulated."

There were sounds of laughter again.

"Cease mocking me! I'll not accept good wishes for a girl child. Save them for when I gain a son."

"You married a Ridgely, Becon." Prudence's husband was laughing through the words. "They cannot birth sons. Trust me. I know. I've three daughters of my own."

"I would force your pardon if I wasn't exhausted, Master Hallowell. You think to call my son, Henry, a girl? He's every bit a lad. Probably to blame for stealing the lantern, too. Master Esterbrook?"

"I'll be along shortly."

"Don't tarry overlong. We've a feast to eat, and you've rest to get. Don't forget, you have something to speak with my daughter about on the morrow."

"I've little chance of forgetting that, with you holding it over my head."

"Someone's got to make up your mind for you, boy. You were taking too long."

There was more laughter at that. Constant had been lectured long ago about eavesdropping. One always hears what one least wants to; knowing her father was somehow forcing Thomas to ask for her hand proved it. Perfectly.

"Well . . . maybe I want sons," Thomas said beneath his breath.

Constant heard him, but the others were leaving the barn and must not be listening. She shut her eyes. She heard the sounds of movement as Thomas must have followed them, and then the barn door slid closed, plunging the interior back into darkness. She waited, listening as each heartbeat slowed back to normal. She was actually amazed her eyes were dry.

She knew everything Kam had told her was true. The menfolk she'd always looked up to had formed a mob of some kind and tortured a man without even a trial. They were compounding their injustice by seeking him out in order to finish the death sentence, to avoid prosecution. Kameron must have done something terrible to deserve such a fate. She wondered anew what it was.

"Constant?"

The barest breath of air came with the sound of her name. She turned her head.

"I know you can hear me."

"Yes?"

Kam eased his bulk into the space in front of her. She couldn't see him but she didn't have to. He was warming the air all about them. It was strange that he hadn't made a sound when he moved. She waited.

"You're to tell him no. You hear? I doona' care what

he offers. I doona' care how he offers it. You're to tell him no."

After hearing the fate planned for him, he worried over her marriage proposal? Under different circumstances she would have found it amusing.

"You listening to me? I will na' allow you to give him a smile, let alone a kiss."

"Kam—" she began.

"I'm serious, lass."

His whisper certainly sounded it. Constant opened her eyes. But for his white-blond hair, she wouldn't have seen him. She looked at the darker shadow where his face should be and grimaced at it.

"They were talking about you," she said finally.

"Give me your word you will na' accept him."

Constant snorted.

"It is na' amusing, Constant Ridgely. Promise me you will na' accept that whelp's lukewarm suit."

"How do you know it will be lukewarm?"

"I doona' care if he's as passionate as a sailor newly arrived at port. I want your promise, Constant, and I want it now."

It's amazing the amount of emphasis he can put on whispered words. She sighed.

"Don't you sigh at me. He'll put out pretty words and maybe a look or two, and you're na' to listen. You hear me?"

"Kameron, they were talking about harming you."

"I'm going to do the same to that pip if he does na' watch his back. Give me your word you'll refuse him."

"They want you dead."

"Constant! I will shake you next. You're na' to accept him. You ken? Under any circumstances."

"We have worse troubles. What if they come back? What if they find you?"

He didn't answer for a spell. She heard how angry he was though. It was in the power of each breath.

"You're a rare lass, Constant. You've kept me intrigued for days now with just *how* rare. You're a prize. You ken? That lad does na' deserve you."

"What are we going to do?"

The low rumble sounded as if it was launched through clenched teeth. "For the love of—I want your promise, Constant. Right now. He's na' worthy to be in the same country as you, let alone by your side in wedlock."

"Can we worry about that later? I've got four more sets of eyes and ears to fool. How am I to do that?"

"There are six, and they came on five mounts, and you're evading my question."

"Six?"

"One dinna' speak. He was riding double with the blacksmith. Looks a bit like him, too."

"That would be his brother."

"I assumed it was na' his son."

If he could have seen her look, he'd not have used such sarcasm. "He is married to one of my sisters. You heard him. They have three daughters."

"The smithy is your brother-in-law?"

"Yes."

"'Twas his hand branding my feet."

"I know. I recognized it."

"I see. This does explain your earlier reaction. But it strays far from the subject. You're na' to accept that pip. Give me your promise, Constant. Afore we run out of time."

"We have the rest of the night. You heard them."

He swore, and then a hand wrapped about her arm and pulled, bringing her directly against him to nuzzle the skin beneath her jaw. That was followed by huffs of breath that teased and tickled.

He whispered, "One returns. My guess is it's the

smithy's brother, or your lackluster suitor, Esterbrook. Regardless, I have little time, and I have to make certain you listen to me."

She was listening. She couldn't hear anything else; then his lips touched her neck.

"Will you give me your word you won't entertain that fellow's suit? Nae matter how he asks?"

His words were accompanied by his tongue. It was leaving a trail of fire-ice along her jawbone.

"Kam—"

"Softly, love. One returns. He's just outside."

"How do you know?"

"The same way I ken there are six men and five mounts. I observe. I listen. I watch. I'm verra good at it."

"You eavesdrop?"

He made a sound of frustration. It felt as strange as his whispered words against her throat. "I have excellent hearing. I have acute eyesight. And they were na' hiding much. So, I observed what they offered."

"You're a . . . spy?"

"Damn it, Constant! Quit wasting words! Promise you'll turn down little Master Esterbrook."

"Why?"

"Why?" he repeated.

"Yes. Why? Why must I turn down a proposal from the man I've waited for all my life? Just because you order it?"

"Why? Oh, Jesu', lass! You've nae idea how much I yearn to show you the extent of why! My entire being is afire with it."

He might be speaking the truth, for the heat emanating from him was akin to being near a fire pit. He groaned and pulled her even closer.

"I'm na' entirely certain I can explain . . . but I'll try. Perhaps if I tease a bit around the edges I may be able to survive it. This is madness. Complete and total . . . oh

Lord, but you're a luscious woman, Constant Ridgely. Desirable. Passionate. Exciting. Absolutely perfect."

He slid his hands along her sides, down over her hips, and then back to her waist, pulling at her clothing with each movement. It was as erotic a feeling as anything he'd done, especially with the back of her dress still gaping open.

"That was your first kiss, Constant. She nodded. She knew he felt it because his head was still settled against her collarbone.

"It wasn't mine."

Constant stiffened.

"Doona' let it fash you. I'm attempting a bit of explanation. I'm using words rather than actions, since I— well, I dinna' handle that verra well. I've got little time, and I need to make you see. You have to see! You're too good for Esterbrook. You're too good for any man unless he's headlong in love with you. I tell you I've experience with a kiss, so you can trust me. I've given them and I've received them. There are lots of differing types . . . but the one that just happened atween us? That was na' usual. You ken what I'm trying to say?"

"I don't think I want to hear any more," she replied.

"Oh, Constant! Hear me out. Please? If I explain it badly, it's because I have you in my arms and I'm fighting my own body over it. I've a bloodthirsty mob after my skin and I'm about to be interrupted by the fellow sent to curry and feed the horses. I only hope I have enough time for the explanation, and enough fortitude to prevent anything else. Forgive my thick tongue if I explain it poorly."

Constant frowned and then lowered her arms from the lantern and tentatively slid them down to his shoulders.

"Doona' touch me! Oh . . . Constant!"

She lifted her hands the moment he spoke, for his

hands tightened on her waist until they bit into her flesh, making her shudder match his. And the next moment his mouth slammed onto hers, sucking and caressing and tempting, and stealing every breath. Constant's heart hammered with his, her mouth moved with the motions he'd just taught her, while the pressure from his handhold at her waist increased.

"This is why you canna' accept young Esterbrook's proposal! And this! He doesn't deserve this! Or this."

He was mouthing words along the nape of her neck, breathing heat everywhere he went. He reached the space below an ear, sucking lightly and sending rivulets of sensation everywhere. His hands moved, going lower, molding about her hips and thighs, bunching and pulling material up at the same time.

"He will na' give you his all, Constant. He canna'. The act of love . . . it can be so wondrous. It can be—oh Lord! This is beyond me. I—I . . . uh, you see . . . if a man's forced, it's different. It's hell on earth. Trust me. I've seen it. Oh . . . no, *please*!"

His voice cracked on the plea as Constant curved her body into him. She molded her breasts to his chest and her belly to the rod that began thrusting at her, sending trills of heat and oceans of thrill in its wake.

"Stop me, Constant. Help me! Dear God, stop me."

His pleas didn't match his actions. He lifted her up and then slid her back down his torso. And Constant helped, her leg locked about his hips. Kam was shoving her clothing up and out of the way, then delving along the backs of her thighs, kneading and molding the flesh with fingers that shot liquid heat. And then he was pleading again.

"Stop me, Constant. Please stop me. We must stop! You doona' ken! We canna' do this. I will na' compromise—"

Fingers gripped her upper thighs and Constant

pulsed into the support. Kam jerked onto his back. It had to hurt. He didn't seem to care. The new position meant she could grip him with both legs, clenching her knees tightly to both sides of his hips while bucking into him, her mouth open and gasping for air.

"Oh, sweet! Right there! Right! I mean, nae! Oh God, *nae*!"

The last word was a long, drawn-out whisper. It had barely finished before they both heard the barn door open.

Constant froze in place. So did Kam. The thunder of his heartbeat matched hers. Loud. Harsh. Strident. Below them came whistling. The jingling of harnesses. Shuffling noises. The whinny of horses. The sound of a currycomb at work. She felt the cold night air on her nakedness, contrasting with the molten heat of the man she lay atop. Constant lay unmoving, while every nerve ending on her body twitched and pinged with some-thing so elemental and raw it was difficult to stanch. Her flesh was alert with spark-driven tension that throbbed in little sequences, especially where she still pressed against his groin. She'd never felt so alive. So moist. So needy. So tension-filled. So wanton. The combination of sensa-tions slowly ebbed. Altered. Subtly and surely. And then they were replaced by vulnerability. Embarrassment. Awkwardness.

Kam began moving, soundlessly and slowly, easing his grip from about her thighs until his hands rested on the backs of her parted legs. That was still too intimate. Everything was. He was blasting heat at her, too. Con-stant closed her eyes tightly and breathed as shallowly as possible. She had to. She supposed this was shock. And with it came a chill so severe, her tremors would've rustled the straw if she'd been on the floor and not atop

Kam. He wrapped both arms about her, sharing his warmth, and slowly the shock transformed into something else: complete and utter self-recrimination and shame.

Constant tried to rein in the rush of sobs, but a moment later they overwhelmed. It took an act of will to keep quiet, but somehow she managed it. She shook with the torrent of tears, gulped back what she could, and still made his chest wet.

Kam left off his embrace, silently moving first one hand, then the other. She felt him pull down her dress, smooth it, and then refasten every hook up her back. He was perfect at it, too. His movements were perfectly timed with the noises from below so as to be undetectable. She should not have been surprised: he'd probably been trained to it.

He had to be a spy.

She'd been harboring and nursing and tending to a spy. No wonder he knew so much about lying. He lived one. Worse, she'd been about to fornicate with him. Willingly. And even worse yet, she couldn't kill the emotion she felt for him. Still. Even knowing what he was.

Constant swallowed her sobs, but more came to take their place. Kam finished the hooks and maneuvered the skirt down to her knees, covering her. Then he started stroking the hair down her back. Softly. Gently. Carefully.

Chapter Thirteen

"Constant? May I see you for a moment?"

Constant looked up from the tub of suds she was elbow deep in and saw Thomas Esterbrook's face, and then her father's right behind him. She looked back down. Thomas had waited until the sun was hovering at midmorn and the others had started twitching and moving impatiently in their chairs beside the kitchen table. She sneered at the bubbles.

She was going to receive the proposal she'd wanted all her life and she was as unenthusiastic about it as Thomas appeared to be.

"Constant?" her father asked.

"I will be right with you, Master Esterbrook," she replied, pulling her hands out to dry them on her apron.

"It's a pleasant morn. I would like to take a walk with you. Would that be to your liking?"

Constant tipped her eyes to his. Thomas had clear, bright green eyes, close to the color of a new leaf. They'd always been bright with mischief. Right at the moment, they looked glassy and dull. She looked away and embraced the surfeit of color in her cheeks. She reached for her shawl and slipped her feet into boots.

He was going to ask for her hand in marriage . . . and he hated it. What was it Kameron had whispered to her at some point? That a man forced into a relationship he doesn't want would turn something as beautiful and passionate as what Kameron and Constant shared into a thing of ugliness.

The snow wasn't going to last into midafternoon at the rate it was melting. Constant noted it in her thoughts as the door shut behind them. She looked down at the same porch she'd been standing on to churn butter only five days earlier. So much had happened! So much had changed!

So much was still unchanged, too.

She had no future with Kameron. According to him, he was wanted by, and had loved, many women. She would be just another conquest. In fact, she almost had been.

Despite the chill in the air, Constant blushed. Beside her, she felt rather than saw Thomas scuffle his feet, much as he used to in Sunday school class. She knew he was nervous. She glanced at him, then away. He hadn't lost a bit of his handsomeness, although it wasn't affecting her as it used to. Thomas Esterbrook had four girls trying to court him . . . five, if she counted herself. It wasn't because he was an ugly sort. He had coal-black hair with streaks of midnight blue running through it. He had a widow's peak at the apex of his forehead. He had high cheekbones that led to a pointed chin he disguised with a bit of black whiskers, and he had those vivid green eyes. He was also a good two inches shorter than she was.

Constant snickered, then caught herself.

"Well, come along. This isn't going to get easier the more I procrastinate."

He walked off the porch, expecting her to follow him.

And Constant did. She lifted her skirt hem and followed. She was so torn! Everything she'd been dreaming of for years was going to be handed to her, but it wasn't what she'd envisioned. The reason was quite clear. She now knew how it felt to be in love.

A man doing something he detests turns it evil.

The words came to her before she reached the mud. Wasn't that what Kameron had told her to remember before she'd finally left him?

She'd fallen asleep atop him. In fact, she'd been there most of the night. He hadn't moved. He simply held her and whispered to her. He wanted everything to be different. He wanted her to know her worth. He was sorry, and yet he wasn't. He'd been very close to losing control and he wasn't the type to lose control. If that wasn't proof of how desirable she was, Kameron didn't know what was. Constant had stayed in the enclosure of his arms and pretended to sleep while he whispered to her. After a time, it had actually worked. She'd slept. Oh. Sweet heaven! She'd slept in a man's arms! A man who had handled parts of her that only her mother had seen. It wasn't conceivable, but it was true. Constant Ridgely, the girl known as a quiet, shy, mousy sort, fit more for house and farm work, had almost been loved, in the way a man loves a woman, by a man who had to be the most handsome, virile, and masculine fellow ever birthed.

She looked down at the muck Thomas was leading her through and tried to temper her thoughts. It wasn't possible. Her body still felt Kameron. Every bit of him! She hadn't wanted to leave. Worse than the sin of almost fornicating with him, she'd wanted it. She lusted for him with a need and longing that didn't seem to diminish, regardless of the hours away from him. At one point early this morn, she'd almost opened her mouth and begged Kam to make love to her—even though she knew the consequences, and what she'd lose. She'd wanted him to love her so badly her body still quaked with the memory of it.

She was actually thankful Thomas Esterbrook was walking in front of her rather than at her side. Constant wrapped her arms about herself. She couldn't believe this! She was about to receive an offer of marriage from the man she'd wanted for over thirteen years, and her mind and body were yearning for someone else! Would that Thomas had asked for her to walk with him a week ago! But no . . . then she'd not have understood what a man was like if he was forced into marriage. She'd never suspect that if he touched her with loathing it wasn't her fault. She might never know what desire and passion and sensual craving really felt like, either.

Constant looked at Thomas's back, watched his gait, how sure-footed he was, how his breeches molded to him, the narrowness of his waist . . . the lengthy queue of black hair down his back, and couldn't detect one ounce of interest. She wanted to be back with Kameron, just as she'd been all night.

All night!

It was still unbelievable.

She blushed at the thought. Kameron had said she had a body that was hard to resist. She knew what he meant. She felt the same thing about his. But he'd kept himself well within bounds, using words to persuade. He'd begged, cajoled, entreated, threatened, and ordered her not to accept anything Thomas offered her. And then he'd started anew. He finally amended it: she could accept, if she could swear to him that Thomas's offer was given freely. According to Kameron, a forced man gains his vengeance from his wife, and it's a lifetime sentence.

He'd told her his parents suffered it. They were barely civil to each other. He dreaded any function that had them in the same room. Most of the people he knew suffered the same miserable wedded life. He wasn't married for a reason: his status at birth had taken his choice away. He wasn't like the colonists, who had the freedom to choose their life's partner.

Constant had lain atop him and listened.

Kameron had finally told her to go ahead and choose Thomas Esterbrook if he created the same sort of emotion and passion in her. Otherwise, he was going to strangle both of them. He hadn't been remotely soft and tender when he'd said that, either.

Constant tripped on an exposed root and took a couple of loud steps before catching herself. Thomas didn't even turn to check.

She frowned at his back. Thomas Esterbrook was a prize catch. He always had been. His family ran the biggest press. They owned a three-story mansion on a very exclusive street in Boston. Why, they even had bricks lining their drive, between the double rows of oak trees they'd planted. Thomas had three siblings, all younger, all female, making him the heir. He had wealth, he was attractive, and he had a fairly well-proportioned frame.

Unfortunately, he wasn't remotely like Kameron. Constant shut her eyes, saw him as clearly as if he stood before her, and reopened them as she accepted the inevitable. She was in love. Deeply. It wasn't healthy. It wasn't smart. It wasn't expected. And there wasn't any way to ignore it. The British spy named Kameron had her heart; he'd almost had her maidenhood. Was she willing to give up a future for him, too? Was she willing to await another life partner if she turned down Thomas?

What if that never happened? Was she willing to tempt fate and become a spinster?

She was so torn!

"It's a cold fall, isn't it?" Thomas asked from over his shoulder.

"We've had colder," she replied.

"True."

He shrugged and kept walking. Constant sighed before following as he looped around the corral, through the stripped-down garden, and then all around the cornfield, their movements easily seen from the house. Constant kept up with him easily. Her skirts weren't avoiding the mud, though, and her boots were ankle-deep in the muck. *All things considered, this isn't remotely romantic*, she thought.

"Constant?"

Thomas swiveled suddenly and she almost ran into him. The difference in height was more apparent at a distance of less than a foot. He looked up at her and frowned, looking as though he smelled something unpleasant. Constant sucked in on her cheeks to stop any untoward reaction that would make him flush worse than he already was. And then she slouched her shoulders and leaned on one hip, bringing her closer to his level.

Even if he was being forced to offer for her, wasn't that better than no marriage and no babies, and no one, once Kameron left?

"We—we've known each other for some time, Constant." Thomas stopped to lick his lips.

Constant smiled. She knew what he had to do, and that wasn't fair; he didn't know she knew. She tried to help him. "Since we were both in dresses," she replied.

The color moved to the tops of his cheeks. It was a becoming reaction. Thomas Esterbrook was handsome. It would be pleasant looking at him, as well as make it easier to do other things with him. Now it was Constant's turn to redden. She had to look away.

"Yes . . . well. It was always expected . . . I mean, I—I always meant to . . . I believe it was expected—"

"Kiss me, Thomas." Constant interrupted his litany of stuttering and stammering.

Those green eyes widened. It wasn't a pleasant look. "K-k-kiss you?" he stammered.

"You do know how, don't you?" she asked.

"Uh . . ."

Constant reached for his shoulders, pulled him to her and matched her lips to his. Then she used exactly the same motions Kameron had taught her. She slid her lips along Thomas's and they didn't resemble anything except polished wood. They were as hard and cold, too.

Constant pulled away. She took a step back, then another, until she was out of reach. Thomas looked exactly as she'd suspected he might. As hard and cold as his lips had felt. She narrowed her eyes as he moved to wipe at his mouth.

"Whatever you have to offer, the answer is no, Thomas," she said finally.

"You should wait until 'tis offered, I would say," he replied.

She shrugged. "Offer then. The answer will still be the same." She tossed her head and turned away from him. The barn shimmered in the distance, as did the house. She started walking toward them. She only hoped no one had seen her humiliation.

"Constant, wait!"

She kept walking, using each stride to pummel the sod.

"Constant!"

Thomas gained her side, grabbed at her arm to stop her, and then jerked her to face him. She was being forced? Constant didn't like it. She looked down at the pincerlike pressure of his hand on her upper arm and then at him.

"Unhand me, Master Esterbrook. Right now."

"We haven't finished our business."

"I have no business with you. I don't think I even know who you are anymore. Good day."

She turned to leave, but he yanked her back around, his strength belying his diminutive size. And then he glared at her, his eyes thinned to slits.

"I have an offer of marriage to make to you, and by heaven, you are going to listen to it!"

"An offer of marriage? Whatever for? You can't abide the touch of my lips to yours. We'd be mismatched. Totally."

"What you did wasn't a kiss, Constant. I know that much. You were after more than that."

"Good heavens, Thomas, what do you think happens between a married man and woman? Nothing?"

"I had no thought to find a hussy within you, Mistress Ridgely."

Her back straightened, putting her two inches above him. "I can't believe I heard you aright, Thomas. I've known you since we started walking. I listened to your tears when you were paddled, and I was there for you when you fell when you tried riding for the first time. I am no hussy and you know it."

"Explain your action, then."

"I wanted to find out if I would be marrying a man. And I found out, now didn't I?"

He sucked in a breath at that. Constant watched it as if she were a hundred miles away and not still held in place by his hand on her arm. She only hoped Kam was asleep and not peeking around the blanket covering the loft window.

"You insult my manhood?"

"If you possessed it, nothing I say would insult it. Now, unhand me. I have chores to finish."

"Your father expects us to wed."

"My father expects a lot of things. I believe he expected more sons, too. He's well versed in disappointment. You should learn the trait. It would be an improvement. Now, unhand me."

His hand tightened. "I am proposing marriage to you, Constant."

"And I'm declining. Good day to you, Thomas."

"You can't decline. I'm offering marriage, for pity's sake!"

Constant's eyebrows rose. Thomas Esterbrook wasn't used to being turned down, obviously. She smiled coldly. "I believe you already made that clear. I hope I was just as clear with my response. I want a man when I wed, Thomas Esterbrook. A man who doesn't run from my passion. I don't believe you're him. Now, unhand me. I have other things to do today."

"You're truly turning me down?"

The surprise on his face was comical. Constant laughed inwardly, and caught the smile. "I believe that is exactly what I am doing."

"But . . . why?"

He loosened his grip enough she could pull her arm away. He had bruised it, though. She could feel it throbbing.

"Because I don't love you. I should think that much is obvious."

"B-but you've loved me for ages."

"I think I loved who I thought you were, Thomas. It was stupid of me, I know that now. Good day to you. You may leave."

"Is it someone else? Is that it?"

Her laughter rang out at that. *Is it ever*, she thought.

She couldn't tell him any of that, though. "Isn't it enough that your halfhearted attempt to secure my hand was turned down? Aren't you relieved?"

He frowned at her. "Why are you acting so strangely? You knew I would offer for you. I told you I would. You always told me you'd accept only me, and no other."

"I'm not acting strangely, Master Esterbrook. I've simply grown up and stopped fooling myself. You're not the man I thought you were. You've changed. I've changed. I didn't realize how much until you failed to return my kiss. You don't want me. You don't desire me. You can't stomach the thought of bedding me. You've been making it plain since spring. I've just not been listening."

"You've a blunt way about you, of a sudden."

"That's probably due to your inability to hear softly stated words. I have to be blunt. So be it. I don't want you either, Thomas. I don't desire you, and I don't wish to wed you. I can't imagine bedding with you. We'd need all the lights out."

"What? I'm insulted now."

"Good. I've done what I set out to do. Now, please leave. I've chores to do, and you're probably delaying some important business, too."

"You're trying to insult me? Why?"

"Because you won't take no for an answer. You're a handsome sort, Thomas Esterbrook. You're wealthy. In goodly health. You are a fine specimen, too. Rest assured I see all that. It's just that it's not enough for me. Not anymore."

"Not enough?" Surprise was written all over him. "What more do you want?"

"A man who doesn't run from my passion. A man who can give as good as he gets in my bed. That's what I want."

"Good Lord! Where did you come up with such a

thing? Gently bred young ladies don't even think of such things, let alone speak of them!"

"Then go find yourself one of them. I'm rapidly tiring of your lukewarm company as it is."

Constant had always attributed a spark of mischief to his eyes. She saw a new look to them. The clear green had darkened and looked bottomless and deep as he stared at her. The flare of his nostrils was interesting to see, too. She hadn't been mistaken. Thomas Esterbrook was very handsome. He just wasn't doing a thing to her pulse, or her emotions. It wasn't his fault, though.

"I don't think I want one of them. I want you."

Constant shook her head to clear it. "What? You can't mean that."

"I do mean it, and it's true."

She rolled her lips in a horselike snort. Everything Kameron had told her about the rug-selling was true. She'd come too easily to Thomas, and he hadn't wanted her. Now that she had turned him down, he wanted her. She shook her head. "But why?"

"This passion you showed. I want to have it. I want it so badly right now, I can't understand it. We won't need to dim the lights, either. Accept my hand, Constant."

Her eyes were huge. "No," she replied.

"I am finished asking for your hand. Now I'm demanding it. I won't take no for an answer."

"What?"

"You heard me. I want you for my wife."

"Ask Rebecca Porter. She's pining for you."

"I don't want Rebecca. I want you. I say it again. I want your hand in marriage. I've spoken to your father. He already accepted me. He listed the dowry he'll settle on you and I agreed."

"All this before you even knew I'd accept you?"

He grabbed both her shoulders and shook her. "You

always said you'd accept me! How was I supposed to know you were changing your mind?"

"Perhaps you shouldn't have left me waiting."

"Damn it, Constant! Accept me."

She shook her head. He was the one pulling her close this time, and his mouth wasn't remotely wooden. It was hot and wet and grasping and felt eternally wrong. Constant shuddered and pulled away. She barely restrained herself from wiping her mouth much as he had done.

She didn't want his passion now that she had it. She knew what she wanted. She knew it was unreachable. Her heart hurt with it. Her entire form pained over it. Her eyes filled with tears.

"Now tell me I'm not manly enough for you."

Thomas was panting; his hands, still on her shoulders, were trembling; and he was flushed clear to his widow's peak. It was just as becoming as before.

"Let me go," she whispered.

"I may have been a bit slow at speaking for you, Constant. I'll make it up to you. I promise. Accept my suit. Let us take the news to your family. I'm begging you."

"No," she replied.

"Good Lord! What do you want from me?"

"I've changed, Thomas. I don't want to wed you anymore. I'm sorry." The tears were spilling over. She pulled from him to wipe at them.

"You have to marry someone, Constant Ridgely. You know it. I know it. I've just seen a side to you I've never seen before. It had me shocked, I admit. It also has me straining in certain areas I won't mention. I just can't believe the change in you, and that I might have missed it. Say you'll wed me. Please?"

She snorted the reaction through her clogged nose. It probably looked as unladylike as it sounded. She lifted her apron to wipe at her face and eyes.

"Well? Please say yes. Don't leave me in this sort of agony. It's not fair."

She couldn't believe it. Thomas Esterbrook had started out detesting everything about asking her, and now he was not only asking, but he was demanding, and then begging her? What a strange morning it was turning out to be.

"I already told you my answer, Thomas."

"Say you'll think about it. Please?"

"If I say that, will you cease this and go about your business?"

"Only if it's true. Look me in the eye and tell me you'll think about it. I'll know the truth of it that way."

What harm was there in that sort of answer? After Kameron left her and things settled into a loveless existence, perhaps what Thomas offered her wouldn't be such a poor substitute. She put her apron back in place and lifted her head. The uncertain look on his face almost made her laugh.

"I will think about what you've said to me this morn, Master Esterbrook. You may tell my father of it."

"Will you kiss me again, too?"

Chapter Fourteen

Constant took special care with her appearance that evening. It wasn't due to her father's possible return. It hadn't anything to do with Thomas Esterbrook and his aborted proposal that very morning. Her eyes flicked to the bloodstained and torn, but still recognizable, red British jacket lying across the chair in her bedroom.

It was because she was saying good-bye to Kameron.

Constant smiled over at Stream before turning back to the mirror. She had to turn before the smile became something else. She looked down at her work-worn hands, examined the chipped nails, the rough calluses, and the red spots that would become sores if she didn't keep them out of water. That always happened when winter came. She turned each palm over and frowned. She didn't have attractive hands.

It had never bothered her before.

Constant looked up. She did have large eyes, and right at the moment, they didn't look remotely turquoise. They looked dark with her emotion, and awash with tears. She reached to whisk the wetness away. Tonight had to be her last night with Kameron. Anything else was too risky.

She didn't want to waste a moment crying. She had years ahead of her for that luxury.

She reached for her coronet of hair and slowly unwound it. She'd put her hair into two braids yester morn, and as she uncoiled each one, her hair sprang into ripples of dark brown. Kam had asked her what color it was and she hadn't lied. It was dark brown. She hadn't been gifted with one strand of the Ridgely reddish-gold hair. She hadn't been cheated, though. Hers was striped throughout with a dark auburn-looking color.

Stream made a sound. Constant smiled at her in the mirror. She knew what her sister was saying, although no words came with it. Stream was warning her. Constant wasn't going to listen. She had years ahead of her for that, too.

She picked up her brush. Her hair was always unmanageable the day it was washed, strands going everywhere but into the braid. By the second and third days, her hair was shiny, thick, and easy to coax into any configuration. She brushed it until the waves cascaded to her waist.

Kameron wanted to know what color of hair she had. Well, she would show him. Then she would get him ready to leave. She could do nothing else. He was a British spy. She was the daughter of a patriot. The red jacket was a silent reminder. Thomas Esterbrook's banked passions reminded her. Stream even reminded her, with alternating frowns and then wide-eyed surprised looks. Constant tipped her head to let a stray tear wend its way down the side of her face.

Thomas had escorted her back to the house, running his hand along her upper arm in a manner that left Constant in no doubt about how he felt. More than once she'd caught him stopping and sucking in a breath before looking over at her again. She knew exactly what he was feeling. She only wished it was reciprocated.

Constant stood and rearranged her skirt. She ignored Stream's folded arms and set expression. She knew she shouldn't go to Kameron with her hair down. She should wear more than a thin cotton dress, held to her waist with an apron. She should be wearing more than a filmy chemise that had come straight out of her hope chest. She already knew all of that. She shouldn't be going anywhere with no pantaloons on, but she didn't care! She folded the homespun, which she'd nearly finished making into trousers, over her arm, picked up his jacket, blew a kiss to Stream, and settled the lamp wick back into the oil. No matter what her future held, there was only one man she'd allow to make her a woman. She dressed this way to make certain of it.

And then she'd help him leave.

Constant slid the stable door open, listening for any untoward sounds. The men had gone and taken most of the horses with them, leaving the stable strangely quiet with just the plow horse, Eustace, inside. Constant slid the door shut and drew the bolt down on it. The men hadn't said when they'd return, only that they would. Constant hadn't really listened; her entire being had seemed attuned to just one thing. Constant didn't know what was the matter with her. She was afraid to look at it too closely. All she knew was the tense, coiled sensation in the pit of her belly had started the moment Thomas put the jacket in her arms, and it had grown until everything she'd done all evening was little more than a blur. She hadn't even remembered what she'd cooked for their sup until she ladled a bowl of ham and beans for Kam.

Constant made certain to block the door with the wagon before picking up Kameron's clothing and his meal. She wasn't going to allow them to be interrupted.

She couldn't. She was creating a memory that was going to have to last a lifetime.

"Constant?"

Her lips twisted at the sound of his voice. He was dreadfully indiscreet. For a hunted man.

"It's me."

She put a foot on the ladder. He made it easier by adjusting the oil lamp, lighting the way to the loft. Like a beacon.

"I've been waiting for you."

She was at the top of the ladder before he spoke again and Constant lost her voice the moment he did. Kam wasn't stretched out atop a log, or two saddles, or anything else. He was sitting facing her, leaning against a bale of hay. He had those massive arms folded across his chest and was looking entirely too masculine for a man with frilly, albeit dirtied, feminine underdrawers looped across himself.

She had to look away as he just watched her, his mouth set.

"You wore your hair down," he finally commented.

Constant put the tray on the straw in front of her and maneuvered herself over the top rung without giving him a glimpse of her lack of underclothing. She was on her knees next, shivering convulsively. She was already regretting every bit of her preparation.

"I hope it wasn't for me," he continued.

Constant pulled the jacket off her shoulder and held it toward him. "I've . . . brought your clothing."

"Was it for me, Constant? And if so—for pity's sake—why?"

She didn't answer. The hand holding out his jacket shook so much that it was obvious to both of them. Kam leaned forward, grimacing a bit at the movement, before plucking the jacket from her fingers. His golden-brown eyes never left hers. And then he moved them to his jacket. She watched with him as he turned the sleeves inside out and flipped it over, making it a nondescript black.

"This is a special coat," he remarked.

"I heard," she replied.

"It's sewn with two sides. One red, as you've already seen, the other black. It's known as a turncoat."

"I know. They told me."

"Such attire makes it simple to infiltrate groups where I wouldn't normally be welcome. Verra handy for finding out what you colonists have planned next."

"I already told you. I know. They told me."

"I actually have several of these turncoats, in varying shades. I even have a homespun-looking brown one, a bit like that hank of material you brought. Helps me fit in with farmers and such."

"Like my family?" she asked in a quiet voice.

"Exactly. I've done it an entire season. I thought I was verra good at it. I've never been caught afore. Shows a certain stupidity, does na' it?"

"I think you've been lucky," she replied.

"This is luck?"

"Not to have been caught before."

"Oh. My thanks. Remind me if I've need of a compliment, na' to come to you."

"How can you expect to fit in? You're too big, you're . . . overly handsome, and you talk strangely."

There was complete silence for a few moments. And then he answered.

"People see what they want to see, Constant, so I give them what they want. Aside from which, I am prone to hunching, I wear a large-brim hat, I put pomade in my hair to darken it, and I keep my mouth shut. That's how."

He shoved an arm into a sleeve with enough force

both of them heard the seam rip. "Look at that. It's in deplorable condition, too. I suppose that's justice for you. It matters little. It'll still cover me."

"I've been tasked with sewing it into a quilt, using the alternating black and red in a starburst pattern."

"Fancy that. I wonder who'd ask such a thing. Nae doubt it was the little black-haired fellow that enjoys breaking legs?"

Constant's eyes flared at the way he spat the words. She watched him pull the jacket off and place it carefully beside him.

"Is that the same fellow you were with this morn, walking about the fields as if you had na' a care in the world?"

She nodded and moved her gaze to the straw in front of her knees.

"I suppose that's your erstwhile Thomas Esterbrook?"

She nodded again.

"I gather congratulations are in order. When's the momentous occasion?"

"I didn't accept his proposal," she said quietly.

"That was na' what it looked like to me."

"He wouldn't take no for an answer."

"So you had to ply him with kisses to find out the truth of his offer? What do you take me for? A complete simpleton?"

Constant lifted her head in surprise. Kameron was as angry-looking as his words sounded. She stared.

"Well?"

"I thought you'd be pleased."

"Pleased? Me? Good Lord, why?"

"Be—because when I . . . turned down his offer, he reacted just like you said he would. Back with the rug-seller story, remember?"

"I've been more than stupid, worse than incompetent, and now you toss it in my face? My thanks, but I'd as

soon na' ken anything about your courtship with him,"
Kameron replied in an acerbic tone.

"I don't understand," she said.

"You never understand. I used to think it was refresh-
ing and rare and entirely too enticing. Now, all I can
think of is the hell I've gone and created for myself. You
doona' understand? So what? Puzzle it out."

Constant's eyes filled with tears. The straw beneath
her melted and blended together until it became a
golden-hued mess, akin to the shade of his eyes. She
blinked rapidly to clear them.

"Did you bring your skean—I mean knife?"

She nodded.

"Good. I'll be needing it. I think 'tis time I sliced my
legs free and went on my way. They've swelled, but they're
na' broken."

"I know," she whispered.

"Oh. Listen to that. You actually know something?
What a nice change. So what say you be a good little lass,
hand me your skean, and then go fetch me a length of
cording. Can you do that?"

She swallowed. *A good little lass?* She repeated it to
herself in disbelief. "You want a length of cord?"

"Aye. An auld bridle, a bit of rein, some baling twine.
Something along that line."

"Why?"

He sighed heavily. "Again with the why? I need a cord
to finish this splint I've fashioned for myself. Your loft
was na' built verra well. Either that or I was angrier than
I thought."

He lifted a thin, jagged-edged board from the straw
at his side.

"Where did you get that?"

"I just told you. I pried a board from the loft floor with
my bare hands. It gave me something constructive to do

with them instead of—oh, Christ. Stop me before I say another God-damned thing. And I'm na' apologizing for one word. You ken?"

He stopped and then swore some more. Constant didn't dare look to see what was wrong with him now. A long, uncomfortable silence followed his tirade, and when he spoke again, his voice was even colder.

"It's na' going to be perfect, but it should hold my injured leg in place so I can move. But nae splint will stay against my leg without a cord. Why are you still sitting there? Get something to strap it with."

Constant scooted back from him on her hands and knees. She was afraid in this position she was showing too much bosom—after all, she'd chosen the gown for that effect—but she didn't dare stand. The gown was sewn from thin cotton and clung everywhere. She heard his groan as she climbed over the top rung of the ladder.

She looked across at him.

Kameron was ripping the bandages from the backs of his legs, regardless of how painful it had to be. His blisters weren't totally healed. She turned away before he saw her watching, clambered down, and slid over the bottom three steps, landing in a heap. It wasn't but a moment before she was on her feet again. She couldn't believe she'd dressed seductively for him. Kameron had changed since this morning. It didn't seem possible. He wasn't romantic or loving. He was a monster.

She grabbed up Eustace's harness and tossed it up to the loft. Then she found a coil of rope. She tossed that up, too. She grabbed a bridle and the reins that went with it. She was preparing to toss it, too, when he spoke again.

"Are you attempting to knock me senseless?"

"It would be an improvement," she answered, and flung the entire bridle up and over the ladder.

Silence. Her answer was nothing but silence. Constant gathered her skirt in her hand and started climbing again. She still had to finish fitting his trousers. She'd use large basting stitches. That would make it go faster, and grant her less time in his presence. She gritted her teeth. She couldn't believe she'd been in a haze of anticipation as she prepared for this evening. She'd been a fool. Naïve. It was obvious. She'd been an easy mark for him; little more than a plaything to toy with while he recuperated; a way to pass the time. Every low description she could claim, she gave to herself before reaching the top rung.

"Do you have any more of this bandaging cloth?"

He had his legs atop the board, while he wadded up the bloodied, used cheesecloth. The motions made every muscle ripple and flex. Constant swallowed, averted her eyes, and crawled over the top of the ladder, carefully keeping her skirt to her ankles. When she looked back over, she caught him staring, unblinkingly, while his entire torso seemed locked into a display of strength and power. Her heart reacted, jumping so it filled her throat, then dropping to her belly to pound thumping pulse beats from there. She was being ridiculous.

"Well?"

"Bandaging cloth?" She wasn't following his words. There was something vibrating through the loft that felt a lot more urgent. More visceral. More vibrant. Heated and immense. Ground-trembling. Breath-stealing. It felt as though even the air was weighted, making it difficult to breathe.

"Everything has to be repeated to you. And then it has to be explained, and even then you fail to ken. This is bandaging cloth. I need more of it."

He threw it at her. Constant dodged sideways and then turned to watch it sail to the barn floor.

"That is a length of cheesecloth. I stole it from the

dairy shed. I've yet to see any of it washed and replaced. I guess I'll worry about it once you're gone."

"You in such a hurry to see me go, are you?"

"I wasn't before."

"I think that's the best thing I've heard all eve . . . so *do* you?"

Constant went to her knees as she looked at him. She still didn't know what was wrong with him, but the entire strange aura in the loft seemed to be emanating from him. Directly toward her. The hair on the nape of her neck stood up.

"Do I . . . what?" she whispered.

Kameron closed his eyes, shuddered, and then re-opened them. Constant watched as he slid his glance down to her waist and back. And she could've sworn he paled.

"Do you have any more cheesecloth?" he asked, his lips in a snarl that revealed clenched teeth.

She shook her head.

"Can you get some?"

"There isn't any more to get. I have to wash it. Didn't I just say as much?"

"Give me your slip then. I have to stay the bleeding. I canna' wrap it until I stop that."

Constant glanced down. "I'm not wearing one," she replied to her lap.

"Oh Lord . . . doona' say so! Doona' even mention it. Doona' remark on it. Doona' say another blasted, God-damned thing. Damn you, Constant! Give me your pantaloons, then. Damn you for making this harder than it already is."

Constant looked up at him. He was still sitting up, but he had both arms about his thighs now, trying to keep his lower legs from contact with anything. Since that position stiffened every bit of him, and every bit of him was exposed to her, she reacted. Her mouth opened, her breath came in little pants, her breasts seemed to enlarge, chafing against the confinement of her bodice, and her eyes roamed over every inch of his body before returning to his face.

"I'm not wearing any of those, either," she whispered.

His eyes went wide and he choked. Constant would have approached, if he hadn't stopped her with a growl.

"Good God, Constant! You vixen! You fool! You ken how much I crave—you little—how can you do this? You ken what you do to me! I *told* you as much last night. Ah . . . Jesu'."

"I have my apron. And . . . if that isn't enough, you can have my . . . chemise. Here."

"Doona' offer, Constant . . . please?"

She held out her apron, and when he didn't move, she tossed it to the straw beside him. Then she reached behind her for the knife.

He didn't say anything as she crawled to him. It sounded as though he was coming up for air each time he sucked in a breath, and then he was exhaling strongly enough to blow out several candles at once. Her hands shook as she spread the apron beneath his legs. He didn't move. He didn't react. She didn't know what to do save what he'd requested. Cut his legs apart.

She put the knife blade under the ropes at his ankles and sawed.

She had to guess how much it pained him as the first rope gave. He hadn't been able to move either leg for five days now. The swollen one shifted a bit from the other, and at that Kam swiveled, going down onto his side with his back to her.

That was troubling for Constant. He hadn't much covering on the front of him. He had even less on the back. She looked at the honey-herb encrusted bandaging still stuck to reddish striping all about his back, and then down to where the ridges of his spine flowed into the tops of his buttocks. She put her fingers out to trace the path her eyes had just followed, but his words stopped her.

"Constant?"

He didn't sound like himself. He sounded like a wounded animal. She lifted her hand.

"Yes?" she replied.

"Cut the next one now. Doona' let me know. Just cut it."

"All right."

She scooted down and gently pried the cut rope from around his ankle. The purplish leg was black where the binding had been. She didn't know if that was a good thing or not. She started sawing on the next rope.

"Constant?" He whispered again.

"Yes?"

"Why did . . . you kiss him?"

The cutting stopped. She lifted the knife away and watched it tremble in her hand. She waited for a few moments before answering, but her voice shook anyway.

"I wanted to see how it compared."

"Compared?"

"To one of yours," she told him and held her breath.

"Curiosity? That's what you're telling me I witnessed?"

"I had to see if it would feel the same."

"You were just seeing if it felt the same," he mimicked, not sounding the least bit hurt. He sounded judgmental and harsh. "And I suppose you kept kissing him for the same reason?"

Constant hacked away at the rope, letting her anger move the blade, and when it sliced open, he groaned before rolling farther onto his stomach.

"I didn't kiss him more than once, Kameron."

The words were little more than a whisper. She didn't

know how she got her throat to work. Regardless of how cold and rude he was, she loved him, and he was still injured. His leg had to be extremely painful. The extent of the damage was even more visible when compared to his good leg.

"What are you waiting for? Get another one off. I canna' leave this godforsaken loft until I can move, and you sit and tarry. Get your skean busy and saw."

"But . . . your leg, Kameron. I don't know what to do. If we don't get you to a doctor, any doctor, you might lose—"

"I saw his hands all over you, Constant. That was more than a kiss from your little beau. That was full-out seduction . . . by mouth," he said, interrupting her.

Constant looked down at the next rope and tucked the blade under it. His words were offensive and said with an ugly tone. And then she realized what he was up to: he was trying his argument ploy again, to take his mind off the pain. He was good at it, too. She studied his legs. At least the blisters weren't bleeding. They were weeping a bit of liquid, though. That was his fault. He'd yanked off the honey-encrusted cloth. He should have waited for her to help.

"It was just a little kiss, Kameron." Constant started sawing as gently as possible at the next rope.

"Oh. *Please.* Doona' take me for a blind fool. If I'm na' mistaken, you have bruising everywhere he touched. That was nae mere kiss."

"I think I know what's wrong with you."

"Good for you. So do I. And it is na' pleasant."

Constant frowned. "I'm being as gentle as I can, Kameron."

"I don't want your gentle touch . . . except maybe in one—God *damn* you, Constant Ridgely! Just saw with the bloody knife and help me get these ropes off."

"What did I do wrong now?"

"I'm tired of your naïve posturing. It's wearing thin. I want you to ken that. Anyone who launches herself at a man like you did that young pup doesn't need instruction or explanation of her charms. She needs a swift spanking. That's what she needs."

Constant drew back. "A spanking? Whatever for? He asked me to wed with him. How was I to know if we'd suit or not? Surely that sort of decision deserves at least one kiss. How would I have known to decline otherwise?"

"That was a declination? God help the poor ass you do accept. He'll need sustenance to survive the betrothal party after being subjected to you."

Constant attacked the next rope with a vengeance. She had it sawn clear through and pulled from between his legs without a bit of compassion. She slid it roughly against his skin without a twinge of conscience.

"I want you to know I do not appreciate what you say, Kameron. I don't. I think you're calling the kettle black. And it isn't fair. You told me not to accept him unless he made me feel akin to how you do. So, I did that. I checked. And I wasn't the least bit passionate about it, either."

"You're a born . . . seductress. You ooze passion . . . with every breath coming from your body. I only wish . . . it was working."

"With what?" she asked icily.

"Taking my mind off this God-damned, bloody pain."

He choked through what could only be a sob, and Constant was instantly at his side, bending over him.

"Kameron?" she whispered.

He didn't answer. He just shook his head while his entire frame jerked. Constant watched him for a moment, wondering how she could have missed something so innately raw and obvious. She reached for his head and turned him. He didn't stop her. His face was scrunched into lines of agony, and there were tears streaking down both cheeks.

"Oh, Kameron. I didn't know. Why didn't you say something?"

"Because I'm a strictly reared, stubborn, bloodless Highlander, that's why. We never admit pain. Or injury. Or hurt. We embrace it. So, why doona' you cease pitying me and finish with the ropes? I already told you, I canna' leave your loft without the use of at least one leg. Perhaps you could keep up your end of the argument and assist me with it rather than stare at me like I'm a lost yearling pup. Unless you have a better idea?"

Constant sat back and studied him. Then she reached behind her back and started unbuttoning her dress.

Chapter Fifteen

"Oh no! Na' that. Nae, Constant, please. Na' that. God, nae. Nae. Anything but that. Anything. You can just stop. I forbid it."

As Kameron talked, Constant kept unfastening hooks. Then she sat on the floor to pull her boots off. She kept the thigh-high stockings in place. She'd worn them because they were the match to her chemise and had lacy tops with large bows. They made her legs look long and shapely. The boots were no loss. They'd ruin the image she wanted to project.

She stood.

"Nae, Constant. Please. I canna' let you do this. I will na' allow—doona' you dare take that off! Doona' even think of it! I forbid it. Doona' so much as think of—"

His voice continued as she turned her back to him in order to peel the dress off her shoulders. She knew she was blushing. She knew what she was doing was inconceivable. She was still doing it. She'd pretend. It was akin to a daydream. It was a delicious dream, too. One she'd treasure forever. She dropped the dress to her ankles and stepped out of it.

There wasn't much to her chemise, although it was

woven with strands of flax linen. It barely covered her buttocks. She was very proud of the weave; she'd done it herself last year. Candlewicking embroidery made a large butterfly between her breasts to support and cup them. It was her design. Constant pushed her hair off her shoulders and swiveled around.

Kameron's words stopped. His mouth dropped open. That was gratifying. Almost as much as the wide, round, golden-brown of his eyes in his tear-streaked face. She could see every bit of the amber color. She was definitely shocking him into thinking about something else.

"Well?" she asked.

"Oh . . . dearest God," he whispered.

"Are you thinking of something else now?"

He gulped. She watched his throat make the motion.

"I hope so, because we've got some more ropes to carve away, and I've got your trousers to finish fitting. I wasn't certain of the size. I'm probably close, though."

"My . . . trousers?" he repeated.

His eyes were still huge, watching her without once blinking. Constant took a step toward him and watched him tremble.

"I've fashioned trousers for you from my homespun. They're crudely cut and sewn worse, but they'll cover you. When I'm finished with you, that is."

He choked on whatever the reply was. Constant hovered above him, allowing him a very good view up her legs. She could tell he was looking, for there was a flush starting from his neck and going over his shoulders as she watched him. Then she sank, as gracefully as she could, to her knees beside him.

"Where on earth . . . did you procure this outfit?" he asked.

"From my hope chest."

"Your hope chest? What on earth were you hoping for?"

"A large, handsome, strong, golden-eyed Adonis of a man to fall into my life. What else?" She shrugged, lifting the material along her breasts, where the nipples hardened almost instantly.

Kameron saw it, too. She watched as his eyes moved there and stayed. Constant took a deep breath, pushing her breasts more fully against the material, and watched him twitch. Then, ever so slowly, she bent toward him, angling her arms together to further emphasize her cleavage. She knew she had an ample bosom. Charity had been making snide remarks about it since Constant had grown breasts. She thought she knew now why they were as large as they were. It was for this. Kameron.

She watched him as he watched her, and couldn't believe how amazingly wanton and luscious it all felt.

She put a hand beneath his chin to lift his jaw. Her pulse beat loud and fast in her ears. Eons of time hung suspended. Glow and warmth imbued everything. And then she moved in ever so slowly to match her lips to his. The moment she kissed him, a moan resonated through the loft, and it came from both of them.

Constant pulled away first, settled back onto her knees, put her hands on her thighs, and regarded him, waiting for her heartbeat to calm enough she'd be able to hear over it. Kameron was probably in shock. Or something. He wasn't moving. He wasn't blinking. He didn't even appear to be breathing.

"I told you there was no comparison, Kameron, and there still isn't. That was what I was finding out."

"I canna' allow this to continue."

He might be speaking of denial, but he'd dropped his eyes, speaking the words to her breasts, and then licked his lips, causing her to smile. Constant lifted her shoulders in a shrug and watched him stare where her bosom pushed against the material.

"That would be a shame, I think."

"You doona' ken what you're doing, Constant."

"Not this time, Kameron. I know exactly what I'm doing. I think it's you who is in need of instruction."

"Oh nae. I am na' going to tup—nae. I canna'. You doona' understand. I refuse. It would be a sacrilege . . . of the highest order. You—you're my angel. The woman who sheltered me. I'm na' so much a beast as to repay that with ravishment. I canna'!"

"I'm not an angel, Kameron. I'm a woman. And right now, I'm a woman . . . in need."

He groaned. Constant leaned forward, bringing her bosom close to his face. He was right. She didn't have any idea what she was doing, but she was following something beyond experience and training. Something primitive and basic, and completely immersing.

"I'm na' an honorable man, Constant. I should ña' be allowed anywhere near a young, impressionable maid. I'm a fornicator. I get drunk on occasion. And I'm a thief, for pity's sake."

"A thief, too?"

She clucked her tongue and slid her left breast, ever so slightly, along his cheek. He shuddered in response. Whispers of gooseflesh slid all along her limbs.

"What were . . . you stealing?"

Constant managed to ask it, although she lost her voice midway. She'd never felt like she did right now. Excitement seemed to spring from the peaks of her flesh and shoot all the way through her.

"Secrets," he answered.

"Not hearts?"

She felt every one of his tremors, and it was making her body sing with anticipation and energy. She felt as though she could do all her daily chores in less than an hour.

"I'm trying to do the noble thing here, Constant. This

is na' helping. Pray doona' add to the list of sins I need atone for. Please?" He choked out the words. His body was immobile. Taut. Statue-stiff and unmoving, even as she neared his mouth with a nipple.

"But, what of me?"

"What . . . about you?"

"Everything you've said is about you. Your sins. Your atonement. Your thwarted needs and desires. And nothing about me. I'm not doing this for you, Kameron. I want you. I need you. If it's all I have in my future, then so be it. And you're not in charge at the moment," she finished before her voice gave out. "I am."

He gave an incendiary growl, and then her nipple was in his mouth, still covered by her chemise, shocking her to the core. Constant grabbed his shoulders and did her best to keep from screaming. Kameron rolled her nipple in his mouth and then sucked, gifting her with rivers of ecstatic pleasure.

Then he pushed her away a fraction in order to blow air atop the moistened peak. She moaned, then moved to hold his head, clamping her palms to his ears, filling her fingers with his luxurious long hair.

Then Kameron was feasting on her other breast. Constant writhed. She reeled in place. She cooed. And then she crooned as reality faded away. She wasn't in a loft. There wasn't a bed of straw beneath her. There was just Kameron. And what he was doing to her. She might be floating. She could even be flying.

Kameron moved then, pressing her onto her back atop the hay beside him, where he sent breath after huffing breath into the valley between her breasts.

"Constant Ridegly, you are a viciously desirable creature. I suspected it when I got my first look at you, and now I ken it for certain. You've tapped every reserve I can claim. But I still . . . will na' compromise you. I canna'. It goes against everything I hold sacred. I've sins I doona' even remember to repent. I will na' add tupping you to them. Please? I'm begging here."

Constant lifted her head and brought him into focus. "You mean there's more?" she asked in surprise.

Kameron's laughter made both breasts quake with it. Constant had to hold to their sides to keep them from jouncing.

"What did I say?" she asked.

"Oh, love, there's mountains more. Oceans. Continents. The heavens and the stars. I only wish I was the man who gets to deliver them to you."

"But . . . you have to be the man, Kameron. I couldn't let any other man near me. Surely you know that."

He sobered and lifted his face from where he'd been pillowed. There wasn't anything carefree about the look he gave her. Lines etched his forehead, and there were shadowed areas about his eyes.

"I canna' take your maidenhead, Constant. Na' tonight. Na' ever. It belongs to the man you will wed, whoever that might be. It will na' be me. I canna' offer you a future. I never could."

"Did I ever ask for one from you?" Her reply was a bit breathless but crisply delivered despite how everything that was good and virtuous inside her got stood on end from his statement. She hoped she hid it well enough.

"What is it you do want, then?" he asked.

She forced herself to continue with the same tone and inflection. "I was taking your mind off your pain. What else?"

His groan came from the depths of him. She felt it. Perfect golden-brown eyes bored into hers and Constant watched as they seemed to fill with black.

"You are severely testing my resolve, Constant. I want you to ken this. I thought I was impossible to break. I doona' cave in to force. I have the scars to prove it. But this is beginning to feel worse than a torturer's embrace. I'm known as a heartbreaker, a man who can love a woman and leave her without a backward glance. I will na' do so with you. I will na'."

"And that means?" she asked.

He chuckled, blowing air across her again, and he watched her nipples tighten. His face twisted. "It means I've had about as much of this as I can stand. You are going to have to move. Now."

"But you're atop me," she replied.

"And you're about to find out what being beneath me means. Out before that happens. Now."

He started to lift himself with his arms, just like always, but his sudden intake of breath, and the way he collapsed, told her something was wrong. As did his groan.

"Kameron?"

He was puffing the air from between his lips, his eyes squinting.

"What?"

"Are you in such pain?"

"Nae," he replied.

"You are going to have to work on your lying."

His eyebrows rose at that and he opened an eye. "You're teasing with me. I happen to be a perfect liar. Always was. Always will be. It's one of the myriad of sins I'll be repenting."

"Are you ready to cut through another of your bonds, then?"

His other eye opened. "You are na' to move for a bit, Constant. Just . . . doona' move. Fair?"

"But why?"

"Because there are some parts of a man that just will

na' listen to his intentions, good or otherwise. Doona' move. I forbid it."

She wriggled slightly and felt him tense.

"Constant, I'm warning you—"

"About what this time?"

"I think you have sadistic tendencies, Constant, my love. And here I thought you the most compassionate woman birthed."

"And I think you think too much. Roll off me and let me proceed."

"I canna' *roll*. I can barely continue breathing."

Her eyes widened. "Your ribs. I clean forgot. Does it pain terribly?"

"Hell, yes. I mean nae. Oh Jesu'. Just get out."

He shoved himself up and off her with a wrenching motion. He grunted as he came in contact with the hay-covered loft floor. Constant turned to her side to face him and supported her head on her upraised arm.

"If you're not in pain, do you wish me to continue?" she asked when he wouldn't look at her.

"What? Nae. Yes. Go away."

"Go away? But I have to help you."

His reply came between clenched teeth. "Are you still there?"

"Yes."

"Then you need to finish. Pick up your skean and cut me free."

"Do you want to support your leg with the splint before I release it?"

"Nae," he answered quickly.

"It will hurt more if you don't."

"Right at the moment, I doona' care. I'm looking for pain. I need an entire existence filled with it."

"I don't understand you at all." Constant moved into

a sitting position, crossing her legs before her. "You asked me to take your mind off pain. And now you want it back?"

"Well, you certainly managed that. My mind is definitely on other things."

"Really? Like what?"

Another groan, and then he turned his head toward her. She watched as he ran his eyes from her head to the shadowed area below her chemise and then moved back to her breasts. He shuddered. He gulped. Then he closed his eyes and took a huge breath. This time when he opened them again, his eyes were glassy and without expression.

Constant stared.

"Things such as that truly bountiful bosom of yours. However did you keep it hidden from me for so long? I usually ferret out such things quicker. I must be losing my touch."

She barely kept from crossing her arms about herself at his words and his tone. He made it sound ugly and sordid. "It wasn't something I wanted noticed," she answered.

"Classic mistake, Constant, my love. Any man looking at what I am would give you anything you desire."

"What if I . . . desire you?"

His eyes widened a fraction and the opaque sheen slipped. Then it was back so quickly that if she'd blinked, she'd have missed it.

"A child's wants can be confused for many things, Constant, my love."

"Who are you calling a child?"

Constant straightened her back, angling forward into the sodden areas of her chemise. She knew it worked as Kameron's eyes cleared back to golden brown and he focused exactly where she wanted him to.

"You temptress. You vixen. You wanton."

Constant tilted her mouth into a pout. "You . . . knave. You thief. You spy." She answered in the exact same tone of voice he'd used.

Kameron's lips twitched. Then he was grinning. Then he was heaving himself onto his arms and lunging for her. Constant was more than prepared for him, allowing her knees to drop to make it easier for him, when sudden agony laced across his features and he fell.

She was instantly on her hands and knees beside him.

"Kameron?" she whispered.

"Come here."

He accompanied the command with his arms gathering her, rolling onto the side with his good leg in order to hold her against him. Then he was sliding down to her bosom again and nuzzling. Then he was kissing and caressing, and then he was sending his words to her breasts again.

"A man who has just partaken of your bounteous bosom needs more, Constant. An endless supply of more, God help him."

"Really?" Her eyes narrowed and she licked her lips.

"Allow me to demonstrate."

He was more than demonstrating. He had her squirming against him, pulling at his hair, her body heaving against him while he lavished attention on her. And when he'd finished and was licking each nipple in turn, instead of sucking and pulling, Constant was such a trembling mass, it took her some moments to decipher exactly where she was, and why.

Kameron wasn't unaffected, either, although he'd done his best to keep his still-covered male part away from her. Constant had tried to maneuver herself near it—she'd even opened her legs and tried to force him between them—but he shoved himself into the space between her knees and just settled there, where his male organ pulsed in place.

He was too big, and he was too heavy, and he was taking all her desire and turning it into such a conglomeration of heat that her breasts felt as though they'd doubled in size—and that would be enormous. Constant put her hands on his shoulders to stop his incessant caressing.

"You must . . . stop," she whispered.

"Lord, doona' I know *that*. We've bent the bounds of decency too far already, and everything on me is angered and yelling at me over it. I ken we have to stop. I just doona' want to. The word is na' in my vocabulary at present, I'm afraid."

"But I have . . . to cut your bonds . . . while I still can." The words were panted. Wheezed.

"Verra well. We'll stop. But doona' look at me like that again."

"Like . . . what?"

He slid his gaze sideways to her and Constant felt certain he'd see the flip her heart made as their eyes connected. Then he slid away, settling with an awkward-looking shimmy into the hay.

"You've a wild and sensuous look about you, Constant. Feral. Passionate. My body recognized it instantly, although my mind did na' put it together for me until tonight. 'Tis verra rare. Afore long, you're going to have males falling about your ankles just for a chance to taste what I've tasted and dream of what I dream. Mark my words."

"I will?" she asked.

"Aye. I'm afeard of it, too. Listen to me . . . afeard? I'm turning into a bairn. You'd best start your cutting. It might save me what's left of my self-respect. What are you looking at? Get your skean and start carving. I'm sufficiently fortified to withstand it."

He turned his head away, and his back was clenching and unclenching spasmodically, making the cheesecloth flex and warp where it was stuck to purplish-red lines.

Constant crawled toward him, using one arm to support her breasts. She looked down at them. She hadn't enlarged. It only felt that way. Actually, she'd never felt so attuned to her own body. She knew if she listened, she'd be able to hear her own blood pumping through each breast.

"Well? What's keeping you??" Kam asked, with a slight edge to his voice.

"I feel different," she replied. "Bigger. Lots bigger. I wanted to make sure it was my imagination."

"If you get much larger, Constant, I'll need an assist to hold you. I've large hands, but—"

His words halted the moment Constant straddled his lower back, facing his feet. Underneath her, she felt him react with such an upward lunge she had to clench both knees to keep from falling, while an unearthly groan came out of his chest.

"Good Lord, Constant! I'm only human. Doona' do it this way, please? It hurts."

"But I haven't even touched you yet," she replied.

"It's na' my legs!"

"It hurts in places other than your legs?"

His answer seemed to be a couple of puffed breaths followed by a string of curses. She slid to his side, and that's when she saw his distended rod, still encased in her old pantaloons. She covered her mouth with a hand to keep any sound inside. Kameron was glaring at her as he used one arm to flatten himself prior to lying down again. Constant leaned forward to watch, and then sat up once he was settled.

"Is this interesting you?" he asked.

"Does it feel like my breasts do? All aware . . . and full and sore?"

He rolled his eyes. "Nae. Will you just cut the rope?"

She moved down, hovering above his knees and slid the knife under the rope. The flesh where she'd taken the rope off him earlier wasn't quite as black. It was more purplish, like a bruise. She started sawing. He tensed only once before she was through the rope and had it eased from beneath his knee, although he had to lift his leg for her, and that couldn't be easy for him.

There was only one more rope holding his legs together. She put the blade under it.

"Constant?" The word stopped her. It sounded choked.

"Yes?"

"Come up here. Now. Please?"

She scooted up toward his head.

"I need a reminder."

"I hurt you, didn't I?"

He reached a hand out and slid a strap off her shoulder. Then he removed the other. Constant watched him watching her, as the material held for a moment to the peaks of her breasts, before falling to her stomach. He half lidded his eyes, shook for a moment, and then opened his eyes fully. Gooseflesh started and continued all over her as he looked, and kept looking. He didn't touch. He just looked, licked his lips occasionally, and then looked some more. And then he spoke.

"Now, what were you asking me?"

"If I . . . hurt you."

"Oh. Nae. Not now. There's naught bothering me at all, sweet."

"Then why did you ask me to come up here?"

He half lidded his eyes again, while a tremor shook

him. Then he opened his eyes again and moved his glance to hers. "Do you really need to ask?"

She shook her head and moved to lift her straps back up. He stopped her with a hand atop hers. At the touch, Constant stilled.

"Leave them be. For now. It'll give me something to think on. Finish unbinding me. We're at the last one?"

She nodded.

"Go then. I'm ready."

She slid back into place, although her garment didn't make the move with her. By the time she reached Kameron's hip, the chemise was dangling from her knees. She wondered if he'd planned that. The straw was scratching her everywhere, the blades prickling and tickling and awakening sensations where they touched. The air might have a hint of frost to it, but it wasn't cold. It couldn't break through the haze that enveloped her with a glow every bit as warm and golden as his gaze.

Her breasts felt odd, as nothing but air met every movement. They felt heavier, too, without the meager support of the chemise straps. She slid the knife under the last rope. It was thick with dried honey, and encrusted with filth. There wasn't a hint of a blister near it, however. Constant closed her eyes in thankfulness for that, reopened them, and started sawing. She felt Kameron tense with each movement of her knife.

Then the rope sprang loose and his legs separated, and he was shaking with what could only be agony. Constant put her hands on his legs and tried to hold them together.

"Constant?" It sounded as if he was strangling on her name.

"Yes?"

"Come here. I need you. Now."

The chemise was worse than a binding as it looped

about her ankles and made moving difficult. She kicked it loose before she reached him.

He swore when he saw her. "Where did your clothing go?"

"I—" she began.

"Never bloody mind! Come here. Now."

Constant didn't know what he expected. She was already as close as she could get. Then she knew, as he gripped her, pulling her so he could settle his head between her breasts, while everything about him just kept coiling and tightening. Shudders enveloped him. His upper lip lifted. His eyes were scrunched shut. A solitary tear slid from beneath his eyelashes. There was a low hum accompanying all of it. She didn't even realize it came from her.

And then, something changed. He lifted his head, speared her with that golden gaze, and licked his lips.

"You had better move . . . from me now, Constant."

"Now?"

"Pain has a way about it, love. It afflicts with a tormentor's embrace. Then it ebbs to a burn. Then it becomes a throbbing, and after that . . . it finally becomes bearable."

She nodded.

"It's becoming bearable."

"So?" she asked.

"Then other parts of me that are suffering for totally different reasons take over. I'm a man, Constant. I've been teased and inflamed to my wit's end tonight. I canna' think of one thing to keep me from finishing this and taking your maidenhood. Trust me. You have na' got much time."

"But I want you to," she whispered.

His answer was intelligible and came through thinned lips. He'd closed his eyes to say it, too. Constant felt the tremor begin within him, and then he grabbed her shoulders and shoved her downward in order to slam his lips to hers. Her breath intermingled with his, their flesh connecting with fervor and heat. Passion and wanton desire took over, combining to a fury of emotion. It stole her thoughts, her emotions. Her morals. There was only Kameron and the erotic and exciting sensations he evoked with his mouth. She squirmed against him, undulated her nakedness to every portion she could touch, and his response was a guttural grunt as he rolled onto his back, pulling her astride him.

"Damn you, Constant. Damn you. Damn you. Damn you."

He murmured the curses against her lips, and Constant caught them with kisses. Her body was aflame with need and desire and craving. Massive craving. Immense yearning. Unbelievable want. Her hands slid down his belly, reaching for the pantaloon-covered part of him, grabbing and then caressing his hardness as it tried to drill into her hand. Kameron tore one of her hands away, but she was right back, shoving the old pantaloons off and out of the way. She needed both hands to lift him. Hold his rod in position . . .

"Dearest God, Constant—stop!"

In reply, she locked her thighs to him, positioned herself over him, and shoved downward, gasping in shock at the ripping burn she experienced as she encased him, and then the sensation of fiery flickers as he grabbed her hips and held her affixed atop him.

"Oh, sweet . . . doona' move! Doona' flinch! Doona' . . . oh *no*!"

The last word was such a garbled and unintelligible sound and said in such a deep tone, she lifted her head. Kameron's face was a mask of torment and bliss. Those full lips of his were curved into the most beatific smile she'd ever seen as his hips lifted, and then he went to an arc, his throat sending an unearthly sound into the loft, holding it until his breath ran out. He sucked in another breath and groaned through that one, too. Constant experienced the strange pulsing sensation where they were joined, while her palms seemed to thud with the heavy hammering of his heart beneath them.

And then he collapsed back down onto the hay, a sheen of moisture coating his body. Constant had never seen anything like it. She watched him with wide eyes as he took heavy breath after heavy breath, until they finally slowed.

"Oh God. Oh, love. I'm so sorry. Forgive me," he whispered.

"For . . . give you?"

"Aye. Forgive me for taking you, and na' even having the fortitude to do it properly. Oh . . . *God*. There are nae words."

He opened his eyes then, and she watched as they went from almost entirely black, back to the golden-brown color she adored.

"I knew this was how I was going to feel. Damn me, anyway."

"It wasn't pleasant, then?"

Constant watched as Kameron's eyes took on a blank look.

"The fault is entirely mine, Constant. I bear complete blame. You are na' at fault. You ken?"

The voice he was using sounded as false as the look in his eyes. Constant narrowed hers. "I refuse to let you—"

"Listen to me, Constant! I will na' have you think any less of yourself because I could na' control my base nature. You ken? This is my burden to bear and my guilt to live with. And it is na' going to be pretty, either."

"But . . . I love you."

The moment it was out, she wanted it back. She didn't need his severe frown to convince her of it. Or his words.

"I accept full responsibility for that, as well. Doona' fash yourself. I accept it. I knew what I was doing. But I canna' change facts. I am a Scottish soldier, Constant Ridgely. You are a seditionist's daughter. I doona' offer a future. I canna'. I need warn you there could be consequences to what we've just done. One time is usually safe, but na' always. A bit of quickness is needed. A prompt washing. You need to move and then you need to handle it. The sooner, the better."

"You care for me. You do. Admit it, Kameron. That's all I want. Be honest with me here and now. Admit it."

He blinked. The glassy sheen in his eyes didn't shift.

"I really need you to move. My leg is starting to pain again. I still have to bind it. I canna' leave until that is done. And I need to cover myself. As do you. Now. You've brought trousers?"

Constant slid from him and gathered her discarded clothing in hands that didn't feel like her own. She tossed him the trousers. They weren't finished, but she didn't think her fingers would cooperate enough to hold a needle. He'd just have to do with what he had. She didn't speak to him. She didn't look at him.

Chapter Sixteen

Constant wiped another of her incessant tears away with the back of her hand and returned to chopping onions. She'd volunteered for the chore with alacrity because it would hide her emotion better than anything else she could've done.

When she'd returned to the bedroom she shared with Stream in the predawn, she'd barely been keeping the tears at bay. Stream had taken in Constant's bedraggled state, her weepy, red-rimmed eyes, and had done nothing more than hold out her arms. Constant hadn't been able to stop the tears. Now, hours later, she still couldn't.

"We need those onions for a stew tonight, Constant."

Mother looked into the darker corner of the kitchen. Constant nodded and kept her face averted.

For a magical span of five days, her entire world had been alight with a sense of joy, anticipation, and excitement, and in the hours before dawn it had ended. Kam had said more after she gave him the trousers. A lot more. He'd said he didn't want her knowing anything more about him, or where he was going, or how he was planning on getting there. He wasn't interested in doing anything other than leaving this hellhole as rapidly as possible.

Constant gulped, sniffed, and gulped again. It wasn't working. Tears obliterated the onion in her left hand and the paring knife in her right. She only wished they were doing the same for her memory.

Shame accounted for some of the salt trails down her cheeks. She realized that much as she lifted her hand and wiped again. She'd acted worse than a brazen hussy, and the continual throbbing of her woman area was the result. It added to her punishment for forcing herself on him. Charity had been right about the humiliation part, too. But nobody had said a thing about the heart-sore, bereft portion of it.

Nobody.

Constant gave up, put her arm up to block her eyes, and sobbed. There wasn't any way to stop the moisture, but maybe she could get some of it out of her system before Mother checked on her again.

She'd known Kameron had to leave. She didn't need him to tell her. She knew they didn't have a future. She hadn't needed him to speak of that, either. She didn't like anything about Britain. She'd spent her entire life hearing about the wickedness over there and how class-conscious and full of snobbery they were. She knew he was going back there and she wasn't.

She only wished her heart knew it.

"Constant!"

It was Henry. He'd been running. Constant sniffed deeply and wiped away as many tears as she could.

"These are very strong onions," she commented before turning toward him.

"You must . . . come quickly!" Henry reached for her sleeve. "They've got him."

"Who?"

"They're hurting him again! You've got to come. You've got to do something!"

"Who?" Constant dropped the onion into her bushel barrel of them. Her heart already had the answer.

"Kam. Hurry!" He had her hand and was trying to pull her.

"Who is Kam?"

She used as innocent a tone as she could manage. He looked heavenward for an instant before looking back at her. Constant didn't move.

"The bird-man you had in the stable loft. You know who Kam is! Hurry! They're going to *kill* him!"

Her eyes flew wide and she stood. "Who is, Henry?"

"Everybody. Please hurry! They've got him strung up at Middle Oak. We're going to be too late!"

"Oh, dear God! Not that!"

Constant didn't bother saddling Eustace. It would take too long. She put a bridle on him and placed Henry atop the animal. Then she jumped up in front of Henry and kicked the horse's sides.

Middle Oak was aptly named. It had been used as a landmark for as long as Constant remembered. It was the sturdiest of the three oaks that marked the corner of the Ridgely property. It was also perfect for a hanging tree.

"How do you know all this?" she yelled over her shoulder as the horse settled into his longest lope.

"I watched them. They discovered the loft. They trailed him."

"You watched?"

"Kam's my friend."

"What?" she asked.

"I've been helping him. I brought him water and . . . handled his bucket duties. I visited him during the day. He told me not to tell anyone."

"You kept it secret? Really?"

Constant would never have guessed Henry had it in him.

"He asked me to. He didn't want you worried. You're all he talked about. I think he likes you a lot."

"No, he doesn't. He couldn't wait to leave."

"You're wrong. He was sad. He sure looked it."

"When was this?"

"Just before dawn. Look! You see them? They've strung him up! Do something, Constant! Now!"

The fear staining Henry's cry transferred to her and then the horse. She could see the crowd ahead through the leafless limbs. She clucked her tongue, nudged with her knees, and flicked the rein. Eustace responded, taking the final field like he was a yearling rather than an old plow horse.

"Wait!"

Constant reached the edge of the mob and swung down from Eustace even before he halted.

"Stop!"

There were more men than she had suspected and Constant's nerve would've failed her if she hadn't seen Kameron. He was astride a horse, his hands strapped together on the pommel of his saddle, his neck stretched upward with a noose about it. And he was hurt. Her heart shared every bit of his pain. She'd spent so much time working to heal him, and all of it for nothing. It looked as if they'd taken a strap to every inch of his upper body again, to even worse effect. Thomas Esterbrook was brandishing the two-sided coat again.

The homespun trousers were torn, muddied, and there was a stream of blood dripping from the foot of his injured leg onto the ground. He was conscious, but it wasn't by choice, she decided. He was probably staying aware in order to keep from hanging himself with any slackening of his posture. And one of his eyes was so swollen he might be in danger of losing it.

"Stop this immediately! Father! Thomas! Daniel Hallowell! Stop!"

"Get back to the house, Constant."

Her father had a feeble voice when he'd overexerted himself. This was one of those times. Constant turned on him.

"I will not!"

"You dare disobey your own father?" Thomas asked.

"I dare anything to stop a crime from being committed."

"What crime is it to put a traitor to death?" John Becon asked.

Constant looked at each of them in turn before answering. "And who are we branding a traitor? And why? As we're still an English colony, and that man is an English soldier, how can he stand accused of such?"

"Leave the politics to the men, Mistress Constant. Friend Esterbrook, take your intended wife to task, since her own father is failing to do it."

"Lay one hand on me and you'll regret it, Thomas Esterbrook." Constant spat it toward him. She was just as surprised as they looked when Thomas took a step back from her.

"Your children have been spared the rod too long, Master Ridgely," John Becon said in a loud voice.

"Constant—" her father began.

"Cut him down right now and let him go . . . or I'll bear witness to this. I'll swear to a constable about all of you. And all of this."

Nobody answered. Nobody moved. Constant looked up at Kameron. He was focused on something over their heads. He didn't meet her eye.

"Cut him down. Give the order."

"You'd take responsibility for such a man. Why?"

"Because no man deserves such treatment without a trial. You know this! You're a burgess. You uphold that very right."

"He's a British spy, Constant!"

Constant spun on Thomas. He looked even smaller than usual. "He still deserves a trial. Everyone does! You know the law. All of you!"

"And I still ask why you'd take responsibility for such a man. You failed to answer. We are still awaiting it."

John Becon spoke without the slightest hint of emotion in his voice. Everyone listened until he'd finished. He had a position of authority in Boston. The quality and range of his speaking voice were obviously part of the reason.

Constant flushed as she turned to him. "An injured man is being strung up by a mob! Without a trial, with no magistrate, and not one charge leveled against him other than baseless rumor. I'm stopping it because someone has to. You know this. You're sworn to uphold the law."

"The man wears a turncoat. He is a turncoat. Wait a minute. This is the same jacket I gave you yestermorn."

They all watched Thomas flip the coat inside out and back.

Constant gulped. Then she lifted her chin. "What of it?" she asked.

"You gave it back to him? You?"

She didn't answer. Nobody said anything, and then her father spoke up feebly, with a pleading tone.

"No. Please no. Say it isn't so, Constant."

"I don't know what it is you ask," Constant lied.

"It was you. You had him in our loft, didn't you? You fed and nursed and protected him, didn't you?"

"I—"

"You betrayed your own family?"

"How is helping an English soldier betrayal, Father? We're still English citizens, are we not?"

There was grumbling, but no one answered her outright. Then John Becon spoke up. "Well, gentlemen! We all heard. By her own mouth, she acknowledged guilt."

Constant stepped closer to Kameron's horse and grabbed for the loosely dangling reins. They'd been fashioned of rawhide strips, braided together. She wound them about her fingers, tightening her hand until it felt bloodless. She ignored it. It didn't matter. As long as she had the reins, the horse wouldn't bolt. And that's what mattered. She took a deep breath, stood straighter, and turned to face the mob.

"I haven't said anything of the sort, and there's no crime I stand accused of, now is there?"

She directed her query mainly to John Becon. Charity's husband was a like height. He was twice again as heavy as her, and three times her age. He was still a frightening man. He raised his big, gray eyebrows. Constant swallowed with nervousness.

"You were with a man in a hayloft. Without chaperonage."

She tossed her head. "What of it?"

"Constant, no," her father remarked.

"We strung him up not a moment too soon, I would say," Thomas remarked in a snide tone. "And you can consider our engagement ended, Mistress Ridgely. I don't offer for, nor will I accept, damaged goods."

"We've heard enough. Haven't we, friends?"

John Becon used his orator voice. Everyone seemed to stop and listen. The very air seemed to join in the silence.

"This man is not only a traitor and a spy, but he has compromised a good patriot's daughter. A hanging may be too good for him. We all agreed?"

There was a chorus of yelling. Prudence's husband reached for the reins she held.

"No!" Constant backed closer to the horse.

"Give me the reins, Constant. Go back to the house."

"Wait! You don't understand."

The horse was shuffling and pawing at the muddy ground near her feet. Constant had to continually step away from its hooves.

"Give me the reins."

"You're wrong. All of you! This man is no spy. He never was. He wore the coat to disguise himself, true, but it wasn't to ferret out any secrets. It was to visit with me at night. You have wronged the man, I tell you."

"Constant!" Her father's voice carried every bit of his shock.

"You—you and the turncoat are lovers, then?"

Thomas had an odd look on his face, and was running his eyes all over Constant's frame. Constant moved farther along the horse's side and jostled Kam's leg as she did so.

"Con . . . stant?"

The feeble sound of her name gripped at her heart. She looked up. His swollen eye was bleeding. *Oh, dear God.* Her eyes filled with tears, and she sent them away. Then they filled with nothing but hatred. She turned back to the mob and glared at each one in turn. She'd never felt such hatred. She was vibrating with it. There wasn't one man there she wouldn't gladly take her knife to. But that wouldn't save Kameron. There was only one thing that might. She opened her mouth and said the only thing she could think of to stop them.

"If you hang this man, you are murdering the father of my unborn child. He has done nothing more than that! Nothing!" She was yelling when she finished. It wasn't necessary. There was complete and absolute silence.

The horse shuffled closer to her.

"Is this true?"

John Becon looked up at Kameron to ask it. Kam spat on the ground, and the spittle contained blood.

"Are . . . you actually asking me . . . something?"

"Have you been intimate with this woman?"

Kam's good eye regarded her. There wasn't any expression on his face. Then he looked up again, over all of them. "I never . . . saw this . . . woman afore," he finally answered.

More crowd noise followed his announcement, and Constant used her weight on the animal's reins to subdue it. Shock was the emotion stinging her, stealing her breath and her voice, and then it cleared. Kameron had told her he was an expert liar. She should have expected it.

"He lies!" she shouted.

"He lies? But why would he do such a thing? If admitting to fornication with you would save his skin, what sane man would lie? Even an innocent man would admit to it."

There were murmurs of agreement among them.

Constant swallowed. "Kameron?" She looked up at him. Kam wouldn't meet her eyes.

"She knows his name!" Thomas was pointing a finger at her as he said it.

Constant looked back at him. With his face twisted in murderous intent, he wasn't the least bit handsome.

"Of course I know his name. I just told you we were lovers. Why wouldn't I know it?"

There was a look of absolute shock on every face in the mob.

"And I actually asked for your hand," Thomas Esterbrook said in disgust.

"Is this true, Constant?"

Her father's eyes were old and sad. He was old and sad. Constant looked him over and actually saw him as he was—a feeble old man. She only hoped he still had enough influence to stop the hanging.

"He's the father of your unborn grandchild, Father," she said. "That is the man's only crime. You'd have my child born a bastard?"

There was a long silence.

"Cut him down," Constant's father said.

Her eyes began to tear up and she viciously stifled the reaction. She wasn't letting any emotion get through. Not now. Not yet.

"Cut him down?" Daniel Hallowell asked.

"I'll see my daughter wed to him. You heard her. He has taken liberties with her. The child born of their sin will not suffer."

"He didn't agree to what she said."

"He's a turncoat. His profession is lying. My daughter has never lied."

"She has fornicated, though!"

She didn't know who said that, but the comment caused another round of unrest and mumbling among the men. Constant closed her eyes for a moment to gather strength. All she had to do was see Kam cut down. She'd get him to his garrison. See he had medical care. Then she'd face the consequences of her actions.

She knew what they'd be. She didn't care. No one would ever offer for her. No one would ever shelter her. Not in this town. Perhaps even farther afield. She still didn't care. All she cared about was getting that noose off Kam's neck. She opened her eyes again.

"What makes you think he'll wed her if we set him loose?" someone asked her father.

Constant watched his frame waver with uncertainty.

"Is the preacher still among us?" John Becon narrowed his eyes at her as he spoke.

Constant didn't so much as blink in response.

"Reverend Williams?" someone asked. "Of course he's here. He's just hard of hearing. As always."

"Get him!"

Constant held her breath while Reverend Williams was brought forward. Everyone was watching the drama unfold. Constant should be prostrate with mortification and shame. She wasn't. Everything within her seemed to throb with purpose as she stifled everything except one goal. She didn't have time to be embarrassed. She could do that later. Her entire focus was on saving Kameron.

"You wish a wedding performed? Who is she wedding? A horse?" Reverend Williams asked loudly.

"The turncoat."

The reverend looked up at Kam. "But I thought we already hanged him."

"As you can see, he's still alive. We need him in that condition in order to finish the ceremony and keep a child from the sin of bastardy."

John Becon was still orchestrating everything, using his orator voice. Reverend Williams pierced her with his gaze. Condemning. Judging. Constant started to tremble and halted it with a supreme act of will. She had to get through this before allowing any emotion to vent. All that mattered was Kameron. That's all. Kameron. Nothing else.

"Mistress Ridgely? Constant Ridgely? Is that you?"

She nodded.

"You . . . have been intimate with this man?" He gestured up to Kam.

She nodded again. The reverend's eyes looked down, away from her. She didn't care about that, either. Later she'd let it bother her. Along with everything else. *Just get the noose off Kam's neck . . .*

"Does any among you possess a license? I can't wed them without one."

"Master Esterbrook?"

"I've got a license. It was for my own marriage to her. Here. Take it."

There was some discussion over legalities and such, and then Thomas's name was scratched out and they looked to Kam to supply the rest.

"You want . . . me to . . . speak . . . again?" he asked.

The noose was tight, and that was probably what kept his words short and his voice hoarse. The sneer was entirely his own, though.

"What is your name, sir?"

"Why?"

"We need it for the license. I can't wed you without it."

"You want . . . me to . . . marry this . . . woman?" He wheezed through the words.

"We'll not have any child born nameless. State your name and surname. We've not got all day."

"She . . . carries . . . nae . . . bairn," Kam replied finally, each word requiring great effort.

"But she might be?"

Kam turned his good eye on her and blinked slowly. Constant could sense not only pain but a strange emotion radiating outward from him although nothing showed in his expression. And then he nodded and looked away.

"You compromised Friend Ridgely's daughter, you'll wed her. Reverend? Start the ceremony."

Constant had dreamt of her wedding day. It would be full of flowers and organ music and white roses and a beautiful white dress. It wasn't to be with an almost naked man, beaten nearly senseless, trussed up and about to be hanged, while she stood at his side in an old, worn, serviceable gown and held his hand with one smelling of onions. She glanced to where he was still losing blood and her lips tightened. They could annul it later. She could do everything later. For now, she had to get him free.

"What is your name?"

"Kameron . . . Ballan," he replied.

"Very well. Constant Ridgely? Do you take Kameron Ballan as your husband?"

"I do," she replied.

They asked the same thing of Kam. He took a long time to answer in the affirmative. Someone draped the document across his thigh while he signed with his still-bound right hand. Constant watched him do it. They all watched him.

The license was given to the reverend, who signed it and handed it to her. Kam gazed down at her with his good eye for a long moment before he turned away, looking over their heads again.

"Verra well, 'tis done. Gentlemen. You . . . may . . . finish." Kam choked out every word and then he closed his eyes.

"Proceed!" Becon yelled.

"*What?*" Constant screamed. She no longer cared about holding anything at bay, including emotions. She clung to the horse's reins like a possessed woman and forced the animal to stand still while she burst into a sobbing, shrieking wretch at its side.

"You didn't think we'd allow him to live, did you?" Becon's words came to her over her own screaming. "Leave off the reins, Mistress Ballan. You've a name for your unborn child. And shortly you'll be a widow. Congratulations."

"No!"

Constant's cry wasn't heard over the sound of a military horn, followed by a field full of soldiers on horseback. The lynch mob scattered. Constant didn't note it. She was holding to the reins, using every bit of weight and strength at her disposal to keep the horse from bolting. When she finally looked up, she saw Eustace loping alongside her father's steed, with Henry clinging to his mane. Everyone fled.

And that's the last she saw of them.

The horse finally quieted and stood docilely beside her. That's when reaction seemed to close in, making her weak and giddy. She held to the reins then for a different reason—to keep herself upright. Her legs shook, her arms were next to useless, but her heart soared. She'd done it. She'd saved him!

And then soldiers surrounded them, anger and shock in their every word. Constant barely heard it. She was watching Kameron as he slumped forward, tightening the rope about his neck. And then finally, as if materializing through a fog, somebody using a long sword cut him loose.

Chapter Seventeen

"Well? Anything to report, Lieutenant?"

The voice was as calmly authoritative as it had been all day and into the evening. Constant held her breath in order to listen through the half-open door.

"They're trying to save the eye. He took a nasty blow there. He might not be able to see with it, if they can save it. The surgeons aren't certain, sir."

"Is Thornacre working on him?"

"Has been since he was brought in, sir. Exactly as you ordered."

"Very good. You may go. Shut the door on your way out."

"Yes, sir."

The soldier came out, shutting the door behind him with a little click of the lock. He glanced toward Constant, perched on the long wooden bench, and then away.

He turned, as if on a lightly sanded dance floor, and walked past her, his footsteps echoing loudly on the wooden floor. She watched when he got to the end of the corridor and swiveled smartly to proceed down the next hall. And then she returned to contemplating her apron-and-skirt-covered knees.

The sound of the soldier's footsteps slowly faded. Constant listened until she couldn't hear them anymore. The entire building was filled with long corridors of plank-lined walls and floors. The space echoed loudly with every movement. It also had a strange quietude, so that when no one was about, it felt as if even the sound of her breathing was sucked from her. Constant blinked her eyes at the sight of her apron, felt the burn behind her eyelids before she reopened them, unable to rest even for that amount of time. She wasn't tired. She was exhausted. There was a difference. If she was tired, she'd be able to nap. But her physical and emotional exhaustion left her unable to do more than sit, blink occasionally, and wait to eavesdrop on the next update of Kameron's condition.

It had been the same since they'd brought her here. Constant had informed one of the soldiers that she was Kameron's wife, but he'd only chuckled and continued to ignore her.

They'd assisted Kameron down from the horse at Middle Oak and eased him onto a makeshift stretcher. Constant hadn't been able to see what they did from that point, for soldiers surrounded him. Nobody paid any attention to her. She was left to mount Kameron's horse and follow. She didn't know what else to do. She couldn't go home. Despite how much she detested the members of the mob, she couldn't betray her community. Soldiers were scouring the countryside for the perpetrators. And she was wed now. Her place was with her husband.

And that's why she followed the line of men bearing Kameron's injured body all the way to their garrison.

Constant traced the slight stain on her apron and brought it to her nose. She sniffed, and then remembered. She'd been peeling onions. For stew. To hide her sobs. It felt like a lifetime ago.

Footsteps started echoing in the hall again. Constant turned her head to watch the same adjutant perform the same forty-five-degree-angle turn at the end of the hall and then proceed to the door beside her. He ignored her as he knocked and was bidden entry.

"You have an update?"

"He has a broken collarbone. It's been set. His ribs may be broken. He's suffered internal injury, making a diagnosis difficult. His leg may be broken, as well. It's too swollen to tell . . . and he's lost consciousness, sir."

Constant's heart stopped, and then it restarted, flooding her with a rush of heat. And then such cold, she trembled.

"This is not good."

"Actually, Doctor Thornacre believes it's merciful. The pain had to be intolerable. Lord Ballanclaire spoke of it more than once. He was in constant agony, sir."

"Ballan spoke of pain? Nonsense. The man's a Highlander."

"It was more something about the constant amount of it. He kept mumbling that word, sir."

"What word?"

"*Constant*, sir."

"Keep me informed. You may go."

"Very good, sir."

Then came the same clicking noise from the lock, the same sidelong glance in her direction, and then the soldier was walking down the corridor to do his perfect swivel turn.

Constant looked back at her hands atop her apron, taking in the wrinkled condition of her skirt, and then the unyielding surface of the bench she sat on. It hadn't been constructed for comfort; it was probably intolerable to sleep on. She eyed it. She supposed if she had no other recourse, she could sleep there. She was going to have to go without food and water, though.

For her wedding day, it was certainly strange. She leaned back and tried to keep her eyes closed to rest. It didn't work. She opened them on the plain, smoothly sanded plank walls forming the hall across from her. Undecorated. Dreary. Uninteresting.

They'd called Kameron *Lord Ballanclaire.* Sweet heaven. *Lord* Ballanclaire. She repeated it in her thoughts. Titled lords were only allowed to wed titled ladies. They certainly couldn't marry a farm girl from the colonies. No wonder the soldiers had looked at her like she'd lost her wits when she told them of the marriage.

Footsteps started echoing again in the hall. This time there were two of them: the lieutenant and a fellow behind him who was balancing a large tray. It was the commander's sup.

She knew she wasn't going to get any. She didn't even have to ask. Constant turned her head away as they knocked on the door. She only hoped she could keep her belly from growling.

"Any update?"

"None, sir. We've brought your supper."

"What am I being served this time?"

"Mutton, sir."

"Oh. Very good. Set it and go. Bring me an update when you have it."

There were sounds of cutlery, liquid being poured, a chair being scraped along the floor. Constant's eyes misted over, despite her effort at stanching it. The tears didn't help relieve the hot, scratchy feeling in her eyes.

"Will there be anything else, sir?"

"No."

"Very good, sir. Enjoy your meal."

The door clicked shut. This time, two sets of eyes

looked down at her. Constant met their glances and then looked away. She wasn't able to see them clearly through her tears.

Constant listened to both sets of footsteps as they moved away in perfect synchrony. "Who's the wench?"

"Later."

She heard the whispers before they got to the end of the corridor. As one unit, they both swiveled to continue around the corner, out of sight. She sighed, put her head back, and watched the wall of nothing opposite her.

She thought she may have snoozed when the footsteps began echoing again. She shook her head, straightened. If she'd managed to sleep, it had done absolutely nothing for the ache behind, and inside of, her eyes. She put both hands to them and rubbed.

She had her hands perfectly folded in her lap, and was sitting up straight when the same two soldiers came into view again. They were still in perfect lockstep. They didn't glance her way.

They were given permission to enter at the knock. Constant tipped her head to listen.

"Well? You have an update?"

"His ribs are broken, sir."

"How many?"

"Too many to count, sir."

"Too many?"

"Yes."

Constant caught her hands to her breast to hold the reaction in. *They'd hit him that hard, and that often? Oh, Kameron!*

"But . . . he will recover?"

"He's strong. In good health. Doctor Thornacre

believes he should make a full recovery. The damage can't be mended until the swelling goes down, though."

"I see. Draft a report for his father. I'll sign it. Anything else?"

"What of the woman, sir?"

"What woman?"

Constant's eyes widened. Her breath caught. Her fingers went icy.

"The one who accompanied him, sir."

"There was a woman with him? Why wasn't I informed earlier? She may know something. Fetch her. Fetch her immediately."

"Yes, sir."

It seemed an instant later they were both standing in front of her, looking and waiting.

"Mistress?"

She didn't look at them. She looked at her entwined hands. She gulped. She tried tightening her muscles. Nothing worked. She was afraid to stand. Her legs felt like jelly, and just as strong.

"The commander is requiring a word with you, mistress."

"A . . . word?" she whispered.

"We're here to escort you. Now, mistress."

Constant shifted forward. She put her hands on her knees and silently ordered her legs to support her. The soldiers didn't wait that long. Large, male hands gripped her upper arms and hauled her to her feet.

Constant dangled between them, searching for some feeling in her feet, and that's why she got dragged across the threshold and into the commander's apartments. It wasn't an auspicious way to meet the man holding her fate in his hands, but there was nothing she could do about it.

"Set her in the chair. Gently, Lieutenant."

They put her in a chair. She supposed it was gently, but it was mortifying all the same. Constant sank into the padded wingback chair, folded her hands, and kept her eyes on her lap.

"Now, young woman. Speak up. What do you have to say for yourself?"

Constant looked up. The commanding officer was standing in front of her, feet apart, his bearing stiff and militaristic. He still looked short. There was a large portrait of what must be the king, George the Third, behind him. Shelves full of books flanked the painting. A large fire lit the area from a fireplace on her right, bordered by long, velvet drapes. The walls were covered in dark wooden paneling separated by wainscoting in a lighter shade. A coat of arms was mounted above the fireplace. Compared to the dull, nondescript hall outside, it was awe-inspiring. Constant stared.

"Does she have a voice, or is she a deaf-mute?" the commander asked, without taking his eyes off her.

"Well? Speak up, wench."

They were all looking at her. Constant swallowed in order to find her voice.

"She was at the scene, sir. She had the horse's reins."

"Really?" The commander put a supercilious note on the word.

"She might know who the devils are, sir."

"Has anyone seen to that, then?"

"We didn't know what to do with her. She claims to be, uh . . . pardon the gall, sir, married to Lord Ballanclaire."

"Oh. I'm certain she wishes as much. What else does she claim?"

Constant was grateful she hadn't found her voice yet. She narrowed her eyes and regarded the trio.

"Not much else, sir. No one has spoken to her since her arrival."

"That isn't very comforting. You let an unknown woman wander our halls? Worse yet, a woman who participated in Lord Ballanclaire's beating and near hanging? Where have your wits gone, Adjutant Simpson? Out with the night watch?"

Constant watched a flush rise from the man's high-necked collar. She almost felt sorry for him. She cleared her throat, making them all look to her again.

"I wasn't participating in anything," she told the commander. "I was holding the horse to keep it from bolting and snapping Kameron's neck."

"Kameron?" he repeated, lifting his eyebrows.

She nodded. She watched him consider her. Then he pulled a chair forward in order to sit facing her.

"You know who did this?"

She nodded again.

"And yet, you did nothing?"

Her eyes filled with tears, and she stared without blinking, quivering in place as she struggled to stop them. She failed. She watched as he wavered and blurred in front of her as tears slipped from her eyes and more just kept coming. She was disgusted with herself. With good reason. After staying dry-eyed since the onions, she had to start weeping now?

"Hand her a handkerchief, Adjutant. Yes. One of yours."

Constant ignored the offered linen, lifting her apron instead to her eyes. They waited while she got herself under control. This was horrid. Detestable. She didn't blame them for any low opinion they might have of her. After enduring what she had, she should be able to explain herself without sobbing helplessly. Nobody said anything as she finally squelched the tears, lowered her apron, and looked across at the commander again.

"Are you ready to continue now?"

Constant forced her face into a blank expression that matched his. She'd been told of the English sense of superiority. Their snobbery. An almost inhuman adherence to class restriction and rules. She hadn't known it included lack of chivalry. They didn't even offer her a sip of water. She finally nodded.

"Does that mean you did something about this unlawful perfidy perpetrated on Lord Ballanclaire?"

That was a mouthful of large words. It sounded ridiculous, too. If he was attempting to show his superiority through his vocabulary, though, he should have picked on a less educated girl. Constant studied him for a few moments before nodding again.

"And just what would that be?"

Her eyes filled with tears again. She couldn't seem to help it. What had she done? She'd ruined her reputation with an entire community. The admission in front of all those men today wasn't going to stay secret. She was a soiled woman now. A woman of low repute and loose morals. A Jezebel. An outcast. Constant had to look down, and watched a tear drop onto her abused and soiled apron. Then another one. She swallowed. It scraped along her throat. And then she answered.

"I . . . wed with him," she said.

The commander's reaction was immediate. He choked, and then he was outright laughing. Constant lifted her head and found his amusement helped conquer the unbridled sobs. He wasn't just chuckling, either. He was near to falling from his chair with merriment.

The last tear fell, clearing her eyes. She sniffed the last of her emotion away. And then she just waited.

He seemed to take a long time to sober, but finally he pulled a handkerchief from somewhere in his perfectly starched and ironed uniform, and used it to mop at his eyes.

"You'll have to forgive me, mistress. It's not often a woman claims to be Lord Ballanclaire's wife. His mistress? Yes. His current fancy? Yes. His fiancée? Yes, even that. I've heard it all. But his wife? Oh, please. That is too enjoyable."

"I only know him as Kameron," Constant said quietly and watched his eyebrows rise.

"So you've already informed us. Kameron, eh?"

She nodded.

"Well, I'll have to advise you, Lord Ballanclaire is not a man who'd up and marry the local milkmaid. He has women clamoring about him for the chance of a smile. He would not select a local wench of indeterminate origins and common appearance. Trust me. I know the man. I know the family. Impossible. And yet, you sit there expecting me to believe he wed with you?"

She nodded again.

"Good Lord. I believe you're serious."

"I have proof," she answered.

His eyes went wide and he paled visibly.

"Adjutant Simpson?"

The commander's voice was a bit higher as he spoke the name. Constant lifted her brows slightly.

"Sir?"

"Leave us. Now. Both of you."

As the door clicked shut, Constant didn't take her eyes off the commander. He looked nervous now. Moisture coated his face, reflecting light from his fire. He pulled on his collar more than once. It was amazing what his discomfiture did to her confidence. Her hands weren't chilled or weak, and her legs felt as sturdy as always.

"You say you have proof?"

"I have a wedding license. He signed it. I signed it. It was witnessed."

"Oh, dearest God! I'll lose my commission. How could he do such a thing?"

"He was about to be hanged. I don't think he thought much beyond surviving that, sir."

"You threatened him?"

It was Constant's turn to laugh. She put a hand to her mouth to stanch it. "Do I look capable of threatening anyone, sir?"

"Good Lord! Do you know what you're saying? The Duke of Ballanclaire's only son and heir can't be wed to a wench from the backwoods of the colonies! I'll be in disgrace! I'll lose my commission! I'll never overcome this. Not only do I lose my most influential patron's heir and get him back within an inch of his life, but I've disgraced the entire lineage of Clan Ballanclaire in the process! Oh my God! He can't be tied to a common milkmaid! He can't. I'll be a laughingstock!"

Constant watched his outburst without one bit of emotion showing. She kept the shock inside. She didn't know much about titles and such, but these revelations sounded even more impressive than before. She didn't know how to answer or what to say. The silence following his words stretched an uncomfortable length. She waited.

"Well? What have you to say for yourself?"

"I'm not a milkmaid," she said calmly.

He swore worse than Kameron ever had, and then he raked hands through what had been regimentally perfect, groomed hair. Constant watched as every strand of it looked to be standing on end. He stopped finally, took several deep breaths, and glared at her. Constant tensed.

"Does anyone else know you're here?" he asked.

"Just about everyone in your garrison," she replied. She didn't know if it was true, but she knew evil intent when she saw it. She wondered how Kameron managed to conquer fear. He'd been so stoic and calm even with a noose about his neck. She really wished she knew how he managed it. She'd copy it.

"What do you want?" He smoothed his hair back into a semblance of order as he asked it. Constant looked at him.

"Well? How much? What denomination? What bank? Speak up."

"How much do I want for what?" she asked.

"For that license. Do you have it on—"

"No."

Her interruption stopped his rise from his chair. He sank back down with a heavy sigh. "This is blackmail, you know," he said.

"I haven't asked for a thing. Nor would I take it. That's hardly blackmail."

"Then why are you here, camping at my door?"

"I came with my . . . husband." She faltered on the title. It sounded as strange to her ears as it probably did to his. "I want to see him. I want him to know I'm here."

"Impossible. Your kind nearly killed him."

Her kind? She repeated it to herself in a state of semi-shock.

"And you expect me to give you another chance?"

"But, I would never hurt him. I—I love him," she replied finally.

"Well, join the legions of women with that affliction. I hardly care. I'm not allowing you to see him. I'm not letting anyone to see him. Not until he's recuperated. I have a career at stake."

"You're a selfish man," she answered finally.

"Every commissioned officer is. Especially one whose career is supported by the Duke of Ballanclaire's patronage. If he withdraws it, I'm finished. You don't know how it works, do you? Why do I even ask? Of course you don't. You're nothing but a common wench. A pretty one, but nothing extraordinary. Tell me something, would you?"

"That depends on what it is," she answered.

"Why you?"

"Why me . . . what?"

"Why did he pick you? Women have tried entrapping Lord Ballanclaire since he left the nursery. And yet here you sit. It's insupportable. I don't know what he sees in you. I certainly can't see anything remarkable."

She'd known Kameron's words had been fantasy. The rug-selling story. Her turquoise eyes. Her lashes. Her eyes filled with tears again. Despite everything.

"Oh, bother. You are an emotional sort, aren't you? That's another surprise. Ballan can't abide scenes. That's why he gave off his attendance on the Marchioness of Barclay. She wept and cried and tried to hold him, and he walked out on her, anyway. It was that incident that got him assigned out here to my regiment. Damn him, anyway."

"I don't think I wish to hear much more," she said.

"Why not? Don't you want to know of this man you've coerced into marriage? Obviously it was a lightning-swift courtship, probably held at the end of a musket. Perhaps that was it. You've a bountiful shape. Perhaps that was what intrigued, and then entrapped, Lord Ballanclaire. Well? Was it?"

She didn't so much as breathe. The space about her heart pained too much. "I don't think . . . you've listened to a thing I've said, sir."

"Of course I have. I just have too many problems with all of it. Starting with you. What am I to do about you?"

"If you'll see to my safe passage from your fort, I'd like to leave."

"Oh no. I can't allow that. I lost Lord Ballanclaire for nigh a sennight. If I lose the woman claiming to be his little colonial wife, I might as well commit suicide for the effect it will have on my career."

"You're not losing me. I'm leaving of my own accord. Kameron won't even need to know. I said we'd married. I didn't say we wanted to. I did it to save him. Just as I told you."

He rolled the reply through his lips. She guessed what it was. Disbelief and suspicion. And perhaps a touch of distaste. Constant stood and pulled the marriage license out of her bodice. She unfolded the document, pressed it flat against her thigh to iron out the wrinkles, and then held it out to him. She watched as he read it. Then she turned and walked over to his fire.

"What are you doing?" he asked.

"Burning the proof."

Constant dropped it atop the log. Both of them watched it curl and turn brown, then catch fire. A few moments later, it was gone.

"Why did you just do that?"

He had a stunned expression on his face. She told herself she didn't care, and then worked at making it true.

"I already told you why. I love him. It's true. It will

always be true. I didn't coerce anything. I didn't force anything. I saved him. And now, I'll leave. Could you arrange a safe escort from your fort now? Please?"

And maybe, if she was extremely lucky, she'd make it that far before the uncontrollable sobs overtook her again. Maybe.

OCTOBER 1772—DESTINY

Chapter Eighteen

October was absolutely beautiful this year. Constant looked out the window of her chamber on the bounty of red, gold, and dark green leaves still covering most of the tree limbs. It had been a long, extended summer. It had been hot. Very hot. The cool temperatures of fall were a blessing after such heat.

And she hated every moment of it.

October carried with it memories, and memories carried agony. Constant held Abigail to her breast and tried to hold in her tears. The baby wriggled in her arms, but she always did. Her twin, Benjamin, was the opposite. He liked being held and coddled and crooned to. Constant looked to where Benjamin was sleeping, and smiled.

Memories were even harder to endure when looking at her babies every day. Benjamin and Abigail were not only twins, but they both looked exactly like their father, from the tufts of white-blond hair atop their heads to their golden-brown eyes.

Constant closed her eyes, forced herself to breathe slowly and carefully through a shudder that heralded an onslaught of weeping, and then she managed to stifle it. She felt as though she'd spent an entire lifetime of tears already. Her children didn't need to see more of them. She put Abigail's wriggling form next to her brother and watched as the tot tried to roll over to get nearer her sibling.

Constant smiled again, and then she dropped her head into her hands and gave in to the sobs.

As Widow Ballan, such displays of emotion weren't considered strange. In fact, she was usually smothered with hugs from her employer whenever emotion overwhelmed her and she didn't get to her chamber quickly enough. At times like that, all Constant could do was hold on to the other woman and sob.

She breathed deeply, ending the storm of tears for the moment, and wiped quickly at her face. She couldn't give in to grief. Not yet. Maybe later. As her breath calmed and her shudders subsided, Constant said a prayer of thanks and opened her eyes.

She looked down at her children, brushed a finger across first Benjamin's wisps of white-blond hair, and then his sister's. They had been her salvation. She knew that much.

It hadn't taken long after she'd left the fort to find employment as a cook, for Madame Hutchinson's boardinghouse needed one desperately. There had almost been a riot at the steps when she'd chanced down this street, one of the boarders threatening a fire to match the one left in his innards by the resident cook.

Constant had simply gone up to the kind-faced, plump woman who'd been wringing her hands, and asked if she could prepare an evening supper to help out. And she'd found her avocation.

That had taken care of room and board. Nothing could be done about her severe heartache, though, not until she realized she was carrying Kameron's baby.

That was what kept her from finding solace beneath the ocean waves she could see and smell from the boardinghouse steps.

There came a knock on her door. "Widow Ballan?"

Constant turned from the contemplation of her babies. Abigail had found the spot she usually occupied, spooned against her sleeping brother. It wouldn't be long before Abigail joined him in slumber. That was helpful, since their mother was their only source of food, and she wasn't going to be available to them for at least two hours.

Two hours? What had possessed her to think she could be away from them for any amount of time, let alone two hours?

"I've come to watch the babes. Master Dimple waits below."

Constant checked her image in the mirror. What Kameron had considered turquoise was a stormy blue color today and her weeping had given her eyelashes a spiked look. Constant brushed at them. She smoothed down the skirts of her Sunday best dress. It wasn't Sunday, but she owned only three dresses. The other two were serviceable and plain and not at all what one should wear when a man came courting.

Her heart quailed as she reached for the doorknob. She almost turned back. A man was courting her. *Her?* As if she had value? Constant caught the agony before it became a sob, picked up her shawl, and opened the door. She smiled at Martha, one of Madame Hutchinson's maids.

She could cry later, when there wasn't anyone to witness it except her babies.

"You look lovely, Widow Ballan." Martha bobbed in

greeting. "That Master Dimple is a lucky fellow, I would say."

"Thank you. They've been fed and changed. You shouldn't have any trouble."

"Those two are never trouble, mistress. They're a joy. Why, one has only to look at such beautiful babes to know what angels look like."

Of course Kameron's offspring would be beautiful enough to make everyone, from the fruit vendors to Madame Hutchinson's society guests, gape with surprise. It was obvious, too, that they'd inherited such beauty from their sire. It certainly hadn't come from the wren-like looks of their mother. Any fool could see that much, although Adam Dimple's reaction when they'd met last week gave Constant pause. That's why she'd actually agreed to accompany him on a stroll this afternoon. He'd looked at her with such a thunderstruck expression that more than one diner in Madame Hutchinson's boardinghouse had remarked on it.

Then there was her cooking. That talent had left him speechless, according to Madame Hutchinson.

Constant tried to smooth the front of her gown. It didn't help much. Her figure had always been ample. Now that she was feeding twins, it was impossible to hide the size of her bosom. She crossed the shawl in front of her bodice and slouched forward a bit. Kameron had once told her to find a farmer to wed. He'd advised her to look for a big, strong, strapping fellow.

Well, Adam was big. He was strapping. He was a farmer.

Constant stopped at the top of the stairs and looked down. Adam Dimple had a large physique, although he wasn't as tall as she suspected Kameron was. Adam was muscled, too. He wasn't as handsome as Kameron, but it would be an impossibility of nature to contrive for more than one male with such attributes to enter her sphere. Adam had nice, gray eyes, and owned a bit of prime acreage. He was also pleasant to look at. Madame Hutchinson had literally cooed at him when she introduced them.

Constant started down the steps. Adam Dimple was also attired in his Sunday best, if the shine to the threads at his shoulders was any indication. That suit had seen a lot of wear. It was serviceable, fit him well, and had a few good years left, by her estimation. The man knew quality when he saw it and didn't mind paying the price. Both were excellent traits in a husband.

Her skirts swished out with every step, curving and shadowing the hues from light green to a deep forest color. Constant had fallen in love with the beautiful fabric the moment she saw it at the mercantile shop. She hadn't minded paying the price.

She reached the bottom of the steps and moved toward her caller.

"Good day to you, Master Dimple."

She held out her hand to him and put a welcoming smile in place as he swiveled toward her. She'd forgotten about the errant lock of light brown hair that fell across his forehead occasionally. She watched as he brushed it back atop his head. Then his eyes widened and she watched him take several deep breaths. She wondered what was wrong with him.

"You look . . . uh . . . words fail me, Widow Ballan."

"That doesn't sound like a good thing," Constant replied, reaching his side and smiling up at him.

She watched his gray eyes drop to her mouth, then to her bodice, and then back to her eyes. He licked his lips.

"You're very . . . uh . . . I've never seen you—beautiful," he stammered.

Constant smiled. Beautiful? Her? The man had been out in the sun too long. "Why, thank you, Master Dimple. You are looking very fine yourself."

"Please. Can I get you to call me Adam?"

"Why, Master Dimple, we barely know—"

"Forgive me. I was rushing you."

He looked away. Constant caught her smile. He reminded her a bit of her brother, Henry, whenever he was caught in some mischief.

"I'll be proud to call you Adam," she said, "and you must call me Constance."

"Your name is Constance? That's uh . . . beautiful, too."

Constant put her hand on his upper arm for a moment and then lifted it away. The touch didn't feel right. She looked at her own fingers with surprise. Touching the fabric on another man's suit didn't feel right? That wasn't a fortuitous sign.

She looked back up at him. Adam cleared his throat.

"Perhaps we'd best begin. Which way do you wish to proceed?"

He walked across Madame Hutchinson's lower parlor in six steps, reaching the door to hold it open for her. The outdoors beckoned to her. Toyed. Teased. She hadn't stepped beyond the boardinghouse property for almost a year. It was safer that way. With sentiment running as heavily as it did against the British, and with the two newspaper articles that Thomas Esterbrook had published about a colonial miss and her illicit turncoat lover, it had simply been safer to stay inside and keep busy with the twins and her cooking.

Adam Dimple held out his arm. Constant swallowed before reaching out to place her hand in the crook of his arm. It still didn't feel right. She wondered if that would ever change.

The air was breezy and crisp. Well below them Constant could see a myriad of ships clogging the harbor. The wooden sidewalk beneath them echoed with Adam's steps. Constant was pleased to note that her footsteps made little sound, which she attributed to losing weight after the birth of her twins.

There were loud voices coming from the end of the street. Adam swiveled them around and started back up the other side.

"What is it?" she asked.

"A bit of unpleasantness. There's always a bit of it whenever the locals get a pint too many in them. Pay them no mind."

"But those were . . . English soldiers," Constant continued.

"Of course. Nothing riles up our boys more than the sight of a redcoat. That's all there is to it. A few tavern boys exchanging words with a small regiment. Ever since the massacre two years back, we're more careful. Our boys aren't stupid. The redcoats carry bayonets and muskets and have full authority to use them. And when they do, we already know they suffer no consequences."

"What if someone gets hurt again?"

"I asked you to pay it no mind. Come. The view from the hill is extraordinary this time of year. You can see all of Boston Harbor. You're lucky to live in such a prime piece of real estate."

"I don't have much of a view from the kitchens, Adam," Constant replied.

"Well, we should do something about that. A woman with your beauty should have large windows."

Constant blushed. She couldn't believe she'd heard him right.

"We probably shouldn't walk far. I've got bread rising, and you know how I feel about my bread."

"I know. I heard talk of it before I met you. It's said a man truly can live on Widow Ballan's bread alone. I heard it. I just didn't believe it until I tasted it."

Constant's blush deepened. They were approaching the boardinghouse again. Mistress Hutchinson had had it painted over the summer, in a pale, sunny yellow color. It made it look even more expansive and pleasant.

"One more street?" Adam asked.

"Very well."

Constant had barely got the words out when three coaches turned onto the street, and a fourth one blocked that end. Although they were a nondescript black, there was no disguising the richness of them, or the outlandish looks of the outriders. Her heart started beating quicker.

"Well, it appears someone on Twelfth Street is going to have visitors. I hope they don't intend to rent rooms with Madame Hutchinson. That would be most unpleasant, wouldn't it?"

"Why do you say that?" Constant asked.

"Because she doesn't abide anything British anymore, just as it should be. No good patriot woman should."

"Could we speak of something else?" Constant asked quietly.

He straightened beside her. "Oh. Forgive me. Do you have royalist leanings, Miss Constance?"

"It's not that. I find all this talk of sedition and fighting unsettling. I've got young babies to care for and a supper to put on. I don't have any leanings further than . . ."

Her voice dribbled to a stop. There wasn't anything she could do about it. Two of the coaches had stopped in front of the yellow boardinghouse on Twelfth Street, and Adam and Constant watched as the last one drove past them to turn at this end of the street, blocking it as well.

"This is starting to look positively dastardly, Constance. Come. Madame Hutchinson may need our assist."

A man stepped from the coach, sending a shock through her entire system. Constant turned her face quickly.

It is Kameron. Please, God . . . no. But even as she prayed, she knew it wouldn't change anything. It couldn't be anyone else. His height and his white-blond hair were unmistakable.

"Those fellows don't look English. Still, it doesn't look good. I hope Madame Hutchinson isn't in some sort of trouble."

Constant was trembling. She couldn't take one step, let alone reach the house. She tightened every muscle under her control. She checked her breathing. She did anything she could to avert the shudders that were overtaking her.

Kameron is here.

"Come along, Constance. We'd best reach Mistress Hutchinson. This doesn't look like a social call. Hurry."

Constant was amazed her feet actually obeyed and started moving with him. Adam wasn't strolling sedately anymore. He held her hand against his side and strode purposefully toward the boardinghouse. Constant skipped along beside him to keep up with his long strides.

Madame Hutchinson met them in the front foyer. She had her arms crossed and a stern look on her face. It wasn't directed at Adam. Constant swallowed.

"*Widow* Ballan? There are some gentlemen here to see you. I have placed them in my private parlor. You may attend them there. And when you have concluded your business, I will be speaking with you."

Constant dipped her head. "Yes, madame," she answered.

Constant had been in Madame Hutchinson's private parlor on several occasions, but the hall she had to traverse to get there had never looked longer. Nor had it ever looked so crowded. She felt like the eagerly awaited object of an executioner's ax, walking past the twelve, very large, strangely dressed men lined up on one side of the hall. They were all attired in tightly fitted black jackets that sported large, embossed, golden buttons, while gold piping trimmed the sleeves and epaulets. A sash of red, white, and black plaid material was worn crosswise over each of their jackets, clasped with a large brooch at the shoulder. And beneath that, they wore what looked like short skirts. Not knee breeches. Not trousers. Skirts. They'd been fashioned from material in the same red, white, and black plaid pattern, and every man had a round, fringed, purselike object draped about his hips so it hung to his groin area.

Not one of them looked remotely feminine, however. They were massive, masculine, and rather uncivilized-looking. Every man had a long sword strapped to one side, and a plethora of wicked-looking knives tucked under his belt. Constant didn't need to be told what these men were. She knew what she was looking at. Highlanders. From that part of Britain called Scotland.

Kam had told her a Highlander wasn't remotely English-looking, but he hadn't described how outlandish and impressive they appeared. Each man exuded strength and purpose. Altogether—without one sound uttered among them—the impression was one of solidity. Barely leashed might. Power. It was vaguely threatening. Intimidating. They wore large, feathered hats that further increased the impression of height and power. They all appeared nearly as tall as Kameron.

One of the men reached forward and knocked on Madame Hutchinson's parlor door.

The door was opened inward by a man who appeared to be a servant fellow. He was dressed like the gentlemen in the hall, but he was smaller. Thinner. He was hatless and didn't carry a sword. He bowed and gestured her in.

There were more men inside, making the ladies' parlor look frilly, feminine, and worse than overcrowded. Constant forced her eyes to move slowly about the room, observing and noting each person. Six more men, nearly identical in size and attire as those in the hall, were backed against opposite walls, facing each other.

She got the significance. The large fellows were guards. All these men. They were there for protection and security. For Kameron.

Her eyes shifted to two older, bewigged gentlemen sitting in the center of the room in Madame Hutchinson's finest chairs. One was immense. The other was quite thin. They both wore Highland attire in the same pattern and color as everyone else, but on these two men, it looked less masculine, and a lot less intimidating. A large portmanteau sat on the floor between them. It was open. Another servant fellow stood beside the window, looking at her with absolutely no expression. A man was silhouetted in the window.

That man was Kameron.

The instant Constant saw him the others might as well have been invisible. Kam had his back to her while he looked out the window at the harbor. He was wearing the same outfit as his guards, only on him the jacket seemed fashioned to highlight his trim waist and broad shoulders.

Kam didn't have a sword strapped to his left side. He

didn't look to have any knives tucked in his belt, either.
But he wore the skirt. Only his was entirely too revealing.
Or something. It draped over his buttocks, showcasing
the powerful muscles.

She couldn't seem to stop looking at him. The skirt
led her eye downward. She'd been right about his scars.
He had several wide bands of darker-toned flesh striping
both lower legs. If his leg had been broken it had set
well, though. It looked fully healed. Healthy. And just as
long and muscled as the other one. He wasn't wearing
the feathered hat. His hair was pulled back in a queue,
the color contrasting sharply with his attire.

Constant moved her gaze upward to where he topped
the window casement by a good half foot. She'd been
mistaken earlier. There wasn't a man anywhere in the
boardinghouse to match him. He was just as immense
and stirring and eye-catching as she'd guessed he'd
be once he stood erect.

"Is she here?" he asked the window.

"Yes, my lord."

The door shut behind her. Constant didn't notice.
She hadn't even blinked since setting eyes on Kam. She
watched him sigh, his shoulders and back rising, then
falling. And then, he turned.

Golden-brown eyes devoured her. Constant's eyes
widened as the sensations she remembered hit every
portion of her body. Then she was moving toward him
without conscious volition. Kameron took two steps
toward her, too, before they were both halted by the
bewigged, portly man in the chair.

"Lord Ballanclaire!" the man said sharply.

Kameron stopped, Constant a second after him. She
watched as he scrunched his eyes shut and swiveled back

the way he'd come. Two steps took him back to the window.

"I canna' say any of it," Kameron said.

"No need. Torquil? Make yourself useful. Bring a chair for the lady, so we can converse civilly."

Constant watched as the fellow who'd opened the door moved a chair out for her. She was grateful she only had to take three faltering steps before she could fall into it. She couldn't move her eyes from Kameron's back.

"Allow me to introduce myself. I am the barrister Iain Blair. Beside me is the barrister Clayton MacVale. We are the Duke of Ballanclaire's representatives. We handle all the duke's affairs. We are here today on a rather delicate matter, between yourself and the duke's heir, Lord Kameron Geoffrey Gannett William Alistair Bennion Ballan of Clan Ballanclaire. Miss?"

Constant realized the large man had been speaking. She hadn't heard much, however. She dropped her gaze to her lap and listened as there was a stir of reaction in the room.

"Well, I believe we can all attest we've reached the proper party, even without Lord Ballanclaire's testimony to the fact. Are we agreed, Sir MacVale?"

The other gentleman spoke up. "Most assuredly, although it makes our chore this afternoon a bit more difficult."

"Yes. Well . . ." The fat man cleared his throat. "There is nae better way than to be blunt about our business. We've been sent on behalf of the crowned head of the United Kingdom, India, and the American Colonies, King George the Third; at the request of the Duke and Laird of Clan Ballanclaire; and with the interest of the royal family of the country of Spain, to plead for an annulment of your marriage to Kameron Ballan."

Constant lifted her head and her eyebrows and looked at them with the most innocent expression she could manage. Her heart was the only thing she couldn't control. It felt like as though it was trying to launch right out of her breast.

"My marriage to whom?" she asked sweetly.

"Doona' deny it, Constant. Please?"

Kameron's whisper almost got to her. Constant felt the prickling along the backs of her eyes that heralded a reaction she wouldn't be able to deny. She drew in a trembling breath, blinked long and slowly, and got the emotion back under control. She looked at the two gentlemen as evenly and controlled as possible. She set her jaw.

"I'm afraid I don't know what you gentlemen are talking about," she answered in the long silence that followed.

Chapter Nineteen

Kameron made some sort of exclamation. The servant man near him was instantly at his side and Kameron waved him away. Constant did her best to ignore them. She was grateful her chair was sideways to the window. She didn't think she could continue the pretense if Kameron was directly in her sight.

She watched with a detached feeling as the two barristers exchanged glances. She refused to let in any emotion. And if she could just hold to that measure of self-control, she'd get through this unscathed. She'd worry over the consequences later. After all, she'd survived the dreadful events of last year. She could survive this. She had to. She had Benjamin and Abigail to protect now, too.

The thin barrister, MacVale, pulled a large leather wallet from his jacket pocket. He opened it and pulled out several official-looking pieces of paper. The room was completely quiet as he unfolded one, reviewed it, and then started speaking.

"I have here a signed statement from the commander of the garrison. It reads that on the evening of October 24, 1771, in his official chambers, he observed a woman burn a signed, clergy-officiated, witnessed, and executed certificate of marriage between Kameron Ballan and C. Ridgely. He wasn't certain of the wife's first name because he hadn't had time to read it thoroughly before it was destroyed. Would you like to verify?"

He held the commander's statement out to her. Constant didn't move. After several moments, he refolded it and pulled out another paper.

"Verra well. This is a certified copy of a document, on file at the magistrate's office, stating that a marriage did take place on the twenty-fourth of October, in the year 1771, between Kameron Ballan, groom, and Constant Ridgely, wife. It is signed by several witnesses, none of whom can be verified at present. The names are fictitious. Due to the circumstances, I was not surprised."

"There were no witnesses, then?" Constant couldn't help the note of hope in her voice.

"I dinna' say that. I said they could na' be verified, at present. I'm fair certain, if I do some research, I'll be able to locate each and every one of them. I believe charges would accompany my search. Such charges would lead to sentences, some to the gallows. Lord Ballanclaire is against pursuing that to a legal conclusion. I've abided his wishes for the moment. I can, of course, change my mind. Should I be forced to do so."

Constant whitened. She didn't say anything. She didn't open her mouth. She was afraid of what might come out.

The thin man's face softened.

"It will na' be a difficult search, mistress. We already ken where to begin. We were there but three days past."

"You . . . were?"

"Let me digress for a moment. Lord Ballanclaire has been finishing his recuperation at his ancestral home, BalClaire Castle near Inveraray. He arrived there mid-February. He was . . . severely injured. It took months of rehabilitation. He has periods of melancholy associated with occasional blurred vision in one eye, and he has yet to regain the full use of his right leg—"

"MacVale!" Kameron's interruption startled everyone with its force. Constant jumped.

"My lord?"

"I will na' have my condition mentioned again."

Constant flicked her glance toward Kameron. She couldn't help it. She loved him more than life itself. There wasn't a way to hide it. Her eyes filled with tears. She blinked rapidly and bit the inside of her cheek to control her emotion. Kam was still staring out the window.

Constant turned back to the thin barrister fellow. She knew by the smile he gave her that he'd seen her response. Constant moved her gaze to her hands, folded in her lap. She longed to kick herself. She couldn't pretend ignorance of Kameron if she gave away her feelings every time she looked at him!

"Verra good, my lord. I shall curb my tongue. Or make a valiant attempt to it. Where was I?"

"His Lordship's stay at BalClaire," the portly one supplied.

"Oh. Aye."

The paper was folded and another one opened. He held it out to her. Constant heard his movements, but she didn't dare look up from the contemplation of her hands.

"It seems that while Lord Ballanclaire was recuperating from his injuries—ahem. I mean, while he was visiting at the ancestral castle, rumors began circulating of a marriage that took place between a colonial woman and the heir to Ballanclaire. This missive started it, actually. It is a demand for monies in order to ensure that certain secrets stay secret. It was sent to BalClaire Castle from these colonies. It is signed by a fellow named Simpson. We visited with him earlier this week. He is regretful of the missive now. He is in the stockade, charged with something that is na' blackmail but will carry the same penalty. He dinna' receive any money."

Constant remembered the adjutant fellow from the garrison. She felt sorry for him, and then set it aside. She needed every bit of sympathy for herself.

"Apparently, this Simpson learned of a secret marriage involving Lord Ballanclaire. He believed the duke would pay handsomely to keep the information hidden. That was an impossibility the moment Simpson put pen to paper. The fellow does na' ken the first thing about espionage."

"Espionage?" she repeated.

"It's a newer word. For spying. You see, espionage is the duty Lord Ballanclaire assigned to himself when he arrived in the colonies a year past . . . last summer. He was na' supposed to see active duty. He was na' to put himself in harm's way. He was actually sent here as a reprimand."

"Reprimand?"

The barrister looked uncomfortable. The portly one answered her. His expression carried something akin to distaste, as if he'd tasted something unpleasant. She moved her gaze back to her hands.

"Lord Ballanclaire has a history of . . . ahem. Well, to put it delicately—dalliances. His past is littered with them. There was an uncomfortable scandal following one of his last uh . . . affairs. There were familial repercussions. Most unpleasant business. The lady involved was a peeress, her rank of some stature at court. She wanted to sue for divorce in order to wed His Lordship. That is an impossibility. So, the duke sent his son and heir out here to keep him out of the public eye, so to speak. He was na' sent to practice covert operations or put himself in danger. He assumed that mission himself. The commander of the garrison allowed it. I believe the reason is due to His Lordship's personality. He can be rather . . . uh . . . *persuasive* is a good word, nae?"

There was an uncomfortable silence as if they expected her to either disclaim or agree. Constant watched her hands and kept silent. No one made a sound. The man finally started talking again.

"We doona' hold the commander at fault. The duke is of a differing opinion, however. His Grace holds the man completely responsible for what happened. We canna' change his mind. His son was na' sent here to put his life in danger. He was na' here to prey on unsuspecting young women. The duke believes the commander should have exerted more control over the heir to a dukedom. There will be repercussions, however they doona' concern us at the moment."

Kameron made another sound. Constant moved her gaze in his direction, even as she realized it for the mistake it was. He was holding himself rigid, his hands in fists at his sides. Her eyes lingered over his form, remembering their days in the loft. She returned her gaze to her lap.

"Sir Blair, if you would allow me to interject here?"

"Of course. Of course. Speak up."

The thin man with the compassionate voice cleared his throat. Constant pulled in a breath and looked up and across at him. He smiled.

"Regardless of reason or fault, the facts are that Lord Ballanclaire did spend a good span of time in these colonies last year. He was verra nearly killed. He was rumored to have wed a colonist. The governor is being held liable on all accounts and is expected to make a full report to the House of Lords. We have been sent to . . . uh, handle the situation."

"I still don't understand why you are telling me any of this," Constant said, although her voice wavered. *The governor?*

The barrister reached a finger beneath his collar and pulled on it.

"If such a marriage took place, it has far-reaching diplomatic consequences. Lord Ballanclaire canna' wed. He was betrothed at birth to the Princess Althea, youngest daughter of Philip the Fifth of Spain. The betrothal carries the signatures of King Ferdinand the Sixth and our late monarch, King George the Second. It was a gesture of goodwill atween our two countries. You see . . . the man you know as Kameron Ballan is na' simply a peer. His mother is a member of the House of Hanover on her mother's side and the Oldenburg dynasty of Norway on her father's. Kameron's grandfather was a son of King Frederick the Fourth's second morganatic and polygamous marriage, to Anne Sophie Reventlow in 1712. This does nullify Kameron's claim to either throne, but it does na' alter marriage alliances."

Constant was afraid of the tingling sensation about her nose and mouth. She'd dealt with it before. Never like this. It wasn't possible. She'd heard it wrong. Kameron was *royalty*? Was that what she'd just heard? She parted her lips and forced shallow quick breaths through them, and within moments the prickling receded. She glanced toward Kam again. He wasn't looking at her. She returned her attention to the lawyers.

The portly barrister cleared his throat again. He seemed to enjoy her discomfiture. Constant decided she didn't like him very much. She waited. The thin barrister, MacVale, spoke again.

"Although it was to have taken place a decade past, there was nae marriage performed once Lord Ballanclaire reached marriageable age. This was nae fault of ours. It is strictly due to Princess Althea's weak constitution. We receive quarterly reports on her condition. They are na' encouraging. The princess is nearly forty, and to all purposes, a bed-bound invalid. That does na' nullify the betrothal, however. According to the current Spanish monarch, King Charles the Third, it is but a temporary setback. Spain needs this alliance."

"I . . . see," she whispered. She did, too. Kameron had said he couldn't offer her a future. He'd meant it. And she'd believed him, although nothing could have prepared her for this.

"So. To the matter at hand. Barrister Blair and myself are here at the behest of the Duke of Ballanclaire. We were to accompany his son to the colonies, locate any possible spouse, and dissolve any marriage that might have taken place. We were to spend whatever sum necessary to make certain of it. We traveled the moment Lord Ballanclaire recovered sufficiently from his injuries to withstand the rigors of such a journey."

"MacVale!" Kameron spat the man's name.

To Constant's surprise, the thin barrister seemed to wink at her before pulling on his collar again. "Pray forgive me, my lord. I forgot."

Kameron turned his head and looked across at them, looking first at MacVale and then moving that golden gaze to her. It scorched the moment her eyes met his. And then it caressed. Her heart stuttered. Her spirit soared. While a high-pitched note grew so loud in her ears she couldn't hear him speaking at first.

". . . state my wishes again. I will na' have my infirmities mentioned. I will na' tolerate pity. You ken?"

He turned back to the window.

Pity? Was the man crazed? Every portion of her yearned for him, and he called it pity?

"His Lordship was pronounced healthy enough—I mean, he was prepared to travel, just this August. We left forthwith. We docked eight days ago. We proceeded to try to locate you. We traveled to the Ridgely farm."

"The Ridgely farm?" Constant echoed, with what she hoped was an innocent tone.

The thin barrister smiled slightly. The portly one narrowed his eyes. Constant kept her eyes on them, although from the corner of her eye she saw the man at the window spinning to face them.

"You heard correctly. The Ridgely farm. We were led to believe it was your home. We dinna' ken then that you were unwelcome there following your marriage. We were so informed, however. It was Lord Ballanclaire who came up with the means to locate you. We simply had to look for the establishment serving the best victuals. And found a Widow Ballan. You."

Her culinary skills had been her undoing. Constant could feel Kameron's agitation. She was leery of even glancing in his direction. She stood and regarded both barristers slowly and carefully, and then she smiled.

"This has been a very interesting and long story, gentlemen, but I really fail to see where it pertains to me. I have a supper to get on. I usually expect about fifty hungry diners to my table. Sometimes there are more, and I—"

"Will you cease denying it, Constant? I canna' take much more of this. You doona' ken!"

The pain in Kam's voice almost broke through her resolve. Constant had to swallow around the immediate dryness in her throat.

"Lord Ballanclaire! You are to remain silent throughout the proceedings!"

The portly barrister's order was accompanied by all six of the guards stepping away from the walls. She narrowed her eyes. It seemed the guards weren't there to protect Kameron, after all. They were there to make certain he did what was required of him.

She sat back down.

"What is it you wish of me, gentlemen?" she asked finally, in a voice they had to strain to hear.

"Are you the woman that wed with Lord Ballanclaire?" the portly one asked.

She nodded.

"I'm afraid I can't hear your answer," he said.

"Yes," she replied.

He opened the portmanteau at their feet and pulled out a flat leather pouch. He clicked his fingers and the servant named Torquil walked past to hand the lawyer an ink pot and a quill. Constant watched as the servant uncorked the ink pot. He didn't look her way.

"I will be writing down your statement. You will need to verify it before signing. I'll then read it to you. You can use an X for your signature. We will then witness it."

Constant shut her eyes for a moment to cover her response. He made her sound not only like a woman with no morals but one with little learning, too. Then she straightened and lifted her chin. "That won't be necessary, Barrister Blair. I can read and I can write."

His eyebrows rose. "Is that so? I dinna' ken American farmers were an educated sort, let alone their daughters."

Constant watched him for a long time. Nobody spoke. "Will that be part of my statement?" she asked, finally.

He flushed. She watched him dip his quill. He cleared his throat. "Name, please."

"Constant Ridgely."

"Nae middle name?"

"No," she replied. She watched as he wrote.

"Date of birth?"

"November 12, 1753."

"November twelfth?" It was Kam asking it, a note of incredulity in his voice.

"Lord Ballanclaire!" the portly gentleman bellowed.

The guards moved in another step. Kam set his jaw and turned back to the window.

"Did you wed with Lord Kameron Ballan at the Ridgely property on October 24, 1771?"

She watched him write the question. Then he looked up.

"Yes," she replied.

"And was this marriage carried out under duress?"

"Under duress?" she repeated.

She knew what Kameron meant about not being able to take much more of this. Her heart was hammering, and droplets of perspiration were dappling the hair at her forehead and along the nape of her neck.

"Were you forced to wed?"

"I know what duress means," she replied.

"Well then?"

"I am trying to answer truthfully. I believe Kameron . . . I mean Lord Ballanclaire, was under duress to marry me. I was not."

His large, gray eyebrows lifted. The thin lawyer smiled over at her.

"Should I place that in her statement, MacVale?"

Constant watched as the barristers conferred. She didn't dare look over at Kam. Her eyes were burning and her chest felt like the plow horse, Eustace, was sitting on it. A knot had formed in her throat, throbbing with every heartbeat. A storm of weeping threatened, every moment this meeting lasted. She didn't know how much longer she could ward it off.

They turned back to her. "And was this marriage consummated?"

Oh God! Constant inhaled in pure agony. She looked over at Kameron before she could stop herself. His jaw was set, defining his perfectly sculpted jaw. His eyes were narrowed, yet still seemed awash with a golden glow. She looked away first.

"L-Lord Ballanclaire was in the process of . . . being hanged. He had a noose about his neck, a broken collarbone, broken ribs, and an injured leg. He could barely move. I don't believe he was conscious of the events or the consequences. There was no way a consummation could have taken place."

"Is that a no?"

Despite every effort, a tear slid from her left eye. Constant was just grateful it was the side away from Kameron and that he wouldn't see it. "No consummation took place following the marriage," she replied softly.

"Did one take place before?"

Constant's cry carried every bit of her emotion. Kam's was just as poignant. She dropped her head. She was too used to crying, she decided. There didn't seem to be a way to stop it. She covered her face with her hands.

"I doona' think that sort of information will be necessary, Barrister Blair," MacVale said.

"An annulment can only take place if there was nae consummation of this union, especially in regards to the girl's tender age and probable virginity. You ken the law. The king is demanding forfeiture of BalClaire and Haverly, with all adjoining properties, along with the fine of thirty thousand pounds if this marriage stands. I have to ask the questions. You ken that. If it was consummated, we have new issues. I will ask again."

Constant took a deep breath to control her emotions and her tears. She knew she had to lie. She just didn't know if she could do it well enough. She moved her hands away from her face. She was grateful to be sitting. She feared she'd have fallen, otherwise.

"What was the question again?" she asked.

"Did you and Lord Ballanclaire consummate your union?"

"I—"

"Doona' answer it, Constant!"

Kameron's words stopped her.

"Lord Ballanclaire! One more word and you will be removed from the proceeding!"

"The lass ruined her reputation for me! She deserves accolades and gratitude, and what does she get? Someone trying to ruin her again. Well, I refuse to allow it!"

"Torquil, fetch more men!"

Kameron was guarded by six men already, and they wanted more? Constant opened her mouth and said his name, and that seemed to stop everything. He looked across the room at her.

"What will they do to you?" she asked in the silence that seemed to descend and hover over the room.

He flinched. "Why? So you can sacrifice yourself for me again? I'll na' allow it! Give them the bloody annulment if that's what you want, and end this! I canna' stand much more, I tell you."

"If that's what *I* want?"

"Lord Ballanclaire! You will na' say one more word!" yelled the portly Mr. Blair.

The throng of men around Kameron shifted and moved to subdue him. Constant caught a glimpse of Kameron yanking his arms and swiveling his shoulder as he resisted. If he didn't stop, he'd be breaking his collarbone again—or worse.

"Doona' just stand there, Torquil! Get more guards!"

The servant man was at the door. Constant spoke

quickly to stop him. "Wait! Please. Wait. You won't need more men. I agree to an annulment. I will sign documents to that effect. I will. Please."

"And you'll answer the question?"

"What was it again?" Constant asked.

"Was the union consummated?"

"Damn you, Blair! When I'm duke—"

"No." Constant said it loudly, halting Kameron's words as well as the guards' efforts to hold him. When Kameron cried out, two of the guards stepped away.

"You agree to an annulment, based on the fact that nae consummation of this union took place?"

Constant looked back to the portly lawyer. "Yes," she replied quietly.

"You are agreeing to this of your own free will?"

"Yes," she replied again.

"You will also accept the sum of one thousand pounds, paid yearly to you until such time as your death?"

They were paying her off? Oh no. Never. Her stomach even revolted at the thought. She opened her mouth to tell them no, and then from out in the hall she heard the distinct sound of Abigail's crying.

Oh, dear God, no! Horrified and panic-stricken, Constant stood. "Do you have the documents ready to sign?" she asked.

"You agree to the sum and will never impress yourself on Duke Ballanclaire, or his heirs, or any of his assigns?"

"Yes. I agree. I do. Yes. Hurry."

The crying was getting louder. Constant raced to Barrister Blair's side and reached for the quill.

"Do you wish to read through the document you are about to sign?"

"No. Give me the pen. I agree to everything that's written. Just hurry."

She'd finished and was lifting the quill to blow on the ink when someone knocked at the door. Her heart fell to the bottom of her belly. She looked up, locked glances with Kameron for an instant, and then turned toward the door as it opened slowly.

Martha stood there, looking small and insignificant and frightened. She had a twin in each arm. She looked ready to cry, too.

"I'm so sorry, mistress. I tried everything. Abigail wouldn't hush and she woke her brother. I'm so sorry. I'd never disturb you in a conference, but they wouldn't calm for me. They want their mother."

Chapter Twenty

Everything happened at once. Constant's mind wasn't capable of absorbing it. The moment realization hit Kameron, he shoved through his guards and slammed aside obstacles to reach the twins, and then he just stood there, breathing heavily as he looked down at them. Abigail was squalling even louder. Benjamin had joined her. And Martha burst into tears that rivaled the babies'. The guards reached Kam next and formed a partial wall about him. Someone yelled. Something dropped with a thud. Someone else gave a cry for order. And Constant stood rooted in place, the quill dripping ink down her arm, while she watched all of it happen.

"My God, Constant! You had my child? I mean children? You had . . . twins? And one is . . . my son? You had my *heirs*?"

His voice choked with emotion. She couldn't reply. There wasn't anything she could say. He was searing her in place with those golden-brown eyes. They were glazed over with moisture and thoroughly dazed. And then they narrowed.

"And you weren't even going to tell me?"

Constant's cry came a moment before she fell. Her last conscious thought was that she hadn't been breathing shallowly and quickly enough.

"This changes everything," someone whispered.

The response was just as soft, but argumentative. "It changes naught. She agreed to the annulment. She signed the documents. We have what the duke requires."

"She was under duress."

"She testified otherwise. There is no further issue here. We have her testimony that the marriage was na' consummated."

"Any fool can see that's complete nonsense."

"So?" It was the portly one again. "It will na' be the first time a child is declared illegitimate based on the annulment of his parents' marriage. King Henry the Eighth did much the same to his firstborn. And please recollect, we have nae choice. The Princess Althea still lives. Spain is requiring the alliance take place. His Majesty is demanding a fortune in land and silver. We have nae choice. We have to file the annulment document."

"We canna' do that. It's too obvious it was consummated, despite her testimony."

"Just because a woman possesses children, does na' make it a foregone conclusion they're a product of her marriage."

"You canna' be serious. Another man siring those bairns? They're the image of His Lordship. Nae court in the land would decree otherwise." MacVale clucked his tongue.

"What do you suggest, then?"

"Perhaps the forfeiture of properties and the fine of thirty thousand would be worth it to His Grace."

"What? Losing BalClaire alone would be ruinous. It's

been the seat of Ballanclaire clan power for five hundred years! As for the fine? It would bankrupt Their Graces. We have to think of something else. Too much is at stake."

"There is another option. I have just thought of it."

That was the thin barrister again. Constant held her breath.

"What?"

"Her death."

Constant was afraid she gave away her feigned unconsciousness with the minute slip in her breathing. She couldn't believe she'd heard him right.

"Her death? Even I would na' go that far, MacVale."

"Nae! Think! I doona' mean her actual death."

"I begin to see . . . You're thinking if we get documentation of her death, then His Lordship can wed Princess Althea, as required. Better yet, there is already an heir to Ballanclaire. This has potential. It does. I dinna' ken you had it in you, MacVale."

"We'll also need to do some hiring. We'll need wet nurses, nannies, and such, and I ask you—is na' the perfect candidate here already?"

"You're thinking to hire her?"

"Why na'? She's been attending to them until now."

"His Lordship will never agree. You heard him. He's barely under our control now, and that's with two dozen men."

"Then he is na' to know."

"I'm na' certain I follow your train of thought, MacVale, but I am intrigued."

"Hush! She's waking."

Constant scrunched up her nose and groaned. She blinked her eyes open next and tried to sit up. That's when she saw she was still in Madame Hutchinson's parlor, although someone had moved her to a settee.

She shifted into a sitting position and moved her legs back to the floor. And looked out into the room.

Constant located Kameron easily. He was sitting in the chair she'd vacated, two guards on either side of him. He had a baby in each hand that he then supported atop a knee. He was rotating them slightly back and forth and staring from one to the other in turn as if mesmerized. He wasn't the only one. The twins were almost four months of age, and focused easily now. They normally fretted and cried with strangers, but hadn't any qualms about Kameron. Quite the opposite. Constant watched as they both went from staring at him to giving him lopsided smiles, and then first Benjamin and then his sister started making bubbles as they cooed up at their father.

Constant couldn't help smiling. Every other person in the parlor seemed to have the same expression, except Kameron, who still looked stunned.

"My word, Constant, they're the most beautiful bairns I've ever seen. You ken?"

He turned to look over at her. She gulped, thought of any lie she could invent, discarded them all, and finally nodded.

"And look. They even have my eyes." He turned back to the babies to watch as they followed his face.

Constant sighed. "They take after their father, Kameron. It isn't a far stretch to see where their beauty comes from."

"That maid spoke of Abigail and Benjamin. I have one of each? Is this one my daughter, then?"

He put the babies against his chest and stood. Constant watched as he walked over to her and sat beside her. The guards formed a corridor of sorts to allow it. The twins weren't used to being carried on a man's forearms, but neither one seemed to mind, she noticed, as Kameron put them back atop his knees. The guards moved, forming a semicircle behind them around the settee, hovering. Watching. It was an odd feeling.

Kameron rolled his hand, moving Benjamin. "Is this one my daughter?"

"No."

"This one is . . . my son, then?"

His voice warbled. Constant reached out to stroke Benjamin's hand. His fingers closed on one of hers.

"Yes. This is your son. His name is Benjamin," she answered.

"That's it?"

"Yes."

"No son of mine has only one name. I actually have six."

"I know. I just heard them," she replied.

"We'll correct it when he's baptized."

"Pardon the interruption, my lord, but there seems to be a bit of difficulty with that plan."

"Difficulty?" Kameron looked up and frowned at the two barristers standing in front of him.

"Yes. This woman has signed an annulment. The children no longer have your name. They canna' be baptized and given it. They're bastards."

"That's nonsense. You ken it as well as I do. My children are as legitimate as they come."

"Na' with an annulment, my lord. We have our orders."

"Well, I'm changing them."

"You canna' change them. His Grace was most specific."

Kameron looked down at the babies and then he handed Abigail to Constant. She watched as he cradled Benjamin against his chest. Kam looked across at the two barristers. The thin one tugged at his cravat again. The portly one grew red.

"You have annulment paperwork signed by my wife. Burn it. I'm ordering you," Kameron said in an authoritative tone she'd never heard him use before.

"But, the duke—"

"If my father wishes to see me again, he'll concede."

"You doona' seem to understand, my lord. You have nae choice. We brought twenty-four men to make certain of it."

"You could have brought a hundred. It would na' stop me. I agreed to this if Constant wanted it and if she was na' harmed. Well, now I add further stipulation: my children are na' harmed. Having them declared bastards harms them. Gentlemen?"

Constant watched as the two lawyers conferred. She knew what they intended. She just didn't know how they'd present it. They turned back.

"We have a proposition, my lord."

"Verra well. Propose it."

"The duke demands that this marriage be annulled. He does not wish to lose your ancestral estates or so much silver to the crown. We were to gain an annulment at whatever cost."

"So?"

"Your father has na' had the choice of losing his grandchildren put before him. He may come to the same determination you have. We will na' know unless we ask him."

"Then, go. Ask him."

They started conferring again. Constant watched with wide eyes. Kameron was willing to turn down a royal bride, lose several estates and the land with it, and pay thirty thousand pounds—an amount she couldn't even grasp—just to remain wed to her? She was reeling over the amount he stood to lose if he did so. She put her hand on his arm. He looked down at her long enough for her to feel her pulse quicken along with her breathing. Then he turned back to the lawyers.

"Well?" he asked.

"We believe the best way to put this option before the duke is to present it as a *fait accompli*, my lord."

"Which means?"

"We believe if the duke sees the children, he may agree with you. We believe you may have the upper hand in your bargaining if you present it that way."

"So the children travel with us? Is that what you propose?"

"We also propose that the annulment be enforced as if it were legalized, as it will be if your father does na' agree."

"What?"

Kam stood. He was fortunate he had the compliant twin rather than Abigail. Benjamin simply rested in the crook of his father's left arm and watched everything from that angle.

"We are under orders from your father, my lord. He's our laird. We're sworn to uphold his wishes. As Ballanclaire clansmen. You ken the law."

"What will this mean for me?"

"The mistress and her children sail with us, but she travels as one of the wet nurses. This is a platonic voyage, and there will be nae marriage in force unless His Grace decrees it so at the end of it."

Constant was blushing.

"That is ridiculous. Worse than ridiculous," Kameron muttered.

"Would you rather she became known as your mistress?"

"Never. She is my lady wife. I will na' abide that word

in any context attached to her name. You use it again at your own peril. You ken?"

Kam's threat was stated in the same authoritative tone he'd used earlier. Constant felt an immediate flare of emotion, followed by a glow. Then an infusion of absolute wonder.

"Please understand, Your Lordship. We have signed paperwork. We have full right to file these documents and make this annulment legal today. We are offering to hold off doing our duty for the time being. We are agreeing to let your father decide the issue, rather than follow his orders outright. Doona' force the issue. We are still His Grace's men. Please." Barrister MacVale was speaking. He looked as though he spoke the truth.

"You want me to travel with Constant and na' let anyone ken who she is? Be unable to claim her as my wife? Not converse with her? Or touch her? Nor claim my marital rights? That is holding me to the extreme, gentlemen."

"If there is the creation of another child, it might simply be another bastard, my lord. You will have three children you canna' claim, rather than two."

. . . and the lie about my death would blow up in your faces, Constant supplied in her mind.

"And I can walk down the street right now, find another magistrate, and marry her again."

"You would na' get through your guards, Lord Ballan-claire."

"That sounds like a challenge," Kam replied.

She had to do something. It looked as if warfare was about to erupt. His guards had their hands on their swords. Kameron looked tensed and ready. Even with a babe in the crook of his arm.

Constant stood. "Kameron. If you're going to fight, hand me Benjamin. Right now."

He looked down at the babe as if he'd forgotten him. His features softened.

"Perhaps we can compromise?" she asked in the silence that followed.

"With what? Their plan? You're my wife, Constant."

"We'll be on our way to your country. All of us. It's more than I had before."

"Constant—"

"How long is this voyage, gentlemen?" she asked, interrupting him.

Less than a week out, she knew the voyage was too long. To know Kameron was on the same ship, out on the same span of ocean, and be unable to speak to him, ruined what sleep she got and made every meal unpalatable on her tongue. She knew the solution she'd overheard when the lawyers thought she was sleeping was the only viable option. Kameron was living a fairy tale. It wasn't going to have a happy ending. No duke would accept her as a daughter. She was better suited as a wet nurse. The barristers and the guards saw it clearly enough.

All of which meant that Constant was being offered the role of caring for her own children. She understood and accepted it. Only at night would her guard drop. By the fifth night, it was punishment to try to sleep. The twins had their own cabin, down the corridor from her. They each had a nanny for the voyage. They had a nurse. There were even two more wet nurses, because the barristers had insisted on hiring them. All of which meant her babies were being loved and fed and crooned to by someone other than her. It was depressing. It was maddening. It was frustrating. And each day it got worse. She endured it only because her children were not suffering.

In fact, Constant's anxiety had caused her to produce less milk, so she was glad her children were well fed.

She wasn't being mistreated. Far from it. She was aboard a large caravel. She had a luxurious berth with a double-size bed. She had the soothing motion of the waves beneath her. She had beautifully sewn lawn night-clothes to wear, but they strangled and choked her flesh until she tore them off.

Constant knew that even though they finalized the annulment, and she was no longer Kam's wife, she still hungered to be in his arms. She'd struggled with her feelings even before he came back into her life. Now that he was near, she was a bundle of ache and frustration, with no release in sight.

Constant stopped, her hand on Kameron's actual doorknob, and slowly backed away onto the deck. *Oh, dearest God!* It was only the sixth day out! They had five weeks left to sail . . . except for her. She didn't have five weeks. She knew what she should do; she'd suspected the moment she'd heard the lawyers' decision to have the Duke of Ballanclaire determine the future of her marriage. If she didn't take the only option available to her during this voyage, she was going to spend her life watching her own children grow up and take their places in high society, while she stayed hidden in the shadows somewhere. She was never going to be able to claim Abigail and Benjamin. Or Kameron.

Constant looked over at one of the three ships accompanying them. Perhaps she should ask if she could move to one of them. Maybe then she wouldn't find her hands idle at her sides, her feet taking her where they shouldn't, and her entire being yearning for something she could never have.

Constant dropped her gaze to the waves. The ship was large, resembling a small town of industriousness. She wasn't even seasick, although one of the nurses had the affliction. She was grateful. The large ship rode the waves like a great bird gliding with the wind. Elegantly. Graciously. Once they'd cleared Boston Harbor, the waves had become more elongated, choppier, and darker green in color. She'd spent a good portion of time looking down into the ocean. Pondering. Preparing. Gathering courage. Each day, the water looked more ominous, the depths blacker and deeper.

There wasn't any other path open to her. There never had been. Kameron Ballan was out of reach. He always had been. Regardless of what he wanted, it wasn't to be. Constant Ridgely didn't need some old, pretentious, bewigged and gem-covered duke telling her she wasn't good enough. She knew it. She wasn't a princess. Why, she wasn't even a wife anymore. If she continued living, she would be the unwed mother of twin bastards.

She'd heard drowning wasn't a difficult death, especially if one didn't know how to swim.

Constant's vision wavered on the ocean water that was going to be her grave. It was nice that there was a greenish opacity to every wave. And then she turned away. She still had five more weeks. Five. She just had to prevent her own feet from coming this way again. She didn't think she could stand it if Kameron gained even a hint of what she was planning.

She retraced her steps back to her own cabin, taking malicious pleasure in hammering each heel into the deck beneath her, and that was why she didn't see his boots until she was almost upon him.

Chapter Twenty-One

Constant instantly knew who blocked her. She'd once held a foot that size in her hands. She pulled in her breath and moved her gaze up. Kameron was wearing a long, plaid skirt, and his shirt wasn't correctly fastened, for it gapped open to mid-belly. She couldn't seem to move her eyes. He hadn't grown his chest hair back.

"I've been watching for you," he said.

"You shouldn't be," she told his chest.

"I ken as much."

She glanced up, gasped, and immediately looked back to his chest. It was safer. That one glimpse was almost too much. He hadn't pulled his hair back, and he had a black patch covering one eye, taking some of his angelic beauty and mutating it into a rakish, harder visage.

Constant's breasts swelled, growing heavy with liquid and tender with the pressure against her gown. She was afraid it wouldn't pass notice. When she dared to look back up, she knew for certain, as the one golden-brown eye moved from her face to her bosom and stayed there.

"You were there, Constant. You heard them. You even agreed to this compromise. This is a platonic voyage."

"Yes," she answered.

"I understand platonic. I just canna' get the rest of me to understand it."

He was growing more agitated, if the quickening breaths were any indication. Constant bit her lip.

"I . . . I wasn't looking for you," she said.

"As always, you need to work on your lying. You're in clear violation of rule number one."

"What?"

"Doona' lie if the truth is staring you in the face."

"I'm not lying."

"You just came from my cabin."

"No, I—"

"You just came from my cabin *door*. I ken. I just said as much. I've been watching you."

"I needed . . ." Her voice stopped. She couldn't finish. She couldn't think.

His groan was audible and very stirring. As was the motion of his chest. "Are you tormenting me on purpose?"

"I . . . no," she answered.

"I haven't had a woman in some time, Constant."

He took another step nearer to her as he spoke, shrinking the corridor they stood in, and making her pulse leap.

"I know. It's been at least six days. I don't know how you manage." She tried to answer flippantly but failed.

He was frowning. The one eye she could see was narrowed at her. "I have na' had a woman since you, Constant."

"A whole year?"

He put his hands on the wall on either side of her head and leaned toward her. Then he was speaking his words to her neck.

"It's my bane, if you will. I was wounded and out of

commission at first, but once I wasn't, I found that other women meant naught to me anymore. Only you. It's a constant thing, too. Constant problem. A constant desire, constant craving, constant longing. You probably should na' stay this close to me much longer."

"I know," she whispered.

"You're going to get singed."

"So are you."

One leg spliced between hers, leveraging her upward, while his hands helped. They were against her waist, then her hips, lifting her atop his bent leg, bringing her face level to his.

"I suggest you say something to stop this. I suggest you do it now, Constant."

He had his nose against hers as he said it. His lips were hovering above hers, and his breath mingled with hers.

"Why do you wear a patch?" she asked, between gasps of breath.

"Bright light affects my vision."

"Bright . . . light?"

She leveraged her mouth the slightest bit toward his. She touched her tongue to his bottom lip. Kam started trembling. She felt it in every bit of him she touched.

"Constant . . ."

"What kind of light?"

Constant slid her lips along his cheek and from there to his throat. His tremors increased. The cords in his neck were intriguing, as was the chest heaving under her hands.

"Light?" he asked.

"Your patch." She murmured the words against his skin. She was glad he wore his hair loose. That way she could taste it as she maneuvered her way toward an ear.

"Oh. Bright sunlight . . . on the waves . . . blurs things. My eye waters. Things . . . like—Constant?"

"Yes?"

"I will na' make you my mistress. I-I-I . . . refuse."

Constant had slid her tongue around the edge of his earlobe, causing him to stammer. "I'm not asking you to."

She was having as much trouble breathing as he was. Her mouth reached the juncture of his jaw. He moved, burning her lips with his whiskers just before his lips reached hers. Then, nothing burned as hot as his mouth devouring hers.

Constant helped him, too. She lifted her legs, wrapping them about his waist, and brought her hands over his shoulders.

"Oh, love. Oh, Constant. Oh, sweet . . ."

Kameron was murmuring love words all over her, trailing them down to her chin before he nipped at the top buttons of her blouse. Then he looked up, pinning her in place with that one golden eye.

"There's nae constable in sight," he whispered.

"Constable?"

"Solicitor, barrister, servant, sailor, wet nurse, nanny . . . guard. You ken. Constables."

"Oh. Those."

"You are still nursing the bairns?"

She wrinkled her brow. "Some. Why?"

"'Tis na' easy to get you with child, if you are."

Her eyes widened. "It isn't?"

"Nae."

She licked her lips. His shudder went right through her frame, too. "We might get caught," she whispered.

"We might not."

Now it was her turn to groan. "Don't tempt me. I can't stand it."

"Me? Look who's prancing through my side of the ship, wearing little more than—what are you wearing?"

"A day gown, a shawl, all the proper undergarments."

"Damn you, Constant. Damn you."

He grabbed her lips with his, alternately sucking and licking. Possessing. Constant helped. They were well into creating a whirlpool of sensation when the ship's bell rang.

Both of them lifted their heads.

"Another ship," Kam informed her.

"Are they . . . friendly?" she asked, between pants for breath.

He turned and put his uncovered eye on her. "Right at the moment, I'm na' inclined to care. You?"

Constant shook her head. He put both hands beneath her buttocks and held her to him as he started walking.

"I've had a gullet-full of this. I'm your husband. You're my wife. I doona' give a damn for any annulment papers or property forfeiture, or fines. I want to be buried deep in you, love. I intend to do that very thing. Here's your cabin."

He shoved the door open, shut it with the bottom of his foot, settled her to one side in order to free a hand, and drew the bolt down with it.

"I don't . . . want this." It would be more believable if she wasn't pushing her loins into him, and gasping through the words.

"You do."

"No . . . wait . . ."

Her request came on a moan, belying the words. No place on her body wasn't wanting. Needing. Desiring. He had her atop the bed now, pulling her cap off and then running his fingers through her hair. Constant hadn't braided it last night.

Kameron had her splayed across the coverlet, then just stopped. The expression in his eye made her heart skip a beat. He held himself from her on his elbows as he just kept looking. And then he began shaking. The wooden platform beneath her feather-stuffed mattress rattled with it.

"Look at me, Constant. Just look. I've bedded more women than I can remember, and yet I'm tense and anxious as a virgin with you. Just you. Why? What is it you do to me?"

"I love you," she replied.

"Oh, darling. If I had words to tell you the depth of my love, I'd speak them. I would."

He accompanied each of his words with a stroke—on her face, down her arm, across the swell of a breast, making Constant a writhing mass of nerves, and he hadn't taken one stitch of clothing from her.

"We probably don't have enough time."

"Then, make time," she replied, and started yanking up on his shirt.

"I'll na' take you quickly. I'll na' lose it again. I'll make it as enjoyable for you—stop that!"

Constant had his shirt opened and shoved down his arms, while her hands ran over every inch of him, as if he was displayed just for her. Every glorious, rippled inch.

"You haven't grown any hair back?" she asked.

His lips twisted. "I told you . . . I'm a towhead. Now, wait!"

He put his hands where she was unhooking his belt, but had to use sheer force to stop her. Constant grinned up at him as he held her hands away from him.

"Na' so fast, sweet. I've a debt to repay."

"What debt?"

"A little thing called stealing your virginity, and na' even doing it properly."

"There is a proper way? But—oh!"

Constant lost the rest of her words in a squeal as he held her, a bent leg atop her hips to make certain of it, while the fingers on one hand started slipping her blouse buttons out of their holes.

"There are a thousand proper, and highly improper, ways . . . and all of them start with me giving you pleasure. Like this."

Constant was sure she was losing her sanity as Kam tongued his way down the opening he'd created, using his mouth to open and separate the material. He didn't stop until he had her blouse spliced apart, revealing each surge of her bosom as she struggled for breath. He was having difficulty controlling his own breathing, and each breath sent rivulets of warm air over her exposed flesh. He lifted himself over her, one hand on either side, while his legs straddled hers.

He was sending a golden glow of desire with every flick of his gaze. She knew where he was looking, too. At the part that always intrigued him. She arched herself, shoving the peaks of her breasts into the material, and saw it affect him. Kam shut his eyes, a shudder ran through his entire frame, and then he reopened them. His golden gaze moved up to her neck, her face, and finally he locked on her own eyes. Constant had never felt so loved or desired or adored.

"I canna' tell you how much I've dreamt of you," he whispered. "You've nae idea. You're the epitome of womanliness, Constant, my love. There is something about you . . . something intangible, but still there. It must come with the birthday we share."

He moved to sit toward the bottom of the bed, grasping her ankles to carefully remove her boots and adjust her legs in a bent position. Constant wasn't capable of stopping him, although she knew she should. Then he ran his hands up her legs, pushing her skirt out of his way as he went. She barely felt him slide her pantaloons down, over her knees and across her ankles, the movement erotic and hot. Then he was flicking a finger against the tops of her stockings.

"Birth . . . day?"

"November twelfth. I heard you. Same as mine." He was speaking the words to the skin of her ankle, as he slid his mouth up her leg.

"We have the same birthday?"

"Aye. That is na' all we share."

"It . . . isn't?"

"Astrologically, we're matched. Scorpion to scorpion. You ever study that sort of thing?"

"No."

"Trust me. We're matched. We both carry it. We're both cursed by it."

"Cursed?"

It wasn't possible to understand his words. Kam had reached the tops of her stockings, and was moving his tongue onto bare flesh that had never felt the like.

"I speak of desire, my love."

"De . . . sire?"

"Aye. Desire. Wicked, sensual, thirsting desire. Hot, hard passion. Molten, liquid, carnal pleasure. Lust. Eroticism. Sensory delectation at every turn. That kind of desire. You are all of that, Constant. I sense it. I smell it. I want to experience it. I crave it."

He lowered his mouth to her and Constant screamed, and screamed again. She thought she was dying. She knew she had to be dying, and it wasn't horrid, or frightening, or dreadful, or dark. It was light, and power, and wonder. She dissolved into whimpers and turned into such a quivering mass of female, she didn't think she still possessed limbs, before he'd taken his fill.

Kam came back into sight, imprinting his gaze anywhere he cared to, as he looked and kept looking. He held himself above her with one arm while pulling his garments off with the other. Constant didn't have an ounce of argument left in her.

"What . . . did you just do?" she whispered.

"Prepared you."

"For . . . what?"

"Me."

His lips went to a pout. Constant reached a hand out to touch them. He groaned, then he nipped at her fingers, then he was sucking two of them into his mouth, and she was wide-eyed at the sensation before she could snatch her hand away.

His groan deepened, blending with the sound of ripping cloth. Air caressed her and then heat. She felt the length and strength and power of him. Constant tensed for the remembered pain, but all she felt at the first pressured stroke was complete and absolute wonder, and then more of the same.

Constant shoved her arms about his shoulders, clawed at his back, and locked her ankles behind him so she'd have the power to return his thrusts. Kameron knew what she was about, for his motions were accompanied by deep-throated grunts, as he alternately filled, and then hovered and teased, until Constant was ready to scream again, this time with vexation.

She knew absolute bliss awaited her. She didn't have to question it, she just knew, and with each of their thrusting movements, it grew closer, harder, more heated, more fluid, and more carnal. She was probably waking the entire ship with her cries, but she no longer cared.

And when it hit, Constant slammed her eyes shut and arched her head back in order to give it room. She was keening. She was soaring, floating . . . and it wasn't on any ship. It was on a journey that wasn't going anywhere but straight to Kameron. It didn't have anything to do with deceit, forfeiture, loss, or death. It was full of nothing but life.

She knew Kam was going to achieve it, too. She held him to her as closely as she could so when it came, she could feed the strength and power of it right back to him, quivering the entire time, while the long cry he gave filled her ears, the room, her heart.

Awareness came back slowly. Her breathing calmed to a manageable level while the moisture on her half-clothed body cooled. She had to force her neck to lift her head so she could look over at where his head rested beside hers. She was replete. Satiated. Liquid. Weak.

"Oh, Kameron," she murmured. "We shouldn't have done this."

He chuckled, and then he was chortling. Constant had to tighten her knees around his hips, keeping his movement to a minimum. She watched as he moved his arms into the position to push up. She was amazed to see him tremble when he tried. All he managed to do was roll his head toward her, before he fell back down.

"Oh, you are so wrong, my love. We most certainly should have. We probably should have warned everyone first, though."

Constant snorted. Then she was laughing with him. Then she sobered. "They're going to know what we did, Kam."

"They damn well better. If na', I'll tell them."

"I—you wouldn't!"

"Rest assured I will. You're mine, Constant Ballan. You're my lady, my wife. Mine."

"But . . . this is a platonic voyage."

"And I still doona' ken when I agreed to that. And if I did, I'm reneging. I'll na' continue with self-denial. You're moving to my cabin. The moment I have enough strength to lift from you and get there myself."

Constant snickered.

"Oh, darling, do you ken what we have together?" he asked.

"I am not stupid."

He opened his eyes and smiled at her. It was one of the most moving, gentle expressions she'd ever seen.

"You're na' remotely stupid, my love, just inexperienced in what I'm referring to. Forgive me for saying it in such a fashion. I only meant that what we have is a gift. The greatest gift. I should know. I'm na' exactly virginal."

"I heard all about your exploits at Madame Hutchinson's boardinghouse."

"That was a partial rendering, love. But hear me out afore getting testy. Women have always chased me. All kinds of women. All types. Using all the excuses. They gave me keys. Invitations. Room directions. I would go to house parties and collect so many keys I dinna' recollect which one belonged to which lady. I made a game of it. Whichever door opened first, that was my lover for the night. All night. Every night."

Constant told her body to stiffen, but only her legs twitched. Nothing worked the way she wanted it to. She settled for turning her head away and speaking as coldly as she could. "I don't care to hear more, Kameron."

He reached for her chin and turned her back to him. She didn't open her eyes, even when he blew the sigh across her nose.

"Forgive me, love. I was na' trying to offend or insult, I was doing a bit of explanation. I should mince words, but I canna'. I swear to you, I have never felt as I do with you. I would have wed you without a noose about my neck, darling. I would do it again tomorrow. Today. I swear it."

"Oh, Kameron." She sniffed.

"Doona' take that tone. Please? I am trying to speak a declaration here."

Constant opened her eyes and had to narrow them slightly at the luminous, golden-brown gaze of both of his.

"Where did your patch go?" she asked.

Kameron lifted onto his forearms, his muscled stomach resting against her. She lost air with the weight of him. She was moving to push him off when he rolled, pulling her atop him.

"My guess? 'Tis gone to the same place as your wardrobe," he finally answered.

"But I'm still clothed."

Constant tipped her head to look down and then looked back, her eyes wide. Her skirt was bunched about her belly, and the edge of one stocking dangled from her toes. She wore nothing else.

"You were saying?" he asked, with a slight smile hovering on those full lips.

"Where did my clothing go?"

"The same place as my patch. My shirt. My kilt. They're another casualty of our passion. It hardly matters. I'll find it all later. And if na', I'll see to replacements. I have more."

"Well, I don't. I have three dresses to my name."

"Na' to worry. I'll order more. My duchess has to make her bow before royalty. She has to have hundreds of dresses."

"Your—your . . . ?" Her voice stopped.

"One day, you'll be my duchess. Strawberry leaves and all. I hope you're na' too annoyed."

"Strawberries? Why?"

"It's a coronet. Duchesses are distinguished by the golden filigree they wear to state occasions. It's shaped to look a bit like strawberry leaves. The Duchess of Ballanclair owns four sets."

"Oh, Kam." She buried her head into his neck.

"What is it, love?"

Constant shook her head, trying to hold back the tears. She was never going to be his duchess. She couldn't do that to him, or to his heritage, or to her own children.

"Constant, what we have is the most heaven you can find on earth. I guarantee it. Do you know something else?"

"What?"

Kameron opened his mouth to say something, but the heavy knocking on her door forestalled him.

"Lord Ballanclaire! Your presence is required in the captain's quarters."

It was Barrister Blair. He didn't sound amused. Kam looked at the ceiling and blew the sigh. "I think we've been found out," he said.

The heavy knocking came again. "Lord Ballanclaire!"

"Stop pounding. I can hear you."

Kameron's voice sounded strange coming through his chest. Constant set her ear atop him and listened. Thrilled. Committed it to memory.

"I have to go now, love. But I'll be back. You've my word. The next knock at your door will be me. Be ready."

"Immediately, my lord!"

"Damn it all. I should have been born a commoner, the lucky devils," Kam remarked as he rolled from beneath her.

Chapter Twenty-Two

It wasn't Kameron knocking at her chamber door. Constant hadn't really expected it, despite his assurance. She knew the truth. They weren't sailing toward anything certain. There was only a vague hope of a future at the end of it. Love didn't matter in the world Kameron had been born into. He couldn't change it. Nobody could.

Constant grimaced in the mirror, taking another deep breath before answering the knock. She didn't know what to feel. She should be feeling everything from anger to embarrassment to resignation. She was doing her best to stifle any emotion. Despite everything, they had broken the rules. She knew they were going to be punished for it. She hoped Kam wasn't fighting it unduly. She didn't want him hurt. She never wanted him hurt. She would rather take all the pain on herself. She should have been stronger. She should have resisted him.

Constant blew the sigh over her lips. She couldn't resist him. Kameron was more than handsome. He was honorable, loving, generous; claiming her and their babies regardless of the consequences. He was every inch a desirable husband. He was also masculine and virile. He made her feel very much a woman. Resist him?

Impossible.

The knock came again. She told herself she was ready, but her hand was shaking when she reached for the door bolt. She put her hands together and blew on them to warm them, trying to mitigate some of her fear. She reached to pat the newly braided modesty of her hair, once again hidden beneath a cap.

She opened the door. Barrister Blair stood there, with more guards than she could count lining the hall. Constant looked down, supremely embarrassed.

"Mistress Ridgely?"

"Sir," she said to the floor.

"I have come to escort you to the sister ship, *The Destiny*. You are being moved. I would suggest no untoward reaction over it."

"I understand," she mumbled.

"This is for the duration of the voyage. You will be allowed to see your children on a contingency basis."

The floor blurred. "Contingent on what?" she asked.

"On your cooperation. If you would follow me?"

Constant squared her shoulders and lifted her chin. They were segregating her and withholding her babies. She should've expected it. She followed Blair to the railing and sat calmly in the large, woven basket that lowered her into a waiting skiff. She didn't look at anyone as she took a seat on one of the benches. The barrister was accompanying her, along with a retinue of guards. No one said a word.

Four rowers moved the skiff along swiftly, and Constant watched her own hands sway on her lap as they neared the ship that was her new home. Almost as an afterthought, she looked up at the wooden hull. *The*

Destiny was smaller than the ship they'd left, but not by much. There were cannon holes along the sides, something she hadn't seen on the flagship.

Constant glanced back once at the ship that held her heart and her babies. When she turned back, she caught Blair's gaze on her. She couldn't prevent the longing that had been on her face. She knew he'd seen it. She looked back at her entwined hands.

She probably should feel grateful to him. It was going to be akin to cutting her own heart from her bosom to leap into the water when the time came. This enforced separation might actually help her resolve. She set her jaw and looked back up, doing her best to give Barrister Blair an expression devoid of any emotion whatsoever.

Constant rode in the basket from the skiff onto a deck that looked almost exactly like the one she'd just left. She ignored all the looks coming her way. There seemed to be men everywhere. They didn't appear to know the significance of her arrival, or that she was, in essence, Lord Ballanclaire's mistress. She intercepted more than a few of them looking in her direction before she settled on watching the polished deck beneath her.

"Come along, mistress. Your berth has been prepared."

Constant kept her vision squarely on the back of Blair's heel, doing her best to ignore the reaction taking place all about her. It felt as though every sailor stopped what he was doing to stare.

Maybe they did know her place. That was disconcerting.

She'd been given the forward cabin, reserved for the highest class of passenger. Constant stood in the doorway and waited for her heart to calm. The white spread on her new bedstead was of quilted satin. The porthole was overly large, allowing sunlight to stream in. There was a large rug between her and the bed, a mirrored stand with ewer, a large armoire, and what she could only assume was a maid. She almost turned back around.

"There has been some mistake," she said when all Barrister Blair did was stand there.

"Yes, there has. Unfortunately, it was His Lordship making it. This suite is yours for the duration of the voyage. Your luggage will follow shortly. I hope you'll be comfortable. This is Lucilla. She's to see to your needs."

The maid, a small woman with a well-lined face and a round shape, bobbed into a curtsy before her. Constant's eyes went from the woman to Blair and back.

"My needs?" she asked.

"You're to start with the basics. Lucilla has instructions to see to your skin. That is our number one priority. I doona' ken what you've been doing to it, but nae lady of the realm has skin resembling a tortoiseshell."

Constant's eyebrows lifted.

He smiled. It didn't reach his eyes.

"We are going to turn you into a lady. Barrister MacVale and I are agreed on this. We canna' take you in front of His Grace unless you possess the rudimentary skills. Well, we can, but it will na' assist our cause."

Constant looked down again. What could she say?

"Lucilla? This is the lady we spoke of earlier."

Barrister Blair spoke in Spanish. That was surprising, not only for his ability but the ease with which he spoke.

The maid nodded. Constant watched.

"I wish her bathed, dressed, and ready to be presented at eight."

Barrister Blair turned back to Constant. He had another disdainful smile on his fat face. Once again, it didn't reach his eyes. Constant waited.

"I have given instructions to your maid. She's Spanish, but speaks rudimentary English if you need to communicate with her."

"*Gracias*," Constant answered in the same language, and then continued. "But it shouldn't be a problem for us, *señor.*"

"You speak Spanish?"

Constant regarded him for a few moments. It was rather entertaining to discomfit him. She smiled in the same emotionless fashion he used. "Yes. I do. I read. I write. I speak fair Spanish. And I'm versed in French," she replied.

"French?" He choked on the word.

"*Oui,*" she answered.

"I had no idea." His eyes were round.

"Somehow that doesn't surprise me, sir. You had me dismissed on sight as a backward woman, with no learning and no culture and little in morals. You are wrong."

"But this is excellent!" He clapped his hands. "It makes my job so much easier. I canna' wait to apprise Clayton. He was halfway leery of my plan, because of the language barrier."

"Your . . . plan?"

"We will speak of it when the time is right. For the moment, you need to concentrate on one thing. One."

"I already know what you require of me," Constant replied quietly.

"We need you to become a lady. Better yet, if you could become a peeress without equal, a virtual queen. That is what we need from you. Can you do that?"

Constant's mouth was open. She had to command it to close. "I don't understand," she whispered.

"All in good time, my dear. All in good time." The change in him was remarkable. "You doona' ken the Ballanclaires. The duke is arrogant, conceited, pompous, and presumptuous. His wife is worse. They will na' accept anything less for their daughter-in-law. Trust me."

"They won't accept me, then," Constant replied in the silence that followed Barrister Blair's description.

"We must make certain they've nae choice. Enough said. Lucilla!" He turned to the maid who jumped at the sound of her name. Constant guessed it was an exaggeration that the woman spoke rudimentary English, for Lucilla looked as surprised and confused as Constant felt. "You are to prepare this lady to be presented. I will call for her at eight—"

"Presented?" Constant interrupted. "Before I agree, I would like to know for what, please?"

"Oh, that. It's the term for preparing oneself for the dinner occasion. Everything a lady does is in the form of a presentation. From the moment of awakening, to the time you reach your bed again. It will encompass all your time. You'll see."

She did see. One week became two, then three. Constant lived in long gloves that reached her shoulders, to hold the creams against her skin. She wasn't allowed outside except with a parasol, since the dusting of freckles across the bridge of her nose branded her a commoner the moment anyone saw them. She lived with a thin board strapped to her spine in order to correct her posture, and during the day she wore a corset about her midriff to create the proper shape of a woman. She suspected it was more to make her breathless and thus unable to speak above a whisper, which the two barristers had to lean closer to hear.

Through it all she was denied contact with her children. Constant only brought it up once. Both men had exchanged glances and promised she would see them once she mastered the art of dining. Art of dining? It was more a theatrical play. Constant had never seen such an array of silver or a stacking of plates such as she faced each and every meal. Then she was instructed on the proper etiquette. Never touch anything until the hostess has been served and has picked up her own silverware. Never speak loudly, or across the table. Converse softly with the diner either to your left or your right. Never take more than three bites of any course. That was a ridiculous requirement, but with her board firmly in place and her stomach sealed into a corset, she couldn't hold more than three bites anyway.

She had it mastered by the end of her first week, and then the requirement was changed. She could see her children when she accomplished a courtly presentation, with a curtsy and then a slight nod. Constant knew the game, then. She wasn't going to be allowed any contact with her children, Kameron, or her past.

Unless the Ballanclaires decreed it so.

So the first week limped into the second, and then the third, and before Constant knew it, she had only two weeks left. She hung on to the rail, holding her cloak tight against the chill, while her gaze roved the bobbing and weaving decks of Kameron's ship. She didn't see him. She never did. That didn't stop her looking and searching. She sighed, nodded to Lucilla, and walked across the sway of *The Destiny*'s deck until she faced the opposite side to look for the phantom ship that both barristers had told her she was imagining.

Constant squinted at the encroaching dark gray clouds, catching sight of what could be a ship, or a bird, and she hugged her cloak closer, sealing out the wind. She was only allowed outside twice, for a total of exactly twenty minutes, every day. Blair and MacVale told her that any longer and she'd destroy what Lucilla had accomplished with her skin.

It was such a waste of time. She was beginning to

wonder if the plan was to change her into a creature of pomp and leisure and then settle her among the Spaniards, or even the French. Constant wrinkled her brow, although she'd been nagged at not to. Every afternoon was devoted to Spanish and then French, until she could speak both fairly fluently, with an aristocratic tone that was accompanied by an upward tilt of her nose. And all of it came with a breathless quality that both men approved of, but was really owing to the corset.

A mast silhouetted itself on the horizon, a bolt of lightning revealing the perfection of shape. Constant watched until it faded. She knew there was a ship out there! It had been paralleling their course for weeks. Both her mentors told her she was imagining things. The last time she mentioned it, they hadn't let her out of the cabin for a full day. A full day when she couldn't even look for Kameron. She wasn't risking that again.

"Come, *señorita*. It is time to return inside." Lucilla spoke at her side. "You heard the sailor's warning."

Constant turned her head. "*Uno momento?*"

"*Sí*, although I'll regret it with this wind and the coming rain. You heard them."

"I know." Constant turned from the railing. "We're expecting a storm. A big one. They've been waiting for it. They've been planning for it. They've been expecting it. I just don't know why."

"It was a red sky this morning. You heard."

"*Sí*," Constant replied, although that wasn't what she'd meant. Lucilla hadn't any aptitude for intrigue. Otherwise she'd have noticed the barristers checking conditions throughout the day. Constant had overheard Barrister MacVale at luncheon, speaking in whispers about wind direction and speed, and when she'd been at her porthole earlier, she'd seen Blair lowering a pole into the water over and over again, measuring wave heights.

All of which was as mystifying as their denial of the other ship.

"Now, *señorita*?"

Constant turned back, balancing herself with both hands on the railing to get back to her cabin. She would welcome the four walls about her for the rest of the day, she guessed, although it was beginning to resemble a cell the longer she stayed in it. It was luxurious, but a prison nonetheless.

Lucilla needed help to latch the lamp onto the ceiling beam. Constant forced herself not to interfere as one of the men Lucilla had called for help assisted. It was getting difficult to keep her balance and she finally sat on the bed for stability. The man gave her a sidelong glance before leaving, and Constant reddened. Over the weeks it had happened again and again. She guessed the cause. They knew who she was, and why she was here.

She was Kameron's mistress.

"Bah! These men! They have no refinement. No elegance. No civility. No Spaniard would make interest so apparent. Why, if we were in my native Castillion, you would see much more emphasis on courtly gestures and subtle glances."

"What men?"

"What men? All of them!" Lucilla clucked her tongue before putting both hands on her hips. "They see a beautiful woman and they cannot keep their tongues in their mouths, or their eyes to themselves."

"When?"

"Do not tell me you have not noticed. I have seen them, and I have said nothing, but it is hard for me. I see them all the time. Everywhere you go, and every time you leave the cabin. I try to keep you inside as much as I can, and still they gawk when they see you. They are pigs. These Scotsmen!"

"The men . . . gawk?" Constant stumbled on the word.

"Not just gawk—they leer, they ogle. It is deplorable! No Spaniard would be caught doing so. They are much more subtle if they see a woman they desire."

"But why would they do such a thing?"

Lucilla stopped her tirade and stared at Constant. "Because you are on deck. That is why."

"Me?"

"Of course, you. They certainly are not acting that way over Lucilla. I assure you."

"The men . . . desire . . . *me*? But why?"

Constant was imagining this. She had to be. She was having an insane conversation in a wildly swaying room, slivers of gaslight sliding back and forth, with a woman who couldn't know what she was saying.

Lucilla huffed out a breath of disgust. "You never look in a mirror. I have waited upon you and served you, and never once have I seen you look at yourself. You avoid it."

"I already know what I look like," Constant answered.

"You know what you used to look like. I think you will be surprised. You have not the first idea of how to be vain. It is a welcome thing, and yet unbelievable at the same time."

"You can't be saying these things to me. I am foolish to listen."

"You are very beautiful, mistress. More so now than when you first arrived, and that was impressive. Your skin has become alabaster smooth. You have been blessed with glorious hair that has streaks colored like the darkest of red sunsets through it. You have very blue eyes, and dark lashes that require nothing to enhance them, and let us not forget the most obvious. You have a womanly shape that is beyond compare. I have served other ladies, but never one so fair. That is why the men stare and gawk and ogle and fall over their own tongues."

Constant stared. "I am those things?"

Lucilla tossed up her hands and then pointed at the mirror above the ewer. "If you can walk to it, look for yourself. I still have much work to do."

She opened the armoire and bent down to pull a trunk out. Constant watched as it looked like every dress she owned was pulled out of the armoire, folded, and settled into the trunk.

"What . . . are you doing?" she asked.

"Preparing for the storm. I have my orders."

"You have to pack everything for the storm?"

"You will be lucky if I do not have to strap you to your bed. Speaking of which, you might as well begin preparing for such. There won't be further lessons tonight. I have been told."

"Strap me to my bed?"

"Haven't you felt the waves? Heard the wind and the rain? It is getting difficult to talk in here, the sound is so loud."

"But why would my things need to be packed?"

Lucilla shrugged. "I do not know the why of such things. I only do as I'm told. I received my orders. They are strange, but I don't question them. You could have, if you wished to."

"When was this?"

"You look when you are on deck, but you see nothing and hear less. The thin one told me of it. Every hand that is capable is required on deck tonight. Anyone without business outside their cabin must stay inside. Stepping out may mean being swept overboard and into the sea. I have been through these storms. They are not pleasant. There. I have finished. If you will stand, I will unhook—"

Lucilla's words were cut off when the door was wrenched open and slammed against the wall, then sprang back into the man who stood there, a seemingly ceaseless stream of water running onto the floor. Her maid screamed. Constant didn't have access to that much air. She gasped. It was the most she was capable of in the corset.

Chapter Twenty-Three

"Constant? Come here."

"But, Kameron—"

"Dismiss your maid, and come here. Now. I am beyond argument."

She didn't doubt it. In the slivers of illumination cast from her lamp, she could see his chest rising and falling with exertion, his jaw was clenched, and he was angry. Constant shivered.

"You know they won't let us—"

"They? What *they*? I have just evaded a hundred *theys*. I've swallowed my fill of ocean and single-handedly rowed myself to the wrong ship twice. You are my wife, and I've tired of being held prisoner in my own life! Dismiss your maid and come here. I am not saying another damned word."

Constant turned to Lucilla. The maid was looking at Kameron with the same openmouthed expression all women probably had when they first saw him.

"Lucilla?" She had to say it twice to get the maid's attention and the second time was sharper. "Lucilla!"

"Mistress?"

"You may leave now. I will not require your services until morn."

"But, mistress—"

"You dare argue with me?"

"This man—"

"This man is my husband."

That got her a wide-eyed stare. Constant waited for the information to sink in.

"This giant . . . he is Lord Ballanclaire?"

"*Sí,*" Constant replied.

"The duke's heir?"

Constant nodded.

"Oh my. Oh dear. They did not tell me."

"Tell you what?"

"That he was this immense, nor so . . . so masculine. Nor so handsome. My goodness, no wonder you have been so sad. The man is beautiful. No. That word is not sufficient. He has the countenance of an angel. But he does not look so angelic now, does he? He looks and acts more like a Spaniard, what with breaking doors down to get to his lady and looking as if he actually swam over to do so. I am very impressed."

"Constant? What are you saying? Why has na' she left?" Kameron interrupted them.

Constant looked across at him. He obviously did not understand Spanish. "We haven't gotten that far, Kam. She is still amazed, I'm afraid."

"At what?"

"You. She is in raptures over your handsomeness, your size, and the forcefulness of your appearance."

"Oh, for the love of God!"

Constant snorted in amusement as Kam actually looked away. She couldn't see his expression because of the haphazard lighting, but she guessed that he was embarrassed.

"I do not know what you say, but he does not look the type to argue, *señora*. You'd best save your breath. You will need it, I think. I have orders about this, but I can give you one hour. I will return then. I will tell no one."

"One hour?" Constant repeated. "But it is near eve, a massive storm is brewing, and we've no lessons. Surely you can give us more than one hour. Please?"

Lucilla looked from one to the other. Kam had lowered his jaw and sucked in on his cheeks as he watched them with hooded eyes. Every time the light snaked to where he stood, feet planted apart to keep his balance and hands on his hips, Constant felt the shivers again. She barely kept from wrapping her arms about herself.

"Very well, *señora*. I will give you two hours. I cannot do more, I am afraid. I have orders. I would not waste time, either. He does not look the patient type. He is also soaked through and needs that clothing removed. Once you have taken it from him, knock on my door. I will see it wrung out and hung. It will not be dry, but that is the best I can do."

Constant's face was flaming.

"Now what is she saying?"

"She wants your clothing."

Kam's head shot up. "What?"

Constant chuckled. "She will see it hung out and dried. She won't tell anyone of your presence here." She didn't say anything about the two hours.

"Remind me to double her salary when I'm duke," he replied. "She's worth every shilling. What is it now? I certainly hope you haven't agreed to see me stripped out of them while she waits."

"Oh no. That pleasure is all mine. Lucilla?"

She turned to the woman and spoke in Spanish again. There was a door to another chamber where the maid slept. Constant waited until the door closed before turning the key. She left the key in the lock, to make it difficult for Lucilla to see through the keyhole, if she were so inclined.

"Well?" Kam demanded.

Constant turned and looked across the crazily swaying room at where he still stood in the doorway. "Well, what?"

"You were given an order to come here. I'm still waiting."

"Oh."

Constant started walking, stopping after each step to regain her balance as the ship tilted. The light was swaying from one side to the other, showing first where Kameron stood, then the bed. Then Kameron. Then the bed. Over and over, like a pendulum of desire, want, and promise.

Kameron wasn't standing still. Every time the light touched him, he'd moved. First to shut and bolt the door, then to unfasten the large cloak that covered him and drop it at his feet. A dark glitter of moisture trailed from it in a zigzag fashion with each roll of the ship.

He slid the buttons of his doublet as she neared, never taking his eyes from hers. The floor was still weaving and roiling beneath her, but she was more sure-footed and steadier the closer she got to him. In the dark his eyes looked like shimmering black agates, surrounded by more shadowed black. His last button was undone. Constant stood less than a yard from him as he pulled his arms from the sleeveless outer garment, dropping it onto the cloak at his feet. He wore a wide-sleeved, broadcloth shirt beneath it. The material was plastered to his body, defining every bit of him. Constant stared and had to consciously command herself to gather one breath, and then another.

Kameron began unbuttoning his cuffs. Constant moved closer, reaching out for him. She gasped when he caught her hands and brought them to his lips, holding them with cold hands that shuddered along with the rest of his body.

"You're freezing cold," she told him. "Why didn't you say something?"

He raised both brows, softening the black shadows around his eyes, and then he grinned. "We're in the Atlantic Ocean, love. The water resembles ice. I should ken. I was out in it."

"You shouldn't have risked so much. You shouldn't be here. We'll be punished again. I should make you go."

"You doona' want me to stay?"

"I—I—" Her voice stopped. How was she to answer that?

"If you're going to lie, my love, let me remind you to first remember rule number one."

It was Constant's turn to shake. She tried to tell herself it was due to the temperature of his lips as he spoke the words against her knuckles. But his hands were warming the longer she held on to him, and his shivers seemed to be easing. She knew it wasn't anything to do with any chill.

"I like your new clothing, love. Puts everything on display. I'm na' sure that will be a good idea in polite company, however. In fact, I'm certain of it. Your gowns will be sewn from thick velvet in the future . . . double layered. Remind me of that, will you?"

"What?"

"Either you're cold, or you're just as needy as I am. Tell me you're cold. I'd be interested in hearing that prevarication."

Constant wasn't remotely cold. She knew what he was talking about now, especially as the light showed exactly where he was looking every time it reached his face. The corset pushed everything out where it was eye-catching as well as unseemly. She'd complained and reddened just about every time she was strapped into it. Those times were as nothing to how her face flamed now. In fact, her entire body was on fire.

"Kameron," she whispered.

He shut his eyes when he heard it, feathered a breath across her fingertips, and released her. Then he opened his eyes, a stray beam of lamplight illuminating the golden brown before it moved away.

Constant felt the reaction clear to where her ankles and feet were strapped mercilessly into pointy-toed boots. Then the shivers were climbing, stealing up her spine and causing a riot of gooseflesh at the back of her neck.

"Doona' move, love. Just stand there and watch."

"Why?"

"You really need a reason?"

That wasn't exactly an answer. Constant dropped her hands to her sides as Kameron went back to unfastening a cuff. She couldn't prevent her glance from roving to where he'd released one sleeve and then lifted the other arm. The sodden material showed every nuance of him as he moved. She sucked in her lower lip as she watched him.

Then he was unfastening his shirt, stopping to peel the opening wider with every released button. Constant found her breath catching with every motion. Kameron had the strangest expression as he pulled the bottom of his shirt from beneath his belt.

Constant released her lower lip with a sucking sound. She watched as a shudder ran through him. The final button was undone, and he stopped. Constant kept her eyes on his, although she could see the V-shaped opening he'd created, allowing her a glimpse of that rippled, muscled belly and chest every time the light allowed. It was almost torturous to try to ignore it, she decided.

"Can I ask you something?" he asked softly.

She nodded.

"Will you answer truthfully?"

"You will know . . . if I don't, I think," she answered. The only voice she had left was the breathless whisper. It wasn't the corset's fault this time. It was Kameron.

"In the loft, when you shaved me . . ."

He was talking as he twisted the shirttails, and the high-pitched ringing in her ears was making it difficult to hear. Constant blinked, swallowed, and forced herself to listen to what he was asking.

". . . why did you do it?"

"I had to get the tar off," she replied.

It was probably a smile curving his lips, but he was doing his best to keep it from showing. Constant's brows drew together.

"You didn't have to shave my chest. True?"

She caught her cry as he moved his fingers to rub them down the opening he'd created, making certain she knew what he spoke of.

"I—" Her voice stopped.

"Yes?" he prompted.

"Uh . . . I . . . You're very impressive, Kameron."

"And?"

"And . . . I wanted to be able . . . to see all of it."

It was definitely a smile, as white glinted off his teeth.

"In that event, you're forgiven," he replied, and split the fabric apart.

He peeled the wet shirt off and tossed the garment atop the pile at his feet. He was covered with mounds of muscle, valleys of shadow-molded strength, and not a bit of hair hid any of it. There were also two raw-looking spots on either side of his chest, just below his armpits. Constant's eyes widened as she saw them.

"What . . . have they done to you?" she asked.

"Oh, those? Just a little reminder of my place in life."

"Your place?"

"I'm a prisoner, love, just as you are. I gave my word I'd come for you. I dinna' stay away of my own free will. I had to be forced. I have a bit of trouble staying in my room. These marks are from the bonds to keep me there."

"They hurt you? Oh, Kameron."

Constant felt the tears hovering near the surface. She'd known he shouldn't be here, although every part of her balked at the thought that he might leave. He was going to earn far worse treatment if he was caught.

"You're na' about to cry, are you? Please. I dinna' risk a drowning in saltwater to reach your side and watch you cry. Besides, I've been through worse. You ken. You were there."

"I know, but . . . I can't believe it. You're the lord and master, aren't you?"

"Oh, rest assured, I will be. I think they're verra aware of that. That explains their largesse to me."

"This is largesse?" she repeated.

"They lined my straps with padded silk. It does na' change much. Straps are straps."

"You shouldn't be here. I won't see you punished again. Please go. Now."

"You truly want me to?"

Constant tried to lie. She forced her eyes not to look him over, and not to guess at the parts of him he'd yet to display, and not to shiver with the remembered ecstasy of being clasped against him.

"Yes," she whispered.

"You're a lousy liar, love. Always were."

He stepped into the space in front of her, kicking his discarded clothing aside. Constant lifted her hands, put her palms against hard sinew and chilled flesh, and fell into the embrace. She couldn't help it.

The tears wouldn't stay away as he enfolded her in his arms. She shuddered with suppressing the weeping, pressing her forehead into the center of his chest, below his throat. She could hear his heart beating, and held her breath to listen.

"Oh, Constant, love. We should try to forgive them. We really should."

"Never."

"But they doona' ken how it is. I canna' fault them. Orders are orders and I doona' have the capacity to make them understand, although I do try. I'm fair certain Blair and MacVale tire of hearing it every time I open my mouth."

"Know how what is?"

"A love such as you and I share. True love. The kind poets write sonnets of, minstrels of old lamented over, and men gladly go to their deaths for. That's what we have. There are nae straps that can hold it at bay, either. There is naught that would. Life is na' worth living if I have to do it apart from you. They doona' understand because they've never felt it. I pity them, actually."

"Oh, Kam . . . eron."

Constant almost got his name out before the emotion overtook her, leaving her sobbing against him. Through it all, Kameron held her, swaying with each roll of the ship, his hands at first holding her sides, then caressing her all over until he stopped at the board at her back.

She caught a ragged sob as he knocked on her back-board with his knuckles.

"This feels like wood. Please doona' tell me they've got you strapped to a board."

She nodded.

"By the saints! At least I only had bonds to keep me

from escaping. You have to wear yours on your back! I swear on all I hold holy, every one of these men will reap the penalty. I swear it."

"It's not punishment. It's to improve my posture."

He pulled back in surprise. "Why? There's naught wrong with it that I can see."

"They're trying to make me into a stiff-backed duchess."

"Truly? I may have to rethink the tortures I was planning for MacVale and Blair. I may even have to consider returning to my prison without being forced. Speaking of which, we still haven't finished getting my clothing to your maid, have we? Lucilla, wasn't it? She's Spanish?"

Constant nodded.

"I recognized the language, even if I failed to learn it. You're verra good at it. But I recollect that from the loft. French, too. Right?"

"Yes," she replied.

"See, I dinna' spend every moment pleasuring my eyes and dreaming of this body of yours, although it may have felt like it. I listened to you, too."

"Kameron!"

"What? Please doona' tell me you have nae notion of what I speak, for I'll not believe a word of it. You ken exactly what I refer to. You were born to the art of passion. It does na' have to be learned. You only have to close your eyes."

"Kam—"

"Close them and listen. I'll prove it."

Constant did as he asked, although she made certain she had a hand firmly about his upper arm. The roiling of the deck wasn't conducive to standing securely with both eyes open; it was frightening and awkward with eyes closed.

"I need you to listen, Constant. Just listen. It'll be easier if you are na' watching while I say it. Trust me.

MacVale thinks me stupefied with it, and he's heard but a portion. You might think me crazed, too. So be it. Maybe I am."

"I don't understand."

He sighed, and blew the breath across her nose. "I love you. I do. 'Tis of an immense nature. The love I feel for you is akin to Homer's for his creation—the enchantress, Circe. It's the same as Romeo's devotion to his Juliet. My love is right up there with the emotions the composers bring to life with every note. You are the missing piece of my life. The soul of it. The heart. The fire. Everything I reach for. If I have a dream, you are at the root of it. I close my eyes and feel you . . . I can almost smell you. You are the center of every thought I have."

"Kameron, please." Constant spoke to stop him, but her voice trembled.

"You can try to stay me. 'Twill na' work. I torture myself with this almost every waking moment and most of my sleeping ones. I've been strapped to my bed with little else to do. My days are filled with thoughts of you. My nights are torment. You have to ken it. You have a body made for caresses . . . my caresses. I find myself shaking simply at the thought of taking every stitch from you. It may take me all night to do so, I think."

"But why?"

"To prolong the moment, love. You would na' believe how I spend every day. Well . . . maybe you would, but I intend to make certain that I have even more to dream of for the duration of the next two weeks."

"Kameron!"

"You think me wicked? Well, come and be wicked with me. But doona' open your eyes just yet."

"Why not?"

"Because I was strapped at the hips and across the

lower legs, too. 'Tis na' a pretty sight. The saltwater I just bathed with stung, too."

Her eyes flew open. "They put straps on you there, too?"

He chuckled down at her. "'Twas my own fault. I would na' lie passively as they expected. How could I? I'd promised you, and I'm na' an easy man to dissuade. I'd as lief say these are wounds from fighting and it took a dozen men to subdue me, but it would be a lie."

Her eyebrows rose.

"It only took one. With a club. They cheated."

"They hit you? Oh, Kameron, does that hurt, too?"

"If you will take my mind off the pain like you did last time, I will admit to it in every excruciating detail. So, what say you?"

"Take your skirt off and let me see."

"Kilt, love. Kilt. Please. This here is a kilt. Or *feileadh-breacan*. 'Tis na' a skirt. It's a kilt. You ken?" He corrected her, but he was grinning as he started unwinding the cloth.

Chapter Twenty-Four

Lucilla didn't hide her desire to peek. Constant had to give her that. Any woman would have done the same. Kam was hidden behind the open door of the armoire, his feet, lower legs, and upper body visible. He rested his chin on his arms, which were folded over the top of the door, while he waited. Constant watched as Lucilla looked over what the swaying lamp revealed, licked her lips, and then sighed.

"Here are my husband's clothes." Constant held out the sodden bundle, trying not to get wet. It was futile. Her thin, damp muslin gown clung to her curves.

"*Sí, señora,*" Lucilla whispered, but didn't move.

"You are to press the water out as best you can, and hang them."

"*Sí, señora,*" she said again.

"You are to do it now, Lucilla."

The woman finally moved her gaze from Kameron's area of the room and opened her arms to accept the bundle of clothing.

"This will take some time, mistress."

Constant shrugged. "I still have my two hours left, or most of them. That is enough time."

"His Lordship brought the sea in with him. Does he need toweling off, too?"

"I have it under control, Lucilla. You may leave."

"You do not wish me to assist? He will be chilled if he does not dry off well. I will be honored to assist."

"Oh, I'm certain you would. He is very handsome, isn't he?" Constant couldn't resist. She almost bit her own tongue for saying it, though.

"*Madre de Dios!* He is a god. I cannot believe such perfection in a man, of all creatures. If I had a man such as he . . ." Her voice trailed off, leaving it to Constant's imagination.

"What is taking so long? It's na' exactly warm over here," Kameron called from the other side of the chamber.

"It's your fault," Constant replied over her shoulder.

"Mine? How do you come up with that?"

"Lucilla is in raptures over you, Kameron. Perhaps you shouldn't display so much of yourself next time you visit me."

"Constant, I'm warning you."

Constant smiled wryly. "He isn't a patient man, Lucilla. Thank you for taking care of his clothing. I will call for you." Constant was holding the door open, and when that didn't work, she had to turn Lucilla and give her a push. She was rolling her eyes by then. Kameron had warned her. He really *was* desired by any and all women.

"Damn it! This is ridiculous! I am a married man."

The armoire door slammed as she turned the lock. Constant swallowed before turning around. The reply died in her throat. Kameron's nakedness was caressed by the light every time it swung over him. He had his arms folded across his chest; feet planted apart; his hair tucked behind his ears, leaving it to curl slightly on the mounds of his chest; and his chin lowered to glare at her—and those were the parts of him she managed to look at without blushing.

Constant caught her breath at the sight. "You may be married, Kameron . . . b-but you're still the most handsome man I've ever seen. I can't fault the others for noticing. I can only join them."

"You really think so? Even with my scars? My deformities?"

"What scars? Where?"

He turned around, flaring his back. Constant's eyes widened at the myriad of jagged, brownish-looking stripes across his skin. She only wished it detracted from him a little. He was still handsome, muscled, and very much naked.

"The honey-herb salve didn't work?" she whispered. "I'm so sorry." She was, too. Her eyes filled with tears.

"The Brits doona' stock it, love. Is it that bad?"

"No," she replied, but knew he'd hear the tears she was holding back.

"Damn it, Constant. I didn't escape to make you cry. That's the last thing I want. Believe me."

He turned back. She watched him wince before he quickly stifled it.

"Oh, Kameron, where does it hurt?"

"Forgive me. Wrong leg."

She ran her eyes over his legs, trying to swallow her nervousness. She couldn't see a thing wrong with his legs; they were perfectly proportioned, very muscled, and without one hair marring them from his ankles to his . . .

Constant gasped and looked away.

"I ken. I should na' have brought it up. One leg is shorter than the other, and na' as muscled. Result of wearing a splint for as long as I had to. You can look aside. It's all right."

"Oh, Kameron."

"Constant Ballan, doona' dare pity me! I would na' stand for it in that little cramped parlor, and I definitely will na' now. You hear me?"

She forced herself to look directly at him. He thought she pitied him? With every bit of him displayed every time the dim, golden light slithered across him?

She took a deep breath. "Pity?" she asked. Louder, she repeated, "Pity? Why would I feel such a thing? And why would you believe it so readily? You are, without a doubt, the most beautiful man I've ever seen, Kameron Geoffrey Bennion Alistair . . . uh, Gannett, and whatever-other-names-you-have, Ballan!" Constant stopped to suck in more air. "Pity? What scarring you have only makes you more dangerous-looking, and you don't need any more of that! As for any deformity—to either leg—let me tell you, I can't see it. I only see legs that need some hair on them!" She had to stop to breathe again. "I told you I think you're the most handsome man born. It's still true. Pity you? I have to shove the women away. Pity? I can't believe the stupidity of the word!"

Her chest fell as she used the last of her breath to finish her rant.

His lips twisted. The next time the light caught him, he was grinning. Then, he was moving. Constant seemed rooted to the spot as she waited, her breathing more rapid and shallow as he neared.

"No, Kameron . . . wait—"

She didn't get anything else out as he reached her, pulling her so rapidly into his embrace, she stumbled there. Then he was stealing her breath away with the pressure of his lips against hers. Then he was sliding his mouth across her cheek, teasing her neck, tempting an earlobe.

Constant was trembling. It was far shy of his shaking, though.

"You're cold," she managed to whisper.

He chuckled, and the parts of him that she was pressed against moved with it. Her eyes flew open at the pressure.

"Na' even remotely, love," he answered, whispering against her ear.

"But—but—"

"But naught."

"Then . . . why—"

He bent his neck, tickled his tongue along the edge of her jaw, and Constant lost her question in a sigh. He molded his lips to her chin, moving it upward until she faced the darkness of the ceiling.

"Why . . . what, love?"

She gulped. Kameron moved his lips to toy with the slight movement in her throat.

"Kam . . . ?"

"Hmm?" he answered, moving his mouth to the indentation at the base of her throat before pulling her closer. His hands reached around her, where she could feel them fingering the corset encircling her waist. He groaned against her skin. "The board has to go first," he whispered.

"Board?" Constant repeated. She couldn't think. She could barely remember to breathe.

"I've better ways to improve your posture. Starting with running my fingers along your spine and feeling you tremble. That sounds nice."

He was fitting word to deed, although the only hint she had that he was undoing her hooks was the feel of release at her bosom. She couldn't feel a bit of it along her back, but knew when he finished as his fingers slid beneath the wood and supported each shoulder, curving her more fully against him.

"It's polished wood," he said.

"I know."

"It was carved for this purpose? They make such an instrument of torture?"

"I don't know."

"I'll na' allow one near our daughters."

"We only have . . . one daughter," Constant panted in reply.

It was difficult to keep her mind on what he was saying while he untied the ribbons keeping her backboard in place. She felt it give along her ribs as each one was freed. He slid the piece away from her, dropping it with a thud of wood on wood as it hit the decking at their feet.

"We've but one daughter thus far, darling. I fully intend to correct that deficiency. I have been so warned, you know."

"Warned?"

"Save for the occasional male, your family births daughters. Lots and lots of them. I recollect hearing that. And 'tis my bound duty to give them to you. I fully intend to do so, too."

"But, Kameron, I—"

"Doona' worry, love. I ken the rules. I ken the punishment, too. Trust me. My entire body kens. It's na' likely while you still suckle the twins, anyhow."

"How—?"

"How do I ken such a thing? I'd answer, but I canna' recall. Some woman, in another lifetime, must have told me."

She stiffened. "I didn't mean that."

"If you're going to get all unyielding and argumentative every time I lose my wits and speak without thinking, I'll just have to keep my mouth busy on other things."

"I didn't—"

He didn't let her finish that either, as his lips caught hers again, draining any desire to talk or do anything other than cling to him. She wasn't standing on the floor any longer, and she couldn't recall when her feet left it.

"Oh, God. Oh, love. Oh . . . Constant."

He was breathing the words against her mouth, filling her with such emotion there wasn't anything about her that felt unyielding or remotely argumentative. He lifted her, balancing her with his hands hooked beneath her armpits, his elbows taut against her sides. Constant's hands fell to his shoulders as she was held above him, her eyes wide and staring as he rocked back and forth with the ship's motion beneath her.

"Kameron, we're going to fall," she said.

"You think it possible to fall any further, love?"

"That's not what I meant."

"I ken verra well what you meant, and you're going to have to learn to trust me." He slid her back down him, closed his eyes, tightened his entire frame, and then a glimmer of what had to be pain arced across his face.

Constant held her breath and waited. It seemed to take forever until he opened his eyes, although it was only four sways of the lamp. She stood, confined by his arms and watching through a mist of tears until he met her gaze.

"You are more beautiful than my dreams, love, and that is difficult to believe," he whispered.

"You're in pain," she answered.

"What?"

She didn't imagine the surprise on his face. She blinked, and the moisture in one eye became a tear, wending its way to her mouth. "You can't hide it forever," she answered.

"I am na' in pain, love. Well, mayhap I am, but 'tis the kind that's most enjoyable. I guarantee it."

"You cannot lie to me, Kameron."

"I doona' lie. All right, I lie sometimes." He sighed, and her body moved with it. "Verra well, I lie a lot. But right now, I'm telling the truth. I am na' in pain. Anywhere. I canna' feel anything except my wife in my arms, my body giving me trouble over it, and a center of warmth radiating from where I have her clasped. If that is pain, God but grant me more of it."

"You winced. I saw it."

He smiled, and his eyebrows moved wickedly up and down several times. "I keep forgetting how innocent you are. It does na' seem possible, when you've the body designed by my deepest desires, but so be it. I am na' in pain, Constant, love. I am stifling myself. It is na' easy."

"Stifling . . . yourself?"

He cleared his throat. "Perhaps I'd be better served getting more of you unwrapped."

"Kameron!"

He looked a bit sheepish, although the expression was gone the next time the light touched him. He wasn't meeting her eyes, though.

"You've a corset on?" he finally asked.

"They're imparting the proper shape to me. It has something to do with an hourglass. I wasn't listening. I detest it. It puts . . . uh, certain . . . uh, *things* . . . out where they shouldn't be. I don't need that sort of enhancement."

He was laughing without sound. Constant could tell. Both of his hands began a strange rhythm up her spine and back down. She shivered with it.

"You are right, love. You doona' need enhancement. Of any kind. You're too much woman already. Damn."

"What?" she asked.

"It's a front fastener, just my luck."

"What does that mean?"

"Lower your arms." His voice was husky.

She did what he requested, sliding them down his body. Constant's fingers meandered from his shoulders, over each hump of muscle in his chest and then down his belly, trilling over the ropes of muscle before she reached his hips. Once there, she alternately squeezed and caressed the sides of his thighs before she moved her hands to her own sides.

The look she'd assumed was pain was back on his face, and he had his lips pursed, breathing rapidly. Her eyes widened. She knew what he meant now about stifling himself. It was obvious by the stab of his rod in the vicinity of her abdomen. She waited, trembling, until he regained control.

"Jesu', Constant, but you're a vixen."

"Was it this way in the loft?"

"A thousand times worse and a hundred times easier."

His hands moved, sliding her sleeves off her arms. She helped him, lifting as he reached her wrists, in order to pull her hands through. Constant didn't move her eyes from his face, although she could see where his glance kept going. It was having the same sensitizing effect on her nipples that it always did.

"Oh, Constant! What you do to me! You have nae idea, do you?"

She smiled. "I . . . have some idea, Kameron."

He looked up at that, and there was no stopping the roar of sound she heard as his black-shadowed eyes met hers for the barest hint of time before the lantern light moved away again.

Then she was crushed against him, the thin lawn of her chemise almost nonexistent against the heat of his rib cage. His mouth found hers. Constant gulped at his lips, tormenting with each breath, pushing further into him, and then she lifted a leg in order to wrap it about one of his, grinding her hips against him until she couldn't halt the cry.

"Na' so fast, love."

"Help me!"

"Na' so—stop that!"

He might have possession of her body, but he couldn't stop her hands. Constant reached for him, beginning a stroking motion that had his entire frame ramrod stiff. The unearthly groan he gave emboldened and enticed her further, making her ministrations that much more earnest and intense. She was being sucked into a whorl of wicked desire and lust before he stopped her, reaching down and pulling her away with hands resembling iron. Constant watched the agonized look on his face with a sly smile on hers.

She knew exactly what he was talking about now. Her entire body was afire with it, too.

"Na' . . . so . . . fast." He panted each word.

Constant blew a kiss to the air between them. She watched a shudder run through his frame. Then she couldn't see anything as he slung her over his shoulder and walked straight to her bed, as if the sea was glass smooth and the floor wasn't bobbing and weaving beneath them.

He tossed her atop the bed, where she bounced twice before coming to rest. The ship was seesawing as she watched him crawl onto the bed, settling onto his haunches right beside her so he could rip one of the strings holding her corset closed, and pull it out. Constant's eyes were huge as he held her down with one hand while he pulled strings with the other. As one string snapped, he moved to the next one down.

It was the most intensely arousing thing she'd ever seen. Kameron's chest was rising and falling as he inhaled and exhaled, his muscles were straining as he plucked each string loose, and the hard part of him was shoving against her side the entire time.

"Kam . . ."

"You are going to need another corset, Constant, and I doona' give a damn who kens it."

He had the piece undone and shoved it open. Then he yanked her chemise down, gathering and lifting her with both hands. He arched himself to reach her nipples with his mouth, giving such ecstasy Constant screamed with it.

Kameron lifted his head as he ripped the flimsy material of the chemise from her. He ran his hands all over her, along every curve, down to each foot, and then back again, leaving trails of sensation in his wake.

"I wanted to do this slow, Constant, love. I wanted to know you. *Know* you, and I wanted you to feel it as I did. I wanted to move your world and make you sob with ecstasy. I wanted to show you how it can be. Now, I doona' give a damn about any of that. I doona' want anything more than to be buried in you. I hope you're ready, because I'm na' doing another thing slowly."

He wasn't exaggerating. He was harsh and entirely male as he rolled atop her, pushing all the breath from her as he did so. She had her arms about him, and her heart beat so loud in her ears, she could hardly hear the curses he rained on her as he moved between her legs and slammed inside her. He called her a jezebel, the center of desire and wickedness. He named her an enchantress, a vixen, a siren, a vamp, a wanton, a seductress, and those were only the ones she could decipher between each savage thrust of his body into hers.

Then he wasn't going fast, despite his tormenting words. He was rising and falling with each motion of the waves, the sea deciding the rhythm, and driving her absolutely demented with the effort to reach what she knew awaited her. Constant clung to him, grasping as much as she could with her arms and legs. She held to him. She pushed and thrust and begged, and what she got was more of his cursing, and more of his heated strength, and more of his teasingly slow motion.

And then she reached heaven. There wasn't enough air for the shriek she gave, nor could she gather more in. The sound ended on sobs of emotion. There was a storm sending the bedroom back and forth, with fire and passion and love-imbued power, but it hadn't a thing to do with the ocean outside, and everything to do with Kameron. He'd said he wanted to move her world? Make her sob? It hadn't been an exaggeration. Constant wept, shivering and convulsing with the ecstasy, holding as tightly to Kameron as she could. And all he did was laugh.

That nearly undid her. She opened her eyes to a view of sweat-slickened flesh, bulging muscles, the hard planes of his cheeks, and the solid black of his eyes.

"Am I going too fast for you, love?" he asked harshly, shoving himself against her with each word. "Too slow?"

"Kam . . . eron!" She choked out his name.

He moved, taking her with him as he stood up, lifting her with him off the bed, continuing his slow, maddening motions. He walked with her, using the length of each wave to his advantage. And then he settled her on the ewer stand, balancing her atop the cold edge of the porcelain bowl before planting his hands on either side of her. The chill at her back conflicted so much with the inferno within her that she slammed her eyes shut and convulsed with another eruption of rapture.

"Constant? Look at me. Look at us. Damn you. Look." His voice was a hoarse, guttural racket of sound as he commanded it.

She opened her eyes, fixing them on the half-lidded

slant of his. She had to wait for the next flip of light from the swinging lantern to know his gaze hadn't moved. She couldn't have looked away from it if she dared. The light caught him again, caressed the expression of wonderment on his face, combined with a look of such torment, Constant's heart squeezed with it. She remembered that look from the loft. The ecstasy.

A groan emanated from him as he grabbed her, lifting her upward with the strength of his own release. The timbre of his voice enshrouded her. Her arms tightened about him to hold him close for as long as possible.

And then Kameron shook, giving little warning before falling to his knees, the thump of his landing loud and painful-sounding. Constant's heels bounced on the decking, but Kameron's body cushioned the rest of her.

She moved her hands to his face, slid her fingers over every bit of his perfection, removing stray strands of hair as she did, and then she was stroking at his eyelashes with thumbs that trembled at the wetness she found there.

"I love you, Kameron," she whispered.

"And I you, Constant, love. I do. I love you. I have said it many times in my life, but I have never meant it until you. You have nae idea."

"I have every idea, Kameron," she answered.

"This is na' usual. I swear. What other men and women do together bears little resemblance to this. I dinna' know true love made all the difference. How could I? I dinna' have any knowledge of it."

"Women chased you, offering love, Kameron. Your entire life they've been there, offering this."

"What women?" he asked.

"Every woman. Everywhere. Every night. Remember?"

"If I said that, it must be another lie, love. There's nae other woman in the world save you." He pulled away, swiped at his eyes and looked around. He frowned. "What are we doing on the floor?"

"What floor? I am atop clouds. I have been since I met you."

"You're atop me, love. It's blasted hard on the bottom. Trust me. Cold, too. Which way is your bed? I intend to find it, fall into it and sleep in it, with you in my arms. I got to experience that only once. I still remember how it felt."

"What's that?"

"Sleeping with you. Allowing my mind to caress where my body couldn't. Awakening with you atop me. Damn you, anyway."

She felt him stir within her again.

He swore. "I said I would be sleeping, Constant."

"You've got two weeks to sleep, Kameron."

"True enough." His lips twisted into a smile that left her in no doubt of his intentions. He coupled it with the raising of both eyebrows. "Have I labeled you a vixen yet?" he asked.

"Every time."

"Good. I'd hate to think I'm losing my touch. Hold to me, darling, I'm going to try to stand now. It may prove difficult."

"I don't have a prayer of not holding to you, Kam."

His smile widened. "Let's just keep it that way, shall we?"

Chapter Twenty-Five

Her two hours had to have passed, and then three. Constant lost all track of time. It was mostly due to Kameron. It was such a wealth of warmth and wonder to lie enwrapped in his arms, watching the room tilt and sway, making ever larger and longer motions that rocked them back and forth on the bed. So Constant stayed with her head on his chest, using him as a pillow, while she waited for Lucilla to ruin it.

"Kam?" she whispered.

"Hmm?"

"You awake?"

"Aye," he answered.

"I thought you were going to sleep."

"Foolish idea. I was mad and—as you reminded me—I have two weeks for that nonsense. I'll be strapped back into my bed with naught to do save sleep, and dream, and remember. Besides, I had other things in mind. My wife is an insatiable sort. I am verra lucky to have found her. Verra."

Constant's body flushed for her. She knew exactly what he was referring to. She had been insatiable.

"How did you get loose, since they strapped you?"

"They control me with the bonds once they have me down. I'm allowed up to relieve myself. Think of the mess, otherwise."

"You are very . . . blunt, for a titled gentleman."

"I'm verra blunt for anyone, darling, titled gent or na'. 'Tis nae one's fault save my own. They gave up trying to instill the correct sense of decorum in me years ago."

"Why?"

"Why, what? Why am I short on decorum, or why did they give up?"

"Both."

He shrugged. "I'm an only child. I had inanimate toys to play with, vacant-faced servants to wait on me, and na' one soul who cared. I tried to alter that, I guess. I was incorrigible and I misbehaved and I was randy. Verra. I was a familial embarrassment looking for a situation that would showcase it."

"What is randy?"

"Uh . . . active. Physically. With the ladies. You know . . . lusty."

"I'm sorry I asked." She was, too.

"If it helps, so am I. Ask me something I can answer without causing you upset."

"All right. Why?"

"Why what? Why ask something that does na' upset you?"

"No. Why did you act that way? What were you trying to alter?"

"Oh. Being ignored. My father is the esteemed, regal, arrogant, contemptuous, and verra censorious fifth Duke of Ballanclaire. He's also the laird of Clan Ballanclaire, and revered almost like a god. His word is law. Unimpeachable. Has been for . . . more than fifty years now. He inherited as a lad. He's so steeped in tradition, historic propriety, and heraldic implications, it's impossible to have a conversation with him on any other subject. I doona' think he kens how."

"Heraldic what?"

"Implications. Lineage. Which clan has ties with which. Who wed who and produced whom. Whose line reaches the farthest back into history. That sort of thing."

"That doesn't sound fortuitous for me."

"What do we care? We can leave. I'm na' the duke. I can abdicate."

"What will happen then?"

"What do I care?"

"Kam."

He sighed. "Oh, verra well. I lied. I doona' ken if I can abdicate or na'. That means I will be duke. Eventually. And you'll be my duchess. And our children will all turn out to be perfect examples of responsibility and propriety, despite their upbringing."

"What upbringing? They're three months old."

"True. But there's about to be a severe break with tradition. They will na' be raised at BalClaire, as he was. And I should have been."

Constant stiffened and tried hiding it. *BalClaire was one of the properties he'd lose.*

"It's nae great loss, Constant. The place is a tomb. Solid rock. Verra auld. The foundation stones go back to a time even afore The Bruce. Fourteenth century, or thereabouts. 'Course it's been modernized a bit since then. My mother forced the issue upon their marriage."

"You weren't raised there?"

"I think I touched on this already. I was a bit . . . incorrigible. Undisciplined. I broke things. Caused trouble. Disrupted. There are more descriptors. Need I continue?"

"Where were you raised, then?"

"Pitcairn Tower. 'Tis a wondrous place, way up north. A bit rough about the edges, but filled with all kinds of entertainment and trouble for a lad to get into, especially when he is going to be the lord of it eventually."

"Is that where you first learned about women?"

Kam didn't say anything for so long, Constant swiveled her head to look at him. She had to wait for the light to sway back twice before she saw his expression. He was sucking in on his cheeks, his eyebrows were raised, and he looked anywhere but at her.

"Well?" she asked.

"I'm na' so certain I should answer that."

"Why not?"

"If I say nae, will you say it's a lie? If I say aye, will you get all upset at me again?"

"I'm never upset at you, Kam."

"In that event, aye. I learned early on. I was twelve. She was fifteen. It was brutally embarrassing if memory serves me right."

"I think you should have lied and said no."

"Oh. In that event, nae. I dinna' have any woman until you. I was saving myself."

Constant giggled. She couldn't help it. "What did your mother think of all this?"

"My mother? That woman is a firm believer in being seen, but never heard . . . or should I say, overheard. I doona' think she has a conversation unless it's to shred someone's character, engage in hate-filled gossip, or insert sarcastic rejoinders when they'll do the most damage. She prefers life at Windsor Castle when she's in London and Haverly when she's not."

"Windsor . . . Castle?" Constant paused between the words.

"Aye. Windsor. In London. She's a member of the royal family, Constant. There were probably two things about her that brought my father's offer for her hand. Her royal blood was the first thing. Had to be."

"And the second?" Constant asked.

"She's bonny. Her beauty was legendary. Still is. She's trim. Perfect complexion, thick, white-blond hair, light brown eyes. Gets it from her Nordic father. Some say I take after her."

"Only some?"

"Oh, verra well. I received nearly every bit of my looks from her, but my size comes from my sire. My father is na' much to look at, but he is large. Legendary large. Handled a claymore and hand ax with the best of them. Never lost on the list. Na' even to his honor guard. Make that . . . his auld honor guard."

"What's a list?"

"Field of battle. For jousting tournaments. That sort of thing."

"You still do those?"

"Aye. Usually without the armor. Keeps a man strong. Agile. Battle primed."

"And the honor guard?"

"Every laird has an honor guard, love. They're hand-picked from the strongest and bravest of their clansmen. That's another use for the list—selecting an honor guard. 'Tis how I selected mine."

"Yours?"

"I have my father's skill on the lists, Constant, although you'd never know it."

"I mean . . . where's your honor guard?"

"Oh. My father disbanded them the last time he

disowned me. Nae. 'Twas the time afore that. Doona' fash. I'll reassemble them. They ken it."

"Your father . . . disowned you?"

"Aye. It's a farce. He kens it. As do I. The verra last thing he'd allow is the dying out of the Ballanclaire line. He's still prone to using it as a threat. You've noted my guards? Those staunch gentlemen assisting me?"

She nodded.

"They're part of his honor guard."

"Your father wins them in contests?"

"Na' them. Their predecessors. The duke is auld. Stooped. As I told you, he's na' much to look at, either. Resembles an ogre. His features are so large, they're misshapen. His nose is akin to a turnip. At least it looked that way when I last saw him."

"Kameron!" Constant couldn't stay the laugh.

"Well, it does."

"You aren't very flattering to your parents."

"I'm supposed to be? Oh, verra well. I'll try. My mother is first cousin to the king. She's a legendary beauty, but one who came with a tongue that spouts sulfur."

"Kam!"

"I'm still unflattering? I'll try again. My father is near seventy, suffers gout, heart issues, aching bones, and an overbearing sense of stiff-necked pride. My mother is a bit younger. Actually, for a lady of two score and six, she's amazingly well preserved. I think she has vinegar in her veins. That's probably why."

"Kameron."

"You are verra difficult to please, Constant." He sighed. "I'll try yet again. My parents are both highly regarded members of the peerage. They detest me. Always have. I am a disgrace and an embarrassment according to my sire, while my mother has never loved me. Na' even when I was in leading reins. Or so she says. This sort of thing does tend to make one's offspring unflattering, for lack of a better word."

"Your parents . . . detest you? They couldn't. They didn't. It isn't true. It can't be."

"Verra well, Constant. Have it your way. I was raised at my mother's breast and lovingly escorted into manhood with my parents overseeing every step. I canna' fathom why I turned out like I did. I truly canna'."

"I think . . . I'm beginning to see . . . a little."

"A little? I'll have you know the barristers agree with me, although they'll never say such again."

"Again?"

"We imbibed together on the way to the colonies. It was a long voyage over. I was a tad wary of the end result. Actually, I was terrified of it."

"Barrister MacVale? *And* Barrister Blair? I don't believe it."

"Verra well, Constant, I give up. My mother is the epitome of virtue, loveliness, and charm, while my father is a dapper, much older gentleman, who is a bit self-absorbed. Both of his lawyers are men of honor, and tee-totalers. They would never cheat, lie, or steal. I doona' ken why they'd choose to be barristers. That career seems to require all those traits. They're obviously better suited as members of the clergy. Why, they probably never touch a drop of spirits. Is that what you wish to hear?"

"I would rather hear about the terrified part."

"Damn. I was hoping you hadn't heard that. Hmm. I meant I was a bit embarrassed at having to meet you. I figured you might have forgotten me, although first loves are usually memorable. But blast it all! I may have been the first, but I had done it so terribly, you might have put it down to a verra bad dream. I would have."

"Kameron," she said. "I want the truth."

"You are worse than an interrogator, Constant. That bodes well for our children's future exploits. You wish the truth?"

He stopped and sighed hugely.

"Verra well. The truth. I did my best acting ever . . . in that loft. After . . . I . . . we—well, after. I wanted you to hate me. I thought it best. 'Twas the hardest thing I've ever done, I think. You turned my entire world completely upside down. You've nae idea. And then you showed up at the hanging? And spoke up for me? I've never known love such as you demonstrated. Ever. You proved there was good in the world, and absolute, unselfish love. And then. Then—"

He stopped, cleared his throat. His voice wavered as he continued. "When . . . I woke . . . I asked for . . . my wife. For you. The commander, he said—he said you . . ."

He swallowed. Hard. She heard it.

"He told me you . . . left. You tossed the certificate in the fire and then you walked out. Just like that. You left without even waiting to see if I'd live. With na' so much as a backward glance. And they thought my sobs . . . were from my injuries. Fools."

"That horrible little man! That's not what happened, Kam. It tore my heart out. And he knew it. Ooh. Whatever punishment your father devises for that selfish man, it's not severe enough. He was worried for his career because of you. Those words were his vengeance."

"Good thing he's na' in range. I'll show him vengeance."

"Stand in line," Constant replied, and he chuckled.

"Well. There you have it, love. I had to see you again, somehow ask for an annulment, and all through it . . . act as though it were naught. Terrified is the only apt description. I told the barristers some of it. That was stupid. It made them watchful. I keep forgetting, although it should be ingrained by now."

Constant was glowing. She couldn't believe she wasn't lighting the entire room with how she felt. Her voice sounded it. "You keep . . . forgetting what?"

"MacVale and Blair are the duke's men. They'll always be his men. They think I'm too dense to realize it. They think I doona' ken what they're planning. I do. I'll just have to be smarter than they are."

"What are they planning?" She held her breath.

"They're going to fake your death, Constant. They're going to make me into a widower with two small bairns and an old, weak, Spanish princess for a future wife. Ugh. Worse yet, she'll be ugly. Fat. Smelly. She'll have but one brow across her forehead, and a mustache, besides."

"She sounds delightful." Constant couldn't prevent the laughter that filled her voice.

He cleared his throat. "To get back to the subject at hand; I ken what the barristers are planning, I just doona' ken when and how they'll accomplish it, although this posture-board thing does give me some promising leads."

"Like what?"

"My father settled a sum on you for signing the annulment. It should stop with news of your death, but I'm certain there's a codicil, or something that the barristers will use. There will be enough for you to live quite comfortably. I'm assuming in Spain. I've been racking my mind for potential locations. Ballanclaire clan has property on Palma, but that's too easy. Cadiz, maybe. Or perhaps Portugal, although I have my doubts. They may also place you in France, although it will na' be Monaco. It's too well known. Attracts a large, cosmopolitan crowd. Can you imagine how scandalous it would be if I'm wed to my betrothed, Princess Althea-the-Pig, and then someone discovers my first wife, still living?"

She shivered. "I don't think that bothers them. I'm

going to be given another identity, and the twins don't favor me at all. They look just like you."

"That they do. And that means they look exactly like their grandmother. Lord, but I canna' wait to apprise her of her grandmother status. Wait a moment. You *know* about this?"

"I overheard them."

He hugged her close. "Careful, Constant, love. You'll be mistaken for a spy at this rate."

"I'd be a failure."

"I was na' verra successful, either, if you look at my record. I'll have to get better at it if I'm going to ferret out your hiding spot."

"Hiding spot?"

"I'm going to come for you, love. I'll move heaven and earth to find you. I'll have to keep everyone guessing while I do. We're going to have to come up with a secret code, though."

"Code?"

"For when I find you. You might be verra well hidden. You might be guarded. Contrary to how it looks at present, I have a bit of trouble with guards. They tend to be verra controlling and impossible to escape from. I only managed it tonight because there's a terrible storm tossing us about and they allowed me up to relieve myself. Do you wish the particulars?"

She shook her head. He continued on anyway.

"They usually wait about while I handle nature's call. It's na' verra conducive to privacy. I'm na' the shy sort, but even if I was, spending time in your loft would've gotten that sort of thing out of my system."

"Kameron."

He sighed. "Verra well. I'll keep to the subject at hand. I'm released to relieve myself, and again when they let me hold our bairns. They promised me that, if

I'd cease struggling. They'll be withholding it if I doona' get back afore daylight"

"You hold . . . the twins?" Constant hoped he wouldn't hear the emotional note in her voice. She swallowed it out of existence as he continued talking.

"Every day. Twice. I see them separately. I asked for that. I want to make certain my children ken their father. I love them, Constant. Already. Immensely. When I'm able to, I'll show them how much. I'll buy them each an estate. Will that be enough, do you think?"

"Children don't need things, Kameron. They need love."

His arms tightened on her. "They'll get it, I swear. I also asked for them separately because I wanted to hold them and I wanted to smell them. I imagined you holding them just before me, and that I could smell you on them."

The room was still rocking in front of her, but Constant couldn't see it through the sheen of tears.

"Our son, Benjamin, loves to be held. Abigail took a bit more persuasion. Actually, she prefers to ride my knees and be played with. She must take after her mother with such a temperament. I was ever amenable to rules and authority, so it canna' be me."

"Kameron," she said.

"You are a difficult woman to fool. I would rather face an inquisition than you. Verra well, Constant. Our daughter has a feisty side. It's likely my fault. It endears her to me greatly. Perhaps I should have said that, instead."

"You don't mind?"

"Abigail's temperament? Of course na'. In fact, I find my children such treasures I am at a loss as to what I can give you."

"Give me?"

"You provided me my heir, Constant, and you doubly

gifted me with his sister. 'Tis expected I show gratitude. How about a diamond necklace, with two stones instead of one? Would that suffice?"

"I don't need gifts, Kam. I only need you."

Her response had him holding her tighter. "Truer words were never spoken, nor more needed. You have nae idea. I swear to you now, Constant, love, we will be together as a family. I will na' rest until I get that. You ken?"

She nodded. She didn't trust her voice.

"That's na' a difficult promise to make. I already said as much."

"When?" she replied.

"Doona' you listen when I talk? I canna' wed with any princess. I refuse. If I canna' be with you, then life is na' worth living. That is nae lie. I swear it."

She rolled, in the circle of his embrace, and held herself up by leaning on her elbows.

She looked at him. "What time is it?" she asked.

"I doona' ken. Tuesday?"

"Kameron."

The lamplight touched his face, slithered away, and returned. Both times he had the same gentle expression.

"You may na' believe this, Constant Ballan, but you saved me. I was swimming in debauchery, lechery, and every sort of vice, and then I found you. You changed me. It was na' something I expected. It was na' something I looked for. It certainly was na' something I thought I wanted, but I received it, anyway. To do anything less than commit to you with everything I am—and will be—would be a lifetime of hell. I already ken. I lived through a year of it while I recuperated enough to travel. You make me long to bolt from the life of luxury and lasciviousness I was living, and reach for something else. I was actually ready to till the soil. I still am."

"You can't become a farmer, Kameron."

"Why na'?"

"Because you are meant for so much more. You're related to the king! You can make him listen. You can help resolve the problems they're having in the colony. You can. I know it."

He looked at her, his chin lowered and his eyes glowing every time the light touched them. "Ah, love. I canna' speak to the king. I canna' get near him, nor do I wish to. I'm na' important enough, and let's na' forget, I've been ostracized. I was sent to the colonies for punishment, although I doona' recall why at the moment."

"The Marchioness of Barclay. I assume you two were lovers. She wanted marriage. She must not have known you couldn't marry anyone except your princess. You should have told her; there wouldn't have been such a scandal."

"Oh, hell. Doona' tell me you remember all that?"

"And more."

He sighed. "Could we go back to discussing the king? It's safer, although why we'd care what trouble a few dissidents create, eludes me. We have greater problems."

"They're more than a few and they're not dissidents."

"Must we have an argument over colonial policies now? Because we've little time as it is. It's probably closing in on morning, although I haven't a clue."

Constant's lips twitched. Then she smiled. "Very well, Kameron. You win. We'll speak of it when we're together again."

"It will take place sooner than you know, love. I'm na' fond of being separated from my lady wife. Tonight was just a sampling. The barristers had better take that into account. Two more weeks seems an eternity."

"There's no guarantee after that, Kam."

"Oh, there's every guarantee, my love. I promise you. I may have been a detestable man. I may have been an embarrassment to my parents and my peers and the world at large, but I promise you, I'll be the best husband and father ever. On that, you have my word."

"Oh, Kameron."

This time, she couldn't halt the tears nor keep him from seeing them, since he was mere inches from her face.

He reached his hands to cup her face, using his thumbs to wipe at the moisture. "We have na' concocted a code yet, love."

"Code?" she repeated.

"Blue ribbon."

"Blue ribbon?"

"When we're apart, remember. Send me a blue ribbon. When I see it, I'll come. I promise. Nae matter where they hide you, no matter which continent, I swear I'll search and I'll find you. I'll never cease looking. Ever."

"I love you," she replied in a soft tone.

"And I love and adore you. It keeps me sane, when all about me is insanity." He smiled, leaned forward to place a kiss on her forehead, and then he shrugged his legs off the side of the bed. "You'd best procure my clothing. I'd go myself, but that maid of yours has ideas."

"Really? I don't know about what," she replied, and snickered.

Chapter Twenty-Six

They were waiting for him in the hallway. Constant saw at least six of the kilt-clad men as Kameron looked one way, then the other, then shut the door.

"Oh, good. There's nae one about." He was smiling. She didn't return it.

"Kameron," she replied.

"You say my name like a threat. If the woman who gave life to me had any potential to be a mother, she'd have sounded the same when I needed it the most. At least, I think she would have. I would have liked it, too. I think."

"Kameron," she repeated in the same level tone.

He sighed, the movement taking her with it since he held her to his side. "Oh, verra well, Constant, love. I'll take another look."

He opened the door again. There were probably more than six of his guards, although she didn't count to make certain. She took a quick glance before shrinking back against Kam's shoulder. She longed to disappear back into her chamber.

The line of men stretched along the corridor in both directions. Although the ship was wildly rocking back and forth, it didn't seem to affect Kameron's guards much. Each man had his feet planted apart and rolled with the movement, managing to look like a disciplined soldier. They were soaking wet. Stern-faced. Constant watched as Kameron looked at each one in turn, pulling her along with him while he did so. She wished she wore more than the dressing gown and robe as goose bumps flew over her skin. They returned to her chamber door and Kameron looked down at her again.

"See? Nae one about. Just as I said."

"Kameron, would you be serious?"

"Good Lord, why? I'm afraid you have me at the wrong time if you wish seriousness. Tomorrow morn, maybe. Right at the moment? Definitely nae."

"Please?" she whispered.

He rolled his eyes and sighed again. "Oh, verra well, love. You are a difficult woman to please. I wonder if you realize it. I will humor you. What should I look for this time?"

"Your guards."

"Where?"

He was grinning now.

Constant narrowed her eyes. "Everywhere!" she hissed.

"Well, I was trying to ignore the situation, but if you insist on my noticing how many men callers you are entertaining, who am I to argue? Which man must I challenge first?"

"Kam!"

"What now?"

"They aren't here for me and you know it."

"They're here for me?" His eyebrows rose as well as his voice. "You certain?"

"Kameron, please don't do this. You're making it worse."

"Impossible, my love. You only need to see the humor of the situation."

"There is nothing humorous about it."

"I disagree. I happen to think it verra amusing. You recollect the rug-seller parable I told you of in the loft?"

"What?"

"I have to admit, you certainly put it to use, Constant, love. You make me proud."

"What are you talking about?"

"You, of course. Look about you. What do you see?"

"I see your guards, Kameron. You know I do."

"My point exactly. You certainly came at a very high price, and I gladly pay it. I doona' want you to think otherwise. Do you ken of any other husband that is arrested for visiting his wife's bed? Well?"

"Kam!" She was shocked. It sounded in her voice.

"I did warn you of my bluntness, dinna' I? If na', consider it done. Apologies. As I was saying, most husbands have to be forced *into* their conjugal bed. See there, Constant? I'm forced from it. Verra humorous. It makes all the difference, too."

"Kameron," she repeated.

He sighed hugely. "Verra well, Constant, love. I will try na' to see the humor of the situation. Is that what you want me to say?"

"Would you please be serious?"

"All right, but if you insist on looking at the world with perfect seriousness, my love, at least give me the right to complain."

"I don't think your guards find you amusing, either," she answered.

"Them? They're used to me by now. Are na' you, lads?"

Constant flicked her glance to the row of men and glimpsed more than a few curved lips among them.

"I am embarrassingly inept," Kam said. "Just look. I almost get hanged because I canna' manage to avoid a bunch of provincials with pitchforks, and now I canna'

even evade Ballanclaire men in the height of a storm. I
should never take it up as an occupation. Remind me of
that, will you, love?"

"Take what up?" she asked.

"Escape." He said the word with a hint of drama. "I
used to think I was an ace spy. Covert was my creed. Now
that I've demonstrated how poorly I've done, it's worse
than embarrassing. It's downright criminal."

He tipped his head down and put his nose against
hers. Constant felt the flare in her heart, accompanied
by the blush at having so many observers.

One of the men about them cleared his throat.
Kameron lifted his head but didn't move his gaze from
hers. A look of agony pierced him before it fled, leaving
such uncertainty on his features, Constant wondered why.

"Why do I feel as if this is the last time I'll see you?" he
whispered.

Constant's eyes filled with tears, at his tone more than
the words. She couldn't help it. She shook her head.

"You deny it and yet I canna' shake it. You will na'
leave me, will you?"

"No," she replied.

"Promise me, love. Promise on all you hold holy."

"I promise," she answered. Kameron scrunched his
eyes shut and she felt the shudder flow over him as he
held her, his arms almost too tight to get her next
breath.

"We'd best be leaving, my lord."

One of the men stepped forward. Kameron's arms
and features relaxed, he opened his eyes, blinked away a
film of moisture, and looked over her head.

"What will a few more minutes matter?" he asked in a
rough tone.

"We've been away from our posts too long already. We'll be missed."

"So?" he snapped.

"We doona' want that to happen."

"Why na'?" he snapped again.

"Well . . ."

Constant heard the sound of the man clearing his throat again. She didn't move her eyes off her contemplation of Kameron's chin.

"We came to a bit of a decision after you rowed yourself to this ship, Your Lordship."

"You watched me row myself, and consequently, almost drown? You *watched*?"

Constant could see and feel the reaction in him. Every muscle tightened and a nerve twitched in his jaw.

"We followed you."

"To every ship?" Kam asked.

"Aye, my lord."

"I am truly pathetic at escaping. Adjust your reminder to that, Constant. Embarrassingly inept and pathetic. That's me."

"You have been under observation by at least six of us every waking moment, my lord. The duke ordered it. You could na' have evaded us."

"If that is supposed to make me feel better, you should save your breath and go back to being silent. In fact, I think I would like you better."

The guard who was speaking didn't hesitate to ignore that request. "We dinna' interfere for a reason, Your Lordship. We thought it verra brave of you, especially the third time. That sort of thing deserves some sort of reward. If we had interfered, you would na' have gained it."

"Gained what?"

"Your reward. We came to an agreement on what it would be. You went through so much to spend some time with your wife. We agreed to allow it and na' interfere. We canna' tarry much longer, though. We'll be found out."

"Why was it brave the third time?" Constant asked, turning her head finally to look over at the speaker.

"It was into the wind, my lady. He looked close to swamping the dinghy more than once. We almost had to mount a rescue."

My lady? Oh my. He'd just called her my lady.

"Oh, Kameron." She turned back to him, blinking rapidly. "Why did you do something so foolish?"

He looked down at her, and the light favored her for an instant with a glimpse of his warm, golden-brown eyes, before it moved away.

"You need ask?"

That answer got him what could only be sounds of amusement from the men lining the hall. Constant didn't move her eyes from his.

"Begging your pardon, my lord, but we need to leave. Now."

"Oh, verra well. I must look to my blessings, I suppose. At least I doona' have to row myself back. That thought has merit."

Kam bent to touch his lips to hers in a kiss stained with gentleness. She lost sight of every bit of reality: the storm, the plethora of guards, the damp chill of his clothing against her. She lost herself in a feeling of absolute bliss for an encapsulated instant of time. From behind closed eyes, she could swear she witnessed nirvana opening up before her, wrapping her with a glow of warmth, golden brown in color, and imbued with nothing but adoration and love.

Then, it was gone. Kameron lifted his head, filled her

vision with the same dazed expression she could feel on her own face, and then he turned to the guard who had spoken.

"Lachlan, is it?"

"Yes, my lord."

"Remind me to double your wages when I'm duke. That goes for all of you. And, Constant?" He turned to her and she was surprised to find herself on the threshold of her chamber. She hadn't felt him move. He put his mouth to her ear and started whispering. She knew why. The guards had proved themselves to be human; they hadn't proved themselves loyal. "Farewell for now, love. Look for me in two weeks. A fortnight. You ken? If I have to fake my own death and return to the colonies and take up farming, I will."

"You'd give up a . . . dukedom?"

"You doona' listen verra well, do you? I already told you life is hell without you. Trust me. It is."

He stepped back from her into the hall, and then he shut the door. Constant didn't move for long moments, and then she raced to her bed.

A boom woke her, shuddering through the cabin. Constant clasped both hands to her throat, holding the robe tight as the sound came again. This time, the entire bedstead resonated with it, trembling until the noise faded.

Lucilla's door opened slowly. The maid hadn't undressed to sleep. She tossed her hands in the air when she saw Constant. "*Madre de Dios!* I slept! I am a fool! Quickly, *señora!* Quickly! We haven't much time. We will leave the trunk. Hurry!"

Constant frowned as Lucilla came closer, moving in awkward sliding steps, swinging her arms as she went.

"Quickly! Do not sit there looking at me like I'm

stewed! Up! Grab a cloak. The ship . . . she is sinking! Hurry!"

The ship is sinking? For the span of a heartbeat Constant considered. She wouldn't have to toss herself into the waves after all. All she had to do was close her eyes and . . .

That's when she knew she couldn't do it. She should've known love was too strong to fight. Constant slid to the edge of the bed and stepped into ice-cold water, gasping at the shock. Lucilla held a cloak out to her and tossed it over her shoulders before she started pushing on Constant's back. It took both of them to open the door, because a wall of water blocked it on the other side. Constant followed Lucilla into the corridor as the water reached her waist. Then they were pulling themselves straight up the steps, hand-over-hand, as the water buoyed them.

They didn't waste time with speech. It wouldn't be heard above the roaring sound of the rushing water. As the ship listed, the hall door now opened upward. She helped Lucilla try to open it, but no amount of pushing seemed to budge it.

"Help!"

While Lucilla pounded on the door, Constant held the door handle with both hands and straddled what had once been a stair railing underneath her. The water was now swirling about her hips.

"Help!"

"That isn't . . . doing . . . any good," Constant panted. Then she shrieked as the door lurched up, pulling her up with it, ripping her out of her cloak.

"Thank heavens! Hurry! You were a fool, Lucilla! Another minute and we would not have time! Quickly!"

It was Barrister MacVale. He was stronger than he looked as he yanked Constant from the door and tossed her to another man, who then raced to the ship's side and tossed her over into a small boat.

Their skiff was bobbing and weaving, pelted with rain. Constant slammed against a seat, careened along the side, and came to rest beside the sturdy lower leg of an oarsman. He didn't look familiar, but it didn't matter. She clung to him with hands slickened with fear and slippery with water.

"All here now! Hurry! Get away from the ship! The suction as she sinks will take us all with it! Row!"

It was impossible to decipher who shouted the command, but the oarsman she held on to wasn't waiting another moment. Constant felt urgency transfer through his body as he strained, first forward, then back. She didn't see Lucilla. She was afraid to lift her head.

The onslaught of rain stole her breath, blurred her vision, and stung her flesh with icy pellets. *Kameron had rowed himself in this?* Awe stained the memory, warming her for a moment. But not for long.

The boat was awash. Constant lost feeling in her backside and lower legs. She lost feeling in her hands, then her arms, and then her fingers. And still the sleet hammered at her.

The man rowed for what seemed like hours. Constant stopped counting the times his leg shifted back and forth after she reached two thousand. Still he rowed, the sea sloshing water into the skiff, freezing Constant in place.

Finally the boat bumped against something solid. She sensed rather than heard the collective sigh of relief. Someone helped her move from the spot, although they had to wrench her arms open to free the oarsman's leg. Constant didn't know who helped her—it was too dark to tell, and whenever she looked up, sleet stung at her face.

Someone put her into a large basket affair and it

lifted. Constant rolled into the smallest ball she could and tried to avoid the elements. The higher they took her, the worse it got, until she tried to hold her jaw together with numb hands, fearing the violent chattering might damage her teeth.

Someone was on the deck to retrieve her. Constant wasn't capable of moving. A blanket was wrapped about her and she was carried to a room, where a blast of warmth hit her cheeks hard enough to make her cry out. A fire was lit in an iron depression in the center of the floor. Constant fell to the decking beside it, and from that point, she had to stifle her cries as the heat awakened her frozen limbs.

"Blair!"

Constant recognized the voice as MacVale's, although she'd never heard him raise it in anger before.

"MacVale? What the devil are you doing here?"

"Me? It was you who was to stay with him! Damn you! Haven't you ever read Shakespeare?"

"What the hell are you talking of? It was your responsibility to stay with him. We altered it last night!"

"Nae. We only discussed changing it!"

"You don't think he's bright enough to ken the plot?"

"Na' without knowledge of this ship! He'll think it real! And if that lad takes his own life, I swear to you—"

"Me? We had an arrangement!" Blair's voice was rising.

"The arrangement got changed, and you ken it!" There was a garbled sound at the end of his statement.

Constant hunched her shoulders, trying to absorb the heat as well as the steam that was rising from her soaked clothing as she listened to the men bicker. Her clothing had been frozen stiff and was now melting into sodden, formfitting garments. The blanket was also wet, adding the smell of wet wool. She didn't care. The fire was too welcome. She reached her hands out toward it.

"What are we going to do?" Blair's voice had a desperate tone to it.

"It's your plan, you come up with something."

"It was perfect, too. It would have worked. Damn you, MacVale!"

"Damn me? It wasn't you disappearing if this dinna' work, it was me!"

"Well, now it's both of us. Congratulations."

"Hush! Both of you! This is a matter of utmost discretion. And you create more terror when the *señora* has been through enough. Lucilla? Meet us in the cabin. And get blankets. Warm ones."

The speaker had a cultured tone to his words, spoken in clear, aristocratic Spanish. Constant lifted her head from her own misery and sought him out. He wasn't easy to see, as steam was clouding her line of sight, and the only light came from their fire. He appeared to be dark-haired, dark-skinned, and had a pointed black beard streaked with gray.

He could be considered handsome, but his effeminate manner of dress was unlike any she was used to. He looked silly, bedecked with lace and velvet, and the sword strapped to his side didn't do much to alter it. Constant blinked twice and stared as he fiddled with the lace at his throat.

"Señora Ballan?"

She nodded.

"Count Rafael de la Garza-Montagna. At your service." He bowed, the high feather on his hat dipping as he did so. "I am pleased to welcome you aboard my ship. Please? Allow an escort to your cabin. Gentlemen?"

"My cabin?" she whispered.

He smiled and stepped closer, giving her his arm for an assist. She took it. She decided he was actually fairly handsome. Close to middle age. Lean. Strange-looking. The ship was rocking and swaying as he walked her through a door, down a corridor, and into a room. Lucilla was there, holding up a warmed blanket; a moment later, Constant had it wrapped about her. She turned to face not only the count but the barristers who'd followed him.

"Please, *señora*, sit. You must be exhausted. Lucilla, if you please. Fetch tea now. Strong tea."

He gestured to a large wooden chair. Constant sat. Exhaustion wasn't enough to describe the tiredness sapping her. She watched as Barrister Blair shut the door behind Lucilla, sealing them in.

"Where am I?" she asked.

"You are a guest aboard *La Concepción*."

"Is this a Ballanclaire ship?"

"No, *señora*."

This storm was producing some very strange events. Constant had to close her eyes for a moment, take a deep breath, and then reopen them. Nothing had changed.

"This is the phantom ship you denied existed, isn't it?" Constant tipped her head to eye first Barrister MacVale, and then Blair. Neither man would meet her gaze. "I think you owe me an explanation."

"It is not these gentlemen you need to speak with, my beauty. It is I. Rafael."

"But . . . they rescued me. Why would they do that when they wanted my death?"

"Your death? Never, my lady," MacVale answered.

My lady? Her ears heard it, but it took a moment to reach clarification. They accepted her, too?

"B-but I overheard your plan. When we first met. In the parlor. I know what you expected of me. My death."

"Oh, my lady. You are so wrong. On all counts. We were just hedging our bets, so to speak."

"Your bets? Why does none of this make sense? You didn't expect me to kill myself?"

"Heavens, nae! Your death would kill him. It still might. I am ever so worried! It was Blair who was to tell him. I told you to stay with him, Blair!"

"We changed it last eve! I was worried over the plan succeeding all the way, so I stepped in!"

"Nae! It was your chore to tell him!"

"Damn you, MacVale!"

"Gentlemen. Stop," Constant ordered, and surprisingly they obeyed. And then she smiled. "Kameron won't kill himself. He won't. He has the responsibility for our babies. They'll be enough. Trust me."

Both men stopped, took deep breaths, and then MacVale smiled at her. "Ah. I forgot. He does have the bairns. He'll na' allow them raised by his parents. You're right. Thank God."

"So tell me. How soon can we be together?" she asked.

"We dinna' have an exact time afore, my lady. We only needed to get you hidden and your death reported. That would be enough to satisfy the current laird and settle any problem with that accursed betrothal. It should na' have been for long, either. Is na' that right, Blair? Speak up, mon. It was your plan."

"And a damn fine one. Pardon my language, my lady."

Constant regarded him for a few moments and then smiled. Blair looked as discomfited as he always made her feel. That was odd. Everything was. And then Blair resumed talking.

"The current duke is an elderly gentleman. Unwell. Kameron has informed us—in insufferable detail and at great length—that he'll pay whatever cost is required in order to stay wed with you. Well, that option will be his the moment he inherits."

"He really did say that?"

"And more. There was nae stopping his words through the entire voyage to the colonies to meet you, and near every moment since. It depended on you, however. He was na' at all certain sure you'd want him. We assume that issue has been decided in his favor?"

Constant blushed and smiled, then nodded.

"So then, you see? The plan was near perfect. But then Count Garza-Montagna intercepted us, invited us aboard this ship for a meeting, and outlined an even better plan. One we wholeheartedly agree with. MacVale even volunteered to disappear in order to make it happen."

"He . . . did?"

"'Tis nae great hardship," MacVale interceded. "There's just something about true love that seems to bring out the best in people—even an auld bachelor, such as myself. I was due for a change, anyway. And they tell me Spanish women really like Highlanders." He winked at her.

"But what of the annulment paperwork I signed? What if it's located?"

"Doona' worry a moment longer of that. We burned it."

"You did? When?" She was glowing. Nothing was remotely cold. Anywhere.

"The moment we . . . uh. Well. The moment we discovered Lord Ballanclaire in your cabin."

"You accept the marriage, then?"

"And the legitimacy of the bairns. Aye."

"Then why was he strapped down?"

The eyebrows of both men rose. There was absolute silence for several heart-pounding moments.

"I *knew* I saw Ballanclaire honor guardsmen aboard

The Destiny this eve. I knew it," Blair said finally. He shook his head. "That husband of yours has the most amazing ability to escape, disobey, and rebel. It never fails to astonish."

MacVale cleared his throat, and he was smiling. "In answer to your question, my lady, the honor guards are the ones at fault here. But they are following orders. They will na' shirk their duty, regardless of reason or fairness. To do so means punishment and possible expulsion from the clan. At least . . . until Kameron inherits and becomes laird."

"Enough! You two take too long with your words, and your explanations are a bore! Why is a Scotsman always so taken with the sound of his own voice?"

The count stepped in front of the barristers and flung his arms wide. Years ago, her sister Hope had described a Spaniard's propensity for drama. Constant smiled slightly as she watched the count demonstrate her sister's point.

"Dear lady. You must listen to me. Please? Hear my pleas. I beg of you. They tell of a new plan? It is mine. And you must help me."

"What can I do?"

"You all speak of true love? Well, I know it exactly. I am in that condition. *Sí*. I have been in love for nearly two decades! Two! It is a desperate situation and I beg your help, as I beseeched these gentlemen before you."

"My . . . help?"

"My beloved cannot wed with me. She never could. So, I lived with the situation, and I sailed the seas, and I brooded. And then I heard a rumor. My beloved's betrothed had wed another! It was a love match. It freed us if it stood. I have been following Ballanclaire ships ever since I first heard. And success is finally mine!"

"I have no idea what you're talking about," Constant replied.

"My beloved has pretended an illness her entire life. She is not ill. She is desperate. I know the feeling. Perhaps you do, too."

Constant was so grateful for the chair, she could cry. Her legs didn't feel like they belonged to her. She was shaking, but it had nothing to do with the elements. Everything in her was attuned to what he was saying. She knew his next words before he said them.

"My beloved is the Princess Althea. She cannot wed with a mere count. She has to wed the great British lord, Kameron Ballan. She has been so ordered. She would rather die. She has so informed me. I will not allow that to happen. That is why I hatched this plot. My beloved does not even know, but she will agree. To this faith, I cling. This is where I need your help. Oh, good. Lucilla is here. With tea. You'd best give some to the *señora* first. She looks close to fainting. You don't faint, do you?"

"I never used to," Constant replied, closing her eyes and breathing as quickly and shallowly as possible.

OCTOBER 1773—BalClaire

Chapter Twenty-Seven

"The Princess Althea Esmerelda Consuelo d'Anjou, daughter of King Philip the Fifth of Spain; great-granddaughter of King Louis the Fourteenth of France through her father; granddaughter of the Duke of Parma, through her mother, Princess Isabella Farnese; and the new Lady Ballanclaire through her marriage by proxy to Kameron Geoffrey Gannett William Alistair Bennion Ballan."

Constant waited until the list of her names and titles had been announced before stepping out onto the landing overlooking the great hall of BalClaire Castle. There was an audible gasp from many onlookers. She held herself stiff and straight and supported the four pounds of jeweled comb holding a mantilla atop her head as if she'd been born to the chore. What her new attaché, Carlos Montoya, had assured her would happen was happening, too. She no longer shook at the knees or blushed uncomfortably at having everyone look at her. In fact, she made certain everyone was either in a deep bow or a curtsy before they rose, and looked at no one but her. All the preparation to ensure that she conducted herself as a true princess was paying off.

Kameron hadn't been completely accurate about
BalClaire Castle. Perhaps he was trying to minimize the
effect of losing it. He'd been truthful about its construc-
tion, however. The Ballanclaire ancestral estate was
definitely a rock-hewn ancient castle. She'd only gotten
a peek at it during her arrival that morning, because
she'd been in a closed carriage portraying a princess with
a weak constitution. That one look had been enough,
although it was an overcast day full of rain. BalClaire
had loomed up from a solid rock face right into the sky,
the entire structure like a great brooding beast. It gave
the same impression as her first look at the Ballanclaire
honor guards had, a year ago in Madame Hutchinson's
parlor. Intimidation. Threat. Power. Might. To think of
Kam as a small boy, kept alone inside these walls, had
made her heart ache.

The carriage had taken her across a drawbridge, the
echo of their passage on wood blending oddly with the
sound of pipers. She already loved the long, mournful
sound the pipes made, carried as it was on the air through
the glens and across the moors as they'd traveled.
Kameron was closer now than ever. She could almost feel
him beside her as they'd passed through the barbican and
into the inner bailey of BalClaire. Just this morn.

It felt like days.

The crowd before her separated, creating a passageway
to the far end of the room. She stood and waited, assuming a look of disdain. It was an act. The room was impressive. Jaw-dropping. Constant kept her features perfectly
chiseled and blank, despite the shivers running all over
her as she looked at length at three fireplaces, two along
an inner wall, while a third framed a dais at the end. They
each looked capable of burning an entire tree. She tipped
her chin a fraction to scan upward. The space was at least
two stories high, constructed of more rock. Spans of it

were covered with long, embroidered tapestries, mounted animal heads, and what looked like the glint of ancient weaponry. Far above was a crosshatched wooden ceiling she'd been told was of hammer-beam design. A profusion of chandeliers were suspended from it, their lit tapers denting the space with pockets of light that barely made it to the crowd below. The room was enormous, dimly lit, smoke hung in the air, and it seemed filled with Scotsmen and -women of all clans and allegiances. Colors and plaids vied with each other among the attendees, although the majority wore Ballanclaire red and white on black.

Kameron had told her the castle was modernized. Not this room. The great hall was a medieval banquet for the senses. It exuded might. Strength. Power. The impression didn't fade regardless of how long she looked it over. It was immensely stirring. Heart-pounding. Almost frightening. Definitely awe-inspiring.

The senior statesman in her coterie was Barrister Iain Blair—now impossible to recognize in his guise as Spaniard Carlos Montoya. He'd thinned down, was usually dressed in court attire of velvets and lace and other costly fabrics, and sported a black, curled wig. He'd filled her head with the history, pageantry, and traditions of the castle, but he hadn't done it justice. BalClaire was the seat of the mighty Ballanclaire clan, owned by the dukes for centuries. From this room, they'd dispensed justice. Sentenced enemies. Awarded heroic deeds. This room was the manifestation of the family's history and power.

And Kameron was willing to forfeit it for her?

Chills ran through her at the thought, before she stanched them and narrowed her eyes at the dais. The reigning duchess moved into view. The woman was wearing a silver ensemble, and the strawberry coronet atop her head looked fashioned of the same metal. Surprisingly, the metallic color drained her complexion of color. That was odd. Constant had thought the woman would never appear in anything less than her best light. Apparently, that detailed attention to herself gave her room to criticize, lambaste, and castigate just about everything, and everyone, else.

Days of travel locked inside a coach with the duchess had confirmed Constant's impression. Kameron had been blunt but accurate when describing his mother. She hadn't a loving bone in her body. She reminded Constant of a coiled snake, ready to strike at the first opportunity. Constant found that claiming a weak constitution was the best method of avoiding her, and if that proved improbable, she hid behind her royal persona's inability to comprehend English. She noticed that her interpreter softened many of the duchess's caustic remarks when he translated.

A richly dressed and bewigged man stepped from the crowd near her. She didn't know how she'd missed him earlier. He wore a plaid kilt in the clan's red, white, and black colors; a black jacket; and an array of medals and brooches that signified his position. He was surrounded by men dressed as he was, but he towered over them. He looked every inch a Scot chieftain. He didn't look weak, either. Kameron had been right about his father's looks: he wasn't remotely attractive, and his nose really was the size and shape of a turnip. And he was enormous, although he stooped.

"May I allow an introduction, Your Highness?"

One of her dignitaries spoke at her side. Constant tipped her head in acquiescence.

"This gentleman is your father-in-law, His Grace, the Duke of Ballanclaire. Your Grace? The Lady Ballanclaire, Princess Althea d'Anjou."

Constant listened to the introductions, first in English, and then in Spanish. She waited for them to finish before holding out her hand to the duke. The moment he touched it, she dipped into a deep curtsy. When she stood up, she noticed that she reached the duke's chest. Even with the two-inch heels on her shoes.

Constant busied herself with the arrangement of her skirt, making certain the satin had fallen correctly. The heavy, brocaded white satin of her skirt was overlaid with a gossamer layer of lace that had been embroidered throughout with tiny diamonds. It was the match to her mantilla. Constant pulled slightly on the lace that flowed over her shoulders and wrapped about her elbows, co-cooning the material to make an enclosure that framed the upper body and face. It took grace and practice to wear a mantilla correctly, especially one this heavily embroidered and bejeweled.

As rich as they were, both lace pieces were a far cry from the magnificence of her bodice. That single square of material had been encrusted with so much diamanté, it had no flexibility and left tiny scratches all along the cleavage created by her corset. And all of it was done to showcase the goose egg–sized diamond of her necklace. The dress had skintight, elbow-length sleeves, ending with more lace that fell to enhance her wrists. The design was intentional; her upper arms were spared contact with the diamanté, and the satin bore up well, leaving no snags to mar the surface.

Constant watched as the duke looked her over from head to toe, as if he were inspecting prize horseflesh. Constant waited, calmly holding up the weight of her gown in the stiff-backed position she'd learned. She hadn't powdered her hair. It would have been a travesty after spending a week sitting patiently while Lucilla stained every strand with India ink. The result was worth it. She looked extraordinary and exotic, and exactly like a Spanish princess. The blue-black color contrasted sharply with the pallor of her skin. It also set off the turquoise color of her eyes.

She watched as the duke took in every nuance of her appearance before he returned to her face. She could tell she'd passed inspection. Her lips thinned involuntarily. She had to consciously force them to soften.

"I am verra pleased to welcome you to BalClaire Castle, Your Highness. I only hope it meets with your approval."

She waited for the translation before answering.

"Your minions shall be informed if it does not," she replied in the high-pitched voice she'd affected.

Constant waited through the translation of her words. She knew she'd said it right as the duke stiffened and his brows drew together. Other than his size, he didn't bear the slightest resemblance to his son.

"Come, Your Highness. Allow me to escort you to the dais. There will be a long receiving line. I have sent invitations throughout the Highlands."

Constant waited for the interpreter to finish before placing her hand lightly on the duke's upraised elbow. She already knew about long receiving lines. She'd had to endure one that lasted more than fourteen hours when she'd first arrived at London. Then she'd been put on display and presented over a span of three days at Haverly. *Three days!*

The Duchess of Ballanclaire wasn't about to be outdone by anything her royal cousin did, or anything her husband might contrive later, either. She'd made that clear to Constant, when she wasn't sullying one of her acquaintances' reputations. Constant would have found the three days at Haverly intolerable, her patience at an end, and her tongue sore from biting down on it, if it hadn't been for Lucilla's suggestion that she stuff cotton into her ears. That way, all she had to do was nod vacuously and murmur occasionally. The duchess probably thought her daughter-in-law was hard of hearing and lacked sense. That was better than the alternative. The last thing Constant wished was to be the Duchess of Ballanclaire's confidante.

Constant sighed quietly. The whole masquerade would be unbearable, except that it made possible a life with Kameron. And then nothing could keep them apart.

There had also been the joy of seeing the real Princess Althea's face when she'd finally wed her count and gone to live a life together at his estates. If anyone involved balked at the plan, they had only to recall that the count and his new wife were in love, as two wedded people should be, and nothing on earth was as important as love.

Nothing.

Constant was surprised it had been Barrister Blair who had designed and executed everything, although both of the barristers had been livid when Constant hadn't been able to keep her pregnancy a secret another moment.

That was the reason it had taken so long to turn her into Princess Althea. She had been heavy with a child no one could know about, and until it was birthed no one could see, or know, anything about her. So, she'd been hidden away at the Ballanclaire estate in Palma. Constant had let her baby sustain her, enfold her, and help her through the loneliest days, especially when they let her take up residence in the suite slated for Kameron. It had made her feel so close to him and to her twins, it had been near heaven.

He'd felt closer still the moment they'd sailed. He'd felt so near in London, when the Spanish galleons had been allowed entrance and escorted up the Thames. He'd felt especially close the evening before her wedding. She hadn't slept! Constant had anticipated seeing him at Westminster Abbey; everyone had. It was expected of him to be at his own wedding . . . but he'd failed to show. She'd been wed by proxy to a stranger, in front of the entire royal court.

Constant caught the remembered dismay to her breast and stanched it immediately, before it became an emotion she'd have to deal with. They'd reached the dais. The duke had stopped. There were three steps to negotiate, and four thronelike chairs sat atop the platform.

Four?

Constant's heart pounded. After her wedding there had been a reception at Windsor. Everyone whispered and speculated about the whereabouts of the reclusive Lord Kameron Ballan. Somehow Constant had managed the entire fourteen hours of gossip. It had been difficult, and more than once she'd nearly been reduced to tears. The only thing that saved her was the interpreter, San Simeon. His clear failure to translate exactly was a blessing. Althea's brother, King Charles, must have selected this interpreter for his tact; Charles would not have sent his barely healthy sister into British hands without a man who could deflect the vicious words directed toward her . . . at least, not until she was good and wed, and he had signed documents to that effect in his hands.

Constant's interpreter had been put to the test at Windsor, but not later, at Haverly. There, the duchess had discouraged speculation and gossip by placing only two chairs on the dais: one for her and one for her newest acquisition, a royal daughter-in-law.

Four chairs?

Constant debated which one she should occupy. She negotiated the steps to the platform, holding her skirts with a hand that trembled before she could stop it, while the other rested atop the duke's forearm.

The chairs were of a like character, constructed from

strong, thick wood, with real silver hammered into each arm. The seat cushions were covered with red-and-white-on-black plaid. She selected the second one she came to and turned to face the crowd. Constant smiled to herself as an attendant fussed with her hem and the train of her ensemble. If anyone from the Ridgely farm ever thought about her, or wondered, they'd never come close to the actuality of her new life. She was treated royally, wore clothes that cost more than Farmer Ridgely could earn in a lifetime, and had to wait for an assist before doing just about anything.

It took a certain talent to expect such service, and even more to ignore it as it was given. The old Constant would have been overheated with blushes, and probably in tears at the attention. The princess Althea was unaffected by it and stood, coolly appraising all those in the room as they started moving to one side to form an orderly receiving line.

The duke stopped at the first chair, the duchess behind him, her smile looking pleasant and genuine. It was false. Anyone who met her eyes would know it. She had the same golden-brown eyes that Kameron was blessed with, but hers were as hard as the egg-shaped diamond at Constant's throat. It was obvious Constant was going to be on the receiving end of her displeasure, along with the man at her side.

Constant almost felt sorry for him.

"You have outdone yourself with your ineptitude, Alistair," the duchess hissed as she stepped before her husband, her face a mask of pleasantry.

"I doona' believe you have permission to use my first name, Your Grace," he replied easily.

"I'll use whichever name to call you and at whatever

time I wish, although the one that comes to mind is impossible to voice."

"As always, your bonny face hides a heart of stone. I sincerely hope you realize you are being overheard, and consequently a judgment of your character is being undertaken. Oh. I forgot. As you have nae character to start with, it canna' be ascertained one way or the other, now can it?" he replied.

Constant sucked in on her cheeks. She wouldn't need to expend any pity on His Grace anytime soon. He sounded well equipped to hold his own in a battle of wits with his wife.

"There's no one near enough to overhear. And look. You're inviting comment with the quantity and placement of chairs. You're losing your touch, old man."

"The princess has ears," he replied.

"Her? Oh. Please. She's a simpleton with bad hearing and slower wits. Rather on the same lines as you and your clan. Kameron is rather lucky to be spared any contact. I rather envy him that."

"By your words, may I hope you'll take up a reclusive life, as well? Why, if you'd agree, I'd wall you into Haverly tomorrow. Pray agree. It would be worth the cost of a stonemason."

"Sir San Simeon?" Constant spoke up, using her high-pitched voice to call to the interpreter standing behind her chair. "What is it my husband's relatives are saying?"

He cleared his throat. "It isn't for your ears, Your Highness," he replied in Spanish.

"I wish to know what they say."

"They are greeting each other," he said. "Exchanging pleasantries. Her Grace asked of his health, and he asks of hers."

"Oh," Constant replied. She really enjoyed Sir San Simeon. He had a dry humor and usually interpreted with an added bit of uncanny wit. He wasn't a party to The Secret. Few were. The less who knew, the better. Supposedly that was another of Kameron's rules for lying. It was a good one.

"You need to move on. You're causing comment, gaining stares, delaying the line, and that will delay the dancing and the banquet. All of which I will be deducting from your allowance."

Constant's eyebrows rose. *Dukes' wives get an allowance?* She hadn't known that.

"As it's my dowry paying for most, if not all, of this, I would hope you'd have ceased that nonsense by now," she replied.

"Dowries are in payment for losing one's freedom. Yours was large, I agree. Na' large enough for what I lost, I'm afraid. Move down and cease bickering in front of the princess."

"I already told you she has no wits, and she's woefully inadequate at the English language. Aside from which, where am I supposed to stand? Before which seat?"

"End chair. And I will na' command it again," he answered.

Her perfectly groomed brows rose as she shifted to stand before Constant, portraying what looked like a loving greeting. Constant returned the smile as icily as it was given as the duchess moved forward to kiss the air beside her daughter-in-law's cheek. Constant's smile was a wasted gesture. The duchess wasn't looking at her. She was still hissing words at her husband.

"You leave a chair vacant, they'll talk. I'll take this one." She stood in front of the chair on Constant's other side and smoothed her skirts.

"You'll take the end and cease delaying, or you'll raise more than eyebrows when my son arrives."

Constant gasped, avoiding detection by the duchess's

own gasp. Constant concentrated on her hands, twisting them together. She probably shouldn't have worn so many rings.

"Kameron is attending this eve? Now? *Here?*"

The duchess's voice rose slightly with each word. Constant noticed that she had shifted slightly, however, standing in front of the last chair.

"Of course here. This is BalClaire Castle, the ancestral seat of the Ballanclaire clan. He'll inherit the lands, the titles, and be chieftain one day. Why would na' he attend?"

"Because he hasn't attended a damn thing for over two years now, and you know it."

"Careful, dear . . . such language. We're about to be presented as a family, and you use profanity. What will our new daughter-in-law think?"

"I already told you, she can't speak the language, and she doesn't have any answers even if she knew what we were saying. She's dipped in everything Spanish and you know what that signifies."

"She's related to the ruling house of France."

"Not closely enough, I'm afraid. I've kept her company for weeks now, and I'm repulsed by all of it. I shudder to think it through. Look for yourself. She's dense, unattractive, dark, sweaty, inbred, and ill-educated. If she weren't a princess, I'd have walked by her without even tossing a farthing her way."

Constant's eyes widened and then narrowed. She watched her own fingers wriggling, and kept from making a fist by sheer willpower.

"I think she's verra attractive. I canna' think of a man that would na'. That is probably your prime complaint. And perhaps her unlined appearance. For a woman near in age to you, she has remarkably clear and unblemished skin. You should ask her secret."

"She's been locked away in a tower for decades. No one saw her. She didn't see anyone. A fool could tell that's the secret to her appearance."

"You should na' tempt me," the duke replied.

Constant's lips twitched. "What is it they say?" she asked Sir San Simeon.

"They speak of your clear and unblemished skin. The beauty of your appearance. The duchess wishes your secret to unlined skin."

"Oh." Constant looked over at the duchess and beamed a smile at her. "Please tell her it is a facial paste made of egg yolk mixed with heavy cream. The heaviest. Leave it on through the night. Every night. That is what it is. Tell her. Thank her." Constant waited while the interpreter apprised the woman of her recipe. The duchess set her chin and didn't say anything. Charity had once tried it. She'd awakened with blemishes from her forehead to her throat, and they had kept erupting even after she'd tossed the concoction.

When the interpreter had finished, the duchess glanced sidelong at Constant and the duke. Her look contained nothing but malice. Constant kept a vacant expression on her face. She didn't know what the duke had on his.

"You did that on purpose, Alistair. I'll remember it," she finally said.

"Talk to me after you've tried it. Besides, she's na' going to be your problem much longer, is she?"

"She's journeying to Pitcairn Tower next. I can't stop her. She wants to be with her husband. She doesn't seem to realize that when he doesn't come it's because he doesn't want to. He doesn't want anything to do with her. I can't reason with him. Nobody can. He doesn't care what society thinks. He's a widower. In mourning. I tried to tell the princess of it, but she just doesn't take the hint."

"It must be a woman thing then, for I doona' want you, either, and yet here you are," he replied.

Constant caught her reaction to that, turning it into a cough that she hid behind her hand. It only worked because Sir San Simeon was also coughing.

"Well, Your Grace, we're about to greet our first guests, and with a vacant chair between us. I hope you're satisfied."

"Doona' fash yourself. He'll be here," the duke replied.

"What makes you so certain?"

"I ken the proper persuasion to use."

"You can't use your usual barbaric means of control. I will not tolerate having him bound and dragged in here. That would be too scandalous. I will disclaim you if you try. Surely you realize that."

"He'll be here. He'll be in proper dress, and he'll be on his best behavior. I guarantee it."

"How?"

"I took his twins. I have them here now. How else?"

Constant had to squelch the desire to hit them. Both of them. It wasn't easy. She wadded her hands into fists so tight the rings cut her flesh, while the duchess trilled what was probably a laugh. Constant gulped the anger to the bottom of her belly, where it sat, threatening to make her ill.

"I thought you dinna' allow children into the castle," the duchess finally answered.

"Kameron believes so, too. Very astute of you, although I'll na' be admitting that again. Aside from which, you left me little choice—with our daughter-in-law, Princess Althea, bringing a brat she favors. Why dinna' you tell me she had a godchild, a wet nurse, and assorted attendants with her?"

"Because you never asked," the duchess replied.

Then, everything stilled. All conversations ceased. Constant knew why: Kameron had arrived. She didn't have to have it pointed out to her. She *knew*. She lifted her head, narrowed her eyes at the haze of smoke, and saw him.

Chapter Twenty-Eight

It was Kameron, all right. He moved rapidly toward them, limping slightly with every other step. He was surrounded by men close to him in size. None of them looked ready to attend a fest. Of any kind. They looked road weary, mud spattered, wet, and ready for battle. It was obvious even in the dimly lit, smoke-hazed room. Swords held ready in their hands, they came to a clanking halt directly in front of the dais. She was three steps up from the floor and exactly level with him. Exactly. Constant swayed for the slightest moment. Her lips slipped open to gasp one breath after the other. She was actually amazed she wasn't swooning.

The high-pitched note she hadn't heard in over a year was back, too, overriding just about everything. She could sense the crowd, watching. Waiting. Silent. Kameron lowered his head, speared the duke with a malevolent look that had Constant even more breathless, and then sneered.

"Good evening, son." The duke spoke up, the sound loud. Abrasive. Taunting.

"Where are they?" Kameron asked in a tight voice. "I've checked the nursery, and aside from a newly birthed brat, there is nae sign of my children. I repeat myself, and I will only do it once more. Where are they?"

"Where you will na' find them easily, of course. Allow me to present your wife, the Princess Althea—"

"You'll na' tell me?" Kameron interrupted him.

"Give me three hours of your presence, Kameron. I'll have them delivered back to you. You've my word."

"You never keep your promises to me, sir," Kameron replied. "If I give in to you now, it will be but the first time you appropriate them. My children are na' pawns for your use! They are flesh and blood and beloved beyond measure. I will na' tolerate this! Na' for one more minute." He turned his head to address his men. "Athelrod? Take your men and search the grounds and outbuildings. Greggor? The towers. Zeke? Room by room. Chamber search."

The three men swiveled and jogged as they left, the clank of weaponry fading into stillness. The remaining four flanked Kameron, two on either side. All of them focused directly on the man to Constant's left.

"Who are these men?" the duke asked.

"My honor guard."

"Your allowance was halved last year. How can you support an honor guard?"

"There are some things even your silver canna' buy, Your Grace. Trust. Honor. Duty. Integrity. Heart."

His words gave Constant an absolute thrill, but the duke was angered. Curt. Gruff-voiced. She had chills for a different reason as he spoke.

"You wish your children returned, Kameron? Verra well. Here are the conditions. Take your place beside your new wife and greet our guests. Three hours hence I'll see you reunited with your brats. Three hours. That is na' too much to ask."

"I've ceased being at your beck and call, sir. You knew

it when I returned with my children . . . and without
their mother. I made it clear. I'm warning you for the last
time. If you doona' tell me where to find Abigail and
Benjamin, when I do find them I will leave the country
with them and never return. There may be a new laird
for Clan Ballanclaire, but it will na' come from your line.
I ask for the last time. Where are my children?"

His voice broke more than once. Constant had to
look away for a moment. He was blurry with the tears she
was unable to stifle—and she wasn't even supposed to
know what he was saying!

"You make a scene without reason. I'm na' requiring
much. Three hours at your new wife's side. That's all.
They are safe. I'll never use them again. You've my word.
Now, cease this, and give me three hours."

In reply, Kameron spun on his heel.

"Kameron."

Constant quickly said the name, giving it the slightest resemblance to how she used to say it. She sensed
everyone staring at her. She didn't see anything except
Kameron as he stopped. And then he turned back. Constant waited for him to look at her, but his gaze stopped
at the egg-shaped diamond. She watched him wince.
Then he looked away, the nerve in his cheek twitching
as he turned his head to look at something on the wall
behind his mother.

"That is his name, is it not?" Constant continued, uti-
lizing her high-pitched, nasally voice, chatting away in
Spanish before anyone could move. "Kameron?"

"The Princess asks if this is Kameron, her husband,"
the interpreter supplied. No one answered.

"He is very handsome," Constant continued, as if
oblivious to the tense confrontation in front of her. "He's
very presentable. I wish introductions made, please. You
may do the honors, Sir San Simeon."

The interpreter tried; Constant had to give him that. Kameron dipped his chin, acknowledging that he heard, but he didn't respond.

"I have a gift for him." Constant spoke up quickly, the moment the introductions were finished. Still Kameron didn't move, or even look her way. "A token of my esteem. Here." She reached for the key tied to her elbow. Her hands were trembling almost too much to work as she unfastened the blue ribbon and retied it back into a bow. "Please tell him the object comes from the heart and has special significance to him—just him. You may do so now."

She was holding out the ribbon with hands that were quaking. Kameron didn't glance her way as Sir San Simeon repeated the words.

The interchange wasn't going unnoticed. The sounds of whispers, chuckling, and snickering came from all about them. It was worse than Windsor had been, and a thousand times better at the same time, because Kameron was standing right there! Right in front of her. And if he didn't take the ribbon, she was ready to leap across the dais and shove it at him.

"Please hand it to him," Constant continued when Kameron just stood there, ignoring everything that had been translated to him.

One of Kameron's men stepped toward her and did as she requested. Constant held her breath as Kameron finally took the ribbon. She watched him wind it about his fist, palming the key. She saw him tremble.

And then he turned away and stalked out, his men following, his limp more obvious. If his exit shocked the onlookers, Constant didn't note it. She wasn't aware of anything except Kameron. She couldn't see through the film of tears as she watched him walk out of her life.

"Congratulations, Alistair." The duchess moved closer.

"You've succeeded in embarrassing yourself beyond my fondest dreams."

"Shut up," the duke replied, and he sounded as old and feeble and powerless as Constant's father once had.

"You've managed such a scene in front of everyone . . . and you want me to keep silent? I think not. I couldn't have asked for a greater triumph."

"Pray silence yourself, or I'll have you physically removed from the room. Doona' force me to make good on my threat. I canna' think of anything calculated to entice the rumormongers more than that."

"Your meaning?" she asked, after a slight pause.

"My son stalks out, and my wife is then removed from the dais by my order. What connotation would you place on such a thing?"

"I won't say another word," she whispered.

"Start the reception line," the duke called loudly.

Constant gulped away every vestige of tears from her throat, pasted the royal, vacant-faced look she'd spent a year learning onto her features, and forced herself to endure what had to be endured.

Again.

They'd gone through more than half the receiving line when Kameron returned. It seemed as if hours had passed while her knees pained her, her back ached with the chore of standing and holding up the weight of her attire, and her heart had become a fiery stone that sent agony to plague her. And then everything changed.

Constant knew the moment he entered the great hall. She was holding the hand of an ancient-looking woman with a tottering step and no teeth. The interpreter was just finishing the woman's fulsome greeting when Constant felt Kameron's gaze on her. She *felt* it. She was subtle about checking, though, using the lace of her mantilla to advantage. She caught the movement as he stepped into the hall, dwarfing everyone. He was unaccompanied. A stir of reaction came from those about him; then she saw him move to the center of the opposite wall to lean back against it, fold his arms, and look across the hall, right at her. She saw what he had wrapped about his fist, too—her blue ribbon. Despite her every effort, Constant felt the familiar stain of a blush. She only hoped it wasn't as noticeable as it felt.

"Your Highness? The lady is waiting."

Constant forced her gaze from where Kameron lounged. "My husband has returned," she replied.

She watched Sir San Simeon flick his glance to the opposite wall. A satisfied expression crossed his sallow face.

"He has had a change of heart, I see. Either that or he has located his children. I am hopeful it is both."

Constant swallowed her first response, which was to agree with him. She wasn't supposed to know! "His . . . children? What is this you say?"

"He—uh . . . his children had a mishap. They were missing. You must turn to your guest now." He changed from speaking Spanish to English as he addressed the old woman, mouthing the same platitudes he'd been saying all evening. "The princess thanks you for the gifts. She wishes to acknowledge your presence here. She extends the warmest wishes to you." Constant nodded slightly as the old woman responded with a toothless smile and moved to speak with the duchess on Constant's other side.

"He is very handsome," Constant told her interpreter. "More so than I'd been told, and even that sounded fanciful."

"I am no judge of such, Your Highness," Sir San Simeon replied.

"Oh, come now. You know beauty when you see it. He has the countenance of an angel. I'd heard that, too. I just didn't believe it."

"He is no angel when crossed. That is what I saw."

"Yes," Constant whispered softly. "He is especially wondrous when he is angered, isn't he?"

"He does not appear an easy man to handle," he replied.

"Really? Hmm."

She smiled after the reply and moved her eyebrows several times, and was rewarded with his answering smile. Then she looked to the nobleman who was bowing before her, put her hand in his, and awaited the introduction.

Constant met personage after personage, a blur of plaid-clad clansmen and elegantly gowned clanswomen. Throughout it, she knew where Kameron was. He didn't stay in one place, but he wasn't mingling with the guests dining on haggis, salmon cakes, roast beef slices, quail, and a varied selection of wines. He was moving to various vantage points throughout the room, and always he was watching her.

He'd dressed for the event. He wore attire almost exactly like his sire; only on Kameron it emphasized his perfectly proportioned, athletic, muscled frame. He had a long sword strapped to his side. The purselike sporran. A red-and-white-on-black plaid kilt. A tightly fitted black jacket. A froth of lace down his shirtfront. He'd pulled his hair back in a queue. He was worse than beautiful. He was jaw-dropping. And he had the blue ribbon about his fist. He kept bringing it to his mouth as if in homage. Constant had a difficult time paying attention to the presentations. She didn't see most of them, she couldn't hear above the high-pitched note in her ears, and Kameron kept moving ever closer.

All of which changed when a beautiful green-eyed woman with pale skin, dark red hair, and blood-red lips curtsied before her. The woman had a spectacular shape, too, outlined in her dark green bodice and the contrasting white of her skirt. Constant's eyes narrowed, and she forced herself to listen as the woman was announced, although she already surmised who she was, and why she was there.

". . . of Barclay."

"I have no wish to meet this woman, Sir San Simeon. Tell her that, if you dare."

"The princess is pleased to see you, Lady Barclay. She extends warm greetings, and comments on how beautifully you are gowned."

"If you extend an invitation to any of my homes, San Simeon, I shall make you regret it," Constant said again, smiling and nodding to the overly painted woman. Lucilla had dusted Constant with powder, expertly lined her eyes with kohl, touched the slightest bit of rouge to her cheeks, and reddened her lips. Constant had thought it theatrical and unladylike. She knew the truth, now. She looked fresh and untouched next to the vivid picture the Marchioness of Barclay presented.

"Her Highness extends her warmest wishes to you, Lady Barclay. Thank you for attending. Good eve," he finished.

"I see Kam is here," the woman had the affront to whisper loudly. "I must see him. Surely you can arrange something."

She wasn't speaking to Constant. That much was obvious. She was addressing her request to the duchess. Constant's eyes narrowed.

"You ask too much, Lindy. I have no control—"

"You got him to attend, didn't you? Use your influence. Do something! He won't answer my letters!"

"My son is recently wed, Lindy. To a princess, no less. You are causing a scene. Go. Don't appear desperate. Men hate that."

Her Grace knows enough of men to give advice? Constant wondered. It didn't seem possible.

"The Lady Barclay appears most insistent. Translate what she has said," Constant ordered San Simeon.

"She is requesting a tea with Her Grace," he answered. "I don't believe the invitation will be forthcoming."

"She'd best not look for one from me, either," Constant commented.

The moment the green-eyed siren moved away, Constant was looking for Kameron. She shouldn't; she didn't want to know if he approached his former lover, or what he would do if she approached him.

She needn't have worried. Kam was standing within yards of the dais. He had the ribbon-wound fist raised to his lips and his eyes on no other woman except her. He had them narrowed as he watched her, concentrating. Constant wondered why it was taking him so long to approach her. She hadn't changed that much. True, she'd thinned to a smaller shape, had a veil worth a king's ransom wrapped about her, bluish-black hair combed and arranged into a lattice-style hair covering made of hammered silver strands, and a touch of paint to her face, but she was still the same.

The last fellow in line bowed before Constant. She heard his name with half an ear, recognized that he was a knight of some order or the other, and saw that Kameron was moving toward her. She was breathless as he approached, and incapable of saying any of the fulsome words San Simeon put to voice in her name for the knight. She didn't care, either.

Kameron reached the dais and stood where he had before, his chin lowered and his lips pursed. Constant had rarely seen anything as stirring. She knew it had something to do with how the candles in the chandeliers had dimmed, losing their light in the softening tallow. It also had something to do with the small group of musicians tuning their instruments from behind the curtained minstrel gallery. It had a bit to do with the activity taking place, as servants cleared away the banquet tables and arranged seating along the walls for those who preferred to watch the dancing. But it had the most to do with Kameron's steady regard.

"I see you've returned, son. Saving face?" the duke asked.

"Doona' fool yourself, sir. I dinna' return to save anyone's face, least of all, yours."

"Well, at least you're consistent. I'll have to give you that much, lad. Always did hate me, dinna' you?"

Kam shrugged. He didn't take his eyes off Constant. There wasn't a single indication that he recognized her. Not one.

"You worked to gain my hatred. You must have wanted it. I complied."

"You're verra blunt, especially for a man meeting his wife for the first time."

"Oh . . . I'm verra blunt for any man, sir. That's one of the things the ladies seem to appreciate about me." He smirked. "At least, so they tell me."

"Kameron Ballan!"

The duke's exclamation almost hid hers. Kam lifted his brows.

"I am also in possession of my bairns. I would na' have returned, otherwise."

"I'm well aware of that. I expected nothing less."

"Besides, I've been assured she does na' speak our language. With the words you two spout, her ignorance is a decided blessing. So tell me, does my new wife speak anything besides Spanish?"

There was a bit of consternation between her new in-laws. Sir San Simeon answered, "Her Highness is well versed in the language of her father, my lord. King Philip was once the Dauphin of France before gaining sovereignty over Spain. His daughter speaks French. Fluently."

"*Français?*" Kam repeated.

"*Oui,*" her interpreter replied.

"*Bien.*"

Then Kameron actually asked Constant if she knew the dance steps well enough to couple with him. She couldn't believe her ears, although her heart did. It fell. And then it pounded with increasing fury from her belly. She was incapable of dancing. She was afraid she might be physically ill.

"I am . . . unwell," she replied.

"I will take my place beside you, then. Your Grace, if you please? My chair?"

Kameron's mother looked annoyed at being moved, but she stepped sideways and sank into the end chair. That was a relief. They could all sit. Constant silently prayed not to fall. She had to wait for her attendants to raise the back of her wire-stiffened underskirt. This made it possible to sit at the front edge of the seat, her skirts falling about her ankles, as was considered graceful and proper. She waited as her attendants knelt to each side of her and settled the back of her skirts on her chair, leaving white satin underskirts to cover her. The skirt was arranged to billow about her, and then she nodded, dismissing them. She kept her eyes downcast. She didn't dare look at Kam until she had the blank expression back on her face.

Then he was beside her, although he didn't deign to use the steps. He simply put a foot onto the platform and climbed up, sliding in one smooth motion into the chair beside her. Constant stared straight ahead, although every nerve was aware of him at her side.

"No one spoke of the beauty of my bride," Kameron said in French. "I'm surprised. I had heard . . . uh . . . certain things of Spaniards. I was foolish to believe them, I see."

"What . . . things?" Constant asked. Then frowned. Her voice was a croak. Not remotely lyrical and high-pitched. She had to correct it, but how? Wouldn't heart-break automatically transfer to one's voice?

"Too horrid for your delicate ears, I'm afraid. And definitely too unflattering."

"My . . . lord!" Constant managed to reply.

"You must call me Kam. Please. I will accept no other. We are going to be close, you understand. Verra close. That leads to intimacy. Marital intimacy. You and I. The idea has merit, I must admit."

"You are even more blunt than I suspected, son," the duke interrupted, speaking flawless French from Constant's other side.

"And you are eavesdropping on a private conversation, sir."

Kameron had answered in English. Constant stiffened further. This was going to get even more difficult if she had to remember which words she was supposed to have understood, and which she wasn't.

The duke snorted. "Private?" he answered, again in English. "In a roomful of gossips and hangers-on? You do the duchess proud, although I find myself wondering at it, too. Earlier, you wouldn't even look at her. Why the change of heart?"

"I dinna' get a good enough look. Obviously. Also, my attention was elsewhere at the time. Now, it is na'."

The duke snorted again. Louder this time. Constant did her best to look ignorant of all of it.

"What of your first wife? Your grief? The overdramatic mourning at Pitcairn Tower? Your reclusive behavior? You see a bonny face and forget your first wife so easily?"

"It was time, I think. I've mourned long enough. Time to live again. And you're mistaken. My new wife is na' bonny. She is astoundingly beautiful."

The duke chuckled. "You decided all this, in what? An hour?"

"I had a very good look throughout that hour. The king has seen fit to wed me to a beautiful woman . . . possessing amazing features and a ripe shape. I came to a decision. It has something to do with physical discomfort. I canna' be celibate forever."

"If I labeled you blunt, it was an understatement. You're in luck she doesn't speak the tongue. She'd probably be swooning."

Constant was beyond swooning, although it sounded like a grand idea. The entire room before her felt as if it was reeling in a circular fashion. She just couldn't fathom why she was still sitting upright and stiff beside the man she'd given everything for.

"So tell me, *chérie*," Kameron whispered, leaning close to her ear. "What does the key unlock?"

Constant toyed with telling him a lie, but couldn't think of one. She couldn't think of anything. She swallowed, and blurted out the truth. "*Ma chambre*," she said.

"*Bien*," he replied. "*Très bien*."

Constant watched the myriad of couples forming interlocking circles on the floor before them with eyes that were swimming in tears. She'd spent months preparing for this moment, changing her appearance and her demeanor. But now she was at a loss. What could she do?

She'd just replaced herself in Kameron Ballan's life.

The musicians struck a chord. It didn't match the one she was hearing. The one she heard was akin to glass breaking.

Chapter Twenty-Nine

"That spawn of *el diablo*! I am a fool! An imbecile! And that man! I will never trust him . . . never. I swear it! I think I hate him!" Constant flung the mantilla at the floor. "And to think I have re-created myself for him! *Dios!* I am a fool! And there is nothing worse!"

"There is much that is worse, Your Highness." It was Lucilla answering, and her even tone only made Constant angrier.

"How dare he?"

"You must calm yourself."

"Calm myself? Why should I? No one will care. He doesn't care!"

"He cares."

"He does not! He doesn't even know that it's me!"

Lucilla sighed heavily. "Did you truly expect him to? Look at yourself. Go ahead, take a good look."

Constant's lips thinned, and then she did the same to her eyes. It didn't change anything. She was still getting prepared to be bedded by her new husband, and there wasn't anyone she could blame but herself. Lucilla lifted her hands and pointed.

"Go ahead. Look. I dare you."

Constant swiveled, blinked, and still couldn't believe her own eyes. Three oversized cheval mirrors were arrayed in one corner of her tower chamber, so it was easy to view herself from every angle. Without the mantilla veiling her, it was impossible to miss the tiny waist, the large bosom, and the wealth of blue-black hair that was enshrined in netting woven with strands of pure silver. Her nose had a slight upward tilt at the end of it, the outline of black around her eyes made them look like stones of vivid blue set in the center of a pristine, porcelain complexion, and what Kameron had once called large, luscious lips were just that, especially with the salve Lucilla had spread on them earlier. She'd described it when she'd been putting the finishing touches to Constant's attire. Such a salve contained capsicum, a pepper that was sure to enlarge and redden sensitive tissues like lips.

Lucilla hadn't lied. It had stung for a bit, too, but the result had seemed worth it . . . then. Now it was another unwanted indication she'd be giving the great Kameron Ballan when he attended her. She was displaying that she desired him. Constant watched her mirror image waver for a moment with tears she couldn't cry, and then she sighed.

"Very well, Lucilla. I'm looking. I'm very desirable. I'm very lush. I'm very beautiful. You didn't lie. I look nothing like myself. You have done wonders with your paints and your salves and your inks."

Lucilla tossed her hands in the air. "But I used nothing! A bit of kohl, a dusting of powder and some lip salve. It is the foundation that matters! A beautiful woman will always be so. She will just be more so when enhanced."

Constant turned away from her image. It didn't help. The heartache wasn't because of how she looked, but how well it had worked. She was beautiful now. So beautiful that it had taken about an hour to be replaced in his affections once Kameron had seen the new version of her.

An hour.

"He didn't recognize me," she whispered.

"It has been a long evening, fraught with turmoil. It will be an even longer night for you, I think. We have a filmy peignoir set aside—"

"Must you go on and on about it?" Constant spat, interrupting the recitation. She didn't want to hear about the gossamer gown and robe. She already knew. She'd picked it out. She'd wanted a seductive atmosphere.

"He is a man, *señora*. You are very much a woman . . . his woman. He hasn't had a woman since his first wife's death. I know these things. They gossip about him. They will gossip about you. They already do. I have heard them, and understood with what English I know. It will be a long night. If I was unwed still, I'd envy you. They all do."

"Get them out." Constant eyed each of the other three maids, all wide-eyed and openmouthed as they watched her, uncomprehending looks on their faces.

"I cannot handle your gown on my own, Your Highness. It's worth a king's ransom, and weighs as much. Sir San Simeon waits in the hall to take it under his control. At least give me their assist until we have it taken away."

"Not a moment longer, then. You may proceed."

Constant turned her back to them, facing her reflections in the trio of mirrors again, and watched Lucilla's set chin.

"They can cease looking at me with such envy, too. Tell them to cease. I refuse to allow it."

"You cannot command looks," Lucilla answered.

"Why not? I'm a princess, am I not? I command. Others obey. What use is royalty if no one obeys?"

"They're envious of you. Any woman would be. His

Lordship is known for his . . . uh . . . how shall I say it? Abilities? Yes, that is it. The man had a reputation, although he is a changed man since wedding you in the colonies. He turns away from every woman. It doesn't change what he is, or how he appears. He still is most handsome. Manly. You know. He takes the breath away. He is a muscled, massive, virile-looking male . . . without equal. Any woman would envy you."

"Let them take my place then. *Dios!* I can't believe my own stupidity. I even gave him a key!"

"It was ever so romantic, too. The servants have whispered of little else since."

"I will not be the subject of gossip! I will not! Tell them to stop!"

Lucilla sighed again. "You are a member of the peerage now. They are servants. I am a servant. We gossip. But do not fret. It is not hateful gossip, such as that duchess woman spouts. The staff is very pleased about the turn of events. Very. His Lordship is well liked by the staff. I don't think his *padre* and *madre* are aware of that. It is contrary to how they themselves are regarded."

"I can imagine," Constant replied.

"Besides which, everyone hears of love at first sight. They just never got to watch it unfold before. It is such a romantic story. A forced meeting, a gift of a blue ribbon attached to a key, a bedroom assignation to consummate a union. The story will be repeated for years if I do not miss my guess."

"Must you take so long unhooking my gown?" Constant asked it between clenched teeth that contrasted with the reddened, bee-stung look of her lips.

"You were sewn into it, *señora*, as you well know. That leaves me little room to slip the hooks. Perhaps if you let some breath out it would help."

"It is out," Constant replied. The diamanté bodice

took longer to shed than it took to put on, which was hard to believe. It had been sewn on twice, once on the outside and again from the inside. That way none of her corset-inspired shape would be disguised. Everything had been done to enhance her beauty for her new husband, and bring about exactly what had transpired. The Princess Althea was supposed to get her new husband to fall in love at first sight, especially since he'd been so difficult to coax into a position where he could see her. No wonder the other maids had been giggling and giving her wide-eyed looks.

They actually believe in love at first sight? Well, if there were such a thing, it was on one side only—his.

"There! It's off, and not as easy as it looked. I will hand this to Sir San Simeon. I'm certain he hovers at your door for such a thing. I will return. Try not to frighten your castle maids until then."

Constant whirled and glared at the little Spanish woman. There were audible gasps about them. It probably had to do with her clenched fists and heaving bosom barely shielded by the chemise she was wearing.

"I will not sit and await my fate like a puppet! I've ceased being so pliable! I cannot believe I was so naïve, so gullible . . . so stupid! I will not be so again. Ever. I will find a way to live through this, but I will not sit calmly like a sacrificial lamb while I prepare for it!"

"A sacrificial lamb?" Lucilla chuckled.

Constant's eyes flared. "You dare to laugh at me? With what I'm facing?"

"Oh, *señora*, please. He is so handsome. On that, he hasn't changed, has he? And he looks to be so very strong, still . . . with the same strength that saw him rowing through the sea to your side. That will be yours again. Tonight. You are so lucky."

"I'm so angered I want to break something, and you call it luck? Ah!" Constant finished by slamming her hands onto the top of one of her dressing tables, making bottles and jars dance.

"Your husband is a very virile man. He will not take such anger as easily as I do. He will probably make you pay for such words. You forget, I have prior knowledge."

"That's another huge part of this! Huge! Gigantic! How am I supposed to pretend otherwise? Well? Have you considered that? Of course not. You, the barristers, and the Count de la Garza-Montagna. None of you considered this, did you? I'm supposed to be a maiden!"

Lucilla smiled and shook her head. "What you whisper of in your bed is no business of mine, Your Highness. It will not be so difficult. You'll see. No man, as in love as that man was, will be difficult to persuade. He may not have recognized you yet, but he hasn't seen the unclothed version. For a woman who has birthed three babes, you have changed little, too. He will be appreciative of that, I'm certain."

"Out! The lot of you! Out!" Constant swung her arms wide as she announced it and ended up shrieking it to the ceiling since nobody but Lucilla understood her Spanish commands.

"You've become a very convincing princess, Your Highness. I am certain word will get to Esmerelda, the Countess de la Garza-Montagna, and her new husband."

Constant gasped. She put her head down, set her lips, and looked across at the maid. The princess had chosen to be known by her second name, Esmerelda, once she was wed. She lost every claim to royalty, although from what Constant had seen of it so far, it resembled a luxurious cage. Princess Althea hadn't cared. She was in love. She had been for nearly twenty years.

Constant had seven months of friendship with Althea to thank for that knowledge, before the princess was assured that the plan would work. She'd helped Constant with every mannerism, every movement, every bit of intrigue. Constant learned the entire litany of the royal house of Anjou—every descendant, every claimant, every member of court—just in case Constant met up with any of them. Princess Althea had been so secluded, however, that most of her descriptions were from her childhood memories. Constant knew that part was in her favor; few knew what the real Princess Althea looked like as an adult. So Althea had been free to wed her possessive count and live out life amid the comfort of Casa de la Montagna, far from the prying eyes of the court and the demands of a royal life. It was what she'd told Constant she'd dreamed of all those lonely years.

It was what she'd lose, if any hint of what they'd done ever surfaced—on any level; even a whisper.

Constant closed her eyes, counted to ten, and then she reopened them. She couldn't change the fate set in motion over a year ago; to do so would harm too many. She didn't dare look at the image in the mirror. She'd lost. She didn't want to see what the loss looked like. She looked across at the maid instead. "Go, Lucilla. Give my treasure to San Simeon. I will not betray anyone with my lack of control, least of all my friend, the Countess Esmerelda."

Lucilla nodded and turned, crossing the bare floor to an antechamber and out the door. This tower was an immense affair, the size of the entire house at the Ridgely farm. There were three chambers within this level. On one side was the room known as the boudoir. It was lined with light blue tapestries, the chaise and two chairs were in the same light blue shade, while the carpets covering the floor were thick and white. The boudoir had been designed to hold a woman's wardrobe on long poles along the walls, just as Kam had described a lifetime ago. Since Princess Althea commanded a huge wardrobe, there were more than fifty dresses hanging there, although her stay at BalClaire wasn't expected to be longer than two days.

The wardrobe Constant owned hadn't been an added expense to the crown, although King Charles had sent a thousand silver pieces to pay for his sister's trousseau. That silver had done exactly what it was supposed to, and the count thanked them for it. Count de la Garza-Montagna had wealth, but nothing near the extent necessary to keep a princess from the ruling house of Spain. It was probably still taking all of Althea's persuasive abilities to convince him he was worth it. Men had such a fragile constitution about some things. Constant remembered that much from Kameron's reaction to his being shaved.

She tossed the memory aside before it destroyed Lucilla's handiwork around her eyes. She had enough experience of that already. The burn from tear-imbued kohl wasn't pleasant and just led to more tears.

No. She wasn't going to cry. She was going to get clothed in the expensive, gossamer netting of loosely woven linen she'd selected for the occasion, and she was going to be put on display for when her new husband arrived to claim her. He wasn't going to regret it until later, when he found out how much he'd destroyed in one hour.

Constant watched as one of the servant girls pointed to the silver-blue sheen of her chosen peignoir and whispered. Then all the girls sighed. Constant knew why. It wasn't going to conceal much. Constant and Althea were a like height and weight, but there had been differences, and they were notable. Constant possessed a much larger bosom and a smaller waist. Almost all the clothing had to be altered. And they'd had to wait until her child was born.

Princess Althea had been quite amused over that, but

she was the only one. Both barristers were ready to pack
Constant back to the colonies once they found out. It
was Althea who had come up with the solution and the
move to the Ballanclaire estate. It was also her idea to
invent the story of a godchild to explain Geoffrey's presence in her life.

Constant shut her eyes again. She owed a lot to
Countess Esmerelda de la Garza-Montagna, but the
princess owed her, too. Althea owed her happiness to
Constant. She'd been so happy, it had brought tears to
everyone's eyes when she'd wed her count. Constant had
attended the wedding as the princess, swathed head to
toe in heavy brocaded fabrics, carried into the chapel on
a litter. She hadn't minded. She'd been too large and un-
wieldy with her baby's size to walk easily, anyway.

Constant opened her eyes. The three maids were still
standing in a row watching her. They looked about her
age, and as innocent as she'd been before she met
Kameron. They all had smiles pasted to their faces, and
the same look of envy and awe. Constant whirled back to
the mirrors. She'd rather watch her own reflection.

Through her mirrors, she could see the other side of
the Queen's Room. Benches were set up against a wall
covered ceiling to floor with dark red tapestries, seeming
to frame an ornate door; the one that led to Kameron's
chamber.

She winced. She'd spent so long preparing for this
moment, but it tasted bitter, rather like the aftertaste of
old tea in her mouth. She watched Lucilla come back
into the room.

"You are ready to continue?" Lucilla asked.

"Do I have a choice?" Constant blinked. She wasn't
going to cry. She'd vowed it. It wasn't working.

"You must not cry, *señora*. What will your maids think? They believe in love at first sight. You must not ruin it."

"*Sí*," she whispered, lifting a fingernail to whisk moisture away from her eye before it damaged the kohl.

"I have it on good authority that His Lordship is acting like a caged tiger. He is raging. He is ready. He growls at anyone who crosses his path. He has banned everyone from this wing of the house for the entire night. We must hurry. We must not make him wait longer."

Constant wiped at her other eye, blinked, and wiped again.

"These tears? They are silly."

"I can't help the way I feel, Lucilla. I am very close to weeping, and you call me . . . silly." Her voice cracked on the last word.

"Within a minute of enwrapping you in his arms, that man will know the truth. He'll be ecstatic. He has mourned you for a year. Twelve months! The only thing he lived for were his children."

"How do you know this?"

"I have heard them talking of it, of course."

"Then why didn't you speak of it before?"

"Because I didn't think it needed saying. The man is about to have his every dream fulfilled, and you cry. Here." She handed Constant a handkerchief. "Dab lightly. At the corners. It will not do so much damage that way. I learned this from working for the Countess Esmerelda. That woman could cry. Now turn. We must hurry. His Lordship will be breaking down the door if we do not finish quickly. I have been so warned. All of us have. You should have seen Sir San Simeon run the moment he had possession of your dress."

"I must not keep you, then." Constant turned her back to them.

"Keep us? We are trying to get you ready for your husband, who from all descriptions will be upon us momentarily, and you call it keeping us? I will wash my hands of you yet, you know."

"Hurry then. Wrap me up all nice and pretty, so I may flaunt myself for my rutting boar of a husband. Go ahead."

"You will need to work on your sarcasm, my lady. I must warn you of it in advance." She turned to the other servant girls and spoke in her Spanish-accented English. "Do not stand there. Accept this, and this. You! Bring the gown."

Constant set her lips and watched her transformation from an elegant, wealthy, pristine princess into a seductive siren. The blue sheen of her negligee filmed her body, leaving little to the imagination. Nor was the excuse of a robe much better. That piece of clothing weighed almost nothing.

The silver hairnetting came off last. Lucilla unclasped each hook of it, pulled it gently from her hair, and then brushed it out. Although saturated with ink, the strands were still unruly and thick, brushing the base of her spine before she moved sections over her shoulders to cover her bosom.

"You are very beautiful. He will not be disappointed. We go now."

"Wait!" Constant stopped Lucilla at the door of the antechamber.

"What is it, *ma princesa*?"

Constant dabbed at the outer corners of her eyes. It still wasn't working. She was about to be with the man she'd love forever, the man she'd given absolutely everything away for, and it hurt too much to consider. "Bring me Geoffrey," she whispered.

"Are you crazed?" the maid answered, finally losing a bit of her even tone.

"I need my son. Now. Right now."

"You need another mind, for you have lost yours!"

"If you don't bring him, I'll wrap up in a cloak and search out the nursery myself. Think of the gossip that would cause."

"*Madre de Dios!* You are mad. A man of great passion is coming for you, and you think to bring an infant into the bedchamber?"

"I need to be loved for myself! Right now. That is what I need. I need my son. Now. Only for a moment. Then you can take him away. If you will not bring him, we can all suffer the consequence. Gossip. Whispers. Intrigues." Constant walked over to the boudoir door, preparatory to getting her cloak. She had the knob in her hand before Lucilla answered.

"Very well. I will do as you command. I will not take responsibility for what happens. You make an excellent princess."

Constant felt the door close. The silence and emptiness of the immense chamber surrounded her, seeming to possess a personality of its own. Her shoulders slumped, her hands shook, and she buried her face in the handkerchief. She was absolutely amazed she wasn't weeping.

She felt, rather than heard, the door open.

"You've been quick, Lucilla," she commented without turning around. "That is good. Was he sleeping?"

"I don't speak Spanish, love," Kameron replied, just before he reached her.

Chapter Thirty

"Oh God. Oh, dearest God. Oh God."

Kameron grabbed her to him, enfolded her with those wondrous arms of his, lifting her off the floor, and he was shaking. Then she saw why—he was weeping. Constant's eyes were huge.

"Oh, love. My dearest love. Constant. 'Tis a miracle, and I canna' believe it. I still canna'. Oh, thank you, God. I have been on my knees renewing my faith, and 'tis na' enough. Thank you, God!"

He lifted his head then, blinked moisture away, and Constant had never seen anything to compare as his eyes met hers from a distance of less than two inches. He was gazing with absolute adoration and he was absolutely still.

"Kameron?" she whispered.

"Oh, my dearest love. My Constant. Mine. I still canna' believe it. I canna'."

"You . . . know who I am?" she whispered.

Little lines creased as he smiled. Then he was grinning. Then his mouth was on hers and there wasn't a thought allowed. The moan that surged through them didn't come wholly from her throat, or from his, and it had a timbre to it that made her tremble.

Kam raised his head. He wasn't gazing adoringly at her any longer. He was angry. He was intense. His eyes were changing a darker shade, too.

"How dare you doubt me! Jesu'! I portrayed myself as a lecherous ass for you—and you thought it real? I have never spanked you, Constant, but I am verra near it at the moment. Verra near."

"You were playacting?" she asked.

"Of course I was playacting! And thankful to have pulled it off. Here I suspected my lying abilities had waned, and yet you believed me? I'm actually impressed at myself. What a position you put me in."

"I didn't do anything."

"What?" His surprise was genuine. His eyes widened and no longer looked black; they were exactly the golden brown she loved. "You've just pulled off a major coup and yet say you did naught?"

"I didn't do it alone."

"Lord, doona' I ken that! I nearly throttled Blair when I ran into him."

"You mean . . . Carlos?"

"Whatever he goes by, I recognized him."

"Him? But . . . not me?"

"I dinna' look at you. I had little choice with Blair. I mean Carlos. He accosted me at the stables, grabbed my bridle, and made me look at him. And then he spouted streams of words at me as if I'd understand."

"The stables? You were . . . leaving?"

"I was leaving. And who comes running out to stop me, grinning like an idiot? Barrister Blair. I mean Carlos. Montoya, right? His new identity will take some practice, love. As will the man. He's trimmed down, dressed in some god-awful Spanish getup, and sporting a curled, black wig? Good Lord. He's almost perfect."

"But I gave you a blue ribbon."

"Nae. The Princess Althea Esmerelda something-or-other gave me a *key* attached to a blue ribbon. That could have been coincidental. She might like blue. Who cares what she likes and what she hands me? I have hated her since I was in dresses. And Constant, women have been handing me keys for years! You knew that! How was I to guess it was you? Well?"

"I—" she began, but he interrupted.

"You left me. You died. I was beset with grief. You've nae idea. I could na' eat, I could na' sleep. Good thing my guards were strong. They tied me into my berth aboard ship to keep me from throwing myself overboard. And then they brought me the bairns. Smart men. You might have recognized some of them."

"From where?"

"My honor guardsmen. Earlier."

"All I saw was you, Kameron."

He somehow wrapped his arms even tighter about her. Squeezing. Holding. Protecting.

"I dinna' see much either. I was seeing red. Literally. My own father kidnapped my bairns to use against me? I was ready to throttle the man. You have nae idea."

"Yes, I do. I was there, remember?"

"I doona' remember much of that meeting. I gave an ultimatum to my sire. I took your gift. I left. I had to find my bairns."

"You found them?"

"'Twas na' difficult. That Abigail is a handful. Make that an armful."

"Is she . . . walking?" Constant asked.

"She skipped that and went right to running. Benjamin

has a bit more sense, but he'll still tag along wherever she leads him. It requires three nurses to watch them. All I had to do was look for the most commotion. Father thought to hide them in the creamery. That was na' smart. He lost all of last sennight's creams and curds to her curiosity."

"You have them? Truly?"

"I already said as much to the duke. Were you na' listening?"

"Can I see them?"

"Afraid na'. Right at the moment, anyway."

"But—" Constant began again.

"Sorry, love. I could na' risk another kidnapping. I sent them, under guard, back to where they'll be safe now. 'Tis a place I may have mentioned. Pitcairn Tower."

She nodded.

"It's mine. Always was. Grandmother's endowment, or something along that line. Why do you think I went there the moment we docked?"

"I've met your parents. That's easy to answer."

"You'd be wrong. I'd have liked nothing more than to spit in their faces. But I had to hide and recover first. It took longer than I expected. In fact, I dinna' manage it. I was na' capable of returning to my public duties because I was na' capable of even moving from my chamber. You doona' ken what it's like. Grief saps your will, making it difficult to face each day, because the damned sunlight does na' even feel warm anymore. Naught does."

"Oh, Kameron, I'm so sorry. They were supposed to tell you."

"Oh, I heard that part. Blair says a lot when you're na' squeezing his throat. I mean Carlos."

Constant's eyes widened. "You actually squeezed his throat?"

"I already said as much. He was alive and you weren't? He's lucky he finally decided to speak English. Rapidlike. Whispered. I'll rehire him when he forgives me—if he forgives me."

"That shouldn't be an issue. He's married to my maid, Lucilla."

"What? Has the entire world gone mad?" Kam asked.

"So, tell me. How are they? What are they like?"

"Your maid and Carlos? Who cares?" He was nuzzling his lips along her throat, and the words sounded indistinct and strange.

"Our babies."

"Oh. They're safe. They're on their way to Pitcairn Tower. I already said as much. Why are you wearing so much?"

Constant watched as he looked down at where her breasts were crushed against his chest.

"I'm barely dressed, Kameron."

"You've got material on. That translates to you're wearing too much. You have nae idea of the constant aspect of my desire at the moment. I have na' so much as looked at another woman—I couldn't. And then you show up? Out of the clear blue sky? I'm surprised I dinna' go with my first inclination once I learned."

"What was that?"

"What was it? Getting to you. Ignoring everyone in my line of sight and in my path, and just getting to you. What else? Blair stopped me. As I said, he talks fast. Made sense. I could hardly stalk across the room, haul you from the chair, and sing aloud to everyone that it was my own Constant returned from the grave, now could I?"

"You could have given me some sign," she complained.

"As poorly as you lie? Darling. Please. I daren't allow even a hint of intrigue. And that meant I had to lie. Better than ever afore. I had to enact a 'love at first sight' scenario. Believably. Perfectly. So . . . I prepared. Took a dip in the loch. Dressed in my finery. Blair assisted. I mean, Carlos. I must remember to call him that. And then I was readied. But nae. The first sight of you almost undid me. I *had* to keep my distance. I forced it. I paced myself. I had to traverse the bloody room, ignore everyone and everything in my path, and try to keep under control before I dared get close to you! It was pure torment. Why do you think it took me a bloody hour to approach you?"

"It was crowded," Constant answered.

"The hell you say." He grinned. Then he was kissing her again. When the room began to spin, Constant was scarcely aware that Kameron had lifted her and was twirling with her in his arms.

"Oh love! 'Tis a miracle! There are nae thanks vast enough. We've an entire lifetime together, and all because of some plan I was na' even told about. I still canna' believe it. You're here. You're *alive*. You're in my arms, and you're my princess wife to top it off. Nothing and nobody can take that away from me. No one can change it. You're mine. Forever."

"I always knew that," she replied.

"Get this bloody gown off, love, or I'll na' be responsible for my actions. Bother that. We'll replace it."

He had her atop the bed, and the gossamer fabric separated in his fingers before Constant could answer him.

"I love you, Constant. More than I can say. Or show. And naught is ever coming between us. Nothing. Ever. I promise it. You ken?"

She nodded. It was all she was capable of, since he was opening his own robe, splicing the top wide . . . and then, he stilled. She heard the door opening, too.

"Well, I have brought the child. I still think it the stupidest idea you have had yet—oh!"

It was Lucilla. She was holding Geoffrey, and she was staring openmouthed at the picture that was before her. Constant was grateful Kam hadn't finished opening his robe. If she were the old Constant, she'd have been beet red with the blush, too.

"Bring him here, Lucilla. I'll take him."

"I think I'd better bear him back to the nursery until later. That is what I think."

"Bring him here. I'll get him back to you momentarily. You may wait in the antechamber."

"I believe I'll wait in the hall . . . thank you very much."

She put the baby on the edge of the bed and backed away, because Kam was scowling at her. Constant held her negligee together with one hand as she sat and reached for Geoffrey.

"I doona' speak Spanish, Constant, and you'd better have a verra good reason for this disruption. And I mean verra."

"This is Geoffrey, Kameron. As I recall, that is one of your names."

"What of it?"

"Don't you think he's beautiful?" she asked, unwrapping the swaddling in order to show him off. Geoffrey was awake, sucking on a fist, and kicking. He was also sporting the same blue-black hair his mother claimed, although his was in a tuft at his forehead.

"It's the bairn from the nursery. I saw it earlier. I'm fair certain I mentioned it at the fest. I dinna' have time for a bairn then, and I certainly doona' now. Send it back. Immediately."

"He's known as my godchild, Kameron. He's three months old. What do you see?"

"A healthy-looking bairn. Will you send for the maid now?"

"He has light brown eyes."

"So?" Kameron looked at the baby, then back at her.

"They're golden brown. See?" She lifted her son to face his father and watched as Kam's eyes widened.

"But he has black hair," he said, his voice unsure.

"I have black hair, too," she replied.

Kam plucked Geoffrey from her and held him inches away to examine him. The baby quit kicking, but he was furiously sucking on both fists now. Constant watched as the knowledge dawned. Then Kam was looking at her with such round eyes, she could see white all about the golden brown.

"We have another bairn?" he choked out.

She nodded.

"Oh my God," he replied. Constant had her hands out to catch the baby as Kam slumped onto the mattress beside her. She needn't have worried. Kameron was as sure as he'd always been. Then he was unwrapping and examining their son. Constant watched as Geoffrey and his father eyed each other and then Kam looked over at her.

"He's a lad," Kam said finally.

"Yes. I know."

"Good heavens, Constant! I touched you once, we have twins. I touched you twice, we have a son. This does not bode well for the size of Pitcairn Tower's nurseries. We'll have to enlarge them."

"BalClaire . . . looks large enough," she replied, and held her breath.

"This mausoleum? You jest. Please say you jest."

Kameron lifted Geoffrey with an arm and cuddled him against his chest. Bare skin to bare skin. Without thought. Without even looking. Constant thought her heart might burst with every beat.

"I think it's a grand place, Kam. Worthy of a Highland chieftain. You. I wouldn't take that from you. Ever. I think BalClaire is part of you."

"'Tis cold. Austere. Brooding. Full of ghosts and tortures."

"I think it's awe-inspiring. Massive. Permanent. And yours. It's your heritage, Kam. And I think it's beautiful. It's just missing something."

"Aye. A heart."

"You. Us. The babies. And love."

"You make a grand argument, my lady wife. And I'll bend. I'll consider it. Once I'm duke. Fair enough?"

"I love you, Kam. You've no idea how much."

"I've a fairly good idea, I think. I mean, look. You reinvented yourself for me."

Constant giggled.

"I canna' continue to call you Constant, though. We'll be whispered of. The best lies are the ones that have no telltale loose ends. You ken?"

"One of my names is Consuelo. You should know that already."

"Why, when I hated everything about my princess wife-to-be? Consuelo? I can call you Connie, then?" Kameron looked to the ceiling again. "Thank you again, God!"

"If you'll give me Geoffrey, I'll take him back to Lucilla," Constant offered, putting out her hands. He looked down as if surprised at the babe against his heart.

"He's verra healthy, Connie. Are you nursing him?"

"And risk exposure? I wanted to. I couldn't. He has a wet nurse. She's probably awaiting him."

"I canna' believe this day." Kameron put the baby back in his swaddling and started rewrapping, demonstrating agility at it as he continued speaking. "My bairns are kidnapped. I find my father is behind it. I then learn it's because of my princess wife, who has been chasing me down. She will not leave me alone, although I've given every indication I do not want to see her. Then, I find out she's my beloved Constant. Now, I discover that I have another son and heir?"

Kam was shaking again. Constant watched the baby trembling in his hands. Kam lifted Geoffrey to his face and pressed his nose against the babe's cheek.

He slanted his gaze across at her before returning to his son. "He's beautiful, my love. I thank you. He's just so different from—wait a moment. He's na' dark. He's got light brows. Please doona' tell me you dyed my son's hair."

"I had to. He looked just like you. One glance and anyone would know who sired him. I'm afraid it's permanent, too. Like mine. It will have to grow out."

"It's striking on his mother. I'll na' allow it on any bairn of mine. We'll have it shaved or something. Call your maid. Bother that. I'll get her. Doona' you dare move and expose more of yourself. Our son doesn't need that sort of education from his parents."

Constant smiled. "He's three months old."

"And you've that maid awaiting him in the hall. She's wed to Blair? I mean, Carlos? Good heavens. Will the wonders of this day never cease? I'll be right back, love. I promise. I'm na' going anywhere for about . . . ten hours or so. I promise that, too. For a woman of your experience, it should be obvious. I guess I was na' a verra good teacher in your loft, was I?"

Kameron slid to the edge of the bed and stood, cradling his son in the crook of one arm while readjusting the belt of his own robe with the other. He was right. She was experienced and his desire was obvious.

"Oh, Kam. You were the best," she replied. And it was the truth.

More by Bestselling Author
Hannah Howell

Available Wherever Books Are Sold!

Check out our website at
http://www.kensingtonbooks.com